His gaze bore into hers. It was all she could do not to blush. "Likewise, Blythe."

The sound of her name on his lips sent a warm shiver down her spine. His voice, a strange combination of rough and smooth, was like rich, plush velvet rubbed the wrong way.

She had to let go of his hand, yet pulling her fingers free of his left her feeling strangely bereft. There was something about this man—*Devlin*—that made her feel as though she had known him all her life.

Reluctantly, she bid him good day and left the stables. It wasn't until she was halfway to the house that she realized exactly who he was.

Devlin. Devlin Ryland.

The realization was enough to bring her to a dead stop. No. It couldn't be. That incredible man with that deep voice could *not* be Devlin Ryland. But he was.

Devlin Ryland, the one man to make her heart skip a beat in two years, was the same man who took her fiancé to Teresa Vega and saved his life.

And, subsequently, ruined Blythe's.

KATHRYN SMITH

For the First Time

AVON BOOKS
An Imprint of HarperCollinsPublishers

AVON BOOKS
An Imprint of HarperCollins*Publishers*
10 East 53rd Street
New York, New York 10022-5299

First Avon Books paperback printing: October 2003

Avon Trademark Reg. U.S. Pat. Off. and in Other Countries, Marca Registrada, Hecho en U.S.A.
HarperCollins® is a registered trademark of HarperCollins Publishers Inc.

Printed in the U.S.A.

10 9 8 7 6 5 4 3 2

I'd like to dedicate this book to the following people:

To my mother, Mary, and my father, Elwyn,
whose support has always been appreciated
and keenly felt.

To my editor, Kelly Harms,
for being a treasure to work with.

To Nancy Yost,
my favorite agent in the world.

To Kim Lewis, Janet Villeneuve
and Karen MacFarlane,
who always make me feel like the supreme diva.

And to my husband, Steve,
for everything.

Thanks and love to you all.

Kathryn

Chapter 1

London
July 1817

"You are going."

Devlin Ryland looked up from packing his valise long enough to acknowledge his oldest brother's presence.

"Yes." He took one more shirt from the pile on the bed and placed it in the worn leather bag. His evening clothes were packed as well as extra trousers, cravats, shirts, and one extra coat. The extra coat was his one concession to fashion. There were going to be people at Brixleigh Park who made a point of never wearing the same thing twice. He should at least have a little variety.

Darkly handsome, his features much more chiseled and rugged than Devlin's own, Brahm limped into the inner sanctum of the room. Devlin could tell from the heavy thumps of his cane against the thickly varnished floorboards that his brother's leg was bothering him.

"I thought you were apprehensive about seeing Carnover again."

Buckling the straps on his valise, Devlin shrugged. "We all

have our demons we must face. You told me that." And Lord knew that Brahm had his share of demons.

Both hands on the carved, burnished silver head of his cane, Brahm leaned slightly forward. "But Carny is supposed to be your friend. Not a demon."

"He is both." He didn't have to explain. No doubt Brahm understood better than he should.

A kind smile curved Brahm's mouth—a sight that had been all too rare these few months since their father's death. "What are you going to do?"

Another shrug. He was packed and ready to go, yet he wasn't ready to leave just yet. "I do not know. Perhaps seeing him will be easier this time."

"You mean perhaps the dreams will not come back."

Straightening his shoulders, Devlin met Brahm's concerned gaze evenly. "Yes."

"What if they do?" Obviously Brahm wasn't done with him yet. Was this simple brotherly concern, or was he worried that Devlin might do something to embarrass the family in Devon? He'd have to come up with something fairly outrageous to top anything Brahm himself had done. Pissing in a punch bowl was hard competition.

And somehow, he couldn't imagine Brahm giving a rat's ass about the family's social standing. His brother was worried about him, plain and simple.

"I'll be all right."

Another rare smile. "I do not doubt it."

Silence followed as Devlin turned and picked up the Baker rifle leaning against a chair near the window. He'd been up till three in the morning cleaning and oiling it, polishing the scarred wood until it gleamed, scrubbing the barrel inside and out until the cloth came away without a hint of black. He slipped it into its case and placed it on the cream velvet bedspread beside his valise.

"What are you taking that for?" Brahm asked. "Are you planning to do some shooting in Devon?"

This time Devlin shrugged just one shoulder. "I might."

"You cannot bear to leave it behind, can you?" What bothered him more, the insight or the compassion in Brahm's tone? It probably seemed foolish to Brahm that his younger brother was so dependent on something as inanimate as a gun, but he wouldn't judge him for it. Brahm never judged. Either because it wasn't in his nature, or because he knew he had no right.

"It's part of me." That rifle had been his constant companion for years. It had been there with him when he saw friends and fellow soldiers shot to bits on the battlefield. He had slept with it, eaten with it beside him. Hell, the whole time he had been in the army he didn't even take a piss without the Baker with him. How could he just "leave it behind" now that the fighting was over? He couldn't.

The Baker never turned its back on him, never let him down, and, like Brahm, never judged him.

"You have to forgive yourself for what happened, brother. Forgive and accept."

There it was. As the oldest, Brahm couldn't help but take responsibility for his younger brothers. This included trying to solve all their problems, even when he had more than enough of his own. He always seemed to know what they "had" to do. Unfortunately, he never seemed to know *how* to achieve it.

"Have *you* forgiven yourself?" Devlin asked, slipping the strap of the rifle case over his head so that the Baker rested at an angle across his back. Its weight was welcome and familiar.

Brahm shifted his weight, still resting against his cane. No doubt his leg was aching like the devil. "Not quite. But I'm trying. You have yet to attempt even that."

"How can I forgive what I did?" Picking up his valise, Devlin stepped around the foot of the bed toward the door. Brahm blocked his path.

"It was war."

He snorted. "Was that what it was?" How easy it was for someone who wasn't there to think he knew what it had been like. One had to be there to know, and sometimes Devlin wished to God that he had been sensible enough to stay the hell home.

Brahm's russet gaze was shrewd, and saw far more than Devlin was comfortable with. "Would you rather Carny had been killed?"

"No." But sometimes he wished it had happened differently.

"Of course not. He is damn grateful you did what you did." A thump of Brahm's cane punctuated his pronouncement. "So am I, for that matter. If you had not acted you might have been killed as well."

"Perhaps that would have been for the best." It was maudlin, but sometimes when the dreams got bad . . .

If his brother didn't need his cane to remain upright, Devlin had no doubt Brahm would have hit him—God knew where—with the gleaming heavy oak. The look on Brahm's face was enough to tell his younger brother what he thought of his self-pity.

Contrition swept through Devlin's veins. It had been a stupid thing to say, especially to Brahm, King of Guilt. At least the blood on his hands belonged to a stranger. The blood on Brahm's belonged to their father.

"Are you going to be all right while I'm gone?"

Now it was Brahm's turn to shrug. "Being alone is a demon I must face. Do not worry about me. Live your own life."

With that opening, perhaps now would be a good time to tell Brahm the whole truth about his trip to Devonshire. "Wynter has some property he wants me to look at while I'm there." He'd made a tidy fortune during the war, and his father had left him a generous inheritance invested in the Exchange; why leave it sitting around when he could buy the beginnings of a new life with it?

Brahm smiled, and Devlin knew it was genuine. "I think that would be good. It is time you settled down."

Frowning, Devlin shifted his valise to his other hand. "What about my older brothers? When are the three of you going to settle down?"

"It would take a very patient, very strong woman to live out the rest of her days with me." Brahm chuckled as he pivoted on the heel of his good leg and moved stiffly toward the door. "One who hasn't heard the gossip."

Devlin walked beside him, shortening his strides to match. "That leaves out every woman in England."

Ever good-natured, Brahm merely smiled and nodded at the remark. "And as for our brothers, North is married to his career and Wynthrope, well, he does not speak to me so I do not know why he remains a bachelor. That leaves you. The big hero. You should not have any trouble finding a woman willing to marry you. Women like men who punish themselves for things that are not their fault. It saves them the trouble." He shot his younger brother a meaningful look over his shoulder as he preceded him out of the bedroom.

Devlin's smile was cynical. "There's incentive to marry."

"I am serious, Dev." They walked down the corridor toward the stairs. "I want you to think of yourself for a change. Find some happiness."

As was habit, Devlin offered his brother his arm as they descended the stairs. "I'm not sure I know how."

"You do not need to," Brahm replied with a wince, leaning heavily on Devlin's arm as they took the first stair. "If you look, happiness will find you."

Brixleigh Park, Devonshire

It was he.

From Brixleigh's gold drawing room, Lady Blythe Christian peered around a heavy velvet drape at the carriage parked in the drive and watched as her brother greeted his guests—a man and a woman. A *little* woman, with short limbs and a short waist and a skinny little body to go with all her skinny little other parts. She was dressed like a perfect tiny doll in a gown of rose muslin and matching spencer. Her companion, who was even more perfect-looking than the woman, was dressed in the height of fashion in a dark blue coat and butter-colored breeches.

"Tell me again why Miles felt he *had* to invite him?" She directed her question toward the glass.

It had been over a year since the last time she saw Rowan Carmichael, Earl Carnover, but he was as handsome as ever—a golden Adonis in the summer sun.

The swine. Bounder. *Jackass.*

"Because they are friends, dearest. Surely you did not expect your brother to ignore such an acquaintance?"

Dropping the curtain, Blythe turned away from the window and faced her sister-in-law. Varvara—Varya—Christian was one of those women who became more beautiful with age. Three years ago she had been striking, but motherhood and a happy marriage had given her a luminescence that made her—in Blythe's opinion—one of the most beautiful women in all of England.

And Blythe loved her too dearly to hate her for it.

"Surely Miles does not expect me to countenance being under the same roof as Carny for so long, does he?" Lud, these house parties sometimes went on for weeks, months even!

Varya smiled patiently as she lounged on a chaise of rich amber brocade, her dark purple gown a stunning contrast. "I believe he probably does, yes."

No doubt he did, at that. Blythe's older brother was forever telling her that she should forgive Carny for his betrayal. After all, it had been two years since it happened.

Two very *short* years.

But what did Miles know? He had never had his every

hope dashed by someone he planned to spend the rest of his life with. Blythe had, and she would decide when—*if*—she forgave Carny.

As if she ever could forgive him. She was not a vindictive person by nature, but Carny would have to suffer long and hard before she condescended to forgive his crimes against her.

But at the moment she'd settle for getting out of the house without his noticing her. He would want to say hello, make small talk, or something equally as stupid. He always tried to talk to her as though nothing had ever happened. As though they were still friends. As though he actually thought something of her. She already knew what he thought of her. It hadn't been enough two years ago, and it was too late for it now.

"Who else is coming?" she asked, leaving the window and dropping into a large armchair. She hooked her right leg over the arm and swung her booted foot like a big lazy pendulum.

A slight frown wrinkled the otherwise smooth skin of Varya's pale brow, but it wasn't directed at her. It was Miles who frowned at her behavior and her clothing. Varya merely accepted it, dear sister that she was. "A lot of people. Devlin Ryland for one."

The great war hero and friend of Miles. Blythe rolled her eyes. "Wonderful. Just what we need, another ex-soldier to bore us senseless with stories about how he single-handedly won the war."

Varya took a sip of tea from a dainty china cup with pink roses painted on it. "He did save Carny's life."

"Well, do not expect me to thank him for that!"

The other woman choked on her tea, but managed to get a serviette to her mouth in time.

"Stop doing that!" she cried when she had stopped coughing. "You always make me spit out my tea!"

Blythe grinned, her foot still swinging. "Sorry."

Setting her cup and saucer on the tray before her, Varya dabbed at her mouth and chin with her napkin. Her expression was one of mock irritation. "You are not. You laugh every time."

That was true. The first time Blythe had made Varya choke on her tea had been only shortly after Miles met his wife-to-be. All of London assumed Varya was Miles's mistress, but Blythe had liked her, so when Varya came to call at Wynter Lane one day, Blythe offered her tea. A casual, but impertinent remark had caused Varya to spit her tea all over herself and the table before her. It had been hilarious, even though Blythe had had the good sense not to laugh. After Varya and Miles married, Blythe never refused the chance to shock her sister-in-law into such unladylike behavior.

"Most of our guests will arrive tomorrow, but we expect some of them today, as you have already seen for yourself." Varya spoke as though their arrival was a matter of grave importance. Blythe stared at her dumbly.

Varya sighed, obviously realizing this was not the time for subtlety. "Do you not think you should perhaps change?"

Blythe replied in a manner befitting her name, "Do you not think you should be outside greeting your guests?"

Her cheeks blossoming with crimson, Varya straightened the skirts of her morning gown. "I was concerned about you. Besides, unlike my husband, I have not quite forgiven Lord Carnover myself for what he did to you."

"Of course Miles has forgiven him." Blythe smiled without bitterness. "They are men. They always forgive each other. It is we women they have trouble with."

"Yes," Varya agreed, frowning once again. "And do not you agree that is exactly why you should run up to your room and change into something a little more . . . forgivable?"

Blythe studied her fingernails. They needed to be trimmed. "I am going out."

And there was nothing wrong with what she was wearing.

True, Miles wouldn't like his guests to see her dressed this way, but she could hardly go visit the tenants and help with repairs in a gown, could she? She was wearing what she always wore when there was work to be done—trousers, shirt, and jacket made for her by the town seamstress. Her boots had been made especially for her as well.

Varya raised a hand to her forehead and rubbed. "Oh, Blythe. Why do you bait his temper this way?"

What did it matter if Miles was angry? It seemed lately he spent most of his time angry with her. He was angry because she didn't want to return to London. Angry because she wouldn't forgive Carny. Angry because she had no interest in finding a husband. It was so very tempting to tell him just where he could stick his anger.

She didn't want to return to London because people would talk. They'd talk about the old scandal—how Carny so very publicly jilted her. They'd pity her for still being single and so obviously unwanted.

She had tried very hard to find a husband once upon a time, and when she found him he betrayed her. And it wasn't as though she had her choice to pick from. Most men didn't want a wife their height or taller. In Carny's case, he simply hadn't wanted her. And she was in no way ready to forgive him for that. Not now. Perhaps not ever.

Not that any of it mattered now. In a little under two months, Blythe would have her inheritance, left to her by her father. It was meant to be her dowry, but if she remained unwed by her twenty-fifth birthday, then she got the money to do with as she pleased. And what she pleased was to buy Rosewood, a little estate just five miles west of Brixleigh. She would be independent, and Miles wouldn't have any say in her life at all.

But for now he did, which was why she was hiding in the drawing room, waiting until he was out of sight before sneaking out.

A man's voice drifted through the open window as the guests climbed the front steps. "Will Lady Blythe be joining us for the festivities?"

Blythe's heart stopped. There was no mistaking that honey-smooth voice. Carny was asking about her. The blighter had the nerve to ask about her!

"Yes," came Miles's confident reply. Her birthday couldn't arrive quick enough.

She couldn't be certain, but she thought she heard Carny say, "Good." What did he care if she took part in the party's activities or not? It wasn't as though he could possibly have any interest in seeing her. Not unless his situation had altered drastically since she last saw him.

At the sound of her husband's voice, Varya rose to her feet. "I told Miles I would greet them inside." She didn't sound as though the task would be a pleasant one. Dear Varya.

"Where are you going to put them?" Blythe tried to keep her tone indifferent.

Varya's smile was gentle. "In the west wing, of course."

Blythe watched her leave with a sense of relief so strong she almost sighed out loud with it. The west wing. Good. Her room was in the east. Now she wouldn't have to worry about getting up in the middle of the night and running into Carny.

Or the wife he had chosen over her.

She stank.

Brushing a trickle of sweat from her forehead with the sleeve of her shirt, Blythe grimaced as the afternoon breeze drifted through the thin linen underneath her arm. She was dirty and sticky, and she smelled as though she hadn't bathed in days.

Some of the men working with her, however, smelled as though they hadn't bathed in months.

When she'd left the house earlier that afternoon, she had planned merely to ride out, visit a few tenants, oversee a few minor repairs, and perhaps take tea with one or two of their wives. She enjoyed sitting with these people who seemed to admire her size and strength and ability to work. She liked how the women talked openly and freely about things women of her class were expected not to discuss. She liked how the men included her in their discussions of agriculture and animal husbandry—also subjects ladies of her station were expected to be completely ignorant about. Lord knew she had her share of faults, but ignorance—she hoped—was not one of them.

She had forgotten that today was the day John Dobson planned to put a new roof on his cottage. She had forgotten everything except that Lord and Lady Carnover were arriving that day. Her only thought had been to avoid them. Joining the half-dozen men working on Dobson's roof in the heat of a warm summer afternoon provided ample distraction.

It also gave her one more reason to make certain she snuck back into the house at a reasonable hour. She was going to have to bathe before dinner. She was also going to have to make sure Suki, her maid, made her look as feminine as possible to keep Miles docile. She didn't want to give him anything new to lecture her about.

The roof still was not finished when she excused herself an hour later, but she couldn't afford to stay away from the house any longer. More guests had no doubt arrived in her absence, and she would hate for any of them to spot her as she snuck in through the servants' entrance and stairwells. The servants wouldn't tell on her, but visitors to the park would be bound to comment to Miles on his sister's strange and dirty attire. Her clothing she could almost get away with—after all, many ladies considered it a lark to dress up in male clothing on occasion—but she would not be able to excuse the dirt, sweat, and odor that clung to her. And then there would be hell to pay for not conducting herself as she should. She was the daughter of a marquess, Miles would remind her. As if she could ever forget their father.

Lord, she would be glad when her birthday arrived! Until then she had to be careful. Miles didn't know of her plans to buy her own estate. If he did, he would no doubt try to stop her. She couldn't allow that to happen. Not when all her dreams were so close to becoming reality.

"Thank you for all your help, Lady Blythe." John Dobson flashed her a broad grin as she lifted herself up into the saddle.

Blythe smiled back. It was no secret among the tenants that young Mr. Dobson was infatuated with her, and to be frank, Blythe was flattered. Dobson was in his late twenties, was ruggedly handsome, and had a body that looked as though it had been sculpted by an Italian master. And as far as height was concerned, he would be her perfect match, if only they belonged in the same world and if only she could bring herself to return his feelings.

"Now that you have that new roof, there's no reason for you to put off looking for a wife any longer, John."

His grin widened, his teeth startling white against the tan of his face. Blythe would have to be dead not to respond to it. Dobson was one of the few tenants who did bathe on a regular basis. "Is that a proposal, my lady?"

Blythe laughed at that. Dobson knew the reality of their relationship as well as she did, but that didn't stop him from being a shameless flirt. And there were times, late at night when she couldn't sleep, when her body itched with urges she alone couldn't satisfy, that she thought of taking him up on what he offered, but she had been taught that ladies didn't do such things, and she had yet to meet a man that could make her forget that rule entirely.

Not even Carny.

"There's a better woman out there for you than me, John Dobson," she informed him lightly, spurring her mare,

Marigold, into languid motion, "and I look forward to the day you introduce me to her."

Dobson's grin remained, but something in his eyes changed. There was regret in his gaze, along with a frank appreciation that men of the upper classes usually reserved for women they wanted to seduce. "There may be a better man for you as well, but you know where to find me in case you get tired of waiting." He winked.

Blushing as she took his meaning, Blythe shook her head. His tone had been light, but she knew without a doubt that if she did show up at his cottage late some night, he would not turn her away. "Good day, John."

As she rode away, Blythe tried to put Dobson's words out of her head. They flattered and pleased her, but they also rubbed salt into a very old and raw wound. Why couldn't men of her own class find her as appealing as John Dobson did? Why were her height and strength a detriment in her own world? She knew for a fact that she wasn't ugly, although her features were as strong as the rest of her, and according to some of the tenant wives, men liked figures that were full like hers. A physically strong woman was a good bed partner and could bear children easily. To these people she was perfect. To her own she was defective. At least where the men were concerned.

Even Carny, that golden blond Judas, had married a little woman, after telling her there was nothing wrong with how she looked.

She absolutely refused to think of him. He didn't deserve her attention. Instead, as she guided her mare through the sun-dappled field and down into the sheltered path that wound through the cool, shady trees to the house, she thought only of how glad she was to have Miles, Varya, and little Edward in residence again. As much as her brother plagued her, she loved him, and it felt good to sit and talk to Varya again. Playing with her young nephew brought a deep, sweet joy to her heart.

As much as she loved living in Devonshire, with the smell of the salt sea on the air and the wonderful ocean breeze that blew through her bedroom window at night, sometimes she missed her family. Miles spent all his time in London, and their mother was in Paris for an extended stay. She said it made her feel closer to Blythe's father, who had spent more time in Paris than he had in London before he died—and before Napoleon got out of hand, of course. That didn't stop Blythe from missing her, and often longing for her sage advice. Letters just weren't the same as having her close.

But even more often than she missed her family or, God forbid, London, Blythe appreciated the quiet of Devon and Brixleigh. Here she was free to be herself, and no one judged her. She could roam the beach, swim in the tide, rather than simply "bathe" in it as the fashionable ladies in Brighton did. She could speak her mind and people listened, because in Miles's absence, she was essentially lord here. No woman in her right mind would give up such freedom willingly.

She would rather die than return to London, where every move a person made was watched and discussed endlessly in the scandal sheets. Somehow some of them had found out about the fiasco with Carny and had depicted her as some kind of hulking monster both in picture and prose. Even worse were the ones that claimed to sympathize with her and made her seem a hapless victim.

It had taken months for her to realize she was neither. Realizing she wasn't a victim had come first. The monster bit had taken longer for her to reconcile. It was very difficult to convince oneself that something wasn't true when one was terribly, awfully certain that it *was*.

As she entered the Brixleigh stables—her eyes adjusting to the change in the light and her nose picking up the welcome, familiar scent of horse and hay—she noticed a strange horse in one of the stalls. That was nothing unusual, as most guests brought their own horses, whether for carriages or pleasure riding. What was unusual about this horse was his sheer size.

"Would you like me to take care of Mari for you, my lady?"

"Yes, thank you," Blythe replied, handing the groom Marigold's reins. Normally she rubbed the mare down herself, but she was anxious for a better look at this new horse. She had never seen anything quite like him before. It was almost as if he was studying her, as interested in her appearance as she was in his.

"Tom, the big gray down there, who does it belong to?"

The young groom glanced in the direction Blythe pointed and shrugged his narrow shoulders. "Don't know, my lady. Must've come in when I wasn't here."

Intrigued, Blythe walked toward the stall where the strange horse stood. The scent of warm horse and manure met her nostrils as she breathed. There was something comforting in these smells that, while pungent, were infinitely more pleasant than some parts of London she had visited. Poverty and human waste had a repellent odor that no animal could match.

The gray watched curiously as Blythe climbed onto the first rung of the paddock door.

"There. Now I can get a good look at you." Blythe held out her hand. "Come here, sweetie. I will not hurt you."

The horse lowered his broad nose to her hand, flicking it softly with pink lips. He was deceptively—surprisingly—gentle.

"Lord, but you're big." The white blaze running up the gray's forehead was soft and smooth beneath her palm, his muzzle dwarfing her hand. Large dark eyes stared at her with as much curiosity as Blythe felt. Such soulful eyes for an animal.

"He's not used to women."

Blythe started. Turning her head toward the voice, she

watched as a man came out of the dimness further down the corridor. He was obviously the owner of this magnificent beast. She would have guessed that even if he hadn't spoken.

Horse and master suited each other. Neither was classically handsome, but both possessed a certain attractiveness. Both were long of limb and broad through the chest. Each was also incredibly tall. Standing on the stall door, Blythe was approximately six inches off the ground—eye level with the stranger, who watched her with eyes just as dark as his horse's.

How had he known she was a woman? He must have heard her voice. Normally people who saw her dressed this way just assumed she was a man.

"He's incredible." She glanced back at the horse who stood stock-still beneath her caressing hand. "What is he?"

The man shrugged his broad shoulders and smiled, his thin lips tipping crookedly. "I do not know. I bought him off an Irishman who didn't seem to know either."

Blythe peered over the door into the stall as the man came closer. Her heartbeat seemed to increase with every step he took. He intimidated her a little, this man who was so much taller than herself, who was so big and softly spoken. Yet for all his stillness, all his apparent gentleness, there was an energy that crackled around him that awakened every nerve in Blythe's body.

Better to think of the horse than the man. "His feet are furry and his height is like that of an English Black, but he doesn't have the slope to his nose."

"I believe he's a mix of Scottish and Irish breeds."

The stranger stood beside her, his own hand coming up to pet the horse's forehead. His fingers were long and strong and brown, not delicate and white like those of most aristocrats. His clothing was plain and dark, but well made. His hair, also dark, was thick and too long to be styled in the popular "Brutus" fashion but too short to be artfully curled like a cherub's. But it was his face that really drew Blythe's attention. None of his features seemed well matched—his eyes were dark and thickly lashed, his nose was slim but long, his mouth was narrow and thin, and his chin and jaw were a tad too sharp—yet when put together, these features formed a face that, while it could never be called pretty, was strangely pleasant to look upon.

And here she was staring at him like he was a stallion on the block at Tattersall's! What was wrong with her? She had met plenty of men before, and never had she stopped to study one in such detail—except for Carny. But Carny was a very handsome man. Many people stared at him.

No doubt many people stared at this man as well, especially when he was on the back of such a horse!

"His name is Flynn." He spoke without glancing at her, but Blythe couldn't help the feeling that he had been aware of her watching him.

"Flynn? Not Zeus or Aries, or something equally heroic?"

He smiled at her teasing tone, but it was a sad smile. "I named him after the Irishman who gave him to me."

She knew without asking that the Irishman was dead, and that to this man, the name Flynn was more heroic than Aries or Zeus ever could be.

Stepping down from the door, Blythe stripped off her glove and offered the stranger her hand. "My name is Blythe."

He towered over her as his hand engulfed hers. His touch sent a tingle through her hand, like a tickle, only under the skin. How strange to have to look up to a man—really look up. At six feet tall, Blythe didn't often have to look up at anyone. How wonderful and unsettling it was to feel small!

"Devlin."

She smiled. "It is nice to meet you, Devlin."

His gaze bore into hers, staring at her with a warmth that rivaled John Dobson's attentions. It was all she could do not to blush. She was too old to blush. "Likewise, Blythe."

The sound of her name on his lips sent a warm shiver

down her spine. His voice, a strange combination of rough and smooth, was like a rich, plush velvet rubbed the wrong way—pleasant friction.

She had to let go of his hand and go back to the house or she'd never be ready for dinner in time. She knew this, and yet pulling her fingers free of his left her feeling strangely bereft. There was something about this man—*Devlin*—that made her feel as though she had known him all her life.

Reluctantly, she bid him good day and left the stables. It wasn't until she was halfway to the house that she realized exactly who he was.

Devlin. Devlin Ryland.

The realization was enough to bring her to a dead stop. No. It couldn't be. That incredible man with that deep voice who named his horse after a dead man could *not* be Devlin Ryland. But he was. He had to be. How many Devlins could there be at one house party? It wasn't a common name.

Devlin Ryland, the one man to make her heart skip a beat in two years, was the same man who had taken Carny to Teresa Vega and saved his life.

And consequently, ruined Blythe's.

Miles and Carny had some explaining to do.

In the middle of the Marquess of Wynter's gold drawing room, surrounded by a bevy of party guests insisting that he regale them with daring and romantic recollections of the war against Napoleon, Devlin tried to prove entertaining while his gaze searched the opulent, gilded room for a glimpse of the incredible Lady Blythe.

Miles and Carny had always made her sound like a tomboy, a hoyden. Nothing they told him could have prepared him for the feline-eyed amazon he'd met in the stables earlier. He would never have put two and two together if she hadn't told him her name, even though her height should have been a dead giveaway.

This was the most physically perfect woman he had ever seen. There was nothing fragile about her in face or appearance, but there was no mistaking her femininity. She was all woman.

"I'm afraid I never actually came face to face with Napoleon," he replied, when one female guest asked about the Corsican. She seemed disappointed. Or at least he thought it was disappointment. It was hard to tell when the top of her head reached somewhere in the vicinity of his elbow. "I caught little more than a glimpse of him at Waterloo."

"Waterloo," came the breathy echo, as though it were some kind of mythical place rather than a blood-soaked field where too many soldiers found out just how mortal they really were.

"How very disappointing."

Devlin turned at the new voice, anticipation stirring in his blood. How long had it been since the sound of a woman's voice had been enough to garner such a response from him? Too long.

If Lady Blythe had looked good in trousers and boots, she was even more stunning in a shimmering gown of gold silk that matched the room around them. The low neckline revealed the long column of her throat and enough of her impressive bosom to entice without being vulgar. No cosmetics touched her face. Her skin, pale with a hint of rose along the high bones of her cheeks, was void of powder. Her lashes were naturally dark, as were her sharply arched brows. Her nose was long and straight. Her mouth was full and wide— on anyone else it would look too big for her face, but it suited Lady Blythe. Her hair, which was a rich, deep auburn, was piled on top of her head in an intricate style that added several inches to her already staggering height. Every inch of her was big and bold, and she didn't try to hide herself. He liked that—and he straightened his own shoulders because of it.

Devlin sketched a bow. "It was no disappointment to miss Bonaparte, I assure you, Lady Blythe."

"That is not what I meant," she purred in that husky tone of hers, taking a glass of champagne from the tray a footman offered her. "Every man in the room seems to be talking about that wretched war, even though it ended two years ago. I was rather hoping you might discuss something else, Mr. Ryland."

"What would you have him discuss, Lady Blythe?" the woman who came up to his elbow asked with a snicker. "Crops?"

Blythe didn't even spare her a glance, but Devlin saw a flush of embarrassment tint her high cheekbones. She held his gaze. "I admire the cut of your trousers, Mr. Ryland. Perhaps you can give me the name of your tailor?"

The woman and her companion gasped as Devlin fought to keep from laughing. It was shocking enough that Lady Blythe asked for the name of his tailor, and even more shocking that she spoke of admiring his trousers! He wondered if she really had been, or if she was simply out to appall the matron.

"You shocked her," he needlessly remarked as the woman walked away, taking the rest of the crowd with her.

Blythe's smile was wry. "I must warn you, I have developed a flair for dispersing crowds."

"I don't mind." He didn't either. He'd much rather be the center of this one woman's attention than that of everyone else in the room. Odd, that. He normally didn't like *any* kind of attention.

She eyed him curiously. "No, I did not think you would. When I first entered the room you looked so pained, I thought perhaps Lady Montrose had jabbed you with her lorgnette."

Her dry tone brought a smile to his lips. "She is no different from anyone else who has never experienced war. They all seem to think it an adventure."

"Not I." She took a sip of champagne, pinning him with her gaze.

His smile faded. "Because your brother fought. You know the truth."

"I suspect the only ones who know the truth are those of you who made it home. Champagne?"

Devlin's attention jerked from the woman who had so succinctly summed up what he believed to be true, to the expectant footman who had suddenly appeared at his side. "No. Thank you."

Blythe arched a brow as the man walked away. "You do not drink?"

"I've already had one."

Her smile was something between disbelief and admiration. "A gentleman who does not like to talk about himself, who does not imbibe to excess and thanks the help. You are a rare creature indeed, Mr. Ryland."

It took a great deal of strength not to preen under her praise. "I think perhaps you are a rarity yourself."

Most women would have blushed and batted their eyelashes at such a remark. Lady Blythe looked at him with something that seemed very much like uncertainty in her gaze.

"Because of my height."

The defiant edge in her voice, coupled with the self-awareness in her eyes, wiped all traces of humor from Devlin's face. "Because you are different. Your height affects who you are just as much as mine does."

She smiled faintly. "Perhaps that is why I feel more comfortable talking to you than to people I've known for years. You know what it's like to have to look down at most people."

Oh yes, he understood exactly what she meant. "And now you can look up."

Blythe nodded. "Yes."

"But what about me?" he asked with mock injury, as he leaned closer. Good lord, he was flirting! "I still have to look down."

She looked up at him with a gaze that was part amused, part intrigued, and part coy. "Yes, but not as far."

Devlin laughed. She had him there. But her words conjured up—just for a split second—a vision of himself on his knees before this woman, gazing up at her as though she were a goddess to be worshipped. And with that came the realization that with his face on the same level as her hips, his idea of worship would be no doubt more pleasing for the lady than offering her a dead lamb.

They stood in silence for a moment, simply smiling at each other. By God, he couldn't explain it, but he *liked* this woman. Ever since he had first laid eyes on Blythe that afternoon, his thoughts kept coming back to her. He admired her, though he barely knew her. He respected her, though they were strangers. And he wanted her. As he stood so close, breathing in the heady scent of her, his mind was filled with images of what it would be like to lie with a woman so tall and strong.

A woman, a voice in his head whispered, *who seemed to be made for him.*

"Ah, I see you two have met."

The spell was broken as Miles and Carny joined them. Blythe's face became completely void of expression, and her bright eyes lost all traces of good humor. Why? He'd been led to believe that Blythe was close to both men, especially to Miles, her brother.

"Yes," he replied. "Lady Blythe and I met earlier this afternoon." He intentionally left out the particulars. His first meeting with Blythe was something he wanted to keep for himself, for some strange reason. And was it his imagination, or did she move closer to him when Carny came to stand beside her?

"It is good to see you again, Blythe." There was an edge of hopefulness in Carny's voice that Devlin didn't quite understand.

"Is it?" Her voice was hard and tight, her jaw clenched.

Miles's expression sobered. "Blythe."

There was obviously something going on among the three

of them that Devlin was not privy to. The air was charged with sudden tension. Both men stared at Blythe, one with regret, the other with apprehension, and Lady Blythe's attention was focused solely on him, as though she were looking to him for support.

He would give her whatever was in his means to give, even though it meant opposing two of his oldest friends. Even though he had no idea what he was walking into.

"Might I have a word with you, Blythe?" Carny asked.

Blythe's cheeks flamed as she stared at the carpet. "I would rather eat worms."

His eyes bright with anger, Miles shot an apologetic glance at Devlin. "Blythe, you have forgotten your manners. What kind of impression do you think you are giving Devlin?"

Lifting her head, Blythe looked from her brother to Devlin. She ignored Carny. "Surely Mr. Ryland will forgive my rudeness. No doubt he knows the history between Lord Carnover and myself."

History? Devlin couldn't keep his surprise from showing. "I have never heard anything but good about you from Carny, Lady Blythe."

It was her turn to look surprised. Miles looked murderous, and poor Carny looked downright humiliated.

"Oh, then you don't know?" Blythe's tone was laden with deceptively sweet innocence. "Before he went to Waterloo and found himself a wife, Lord Carnover and I were engaged to be married."

Chapter 2

Humiliating Carny hadn't felt nearly as good as it should have.

In fact, what little satisfaction there was had paled when held up against the tongue-lashing Miles was bound to deliver once he got her alone.

Devlin Ryland hadn't looked too impressed by her outburst either. He'd just stood there, frowning. Who the frown was directed at, Blythe couldn't say, but she had a sneaky suspicion that it was she.

At least he wasn't frowning now. He wasn't doing anything but eating. Around him, seated around the long, food-laden table, people laughed and chatted, but he seemingly paid no heed. He concentrated on his plate, carefully cutting his food, putting it in his mouth, chewing and swallowing. Occasionally he would take a sip from his glass of wine, but by the time most people were on their third or fourth glass, he was still on his first.

Blythe tried not to stare, truly she did, but no matter what she turned her attention to, it always ended up centered right back on Devlin. He intrigued her, and she couldn't quite put her finger on why. The way he looked in the stark darkness of his evening attire might have something to do with it, as the looks of all men were improved by such finery. His height was certainly part of it, but there was more. She liked the way he truly seemed to listen when someone spoke to him. She liked that he treated women the same as men—he didn't flirt or flatter, not even when it was done to him. In fact, such attention from women seemed to make him uneasy, at least from what she had seen over dinner.

And there had been a lot of flirting. Lady Ashby vied with Lady Trundel for his attention, both of them all but hopping up on the table and offering themselves for his pleasure.

"Do tell us, Mr. Ryland, what it is like to be a hero," Lady Ashby urged. "Is it very tiresome having all the ladies swooning at your feet?"

There were a few chuckles at this—mostly from Lady Ashby herself. One gentleman remarked that he didn't think having ladies swooning over him would be very tiresome at all.

Devlin forced a smile. Blythe knew it was forced because both sides of his mouth curved up. In her brief acquaintance with the man she already knew that his natural smile was lopsided.

"I try not to pay much attention to that sort of thing, Lady Ashby," he replied, taking a sip of his wine. He seemed to swish it around a bit before swallowing, as though there was a bad taste in his mouth.

Lady Ashby appeared both charmed and confused. "My dear Mr. Devlin, whyever not?"

"Because if someone hadn't stuck the title of 'hero' on me, most of those ladies would not swoon over me for two hundred pounds."

Blythe opened her mouth to say something, anything to correct him, but Lady Ashby beat her to it. "Oh my dear sir, I am sure that is not true at all. Even without being branded a hero, a big, strong gentleman like yourself has *many* charms that could make a lady weak in the knees."

Good Lord, was she foxed? No, Lady Ashby was perfectly—astonishingly—sober. Her meaning was scandalously clear, and a few of the more ribald guests laughed uproariously, but Devlin did not.

He smiled at Lady Ashby, a more genuine smile this time, but it didn't quite reach his eyes. "You will have to ask my wife when I'm lucky enough to have one. Hers will be the only knees I'll be concerned with."

Oh, she could jump up and hug him! Instead, Blythe settled for laughing. Even Lady Ashby, to her credit, chuckled at his sally, though she didn't look all that amused. It was well known that she had a penchant for young, virile men. At least she wouldn't be able to add Devlin to her ever growing list of conquests.

Why this made her so happy Blythe did not know. Perhaps the instant liking she had taken to Devlin, despite the fact that his act of heroism had brought about her heartbreak, made her want him to be better than other men. Stronger, not so weak-willed or easily caught by a pair of large breasts and fluttering eyelashes. Setting him apart from the rest of his sex was not a wise idea. She had done the same to Carny, and the disappointment still stung.

Devlin must have heard her laughter, for he turned his head toward her. He smiled—crookedly—his dark eyes alight with boyish mischief. It was as though they were sharing a private joke or a moment of complete understanding. Whatever it was sent a frisson of awareness shooting through Blythe's entire being—the kind of awareness a woman feels toward an attractive man.

Oh dear. This could not continue.

"Speaking of marriage," Lady Ashby continued, interrupting the moment. "When are you going to finally settle down, Lady Blythe?"

All eyes turned toward her, but Blythe wasn't the least bit embarrassed. She'd been asked the same question at least a thousand times ever since her come-out and had her answer pared down to the shortest response she could give without seeming rude.

"When I am fortunate enough to find the right man, Lady Ashby."

There were, of course, more than a few chuckles at this. One person not laughing was Devlin Ryland. In fact, he looked as though he would very much like to ask for a description of the "right man."

If she listed the attributes she had in mind, how many of them would he possess?

Oh dear, dear, dear.

Lady Ashby laughed the hardest, or rather, the *loudest.* Somehow she managed to do it without changing her faintly amused expression—probably to avoid wrinkling her delicate ivory skin. Whatever the reason, it was somewhat disconcerting to see a lady laugh without really looking as though she enjoyed it.

"My dear girl," Lady Ashby trilled. "There is no such thing as the *right* man. There is only the *tolerable.*"

How could a woman who flirted with and bedded as many men as Lady Ashby have such a low opinion of their sex?

Perhaps it was because she'd been with so many that she had such a low opinion. The more men Blythe herself became acquainted with, the more cynical she became.

Blythe pretended to find great humor in the other woman's remarks. "Of course! Now I see what I have been doing wrong. I shall lower my expectations immediately. Thank you, Lady Ashby."

Of course, laughter followed her wry pronouncement. The only people not laughing were Devlin and Carny. Devlin's expression was curious, if not pleasant, but Carny simply sat there with a guilty look on his face. It was a little late for him to have regrets now.

You have no one but yourself to blame, Carny. Look as guilty as you want. I am invulnerable to it.

"I think you should keep your expectations as high as you want, Blythe," Varya commented from her seat higher up the table. Miles shot her a curious glance.

Blythe smiled. Trust Varya to always be on her side. "Oh? Why is that?"

Her sister-in-law smiled serenely. "Any man worth his salt would accept the challenge to live up to them."

The ladies laughed, the gentlemen protested, but only one person asked the question that made Blythe's heart falter in her breast.

"Any man worth his salt would already live up to them. Is that not right, Lady Blythe?"

Taking a sip of wine to combat the sudden dryness in her throat, Blythe met Devlin's curious gaze with a level one of her own. "Quite, Mr. Devlin."

He smiled. Was that the sound of a gauntlet being thrown down? And why did her heart beat faster with anticipation rather than dread? It had been so long since it pounded in response to any man but Carny.

This was not good. This was very bad indeed.

Carny was still looking at her as though he wanted to tear his own heart out and offer it to her in penance, seemingly oblivious to his own wife a little farther down the table. Blythe didn't want his guilt, not now. She wanted him to be sorry and mean it. That was all. All the guilt in the world couldn't compare to a smidgen of regret.

After dinner, when the gentlemen were left to their port and cigars and the ladies followed Varya to the drawing room, Blythe took advantage of the lull to steal away for a moment's peace.

She found solitude in Varya's music room. Flopping onto a pale blue sofa, she blew out a long, gusty sigh. She had been too long away from society if a simple dinner party could wear upon her so.

She toed off her slippers. Ahh, that was better. The air cooled her wriggling toes as she fell back into the sofa's cushioned embrace. She simply sat there and enjoyed the relative silence. It would be a commodity hard to come by in the weeks to come.

A little while later she entertained the idea of not rejoining the party. It would be wrong of her not to. But would anyone notice if she spent the rest of the evening hiding in here? Oddly enough, she suspected Devlin Ryland would notice. The thought warmed her far more than it should have.

Oh Lord, how could she have been so rude to mention her and Carny's engagement in front of him? He didn't deserve to be dragged into their mess. He must think her so totally without manners and propriety. And yet, during dinner, he hadn't looked at her as though he found her lacking.

"May I join you?" said a voice from the door.

Blythe froze, trembling ever so slightly.

Oh no. Not now.

Looking up, she met Carny's pale gaze as he entered the room, impeccably dressed in buff breeches and a dark blue coat. His smile was rueful, as though he regretted the scene she had made in front of Devlin Ryland as much as she did.

She didn't bother to stand. "If I say yes, will you run out on me as is your habit?"

There was some satisfaction in watching the color drain from his tanned cheeks. Once, shortly after his return from Belgium—when he returned to England with his *wife*—he had tried to apologize for his actions, but Blythe hadn't thought he was really all that sorry. He had been too blissfully in love to be properly remorseful. Now, many, many months later, he looked almost as sorry as he should be for dashing all her hopes.

Almost.

"We were not betrothed, Blythe. Not formally."

An icy heat crept up Blythe's cheeks, and she resisted the urge to stand so that they were eye to eye because then she might be tempted to smash her fist into the perfection of his face.

"You asked me to wait for you. You told me that when you returned you were going to marry me. People expected it to happen—*I* expected it to happen. Had I known it would have taken being shot to actually get you to the altar I would have put a ball into you before you left."

It was unkind of her to remind him of how he had almost died at Waterloo. Perhaps on some level she even understood how he could have betrayed her after coming so close to death. Devlin Ryland might have saved his life, but it had been Carny's wife—Teresa—who had nursed him, kept the fevers and infections at bay. She must have been like an angel from heaven to him, while Blythe herself became little more than a distant memory.

A distant memory who had commissioned a seamstress to construct her wedding gown while her soon-to-be-betrothed romanced another woman. How she despised him for that. She had been so happy, so young and certain in his devotion— in her own. Never once had she suspected his love wasn't true. Not once. And that was what she hated most. He had fooled her, and that one mistake had cost her so much, hurt her so deeply that she swore never to allow it to happen again.

The next time she fell prey to a man she would have his admission of love long before she ever gave hers. His heart would be in her hand before he held hers. She would not open herself up to hurt again.

That was if she ever met another man who made her want to take a chance on love. Here in Devonshire, the chances of that happening were wonderfully small.

Standing just a few feet away, Carny gripped the back of a dainty French chair. He seemed more interested in watching his fingers curl around the gilded wood than he was in looking at her. Blythe kept her own gaze focused squarely on his face, forcing herself to see him as a man, flawed and imperfect rather than the hero she had always believed him to be.

There were far too many heroes at Brixleigh right now.

"I never meant to injure you," he murmured, his gaze resting somewhere in the vicinity of her nose. "Surely you know that."

"Actually," she replied, "I sincerely doubt I crossed your mind at all. I believe the person whose feelings you were most concerned with was yourself, and while I find that dishonorable, I am afraid I cannot hold it against you."

Now his gaze snapped to hers. The surprise there was almost laughable. "You cannot?"

"No." It was true. She had no idea what he had gone through at Waterloo, had never experienced what war could do to a person's heart and mind. For all she knew, she might have done the same if the roles had been reversed. Although she perhaps would have handled things a *bit* differently.

A portrait of a distant ancestor hung on the far wall. It was tempting to stare at it rather than Carny, but he deserved to have her unwavering attention as she finally told him the truth of what was in her heart.

"What I cannot forgive you for, Carny, is for letting me believe you loved me in the first place. You obviously did not; otherwise your brush with death would have made you realize it, rather than turning your attentions to someone else. You have apologized for almost everything else, but you have never once said you were sorry for deceiving me where your feelings were concerned."

He said nothing. In fact, he appeared to be incapable of speech of any kind. Blythe, on the other hand, was filled with a strange, bustling elation. She had done it. She had confronted Carny. She hadn't made a fool out of herself, nor did she feel any regret for having spoken as plainly as she had. She felt curiously relieved and free. His hold was slipping, but the scars were still fresh and far too tender.

His brow puckering, Carny opened his mouth, but whatever he was about to say was lost as Devlin Ryland entered the room, looking very dark and dangerous in head-to-toe black, save for the snowy white of his shirt and cravat. He begged no pardons for his interruption, nor did he try to pretend he had stumbled upon them by accident.

In fact, he didn't look surprised to see them together at all. It was as though he had expected it. Why? And why should that fill Blythe with such a feeling of guilty unease?

His gaze focused solely on Carny. "Your wife is looking for you."

Carny flushed, as only the fair and beautiful could, like a child caught playing somewhere he had been told not to.

"Yes, of course." He bowed stiffly. "Pray excuse me."

Blythe watched him go with a strange feeling. Was it regret? Pity? She couldn't tell, but she did know that she wasn't the least bit embarrassed to have been caught alone with him. In fact, she didn't feel much at all where Carny was concerned—not as she thought she ought. She was more nervous at being alone with Devlin.

"That was very good of you," she remarked, rising to her feet once she was certain Carny was out of earshot. "To come and rescue your friend like that."

His dark gaze was unreadable even though his expression was completely unguarded. "It wasn't for him."

He came to rescue her, then. Part of Blythe rebelled at the thought. Did she look like the kind of woman who needed rescuing? She was strong and capable and completely independent of needing a man's protection.

So why did her insides turn all warm and tingly at his simple confession? Why did she feel giddy and—damn it all—*feminine* when he looked at her like that? As if he were a knight on a charger and she the damsel in distress.

As she always wanted a man to look at her.

"Would you like me to escort you downstairs?" His tone was perfectly polite, completely unaware that he was treating her in a manner she was completely unaccustomed to.

Any man worth his salt would instinctively live up to her expectations. Wasn't that what he said? Did he realize he had already met one?

Dear God, if she had any sense she'd run from him as fast as she could. This man would be a danger to her. He could make her wish for foolish things that she had no business wishing for. She knew this, and yet she did not run.

"I do not think that would be wise." How calm she sounded, despite the fact that her heart was trying to climb into her throat. "People might talk."

He nodded. "I will follow after you then."

How far? Just to the drawing room or anywhere she wanted? Oh, it was fanciful, romantic thinking, she knew—the kind of thinking that had gotten her into trouble with Carny—but she couldn't stop herself from thinking it. Another reason to run screaming.

She would have to stay away from Devlin Ryland. He was a dangerous man if he could have her feeling a degree of infatuation for him within a day of meeting him. If Blythe knew one thing about the male sex, it was that she had very poor judgment where they were concerned.

"I will see you in the drawing room then." Smoothing her skirts, she moved toward the open doorway where he stood inside, like a sentry guarding the entrance to a castle. His gaze was fastened on her face, but Blythe felt it as keenly as if he had examined her from head to toe.

She stopped beside him and turned, raising her chin to look up at him. For a moment, she savored the sensation, smiling at the puzzlement in his eyes.

"Earlier today when we met in the stables, you knew I was a woman. How?"

The right side of his mouth lifted and curved. His dark eyes brightened with a sudden warmth that made Blythe shiver in response. "There could be no mistaking you for anything but."

Oh. "Thank you for rescuing me, Mr. Devlin."

"Any time, Lady Blythe."

As Blythe turned to run—*walk*—away, she knew in her heart that he meant it.

"Well, what do you think?"

At first Devlin had been dubious when Miles told him he had the perfect estate in mind for him to buy, but he'd met his friend early that morning, when the sun was still low in the sky and dew clung to the grass, and rode west to where this little piece of heaven was supposedly located.

Now he was glad for Miles's tenacity and his taste in architecture. Sitting astride Flynn's broad back, Devlin surveyed the property sprawled prettily before him. They'd stopped for one last look on the ride back to Brixleigh. He didn't even have to look at the powerfully built, auburn-haired man beside him to know his friend's smile was smug. "It's perfect."

And it was. Situated in the gentle slope of a shallow valley not quite five miles from Brixleigh, Rosewood Manor was like a pale jewel placed on rich green velvet. Built in the early years of the previous century, Rosewood was made of smooth, rose-colored stone. Its front was unadorned save for the large, ornately paned windows and double oak doors. It looked like a house that had been well cared for and well lived in—not by some aristocrat who stayed there only when he wanted to shoot animals or have large parties, but by a family who had loved every nook and stone—including the multitudes of flowers, shrubberies, and trees that made up the garden behind it.

The house was large—certainly not anything like Brixleigh, but big enough that he would need either a capable housekeeper or a wife to make sure everything ran smoothly.

A wife. He had never really given much thought to marriage in the past, always assuming that he would marry one day but having no attributes in mind. But now that his mind turned to thoughts of impending matrimony, no one but the right woman would do.

A woman who would not judge him. A woman he could share his darkest secret with, and she would not turn away. A woman who could teach him how to love and give her love in return. Just once in his life he wanted to know what it was like to love and be loved—unconditionally and uncontrollably.

Was it too much for him to ask that he find such a perfect life? Yes, he knew it was. He didn't deserve such happiness. He'd made sure of that the day he'd joined Wellington's army. There was too much blood on his hands to deserve anything but the nightmares that plagued him and the guilt that refused to let him go.

"Is the inside sound?" No more thoughts of the past. It was time to think of the future.

"Very," Miles replied. "There is little furniture but the interior is simple—none of that fussy Frog rubbish."

Nodding, Devlin kept his gaze centered on his future home. "Who do I talk to?"

Miles chuckled. "I knew you would want it. Jamieson owns it."

Now Devlin turned to face his friend. "Lord Dartmouth?"

"The same." Miles's teeth gleamed white against the tan of his skin. "Was it not his brother Thomas whose life you saved at Talavera?"

Devlin's gaze skipped back to Rosewood, a sense of unease washing over him. Flynn shifted as he sensed it, and Devlin calmed himself as he soothed the horse. He didn't like it when people made him sound like some kind of hero. Heroes saved. Heroes didn't kill.

"You make it sound like I pulled him from the very jaws of death."

"Didn't you?"

Devlin shrugged one shoulder. "I pulled a ball from his leg. That is all." He hadn't been the first man to perform such surgery on a battlefield without medical training. He probably would not be the last.

"When there was no one else to do it and infection was already taking hold. If it hadn't been for you, he would have died."

Devlin didn't bother to explain. How could he? Miles hadn't been a career soldier. He'd been an officer who paid for the chance to fight the French for the sake of crown and country. He'd ridden a horse, always had a clean uniform, had always been held separate from the men below him despite his equal treatment of everyone he met. He had no conception of what it was to march into battle, to lie in cold, wet mud for hours waiting for the enemy to walk into your sights. Not that Miles hadn't seen battle—he had, and he had been wounded as well. He'd been tended by Wellington's own surgeon while other more seriously wounded men lay dying in the dirt, their blood flowing like wine from the holes in their bodies. Devlin didn't hold him in lower esteem because of that—it was just the way things were.

Yes, Devlin had pulled a ball out of Jamieson's brother. He had pulled lead out of many men. He'd stitched wounds with the thread pulled from dead men's uniforms. He had also held many a callused hand as that soldier—old or young—slipped away to the supposed "better place" that was waiting somewhere beyond that godforsaken Peninsula. He just did what needed to be done. If that was all it took to make a hero, well, there were better men than he who should bear the title. Men who had been forgotten now that Napoleon was long defeated.

"Does Dartmouth have a solicitor in town?" Devlin didn't feel comfortable using the man's surname as Miles had. Years in the Ninety-fifth had accomplished that. The Rifles had not been a division for the upper crust, no matter that both Miles and Carny had served with them on more than one occasion. Miles liked to think that he had been one of them, but he hadn't been. The men had liked him but they had never accepted the marquess as one of their own. Miles would never know that, however, not from Devlin.

"Yes, there is a solicitor in charge of the sale," Miles replied as they turned their horses back in the direction of Brixleigh. "Man by the name of Adams. I will send word to him today if you would like."

"I would. If the inside is as perfect as the out, I want it." As soon as he said the words he felt as though some kind of order had come into his life. He would have a home, a place to settle. A hole in his life would be filled.

Now if he could fill the ten or twenty thousand others that plagued him from time to time . . .

They filled the ride back to Brixleigh with talk of the area and Miles's family's connection to it. This of course eventually led to talk of Miles's father and mother and finally, his sister.

What had she and Carny been discussing last night when he walked in on them? Their broken engagement? And just who had broken it anyway? He couldn't imagine any sane man walking away from such a woman. But if it had been Blythe, why was there such bitterness in her expression and tone when she confronted Carny before dinner?

And why had Carny looked so guilty when Devlin discovered them in the music room? Was there something going on between him and Blythe? No, he couldn't believe it. He didn't want to believe either one of them capable of such deceit. Especially Blythe.

Never had he felt such a strong and instant pull toward another person. It was physical, certainly. He would have to be dead not to appreciate Lady Blythe's lush curves, but she was Miles's sister, and despite her age, most likely an innocent— unless she was Carny's mistress. Regardless, she was not the kind of woman who had to settle for the youngest son of a viscount. Nor was she the kind of woman who deserved a man as damaged as he. Miles would want better for her even if she didn't.

"Your description of Lady Blythe was unjust, my friend," Devlin remarked, breaking the brief silence as they neared the Brixleigh stables.

"Oh?" Miles seemed surprised. "In what respect?"

Stripping off his left glove, Devlin held it and the reins in his right hand as he raked his fingers through the wind-tangled thickness of his hair. "You and Carny both had me prepared for some kind of hoydenish tomboy."

The heavier man didn't seem to find this odd. "She is."

"She's also a beautiful, interesting woman."

Miles raised his brows. "Beautiful and interesting, eh? Never thought of her quite that way before. She is quite a handful, I will give her that."

A handful? More like two, or four. Maybe if Devlin were an octopus he could get enough handfuls to satisfy his curiosity.

He wanted to ask about Blythe and Carny, but it was none of his business, and he knew it. Besides, if they were having an affair, Miles would undoubtedly be the last to know.

After leaving their horses with Brixleigh's capable grooms, Miles and Devlin made their way to the east lawn where a small group of women had gathered for a morning archery match. Frankly, Devlin was surprised to see so many guests up and around, but country parties generally meant keeping country hours.

They also meant a lot of sneaking between rooms at night, as he'd learned when Lady Ashby had slipped into his the night before. Luckily he had crawled into bed in his small-clothes or she would have seen more of him than he wanted. Still, he probably should have been a bit more delicate with her, but she had awakened him just as the dream had taken hold, and his mood had been less than gentle.

Still, "Get the frig out" was hardly the kind of thing one said to a lady. He wasn't surprised that she didn't even look at him this morning.

Another thing that didn't surprise him was that Blythe was one of the ladies gathered on the grass. Even if her height hadn't made her stand out among the others, her clothing would have.

"What the hell is she wearing?" Miles growled.

Grinning, Devlin watched as Blythe lined up her arrow with her target. "It looks like an old Rifleman jacket."

The sight of the familiar green, so like the one he used to wear, should have filled Devlin with trepidation, should have brought forth memories he didn't want to remember. Instead he felt a certain amount of pride for the brass buttons in need of a good polishing. He also appreciated the way Blythe filled out the coat. It had been tailored to fit her perfectly and accentuated the full globes of her breasts like a second skin.

Her brother was not impressed. "I'll strangle her."

"Relax, Miles." Devlin laid a hand on his friend's shoulder. "There's nothing wrong with what she's wearing, not for a sporting event among friends."

Miles turned to stare at him as if he had announced that Napoleon was riding up the drive. "That was one of *my* coats she destroyed! And she is wearing trousers!"

Devlin shrugged. He couldn't argue there. Blythe was indeed wearing trousers. She looked damn fine in them too. Her legs were long and firm beneath the snug buckskin. A woman like Blythe would have strong legs—legs that would wrap around a man and not let him go until she'd had her fill of him.

Sweet Jesus, he was growing hard just thinking about it.

"The gown she wore to dinner last night was far more revealing than what she's wearing now."

Miles stopped dead in his tracks and turned fully to face him. "That was different. Decolletage is acceptable. All women display their breasts to some degree. They do *not* wear fashions that display their limbs in such a brazen manner!"

Devlin shrugged again, but Miles had already spun on his heel and continued toward the crowd of spectators watching the archers. Perhaps Blythe was displaying her legs, but it wasn't as though they were bare. Personally, Devlin preferred the gown she wore to dinner. A hint of breast was better than trousers any day.

Sighing, he jogged after Miles just as Blythe let her arrow fly. It sliced through the air as a blur and hit the target dead in the center with such force, it vibrated for nearly a full minute before going still.

An appreciative murmur rose from the clapping spectators. Devlin thought their response a little restrained, but that was the aristocracy. He'd been too long out of society to know what was done and what wasn't. He'd joined the army when most young men entered society—social rules and regulations were the least of his concerns.

He stood on the outer fringe of the group, just far enough behind that no one noticed him. Lady Ashby was among the group, and he had no desire to speak to her. Either she'd be rude because of his disregard for her the night before, or she'd try all the harder to coerce him into her bed. Even if she didn't talk to him, someone else would, and he didn't want anything to interfere with his study of Blythe.

She selected another arrow from the quiver and took aim. *Whoosh. Thwwwang.* Another bull's-eye.

"Incredible," he whispered when she repeated the performance a third time.

In front of him, Lord Compton leaned toward his wife and brayed, "Rather mannish, ain't she?"

"She's amazing," Devlin said without thinking. When several heads turned to stare at him, he added, "Hits dead center every time."

Too late he realized he should have kept his mouth shut. Lady Ashby was already prowling toward him.

Her voice was as low as a cat's purr and her nails like claws as she wrapped her hand around his sleeve. "I did not know your taste ran to aging, lumbering spinsters."

Obviously she was still sore over his failure to fall at her feet. She hadn't much liked being forcibly shoved out of his room at two o'clock in the morning. "You would rather it ran to aging, unfaithful wives?"

Once the words were out of his mouth there was nothing he could do about them. It wasn't in his nature to be cruel or unnecessarily rude, but Lady Ashby's remarks about Blythe were undeserved and untrue. It wasn't that unusual for women Blythe's age to be unmarried, nor was she lumbering. In fact, she was uncommonly graceful.

Lady Ashby flushed a dark, unbecoming red. Her fingers tightened around his arm, just enough so that he could feel her nails digging into the fabric of his coat. Were his arm bare she surely would have broken the skin.

If Lady Ashby wanted to play rough, she'd picked the wrong man. Years dealing with enemy soldiers, spies, and all manner of cutthroats had left Devlin with the realization that women could be just as ruthless and dirty as men. It only took being kicked in the privates twice by female Bonapartists before he stopped being chivalrous and started fighting back.

He caught Lady Ashby by the wrist, his soiled glove en-

gulfing her delicate bones hard enough to make her gasp in
pain. Still, she didn't immediately relinquish her hold on
him. He had to bring tears to her eyes before she did that.

Oddly enough, he had the strange suspicion that she actually enjoyed it.

Devlin didn't speak, nor did Lady Ashby. She simply
smiled a coy smile and turned away, rubbing the dirty spot on
her arm where his fingers had been.

He watched her go, knowing better than to turn his back on
the enemy before making certain there was no possibility of
a second attack.

Finally certain she wouldn't be coming back, Devlin allowed himself to relax. He started to turn his attention back
to the archery competition, only to notice Lady Blythe walking toward him. Had she witnessed the scene between him
and Lady Ashby?

She smiled—it lit her entire face. Good God, but she was
arresting. His chest tightened in response.

"Good morning, Mr. Ryland."

"Lady Blythe."

She glanced over her shoulder at the spectators. "I see
Joyce the Jackal tried to sink her claws into you. I trust you
escaped unharmed?"

He couldn't help but chuckle at her nickname for Lady
Ashby. "Quite."

Her expression changed to one of uncertainty. Her bright
green eyes were veiled by the sudden lowering of her auburn
lashes. "Everyone is preparing to go inside to tidy up for
breakfast. I thought perhaps you might escort me inside."

Devlin's brow furrowed. Lady Blythe didn't strike him as
the kind of woman who wanted or needed a male escort to
enter her own house.

"What is it?" he asked. "Are you trying to escape your
brother?" He couldn't help but notice that Miles was watching them. Nor could he miss the scowl on his friend's face.

Blythe grinned sheepishly as she raised her gaze to meet his. "Exactly. Would you mind rescuing me once more?"

This was the second time she had referred to his interruption of her meeting with Carny the night before as a rescue. Perhaps there wasn't anything between the two of them after all.

He was more relieved than he cared to admit.

He offered her his arm. "With pleasure."

Her smiled broadened, and the ache in his chest deepened. What the devil was wrong with him that this eccentric, wonderfully individual woman affected him the way she did?

It wasn't a question he could answer, but as they walked toward the house, there was a lightness in Devlin's heart that he hadn't felt in a very, very long time.

Varya was in the nursery with little Edward when Miles found her. He had yet to change and was still wearing the same clothes he'd worn on his ride with Devlin, right down to his muddy boots. At least he hoped it was mud.

His wife raked him with a critical but loving sapphire gaze. "You smell."

Three years, and he still loved the sound of her voice—low and husky with a smooth Russian lilt.

"You like it," he teased, taking his son from her arms. Edward was two years old and bounced back and forth between being an angel and being a holy terror. He had his mother's eyes, which made it hard for his father to say no, and his grandfather Vladimir's temperament, which made for some interesting power struggles between father and son.

Still, he was the most beautiful thing Miles had ever seen.

"You should be resting," he told Varya as Edward pulled on his ear. "I do not want you wearing yourself out."

Varya scowled and rubbed a hand across the back of her neck. She looked fine, but Miles didn't care how she *looked*.

"For God's sake, Miles. I am with child, not an invalid."

He bounced Edward on his hip. "The doctor said you should be careful."

The scowl deepened. Lord, she was magnificent when angry. The sharp V of her brows was as black and imposing as a raven's wings.

"No, *you* said I should be careful. The doctor said I was fine."

He could hear the edge in her voice, that irritated-female sound that meant she was more than prepared to give him a fight if he came looking for one. A change of subject was in order, because in a verbal sparring match with his wife, Miles *always* lost.

"Ryland said something interesting to me this morning."

He could literally see the tension drain from her shoulders. "Oh? What was that?"

"He said Blythe was beautiful."

Varya crossed to a small dresser with a pile of clean nappies on top of it and started putting them in the drawer. It was a job that should have been left for Edward's nurse, but Varya was one of those rare mothers who had a difficult time allowing someone else to care for her child. "She is."

"And interesting."

"She is that as well." She paused, several nappies in her hand. "Although I must give Mr. Ryland credit for seeing it this early in their acquaintance."

Miles put his squirming son down on the rug with his toys and moved toward his wife. "So you are not surprised that a man finds my sister appealing?"

"No, why should I be? I've known since I first laid eyes on her that she was an amazing young woman."

She did? "Why did you not tell me this before?"

Rolling her eyes, Varya shut the drawer and braced her hands on her full hips. In a few months her condition would be impossible to hide. "You have eyes, Miles. Could you not see it yourself?"

Miles ran a hand through his hair. "I suppose I've always been biased. Of course she is amazing. She's my sister. I thought she was the most beautiful thing in the world when I first laid eyes on her. 'Course I was ten at the time and had yet to meet you."

That got a smile out of her—and a blush. "Flatterer. Why should it bother you that Mr. Ryland finds Blythe appealing?"

Pleased that he could still make her blush, Miles shrugged. "It does not. I think they would be a perfect match."

"You do?" Apparently he could still surprise her as well.

"Of course I do, just as I knew she and Carny would not be."

She wrapped her arms around his waist, stepping closer so that the fullness of her breasts pressed against his torso. "So what is the problem?"

"The problem," he growled, pulling her tight against him, "is making the two of them see it."

She ran her hand up his chest. "Do not attempt matchmaking, Miles. You would not be good at it."

"What would you suggest I do?"

Varya smiled, lifting her face for a kiss. "If it is meant to be they will figure out for themselves, just as we did."

"That is what I'm afraid of."

Her answering laughter was cut off as Miles lowered his head to hers. Then he kissed her, and even after three years Varya's kiss was still able to make him forget everything else—even Blythe and Devlin.

Chapter 3

There was more to Devlin Ryland than Blythe had first thought.

She had expected him to be more like Miles and Carny—talkative, arrogant even. She had expected him to expound upon his escapades during the war—people certainly asked him to enough—but he didn't do that either. He was quiet and solitary. He avoided large groups, and consequently was on his way to becoming a great favorite among the wallflowers, the shy, and the elderly guests with whom he spent a great deal of time conversing.

And one day, while walking through the garden, Blythe spotted him playing fetch with some of the estate dogs while other guests played at pall-mall. It was one of the few occasions since his arrival almost a week ago that he looked as though he was truly entertained.

It wasn't that she thought him distant, but rather that he enjoyed himself more when nothing but throwing a stick was expected of him, or when he could sit back and do the listening rather than the talking.

So it was a bit of a surprise when he appeared in the ballroom the night of Varya's formal ball dressed in evening wear and acting as though he actually intended to dance.

A few heads turned as he entered the room. Several of them belonged to guests already swirling and gliding along the polished center of the dance floor. Why everyone didn't simply stop what he was doing and stare, Blythe didn't understand.

Simply put, Devlin Ryland cut one hell of a figure. There were few men who didn't look good in evening finery, but Devlin took "fine" to a whole new level. His dark coloring was the perfect complement to the austere black of his coat and trousers. The golden tan of his skin made the white of his collar and cravat seem that much whiter. His shoulders were broad—no padding in that coat, oh no. Incredibly long legs ate up the floor with every confident step.

Perhaps that was the most amazing thing about Devlin Ryland—the way he moved. Blythe was used to men like her brother, men born to privilege and power. Miles walked like a man who knew his place in the world—on top of it—while Devlin walked like a man comfortable in his own skin. He was a man who knew what his body was capable of because it had been stretched to its limits in the past.

Blythe envied him. She straightened her own shoulders as she watched him stop and greet two elderly ladies who tittered like schoolgirls at his attention. She stretched her spine and rose to the full reach of her height when two younger, unmarried women joined the group. Such tiny little girls, both of them together wouldn't be woman enough for such a man.

And what? She would be?

It was a sad day when all she could name to recommend herself to a man was her size. Yes, she was freakishly tall. Yes, she was rounder than was the fashion, and she was willing to bet she could best half the men in the room at an arm wrestle, but that didn't make her someone Devlin Ryland would want as a mate. Did it?

Why was she even thinking it? Mr. Ryland hadn't given

her any indication that he was interested in anything more than friendship, and even if he had, she knew better than to let her thoughts run away with her. She would not make a cake of herself again where a man was concerned.

Besides, she'd watched Devlin Ryland enough over the past few days to know why these young things liked him. *Everyone* seemed to like him. He treated everyone exactly the same—with great patience and kindness. Who wouldn't be drawn to such condescension? No doubt, tonight he would partner all those poor women no one else would stand up with.

At least *she* wasn't in that group. The only thing that saved her was the fact that many of the men present were personal friends of Miles. Two of them had already requested dances. Blythe wasn't certain which was more embarrassing; not dancing, or dancing because your brother's friends felt sorry for you.

It wasn't that she couldn't dance—she could. It was her height that kept many men from asking. It took a man very comfortable in his skin to dance with a woman his height or taller. The fact that Blythe had instructed her maid to pile as much of her hair on top of her head as she could didn't help either. It made her even taller.

She had also worn her flashiest gown. It was made of shimmery gold gauze over a pale cream silk underskirt. The low square neckline showed a scandalous amount of her bosom, but was still less shocking than other gowns in the room. She loved this gown. It flattered her figure and complemented her coloring perfectly. This dress made her feel like a woman—or rather how she'd always believed a woman should feel.

Powerful. Pretty.

And she didn't care if she danced. No doubt if someone other than his friends asked her to dance, Miles would try to marry them right there on the spot. She didn't want to explain that Lord So-and-So was only after her dowry or that Lord Fat Pants just wanted her because she had "good hips for breeding."

Besides, Miles might have actually gotten to the point where he was desperate enough to accept one of them! And then that would just lead to more trouble when Blythe refused and then—

". . . dance?"

"Hmm . . . what?" She turned around and found herself staring at a very simply but well-tied cravat and a smoothly shaven jaw. She raised her gaze. Staring down at her, as though she were the only woman in the room, were two gorgeously dark eyes, set beneath long, arched brows and framed by eyelashes so thick and lush any woman would envy them.

His smile was lopsided. Her heart skipped a beat. "Oh. Forgive me, Mr. Ryland."

His gaze was teasing, but there was a touch of flush along his high cheekbones. "Do you ignore all men who ask you to dance, Lady Blythe?"

"Dance? Oh no, you do not have to dance with me, see?" She held up her dance card. "I have several partners for this evening."

He frowned at the card. "It's not full."

Heat suffused Blythe's cheeks. "Well, no, but I do have partners. I am not one of your wallflowers."

Thick brows crept high up onto his forehead as he returned his attention from the card at her wrist to her face. "Wallflowers? Lady Blythe, I asked you to dance because I want to dance with you, not because no one else will."

Her cheeks became even warmer. "Oh." He wanted to dance with her. *Wanted* to dance with *her*. Why?

The answer was simple. She was the only woman in the room that he wouldn't get a pain in his neck from looking down at. Of course he would want to dance with her.

Or perhaps he thought she looked pretty in her gown. Maybe he wanted to dance with her just because he wanted to. Did there have to be another reason?

"Forgive my rudeness, Mr. Ryland. I would be honored to dance with you. Which dance would you like?"

"The first and last waltzes."

The waltz? How long had it been since she had waltzed? The last man she waltzed with had been Carny. Good Lord, she didn't know if she remembered how to waltz! And he wanted the first and the last. With her!

Her cheeks warmed. She would make an idiot of herself, of that there could be no doubt. "I have not waltzed in a long time. I'm afraid I will not be very good at it."

Devlin smiled—a subtle tilt of his mouth. He had dimples. She'd never noticed before now. "Just follow my lead."

His lead? Oh Lord, whenever she waltzed, *she* always tried to lead! This was going to be humiliating at the very least. The wise thing to do would be to beg off.

"All right," she heard herself agree. She even smiled. "I will dance with you."

He looked pleased—so pleased that a shiver of pleasure raced down Blythe's spine. Perhaps—just for a moment—she would let herself believe that he had been nervous about asking her, that for a moment she was a beautiful, desirable woman whom this man wanted to hold in his arms.

But only for a moment. Such thoughts were dangerous, as she well knew. They often led to thinking a gentleman's feelings ran deeper than they did, and Blythe had promised herself never to make that mistake again. It simply hurt too much to find out she was wrong.

As luck would have it, the opening strains of the first waltz of the evening started at just that instant, eliminating the need for Blythe to think of something charming and witty to say.

Devlin offered her his hand. She hesitated only a fraction of a second before placing her pale gold glove in the stark white of his. Even his hand made hers look smaller—delicate almost.

Oh yes, these were dangerous thoughts indeed.

Out into the middle of the floor he led her. Was it her imagination, or did the chandeliers somehow seem less bright? Conversations dropped to dim murmurs as the music swelled until there was nothing but the orchestra and the two of them.

Devlin's free hand came up to her waist and slid around to her back. Gooseflesh dotted Blythe's skin as she fought a shiver at the warmth of his touch. Reaching up—so wondrously far it seemed!—she placed her right hand on his shoulder. She was right about the lack of padding in his coat. All she felt was the unyielding firmness of bone and muscle beneath her palm.

And then he began to move. She followed easily. His steps were so sure, his hold on her so confident and firm that her natural instinct to lead never had a chance to rear its head and embarrass her. He was in control, and there wasn't an inch of her that minded.

They weren't the most graceful of couples. Looking around, Blythe realized that honor had to go to Carny and Teresa, who danced together as though carried by clouds. Strangely enough, she didn't care. She had never felt this graceful, this *right* dancing with anyone before, not even Carny.

For once she didn't have to watch the length of her strides. She didn't have to affect tiny ladylike steps. Devlin's legs were long—even longer than her own—and he made bold, sweeping circles that she followed with ease. He also held her closer than society deemed proper.

Secretly, Blythe liked the way he held her. Liked the occasional brush of his leg against hers. Liked that all she had to do was tilt her chin up and she could study the tiny lines fanning out from his eyes, smell the bay rum he used—wonder what it might be like to press her lips to his.

He met her gaze with a quizzical smile. "What?"

She shrugged. "I am simply enjoying myself."

"You should enjoy yourself more often. It becomes you."

It wasn't much as compliments went—not when Carny had once compared her eyes to pale emeralds—but it hit home all the same. There were no false comparisons, no flowery odes, just the simple admission that she looked nice when happy.

"I usually have to shorten my steps," she admitted.

Devlin's smile grew. "I can lengthen mine if you like."

Blythe shook her head. "People would stare."

Something in his expression changed. His smile faded but his eyes lit with a bright, inner light. It was an intimate gaze—one that caught her breath in her throat. "You deserve to be stared at."

Oh Lord, she was blushing again! How did he do that? How could he take something that had always been an embarrassment, had always bothered her, and turn it into a positive thing? He made it sound as though people stared at her because they admired her face and figure, not that they saw her as an oddity, a woman to be pitied.

Before she could think of a reply, or even mumble an inane thank-you, he did just what he threatened to do. He lengthened his strides, forcing her to lengthen her own to keep from stumbling. Soon they were sailing around the floor with great, wide, sweeping arcs. The couples around them became a blur as Blythe focused on the sparkle in his eyes.

He should enjoy himself more often. It became him.

So fast he whirled her around that once, Blythe imagined he had literally swept her off her feet. He was certainly holding her close enough to do it—she could feel the buttons of his coat through the thin fabric of her gown—but it was impossible. Surely she was too heavy for him to pick up with one arm—oh! He did it again. How did he make her feel so weightless?

Breathless from keeping pace with him, flushed from the sheer joy and exertion of the exercise, Blythe threw back her head and laughed out loud, ignorant of whatever glances came their way. She didn't care who stared. Didn't care who might whisper about them later. Right now she was having fun, more fun than she had experienced in years. Anybody who didn't like it was welcome to look the other way and be damned.

Too soon the music ended. Blythe's stop was less graceful than Devlin's. Her feet tangled in her skirts, and she stumbled into the solid wall of his chest. For a moment, she could feel his breath warm against her temple. For a moment, he held her flush against him, closer than any man had ever held her before. So close that she could feel not just his buttons, but *every* inch of his body against hers.

Oh God.

Then he stepped back, once more putting a respectable distance between them.

Strangely bereft, Blythe managed a smile. "Thank you for the dance, Mr. Ryland. It was very . . . exhilarating."

Devlin bowed. "My pleasure. Until our next dance." And then he did something totally unexpected. He kissed her hand, and not on the knuckles like most gentlemen. He turned it over and kissed her palm, where her glove was warm and moist from gripping his shoulder. It was an incredibly erotic feeling, his lips against her palm—even if there was a layer of silk between them. The pressure of his lips, however brief, warmed her even further. Who would have known that warm and damp could be so pleasant?

Apparently Devlin Ryland had, if the appreciation in his gaze was any indication.

Murmuring a soft farewell, she watched him walk away from her original position outside the circle of dancers, where he had guided her. Could it be possible that Devlin Ryland, a national hero, found *her* appealing?

Well, what was so surprising about that, if he did? While

she wasn't the most beautiful woman in England, she knew she wasn't without a certain comeliness. After all, Carny had found her pretty once. Why couldn't Devlin?

She gave her thoughts a mental tug on the reins. Finding her attractive and falling in love with her were two entirely different things. It was fine to think that perhaps Devlin was drawn to her, but beyond that she could not—would not—imagine. She would develop a sense of caution about men if it was the last thing she did. Never again would she assume a man's feelings matched her own.

And just what were her own? She hardly knew Devlin well enough to fancy herself in love. She liked him, that much was for sure, and she liked the feel of his arms around her and his body against hers. That merely made her wanton, not lovelorn. She would have to be careful and on her guard. Devlin Ryland was the kind of man she could actually imagine going to when those "urges" came upon her. She'd wager he'd not only stop the ache, but fill the emptiness inside her as well.

All of this after only a few days' acquaintance. Good Lord, what state would she be in by the time the house party finally ended?

Heated not only by her dance with Devlin, but by the direction of her thoughts, Blythe flipped open her fan and applied it vigorously to cooling her flushed face. She strode across the dance floor toward the French doors that led out into the courtyard. A little fresh air would set her to rights.

Outside the air was warm, but cooler than that of the ballroom. A soft breeze blew through the west archway. The house was built around the courtyard, forming a square. Arches were built into the east, west, and north sides to allow guests alternative ways in and out of the courtyard.

A kind of garden, the courtyard had a stone floor with a large fountain in the center. Mermaids, a regular topic of conversation in most seaside villages, frolicked in the constantly burbling water. A table and several chairs were positioned under a canopy for the family or guests to dine alfresco if they wished. Rose bushes, potted shrubs, and marble statuary gave the courtyard its "garden" feel and seclusion. The courtyard was huge, and there were many private spots where the glow of the lanterns didn't reach, especially toward the back where lovers could escape for a bit of privacy.

It wasn't Blythe's intention to go looking for such a display. She simply wanted to cool off and put all thoughts of Devlin Ryland out of her mind. Honestly, how foolish was she? A man paid attention to her and she immediately became infatuated with him. Maybe Miles was right. Maybe she needed to spend more time in town. A week or two in London ought to cure her of any romantic fantasies.

"Why are you acting this way?"

Blythe jumped at the harshly uttered question. Where had it come from?

"I do not understand you at all!"

A man and a woman, obviously having an argument. If she wasn't mistaken, the lady was crying. Well, she wasn't an eavesdropper, so she'd give them all the privacy they wanted.

"Teresa, my love. Please do not cry."

Blythe froze. All thoughts of leaving vanished. It was Carny. Carny and his wife who were arguing. Why?

Oh, it was none of her business—in fact less so now than it had been before she discovered their identities—but she couldn't help herself. Quietly, she crept closer to the wall of roses that separated her well-lit path from the dim corner that concealed the couple.

"You make me cry!" Teresa replied in her thick Spanish accent. "You are so mean sometimes!"

"You know I would never hurt you."

Blythe grimaced. She'd heard *that* before. She had no doubt of Carny's sincerity at this moment, but she hoped for Teresa's sake that they didn't go to war again anytime soon, otherwise Carny might find someone he liked even better than her.

Oh, that wasn't fair—not to Carny or to Teresa. Jilting her was one thing, but she couldn't believe even Carny would forsake his marriage vows.

"Just go away. I have to stop crying and I will not stop with you here."

"Teresa—"

"Go!"

Much to Blythe's surprise, Carny did as he was told. Hugging the side of the bush so as not to be seen, Blythe watched him go as a dozen thorns bit into her backside. It was only that she would rather suffer pain than talk to Carny that kept her from cursing.

As soon as she was certain he was gone, Blythe moved away from the bush. She'd go back inside before Teresa—

"How much did you hear?"

—saw her. *Blast.*

Turning, Blythe offered what she hoped was an apologetic smile and not the grimace it felt like. "More than I should have. My apologies."

The little woman nodded, dabbing at her eyes with a handkerchief. She looked so tiny, so fragile. Protectiveness rose up in Blythe's breast, even as her common sense cried out in exasperation.

She did *not* want to befriend Carny's wife. That would be too much, even for her.

"I know I would not be your first choice of a confidante, but . . ." *Sigh.* "Would you like to talk?"

Wide, dark eyes stared up at her from a tear-ravaged face. Another nod. "I would, yes."

Blythe slipped an arm around the other woman's narrow shoulders and led her to a bench further into the courtyard's more secluded area.

Teresa didn't say much about her marriage, and Blythe

couldn't blame her for not trusting her with that immediately. They talked about themselves mostly, about their lives and families. And by the time Teresa's tears had dried and her eyes didn't seem quite so swollen, Blythe had found a friend.

Funny how one found things in the least likely of places.

The sun wasn't far from rising by the time Devlin finally retired to his room. He hadn't spent so much time on his feet since his soldier days. Of course, the ball had been a much more pleasant way to spend his time, not to mention much easier on his wardrobe.

He'd spent much of the evening talking to Miles and Carny and their charming wives, both of whom he had danced with. Dancing with Varya had been a little easier because she was taller, but dancing with Teresa had been sheer hell. She spent most of it laughing at him because he was so worried about doing something that might hurt her. She hadn't been worried at all. Never mind that he was a foot and a half taller than she was, at least seven to eight stone heavier.

No, the only woman he had felt comfortable dancing with had been Lady Blythe, and not just because she was the perfect height—the perfect everything, so it seemed. She hadn't made him feel awkward or nervous, even though it had been a long time since he had waltzed with a woman. And when she tossed back her head and laughed during that first dance . . . well, he'd lost a bit of what little heart he had to her right then and there.

Devlin didn't know much about love. He loved his brothers, and he had felt a certain degree of emotion for the friends he'd lost during the war. He still got a little teary when he thought of Patrick Flynn. And he supposed, in a way, he had loved his parents as well, even though their deaths hadn't wrenched even half a tear from him. One thing was certain; his parents hadn't been overwhelmed with parental love for their youngest son. How could they when he was a reminder of a night both viscount and viscountess would have preferred to forget?

Regardless of his own experiences, he knew of people who had been in love and professed to be in love still. Carny and Teresa, for example. He had watched them fall in love. Miles and Varya still seemed very taken with each other, so maybe there was such a thing as lasting love.

How did a person even know if he was in love anyway? Taking his rifle from its case, Devlin toed off his shoes and sat down in the chair by the window. He took a slightly oily, stained rag from a tin and started polishing the Baker's barrel. Cleaning it every night before going to sleep had become a habit so long ago that it would feel stranger not to do it than to continue.

Perhaps a man knew he was in love when he started spouting poetry or buying the lady flowers. Perhaps it was more of an intuition, or perhaps it was simply sex. A man found a woman he could imagine bedding for the rest of his life, she agreed, and that was it. Maybe love was just really good sex with a nice woman.

It sounded like a good deal to him. His brother Wynthrope would certainly concur. So why did it sound so empty? A life spent with a decent woman—one you could safely call a friend— having a splendid physical relationship sounded like the perfect combination.

The problem wasn't in the woman. The problem was in *him.* He had no trouble imagining being reasonably happy with such a woman, but what about her? He didn't want to be just some nice man a lady thought she could spend her entire life mating with. He wanted to be the sun and the moon to his wife. He wanted adoration, trust, and complete devotion. He wanted to be loved the way the poets wrote about. He wanted to be the most important thing in someone's life.

And God help him, he wanted the same for himself.

He couldn't imagine it ever happening. Couldn't imagine a woman—one such as Lady Blythe—falling in love with a man like him. She deserved so much better than a man as damaged and damned as himself. And as much as he wanted to believe love existed, he couldn't imagine feeling it, or someone feeling it for him.

He wanted her, that was for certain. Seeing her in that flimsy gold gown had only intensified that wanting. He had never been the kind of man who was easily ruled by his loins, but that night he had actually fantasized about taking Blythe into a dark room and making love to her until neither of them could stand.

She was Miles's sister and Carny's ex-fiancée. She was also far too innocent and good to be dirtied by his touch. He shouldn't be thinking about her this way, but none of that seemed to matter.

Even worse, he liked her. Genuinely liked her—what he knew of her. Granted, he had only been in Devon less than a week, but he was more comfortable with Lady Blythe than he was with anyone other than Miles. He even felt calmer around Carny when she was near.

With the Baker cleaned, Devlin slipped the rifle back into its case, washed his hands, undressed, and crawled into bed. He drifted off with images of Lady Blythe in his head, her laughter ringing in his ears.

And for the first time in a long time, Devlin's dreams were almost entirely pleasant.

Not even five hours after going to bed, Devlin was awake again. He rose, washed, and dressed quickly and quietly. A trip downstairs confirmed no one else in the house was up yet. The only activity came from the servants, bustling about their morning chores.

He had a cup of coffee and headed out to the stables where

he spent half an hour chatting with the head groom, a man who reminded him much of Samuel, who had been Devlin's father's groom for many years while Devlin was growing up. He had been very attached to old Sam—he still was. Sam treated him more like a son than his real father had.

After that he saddled Flynn and went for a ride down to the beach. The tide was high, lapping gently against the pebbled shore. Devlin let Flynn run along the water's edge, laughing as the cool water sprayed up over his face and clothes. The wind stung his eyes and whipped through his hair as the sweet salt air filled his lungs. He felt good— better than he had in too long to remember. He wanted to hang on to it, yet he knew better than to believe such happiness would last. He hadn't earned the right to grab on to it and keep it.

But for now, he would enjoy it. Once he took possession of Rosewood he would make riding along the beach a daily occurrence. Perhaps he could convince Lady Blythe to join him.

Good God, could he not go at least two hours without thinking about her? This was foolishness, truly. He strove to put her out of his mind and think instead about Rosewood and all the changes he would make if he managed to take possession. He wanted to see the inside in detail as well; peeking in windows wouldn't do.

By the time he returned to Brixleigh it was late morning, and many of the guests were up and about, taking breakfast, enjoying coffee in the garden, or playing at various games and diversions. Some of the footmen were setting up an expanse for target shooting.

"Ah, Dev, there you are," Miles greeted him as he entered the dining room. "I received word not even half an hour ago that Adams is expected back on Tuesday. Is that fine with you?"

"Of course." It was only Friday now—the house party would go on for another fortnight at least. There was plenty of time to meet with the solicitor, take a more detailed tour, and discuss purchasing Rosewood.

He joined Miles and the others—Varya, Teresa, Carny, Lord and Lady Westwood, and Lord Harcourt—at the table after helping himself to the array of dishes on the sideboard. He was ravenous.

Blythe joined the party a few moments later. She wore a blue morning gown that was obviously for her brother's benefit and had her hair twisted into a neat coil on the back of her head. Devlin preferred it piled up on top of her head with little bits curling free as it had been the night before. What he really wanted was to see the thick auburn mass unbound, but that wasn't likely to happen.

"Good morning, everyone," she said cheerily as she crossed to the sideboard. Obviously she had been up for some time as well. She hadn't the look of someone who had just gotten out of bed.

Now there was something he'd like to see as well. Blythe as she woke up in the morning.

It was enough to make a man hard just picturing it.

She joined them at the table with a plate piled almost as high as Devlin's own and surprised him by taking the empty seat beside him. There were other vacant chairs around the table, why sit next to him?

"You are not going to eat all that, are you?" Carny's incredulity was barely contained, and Devlin could have slapped him for it, were it not for the fact that Carny looked as though he'd like to slap himself.

Blythe regarded him coolly, despite the heightened color in her cheeks. "Why yes, I am. I make it a point to never take or ask for something I do not want."

There was a deeper meaning in her words. There had to be or Carny wouldn't have flushed as he did. Was Blythe referring to their broken engagement? Was it indeed Carny who had done the jilting?

Stupid idiot.

Lady Blythe ate with as much gusto as she danced. That she enjoyed food was obvious with every ecstasy-filled bite. She actually closed her eyes in rapture at the bacon. It was marvelous to watch. And she drank enough tea to satisfy a whole regiment.

"Are there any more scones?" she asked a few moments later when half her plate had been cleaned.

Varya and Teresa laughed, but Lady Westwood looked at her as though she couldn't believe her ears.

"No. They are all gone," Miles replied with a grin. "Besides, you have yet to finish what is on your plate."

"I cannot believe she has eaten as much as she has!" Lady Westwood exclaimed. It wasn't said maliciously, but it might as well have been, given the flush that crept up Blythe's cheeks.

Devlin nudged her with his elbow. "You can have half of mine, Lady Blythe."

She turned to face him, and at that moment Devlin knew what it was to be a god. The smile she gave him was the closest he had ever come to being worshipped.

"Thank you, Mr. Ryland."

As she took the scone from him, their gazes met and held. Devlin didn't know what she could see in his eyes, but he hoped she knew that he didn't care how much she ate as long as she enjoyed it. He would rather have her as she was— healthy and round—than thin and sickly looking like Lady Westwood and others of her set.

After Blythe had finished everything on her plate and after some of the other guests had risen for the day, the group of them strolled outside, all of the ladies save for Blythe shielding their delicate complexions with bonnets as well as parasols.

"Miles hates my hat," she replied when Devlin asked why she didn't wear protection from the sun's tanning rays.

"And I despise bonnets. They make me feel like I have blinders on."

He laughed and offered her his hat if she wanted it. It was old and slightly battered, but it was better than the one she favored, if it was the one he had seen her in. She thought about it for a moment, but declined. Miles would no doubt pitch a fit.

The shooting targets were arranged on the west lawn, facing away from the house and far enough away that safety needn't be an issue. Devlin watched with interest as different men lined up for a chance to display their skill with a rifle. Most of them were hunters and decent shots. A few were former soldiers as well, which gave them a slight advantage. Good shots, all of them. Many struck the center of the target or near it several times—good odds considering that rifles weren't always exactly accurate.

"Good show, Carnover!" Lord Harcourt called when the shooting was over.

Carny smiled. He'd had the best score out of all the competitors. "Thank you, but if you want to see real skill, you should watch Ryland here."

Devlin forced a smile, but inside he wished Carny had kept his praise to himself. For a moment, it seemed as though everyone had forgotten that he was supposed to be some kind of hero. Now they were going to expect him to prove it.

"By thunder, you're right!" Harcourt chortled. "What say you, Ryland? Up to giving us a little demonstration, eh?"

Devlin opened his mouth to refuse, but plans were already being made. He couldn't say no. They wouldn't let him.

"Give him a better target," someone remarked.

"How about a person with an apple on his head?"

"Or in his hand?"

"A cigar in his mouth!"

Scowling, Devlin shook his head. At least here he could put his foot down. "I won't endanger anyone's life."

"Besides," Carny joined in with a grin, "who would be foolish enough to let him do it?"

A voice behind Devlin spoke—so softly that at first he didn't hear what she said. It took a few seconds for her words to sink in.

"I would."

His heart seized in his chest. He didn't have to look to know who the voice belonged to, but he turned to face her anyway. She stood in a patch of sunshine, the bright rays turning her hair the color of flame and making her eyes as clear as an island lagoon.

She smiled. "I would be foolish enough, Mr. Ryland. I trust you."

Devlin opened his mouth to speak. The words were there, right on the tip of his tongue, but they wouldn't come out. Finally, after what seemed like forever, but was mere seconds, he gave up.

"Bring me my gun," he barked at one of the footmen. Christ, what was wrong with him? A woman said she would trust him and he couldn't even form a response?

He turned back to Blythe, who was still watching him with that strangely serene, yet curious expression. It was as though she knew some manner of secret, as though she had seen inside his soul— and she wanted to know more.

It scared the hell out of him.

"Thank you," was all he could bring himself to say.

As he walked toward one of the targets, he heard someone say, "He brought his own gun? When there's no hunting party?"

"Of course he did," came Carny's defensive reply. "He's a rifleman."

Devlin shook his head. He would never understand why Carny saw him the way he did, even if he had saved Carny's life. Why did the man insist on puffing him up? Carny had always had a degree of fascination with the men beneath him in the ranks. It was as though he thought being a regular soldier horribly romantic.

How romantic was it to kill people?

A target was arranged for him, a bale of hay with a wooden target attached to it. Circles were marked on it in brightly colored paint, the center obviously red.

"How many?" he asked tonelessly as a footman handed him the Baker's case.

Carny grinned. "Five ought to show them. Do it like you used to in the drills."

Why not dress some of the guests up as the French and see if he could hit them as well? No, that was unfair. Carny only wanted to show him off. He didn't want to forget as Devlin did.

Nodding, Devlin took his place approximately one hundred yards from the target. It was a fair distance, but he knew the Baker could handle it. She was the most accurate rifle he'd ever fired.

He had powder and balls nearby for reloading. It had been a long time since he shot. Carny wanted him to do it as he used to, but he wasn't so sure he could. That meant three rounds a minute. At one time he could do it easily, but now . . .

Now wasn't the time to think about it. Just do it.

As fast as he could, he loaded the Baker, lifted it to his shoulder, aimed, and fired. Not even bothering to look at the target, he began loading again. His heart began to thump against his ribs, blocking out all other sounds. The smell of burnt powder filled his nostrils as he fired again.

Reload.

Suddenly, he was in a field in Brussels or Portugal or perhaps France. French soldiers were running straight for him, their footfalls thundering between volleys of cannon fire. The blades of their bayonets glistened with blood as acrid smoke drifted around them. Sweat beaded on his forehead and upper lip as he jammed the rod down the Baker's barrel.

Fire.

Reload.

The soldiers were drawing closer. He could smell them now, legions of unwashed men drenched in sweat, blood, and gunpowder. Their language was gibberish in his ears even though he had learned enough of it over the years to be almost fluent. A few words took form in his mind.

Kill. Shoot. Fire. English.

They were going to kill him if he didn't take them down first. Someone was shouting to him. It sounded like Patrick Flynn.

Fire. Reload—hurry, man! Reload. Fire.

Devlin did. His hands sweating, moving with lightning alacrity, he squeezed off another round and reached for more as the French ghost soldiers stampeded toward him . . .

He had no more shot.

A hand clamping down on his shoulder brought Devlin back to the present with heart-stopping clarity. Air rushed into his lungs as his legs began to tremble.

Not real. It hadn't been real.

"By God, man, that was incredible!" It was Carny, grinning like a boasting schoolboy. "I knew you could do it! Five shots dead center. Incredible!"

A small crowd gathered and dispersed around him, each person congratulating or praising him in some manner. Devlin didn't hear most of it. He just stood there, the Baker hanging loosely at his side, trying to return his breathing to normal before he passed out.

Someone pressed a handkerchief to his upper lip. Blinking, he looked down. He didn't have to look far. It was Lady Blythe.

She handed him the delicate linen and his hat, which he had discarded before shooting. "Wipe your forehead."

He did as she bade. What was she thinking? Could she see the fear in his eyes? Smell it in his sweat? Could she see how much he despised the only thing he'd ever been truly good at? How frightened he was of it and what he was capable of doing with it?

If she could, she didn't show it. She simply gazed at him with those startlingly clear eyes and favored him with a gentle smile— the kind he used to wish his mother would give him whenever he'd hurt himself as a child.

"Would you like to tour the park tomorrow morning, Mr. Ryland?"

That was all she was going to say? "Will you be my guide, Lady Blythe?" He was breathless and hoarse, damn it.

She glanced away—just for a split second, but enough to let him know she was pleased that he asked. "If you wish."

"I do."

She nodded. "Eight o'clock? At the stables?"

He agreed, and she flashed him another smile before turning her back and walking away. Holding her handkerchief in one hand, the Baker in the other, Devlin watched her go.

What the hell had just happened?

Chapter 4

"What are you reading?"

Her brow puckering in mild annoyance, Blythe looked up from her book as her brother sat down on the settee beside her. He had a house full of guests to entertain, especially this early in the evening, and her solitude since Teresa left the room earlier had been all too brief. Why was Miles bothering her now? She hadn't done anything to earn his ire.

"It is a book on horse breeds. I am intrigued by Mr. Ryland's horse. I thought this might help me figure out his bloodlines."

Miles smiled, reminding Blythe very much of their father as he did. "Ah, so you have met Flynn, have you?"

Blythe's lips curved as well. "I have. I saw him shortly after Mr. Ryland arrived."

Her brother nodded. "What do you think of him?"

Raising her brows in surprise, Blythe shrugged. "He seemed like a very nice horse." What did Miles care what she thought of an animal anyway? "It wasn't as though we had a conversation or any such thing."

Miles scowled at her sarcasm. "Not the horse! Devlin."

She saw where this was going. Miles wanted to know what she thought of Carny's savior. Well, she wasn't going to blame Mr. Ryland for anything that happened between herself and Carny.

"I have only known him a few days, Miles. Hardly long enough to form a decisive opinion."

He seemed satisfied. That in itself was disconcerting. Miles was rarely, if ever, satisfied by anything. "Did you enjoy the shooting today?"

"It was interesting." She set the book on the small pedestal table beside her chair. Obviously he had more on his mind. "You?"

"I thought it was quite good. Ryland was very impressive, do you not think?"

Ahh, so that's what this was. He wasn't trying to find out if she disliked Devlin, he wanted to ferret out if she *liked* him. It would be somewhat sweet if Miles hadn't been harping on her for the last year to hurry up and get married. Why would she want to ruin her life by getting married? She had all the freedom and independence she could want right now.

"He was very impressive, yes." She draped her arm across the back of the settee. "But I'm not going to marry him just because he can shoot."

"Marry?" Miles laughed—a little too loudly. "Who said anything about marriage?"

He wasn't a very good liar, not when it came to lying to her. Normally she would be quite annoyed with him, but not when he was providing her with the perfect opportunity to find out more about the mysterious Mr. Ryland. They were friends. And as her brother, he was duty-bound to tell her all he knew.

"Miles, what happened to Mr. Ryland?" Ever since that morning, Blythe had been unable to put Devlin or his wellbeing out of her mind. He had seemed so unnerved by the shooting competition, almost as though ghosts from the past had come up to haunt him as he aimed at the target—a target Blythe didn't believe he'd even seen yet managed to hit dead center every time.

Miles was obviously thrown off by her change in subject. "What do you mean, 'happened' to him?"

Good Lord, he wasn't truly that blind when it came to his friends, was he? How had he ever managed to spy for Wellington and the Home Office? Honestly, there were times when she thought him positively thick.

"He was a rifleman, a sharpshooter. That rifle was a part of him, so why did he break into tremors and a cold sweat today after shooting five rounds at a still target?"

Miles's expression became thoughtful, then knowingly grim. "War changes a man, brat. I do not have to tell you that."

He referred to Carny, of course. Neither of them had to come right out and say his name.

Casually crossing his long legs, Miles leaned back against the plump cushions, his fingers absently stroking the sofa's curved arm. "Some men have a hard time leaving behind everything they saw and did over there. Sometimes it can come back to haunt you at the strangest times."

As it had when Miles first returned from fighting. He used to have nightmares, but as far as Blythe knew, they ended long ago. "So you think Mr. Ryland might have remembered something about the war while he was shooting today?" That would certainly explain the shaking and the wildness she'd seen in his eyes.

Miles shrugged. "I cannot say for certain, but Ryland was a soldier for more than a decade—since he was a very young man. He was in a lot of desperate situations and always put others before himself. It was as though he had something to prove by being the best and most fearless. What and to whom, I have no idea."

It was all very interesting and certainly intriguing, but she wanted answers about the man, not more questions!

"I do know this," Miles continued after a second's silence. "Something changed him at Waterloo. He was a different man after that. Quieter, more serious."

Waterloo. Miles hadn't been at Waterloo, so he didn't know what had happened. But Carny did. The question was, would Carny tell her if he knew anything? After all, Mr. Ryland had saved his life. Carny might regard telling his secrets as a betrayal of their friendship.

But perhaps he'd hold friendship in as low regard as he did betrothals.

"Thank you," she said, rising to her feet. "You know, if we did not argue so much, we could talk like this more often."

Miles smiled. "We should. Are you off to bed?"

"I believe so. I am showing Mr. Ryland the park tomorrow, so I want to have a good night's sleep."

"Yes," he agreed, also standing. "A lady should look her best when in a gentleman's company."

Rolling her eyes, Blythe kissed her brother's cheek and left the library. She had to give Miles credit for one thing—Devlin Ryland was a much better choice of a husband for her than some of the other ones he had come up with.

She entered her bedroom to find a lamp lit and the covers already turned down. Not bothering to ring for Suki, Blythe undressed and pulled a fresh nightgown over her head. Then she unwound her hair and gave it a thorough brushing before padding across the carpet to climb up onto the bed.

There was something on it. Reaching down, she picked up the square of soft, folded linen. She turned it over.

B.E.C. Her initials. This was the handkerchief she had given Mr. Ryland that morning. Should she be hurt that he returned it or appreciate his thoughtfulness? It was so difficult to understand men and their motives.

Then a thought struck her. He had been in her room.

Just the idea of him standing there, in her private sanctuary, setting the handkerchief on her neatly readied bed was enough to make the bottom of Blythe's feet tingle. Every pulse point in her body seemed to throb with the picture her mind created: Mr. Ryland, in nothing but his trousers and shirt sleeves, the open collar of his shirt revealing the crisp dark hair that covered his chest and the tanned, strong column of his throat. His sleeves were rolled up, exposing dark forearms. His hair was slightly mussed, falling boyishly over his forehead, and as he placed the linen on her bed, he ran a palm over the soft, ivory sheet, imagining her body there beneath his hand . . .

Good Lord! What was she doing? And how would she know if he had hair on his chest or not! Why would she care what his arms looked like? And why, why was it so easy for her to imagine those details?

Her blood feverish, her body tingling with desire, Blythe flopped back on the mattress and breathed deeply. She forced herself to think about cleaning out the stables rather than about Devlin Ryland's long, blunt fingers. She didn't even know the man!

Sometime later, she rolled over onto her side to turn down the lamp. She hesitated as her eyes fell on the handkerchief, now sitting on her nightstand. Picking it up, she lifted it to her nose and breathed deep. There was a hint of the sandalwood soap she had the laundry maids use to clean her clothes, but that was overshadowed by new, yet familiar scents. Bay rum, horse, and cloves. This was *his* smell.

After extinguishing the lamp, Blythe rolled onto her stomach and waited for sleep to come and claim her. When it did, it found her lying peacefully, breathing in the scent of Devlin Ryland and smiling.

*　*　*

True to their arrangement, Blythe and Devlin met at exactly eight o'clock the next morning. After exchanging greetings, they saddled their horses and set off for a tour of Brixleigh Park.

The morning rang with the sounds of summer. Tenant children played in the fields, their laughter chasing after them. Gulls swooped and soared, searching for their next meal, calling out to their companions with high, mournful voices. And in the distance, the low bleat of sheep answered the commanding bark of a herding dog.

A light breeze blew across the green grass, bringing the smell of salt sea and rich earth with it. Blythe turned her face to the sun and tried to ignore this strange awareness she felt toward the man riding beside her.

Devlin—he had ceased to be simply Mr. Ryland to her last night—had taken one look at her in her boots, trousers, and coat and smiled that little lopsided smile of his. Her heart tilted with it. It was far too boyish for a man with a face like his, but it suited him, as did the dark colors he favored. Most men would look drab and unfashionable in such shades, but somehow they looked nice on him.

And then he had done something wholly unexpected.

"What are you doing?" she demanded when he bent down and cupped his hands.

"Giving you a hand up," was the simple reply as he lifted his gaze to hers. He smiled when she didn't put her boot immediately into his gloved hands. "Surely you've been given a hand up before?"

Actually, no. She'd been getting onto horses by her own devices since she was old enough to ride. Her father thought it was cute, how independent his daughter was, so all the grooms had allowed her to climb up by herself—no matter how long it took.

But she wasn't going to tell Devlin that, so she had lifted

her boot into his hands and prayed that he wouldn't hurt his back helping. She practically jumped into the saddle in her effort to put as little of her weight on him as possible.

Stunned, Blythe sat on her mare's back and watched as Devlin gracefully vaulted onto Flynn's back. His gentlemanly behavior almost made her wish she were wearing a riding habit—something fashionable with a jaunty little feathered hat. Something feminine. For the first time in years, she wanted a man to see her as a woman.

A few days ago she had no idea who this man was, and now she was wanting to look womanly for him? Had she learned nothing from the fiasco with Carny? She had no sense when it came to men; she had to remember that. Devlin's attentions might be nothing more than a man being kind to a friend's sister. Even if Devlin was serious in his attentions, she would be wise to guard her own response and actions.

She'd made a fool of herself over one man; she would not be so quick to do so again. Ignorant in the ways of men she might be, but she knew all too well how easy it was for them to say one thing and mean another. It would take more than a few compliments, heated looks, and one kiss to tempt her now as they had with Carny. Even in her youth she'd given her adoration far too quickly. It seemed that she was bound to pine for whoever paid attention to her. It had to stop. She would not be made a fool of again.

But not because people would talk. She didn't care if people talked. She just didn't want to experience that disappointment, that betrayal, again.

"Are you enjoying your stay at Brixleigh?" she asked as they clip-clopped down the lane that led to the tenant farms. John Dobson grinned and waved. She waved back.

"Yes," Devlin replied, his gaze fixed on Dobson. The two men seemed to be sizing each other up. Or rather, that was what Blythe's fanciful imagination wanted to believe. They were just strangers giving each other a cursory glare . . . er, glance.

"I have never been in this part of Devon before," he continued once Dobson was safely behind them. Ahead were gently rolling hills of rich, verdant green, seagulls swooping overhead in a sky of cloudless blue. "It is very pretty."

"Have you been to the beach yet?" She loved the beach, although she hadn't been there for days.

"Yes, I was down just the other morning. I spent several hours there. Your brother has also taken it upon himself to show me several available properties in the area."

Blythe's heart jumped. "Oh?" She tried to look and sound nonchalant. "Are you thinking of settling here?"

He favored her with that little smile. "I am, yes. Would I make an acceptable neighbor, do you think?"

She blushed. What was it about this man that made her blush like a schoolgirl? It was demmed frustrating.

"I cannot say," she replied coyly. Lord, she sounded like Lady Ashby! "I should like to think so."

They talked a bit more about the area and the nearby villages and towns as Blythe pointed out various landmarks of the park, including the high cliffs that fell in an almost completely straight line to the beach below. Of course, this led to a lengthy discourse on the history of smuggling in the area. It had only been the last few years that she hadn't seen lights on the tide and cliffs anymore.

She wanted to ask him what properties Miles had shown him, but didn't for fear of seeming *too* interested in his plans. She didn't dare tell him of her own plans for Rosewood. He might let something slip to Miles, and then her brother would surely try to put a stop to her buying her own property.

She glanced at Devlin, slouched comfortably in his saddle. He really shouldn't slouch. A man of his height should always keep his shoulders back, as her governess had forced her to do growing up. Even standing at her tallest she still had to look up at Devlin. It was a strange experience. Not unpleasant, just strange. What would it be like to have to lift her chin so a man could kiss her?

He caught her staring and raised a thick, arched brow.

Fighting the girlish urge to blush yet again, Blythe smiled as though she hadn't been thinking of the feel of his lips against hers. "Do you ever wish you could change something about yourself?"

The other brow crept up to join the first. "Are you always so blunt with people you do not know?"

There was no judgment in his tone, only curiosity. Blythe nodded. "Sometimes. Are you going to answer or not? I'll tell you."

He must have found her offer tempting because he acquiesced. "I would change my eyes."

The offensive organs watched her from beneath thick, velvety lashes. "But you have pretty eyes!" She didn't care how forward she was, it was the truth!

He grimaced. "That is why I would change them."

Blythe shook her head. "No, I simply cannot allow it. Pick something else."

Disbelief drifted over his features before giving way to a chuckle. "All right. I would change my nose."

There was nothing wrong with his nose. It was a little long, yes, but it was otherwise straight and slender. "Your nose has character. It is fine just as it is."

He was openly grinning now. Long dimples creased his cheeks. "My feet then."

She glanced down at his boots. "What is wrong with your feet? Warts?"

Devlin laughed. It was a bit rusty-sounding, but it made Blythe giddy all the same. "No. They are too big."

"But big feet are good on a man."

A teasing light she didn't quite understand lit his eyes. He knew a joke and wasn't going to share it with her. "Oh? Why?"

"Because . . ." Well, she couldn't remember exactly why, but she had heard someone say it once before. "Because who would want a man with little feet?" She affected a shudder.

Chuckling, he looked out over the field before them, then turned his attention back to her. "All right. What would you change?"

"That is easy." She smiled—albeit a bit self-consciously. "I would change my height."

He studied her with such intensity that a heat that had nothing to do with the warm weather crept up Blythe's neck. "Why the devil would you want to change your height?"

Wasn't that obvious? "Because I am too tall. Men do not like tall women."

Scowling, he made a scoffing noise in his throat. "Insecure men might not like tall women. Real men like tall women just fine."

Maybe so, but the idea of towering over her husband was unappealing all the same. "Easy for you to say. I'm not taller than you."

"If you found a man taller than you, would you still wish to be shorter?" His dark gaze pinned her. It was impossible to look away.

One look in his eyes and there could be no denying that both of them were very much aware of the fact that he was such a man. "I . . . I suppose not."

One side of his mouth curved upward. "Don't change a thing, Lady Blythe. You are perfect just as you are."

Perfect? Her? Frowning, Blythe stared at her mare's ruffled mane. How was she supposed to respond to that? Did he actually mean it? No. He was just being polite. *Nobody* was perfect.

Or maybe, blast it, he meant it. Regardless, it was nice of him to say it. "Thank you, Mr. Ryland."

"Devlin," he replied with a wink. "After all, you know my deepest, darkest secrets now."

No, she didn't, but she'd like to. And she didn't like *that* one bit.

Perfect just the way she was. Good God, how much more obvious could he be?

Even now, hours after the fact, Devlin wanted to groan aloud at his folly. Fortunately, Lady Blythe's mare had thrown a shoe, and that took precedence. Blythe hadn't made further mention of his remark.

But then he had to go and offer to reshod the mare for her. He was a schoolboy, panting after his first infatuation.

"Would you show me how to do it?" she had asked, all innocent and seemingly unaware of the growing effect she had on him. Could she truly not see it? Then he was a better actor than he thought.

Of course he'd said yes. So they were to meet again later that afternoon—after the picnic Varya planned for the guests—and replace Marigold's shoe.

So now Devlin sat on a rock, eating an apple and watching Lady Blythe as she talked and laughed with a group of ladies sitting on a blanket beneath the shade of a large, leafy tree. As usual, she was bonnetless, but a parasol deprived him of seeing the sun highlight the glory of her hair. The way she sat, with her legs tucked to the side, wrapped her amber skirts about her limbs, accentuating the strong curves of her long legs and the swell of her buttocks.

Was she purposely trying to drive him to distraction? It was bad enough that the gown she wore displayed the flesh of her upper chest in all its creamy perfection, did she have to tease him with hints of the rest of her Junoesque form?

Most men found the sight of a woman in trousers and

boots far more scandalous, and often more sensual, than a woman in the more familiar garb of gowns and slippers, but for Devlin it was just the opposite. Blythe in trousers was definitely appealing, but it was Blythe in a gown that heated his blood and quickened his pulse. The neckline and short sleeves revealed far more of her pale skin than a shirt ever could, and the breeze that caught the hem of her skirts teased him with a glimpse of stocking-clad ankle. A man could slide his hand beneath those skirts. It was more difficult to touch so intimately when the woman wore trousers.

"You are smitten, are you not?"

Devlin spared Carny the briefest of glances before returning his attention to Blythe. "With whom?"

Flipping out the tails of his coat, Carny sat down on the rock beside him. "With Blythe."

"Absurd." He took another bite of apple. A large bite—one he couldn't talk around.

"No, it isn't." The fair man stretched out his buckskin-clad legs in front of him and folded his arms across his chest. Did he always have to look so well put together? Devlin considered himself lucky if his stockings matched. "It would be an example of your extraordinary taste in women."

His free hand dangling between his wide-spread knees, Devlin turned to stare at his friend as he swallowed. "I heard that you once had such taste."

It was none of his business, and normally he wouldn't dream of asking about things that didn't concern him, but he wanted to know what had happened between Carny and Blythe. And damn it, he wanted to know if any of those feelings still existed.

Dark crimson blossomed on the high ridge of Carny's cheekbones. "So I thought."

Setting aside his apple core to give to Flynn later, Devlin plunged ahead. Carny had just confirmed his earlier suspicions. "I know how important honor is to you, Carny. How could you jilt her like that?"

Carny glanced toward the woman they were discussing. There was a wealth of regret in his expression. "There was no formal betrothal. Yes, Blythe and I had an understanding of sorts; I've never attempted to deny that. I thought she and I would make a good match. I had no idea her feelings went deeper. Then I found Teresa and I learned what love really was. I was not going to give that up—not for anyone, not even Blythe."

"Was it worth it?"

Carny laughed sharply. "Yes. Even Blythe's hatred was worth having Teresa by my side. Look at the two of them, laughing together. I hope to God they're not talking about me."

Devlin watched the two women. They did seem to be getting along. How odd they looked together. Teresa was a little hummingbird and Blythe a phoenix. Each beautiful in her own way, but where Teresa exuded quiet maturity, Blythe was innocence and light. Was it wrong of him to want to touch her? To want some of that light for himself? It seemed he'd been in the dark for far too long, and whatever innocence he once possessed had disappeared a long time ago. Nothing could shock him now.

Nothing except his reaction to Blythe. He wanted her. He thought of her constantly. If he closed his eyes and breathed deeply he fancied he could smell her, all sandalwood sweetness.

She hadn't mentioned the handkerchief yet. Surely she must have found it. Did she wonder if he had given it to a maid or if he had gone to her room himself? Did she know that he had touched her pillow and imagined her lying there, her hair streaming out around her?

"You will have to earn her trust," Carny said, interrupting his thoughts. "I fear I have made it difficult for Blythe to put her belief in any man."

Devlin shook his head, his heart leaping at the sound of Blythe's laughter. "I do not understand how you could have let her go."

Carny's hand came down on his shoulder. He seemed sincere, but there was a tightness around his mouth. "That is why you are the better man for her, my friend. If you are developing feelings for her, you should let her know."

Feelings? Did Carny expect him to confess his lust and infatuation? He didn't know if he believed in love, and even if he did, it was too much to ask that someone like Blythe fall in love with a man like him. What if all the darkness inside him extinguished her light? What if she found out what he was capable of, what he had done?

Wasn't it too much to ask of anyone that she love a murderer?

Devlin was already in the stables when Blythe walked in later that afternoon. Thankfully she had had the forethought to change into trousers for her lesson in shoeing. Otherwise, he might have spent more time staring at her bodice than at the hoof in question. As it was, it was difficult enough just standing next to her. He could smell her perfume and the fresh scent of her hair. And when she walked by him to say hello to Flynn, her hand brushed his thigh. It was an accident, of course, but that didn't stop his heart from stuttering or his cock—no, he couldn't be so vulgar where she was concerned—his *John Thomas* from stirring. Good Lord, he was thirty, not thirteen!

"I forgot to thank you," she said, glancing over her shoulder at him as she stroked Flynn's broad nose, "for returning my handkerchief."

So she had seen it! Devlin shrugged, hoping he looked more relaxed than he felt. His brow pulled as he struggled to maintain his composure and not blush like a boy. "I thought you might need it."

She wanted to ask why he had needed it; he could see it in her face, but she didn't ask, and he was grateful for it.

"Well," she said with a cough after a few seconds' silence. "Are you going to show me how to shoe a horse or not?"

"Right." He was making an idiot of himself. "I have a shoe ready. Marigold's a size three."

"Do you measure the shoe against the hoof to judge the size?"

He nodded as he entered the mare's stall. She followed docilely as he led her out into the shoeing area. "The bigger the hoof, the bigger the shoe, obviously. Flynn is a ten."

"Well, he is a big horse."

Devlin grinned. "Are big feet preferable in horses as well as men?"

Blythe colored at his teasing tone. Had she figured out why big feet were supposed to be so desirable in a man? Would she be impressed if he told her each of his feet was over thirteen inches long?

"I suppose they wouldn't be able to stand if their hooves were too small."

No, she hadn't figured it out. Devlin had to chuckle. She was so blunt and worldly in some ways, so deceptively innocent in others. It was a dangerous combination because it made him want to protect and educate her all at the same time.

"I want you to come over here and stand with your back to the mare's head."

Blythe did as he bid. Within minutes he had her in the proper stance, with Marigold's hoof coming up behind her to tuck between her knees.

"Normally you would have to remove the old shoe first, but since that's already been done, you can start by cutting down the frog—the center of the hoof."

He handed her a curved blade and guided her in cutting out a portion of the hoof center. Then he handed her the rasp—a long file with a sturdy handle—to level the bottom surface of the hoof.

"Good job," he praised. "You don't have to hold everything so tightly, though. Relax a bit or she'll sense your tension."

Blythe relaxed her shoulders as she measured the shoe against her mare's hoof. She was as natural to shoeing as a fish to water. Even when it came time to cut the hoof down to match the curve of the shoe, she handled the clippers like an experienced groom. She had a lot of strength in her hands for a woman.

How would those strong fingers feel stroking him? He stifled a groan. Good God, was there no peace from this madness?

"How did you come to know so much about horses?" she asked. "In the war?"

He shook his head. "No. I spent a lot of time with our family's groom when I was younger." He'd spent almost all his time with old Sam. He had been more comfortable with him, felt more loved than he had with his own parents. But that was a subject he didn't want to discuss.

"Now you nail the shoe in place." He handed her the square-headed hammer and a curved nail. "Once you hammer it through, twist the end of the nail off about one quarter inch from the hoof. There are four nails for each side."

"I won't hurt her, will I?"

Devlin smiled at the anxiety in her voice. "No, you won't hurt her."

Once the nails were through, Blythe put Marigold's hoof on the low stool as Devlin instructed and used the dull side of the rasp to make grooves in the side of the hoof for the nails to rest in. Then, using the hammer and a small iron block, she bent the nails over the block and tapped them against the hoof to keep them from working themselves loose.

It was amazing how good a job she was doing for her first

time. Unfortunately, it was taking longer than Marigold was used to, and Devlin was afraid the mare's patience might be coming to an end.

"Why don't you let me finish?" he suggested, picking up the rasp. All that was left was to file the hoof down so that it met the shoe, but Marigold was beginning to shift in agitation.

"I can do it," Blythe insisted. And she did, but just as she was finishing, Marigold decided she'd had enough and pulled her hoof free of her mistress's grasp.

And then she kicked with it.

Luckily for Blythe, it was a glancing blow, but it was still enough to knock her off balance, given the stance she was in. It was good that Devlin had been preparing to take over for her, otherwise he wouldn't have been close enough to catch her.

"Are you all right?" he demanded as she fell into his arms.

Tears welled in her eyes. "Damnation, but that hurts!"

He would have laughed at her cursing were he not so concerned about her. He had to get her to the house, had to check and make sure her leg was sound. He had seen men's legs broken by a horse's kick. Flynn had taken out more than one Frenchman that way.

He hooked one arm beneath Blythe's knees, the other around her back, and lifted.

"What are you doing? Devlin, put me down! I am too heavy."

He hefted her against his chest, grunting with the effort. "You're heavier than a feather, I'll give you that, but I can carry you just fine."

She kicked her feet. "No you cannot. You will hurt your back. Put me down. I can walk. It doesn't hurt that much."

"Blythe," he growled between clenched teeth as he struggled to keep her from slithering out of his grip. "Shut up and keep still."

She stared at him in shocked silence, but at least she stopped squirming. She even wrapped her arms around his neck as he quickened his pace through the path toward the house.

The servants gawked in wonder as Devlin barged through the back entrance, Lady Blythe in his arms.

"They will be talking about this for days," Blythe muttered as they swept through the bustling, humid kitchen.

"They'll be talking about me," he grunted, trying to make light. "You they will forget about as soon as they learn you are not seriously injured."

"If I am not seriously injured, why are you carrying me?"

He scowled at her. "Because a gentleman always carries a lady in need."

Blythe snorted. "In case you have not noticed, Mr. Ryland, I am not a typical lady."

As if he hadn't noticed! "You called me Devlin before. And in case *you* haven't noticed, Blythe, I'm not a typical gentleman. Now, unless you want to truly test whether you can walk on your own, kindly tell me where to take you and then be quiet until we get there."

"The front parlor," she replied petulantly, her jaw tight as she shut it.

Was it a coincidence that the front parlor was the room the farthest distance from where they now stood? Devlin didn't think so. Still, he managed to arrive there with her in his arms, despite the fact that he was losing all feeling in his biceps, and his back was as bowed as a cheap whore's legs.

When he set her on the sofa in the parlor, it was all he could do not to collapse on it with her. Instead, he whipped a blade out of the sheath on his belt and sliced the left leg of her trousers from boot top to thigh before she could utter a word.

"Mr. Ryland!"

"Devlin," he corrected without thinking as he parted the edges of her trouser leg. There was a long, red mark marring the ivory flesh of her thigh. It was wider toward the back where the hoof first struck, and some of the skin had been abraded where the rough edge of the hoof had caught on the side.

"Can you move your leg?"

She did.

"Does this hurt?" He ran the flat of his palm up the front of her thigh.

She jumped, color flaring in her cheeks. "N-no."

"This?" Moving his hand between her thighs, he pressed on the warm flesh there as his other hand slid beneath her injured leg to probe the bone there.

"No."

There had to be something wrong because her voice was little more than a squeak. Then Devlin realized just how improper the situation was. He had only wanted to ascertain the extent of her injuries and hadn't given thought to how a gently bred lady might react to his shoving his hand between her legs, much less to what he had done to her trousers.

He was also suddenly aware of just how warm and silky the flesh beneath his hands was.

Snatching his hands away, he jumped to his feet. "Your leg isn't broken, but I want you to keep cold compresses on it for the swelling, and I'll have the cook make up a poultice to help with the bruising."

"What the hell is going on?"

Devlin closed his eyes and sighed. Miles. At least he hadn't come in when Devlin had his hands in his sister's trousers. Oh wonderful, he had Carny with him. Both men looked like they could cheerfully take his head off.

"Devlin was showing me how to shoe Marigold and she kicked me," Blythe replied, pulling the cut edges of her trouser leg together.

Miles's eyes narrowed. "Devlin, eh?" The intimacy of first names was not lost on him, Devlin could tell. "Is it broken?

And why the devil did you allow her to shoe an agitated horse?"

"She wasn't agitated when we began," Blythe jumped in before Devlin could respond. "Devlin tried to warn me that she was starting to fidget, but I wanted to finish. It is my own fault I was kicked. And no, my leg is not broken."

Miles nodded, much of the tension leaving his features. "Very well. We will have to get you upstairs to your room. Carny, help me carry her."

Help him! Good Lord, a man Miles's size could carry her on his own. She wasn't an ogre, for Christ's sake!

"I can take her," Devlin retorted. Before either Miles or Carny could disagree, he bent down and once again picked Blythe up.

He glanced at Miles as they passed him in the door. "Have someone prepare a cold compress and bring some whiskey to her room for me to clean the scratches. Oh, and a poultice for the bruising."

As he started across the great hall toward the stairs, he heard the two men talking.

"Strong bastard, isn't he?" he heard Carny remark.

"Yes," Miles agreed. "He's going to have to be."

Chapter 5

Blythe did what she was told and spent the rest of the day in bed, after being assured that Devlin would look after Marigold and see that she broke the new shoe in properly. She even took a tray for dinner. And now she was debating whether to go downstairs for breakfast. Truth be told, she was rather glad for the excuse not to join the others. She absolutely could *not* face Devlin again.

After leaving Miles and Carny gaping behind them, Devlin had carried her up to her room, set her down on her bed, and wouldn't leave until he was sure that the maid had properly cleaned the scratches on her legs and that the poultice and cold compresses were applied correctly. It was unsettling, having him in her bedroom, hovering over her bare leg, watching everything that went on it.

No man had ever seen her bare limbs before. They were too long and far too big and firm to be considered the least bit feminine, but still, wasn't bare skin supposed to inflame a man's desire? Devlin hadn't seemed the least bit interested in her flesh outside of the damage done to it. And Blythe had been extremely aware of his hands upon her. His touch had given her gooseflesh, despite the pain she was in.

Her leg didn't hurt as much now. The pain had faded to a dull ache. It hurt to walk, but she could still get around. Thank God it had been nothing more than a glancing blow.

But she couldn't forget what it felt like to be in Devlin's arms. He had picked her up as though she were the daintiest of women and carried her, not once but twice!

He made her feel womanly, delicate. It both thrilled and scared her. She wanted to give in to it, to flirt and hope that he would flirt back. She wanted it to go further. She wanted him to court her, woo her, seduce her.

Love her.

That was what she wanted—to love and be loved. But did she love Devlin? Was it possible after only a few days' acquaintance? Certainly not. She was infatuated with him because he was a hero—her hero. It was the same old trap she kept falling into. She thought it had stopped with Carny. Obviously it hadn't.

And her new friendship with Teresa didn't help things. She had come to sit with Blythe the night before while the other guests played at cards and charades. The way the Spanish woman went on about Devlin, a person would think him ready for sainthood. Apparently Carny wasn't the only soldier who owed his survival to Devlin. There were more. Teresa claimed that he was quite the surgeon. Blythe didn't doubt it. There probably wasn't anything Devlin Ryland couldn't do if he put his mind to it.

Crawling out of bed, Blythe hobbled across the cream and white carpet toward her dressing table, her injured leg sore and stiff, and rang for her maid. Gingerly, she lowered herself to the dressing table stool and began brushing her hair.

Her bedroom door opened, but it wasn't her maid arriving surprisingly soon. It was Varya, barging in like a woman with a mission, the skirts of her violet morning gown swishing violently.

"Oh good, you are up. I was afraid I was going to have to carry you downstairs myself."

Now *there* was something Blythe would like to see! "Whatever is the matter?"

Agitation colored Varya's cheeks and brightened the dark blue of her eyes. "If you do not come downstairs so that Teresa and I can dote on you, I am going to strangle Lady Ashby!"

She would like to see that as well. She ran the brush through her hair. "What has she done this time?"

Varya scowled, her hands clenching into fists at her sides. "She keeps touching Miles. *He* says he does not notice, but I know he is just being polite. He does not want me to make a scene. At least she seems to have left Mr. Ryland alone."

That was good. Otherwise, Blythe might be tempted to strangle her as well. This jealousy was not something she wanted to think about.

Varya wasn't finished. "Teresa cannot stand her either, but it would be rude of us just to ignore her. That is why you have to come downstairs. You must give us a reason to stay away from her."

Blythe laughed. "All right, you have convinced me. I shall come downstairs."

"Good!" Varya's face brightened. "And Miles will be so happy to see you up and about when he returns."

Blythe began coiling her hair into a neat topknot. "Where has he run off to now?"

"He accompanied Mr. Ryland into town. They have gone to talk to some solicitor about buying that little estate just west of here."

The pins dropped from Blythe's numb fingers. "Rosewood?"

Varya nodded, seemingly unaware that her sister-in-law had gone still and pale. "Yes, that is it. It seems that Miles showed the property to Mr. Ryland last week and he was quite taken with it."

Lord, she was going to be ill. Devlin wanted Rosewood? Devlin was going to *buy* Rosewood? It was too absurd! He couldn't. He just couldn't. Rosewood was hers. It was meant to be hers.

"Dearest, are you quite all right?" Varya demanded, her voice heavy with concern. "You are very pale."

"No, no," Blythe assured her sister-in-law. "I am quite well, Varya. Just a little pain in my leg, that is all."

She couldn't tell Varya the truth. As much as she adored her sister-in-law, she couldn't trust her not to interfere. Varya would go to Miles and ask him to help his sister, but Blythe knew her brother. Miles would do everything in his power to make certain she didn't get that property. He wouldn't do it to be vindictive. He would do it because he thought he knew what was best for her.

No, she would just have to be calm and rational. Mr. Adams and Lord Dartmouth both knew how much she wanted that estate. Mr. Adams had told her that she would always have first priority when it came to selling it. No doubt she would hear from him once he had discussed the situation with Devlin. He would tell Devlin that someone else was interested in the estate. Perhaps Devlin would change his mind. And if that didn't do it, Blythe would have to risk telling him her plan. Surely he wouldn't go through with his intent to purchase Rosewood once he discovered how much Blythe wanted it for her own.

There was a knock on the door, and Suki scurried in. Within minutes she had Blythe dressed in a morning gown of bronze muslin and ready to go downstairs.

"Take my arm, dearest," Varya instructed as they made to leave the room. "I will help you."

Blythe leaned on Varya for support as she limped down the broad, morning-dim corridor. The pain in her leg was nothing compared to the tightness in her chest.

She had to have faith that it would all work out. She had to believe that neither Devlin nor Mr. Adams would intentionally do anything that might ruin her plans. There was nothing to be upset over. She would just be patient and wait for word from Mr. Adams.

Everything would be all right.

"There is someone else interested in the property," Mr. Adams revealed late Tuesday morning as he shuffled a stack of papers. "I will have to contact Lord Dartmouth with your offer."

The slight, middle-aged man faced Miles and Devlin from behind a large oak desk that seemed to dwarf him somewhat. The shiny pink of his pate showed through the thinning lines of his neat, sandy-colored hair, and his eyes lost some of their shrewdness behind the gleaming glass of his spectacles.

There was something odd about Adams's demeanor. Miles couldn't quite put his finger on it, but he had never known a solicitor not to jump immediately at an offer as generous as Devlin's.

Devlin, however, appeared unruffled. Then again, Miles couldn't recall ever seeing his friend truly ruffled at all. He sat somewhat slouched in the hard, polished oak chair, his long legs stretched out before him, arms folded across his chest. "Of course. There are several other properties I can look at in the meantime."

Now *that* put a little concern in the lawyer's eyes. "Er . . . yes, of course. I wonder, Lord Wynter, if I might bend your ear for a moment over another matter?"

Miles fought a frown. Something was definitely amiss.

Adams wasn't the type to mix business with more business.

"Of course, Adams. Excuse me for a moment, Ryland."

Devlin nodded. "Take your time."

Miles rose from his own chair—which was deuced uncomfortable—and followed the shorter man outside into the corridor. Adams shut the office door behind them.

"Forgive me, my lord," Adams murmured, not quite meeting his gaze, "but there is something I think you should know about this other probable buyer for Rosewood."

He knew it! "And what is that?"

Adams practically cringed. "It is Lady Blythe."

What? "My sister?"

The solicitor nodded. This time his eyes met Miles's, but briefly. "Yes. She says she will come into some money soon and has asked for first consideration should someone else make an offer."

Well, damn it all. The little brat! She was going to take the money that should be her dowry and use it to buy a house? A house! All those times she told him she'd "consider" going back to London and looking for a husband were just lies. She had no intention of returning to town, and it appeared as though she had no intention of looking for a husband either. Little idiot. Had she not learned that not all men were untrustworthy? No, how could she when she spent her days isolated in a tiny Devonshire village?

Since Blythe's *disappointment* with Carny she'd done nothing but hide. At first she had refused to leave the London house, and then, as soon as she got the chance, she left for Devon. Initially he thought it a good idea to let her get away and lick her wounds. God knew he would have done anything to take away her pain. But that had been two years ago and she was still hiding from the world. He didn't want to see his baby sister end up a spinster, alone in a big house with no one to love her as she deserved.

Her hiding was going to stop now. God help him, but he still had a few options left. It was time to exercise them, even if it could mean earning his sister's hatred. She'd forgive him eventually, especially once she was happily married.

He glanced at the office door. God help him if he was wrong about the attraction between Ryland and Blythe.

"Adams, there seems to have been some kind of mistake."

The smaller man raised bushy eyebrows. "Oh?"

"Yes. I would appreciate it if you would keep what I'm about to tell you just between the two of us."

"Of course." Adams's chest puffed out. "I assure you I am the soul of discretion, my lord."

He was counting on it, because what he was about to tell the lawyer was a complete fabrication, little more than wishful thinking on his part.

"My sister will still be the mistress of Rosewood, even if Mr. Ryland buys it." If Miles had any say in it, that was.

Adams's eyes widened behind his spectacles. "Well, that certainly changes things, doesn't it?"

Miles nodded. "Indeed. In fact, I believe that Ryland's taking possession of Rosewood will only hasten the happy event. Neither you nor Lord Dartmouth need worry about any promises made to Lady Blythe."

The lawyer was happy—and very eager to oblige. "Oh, well, in that case I do not see why we cannot precipitate proceedings. I shall write to Lord Dartmouth and inform him of the sale directly. I am quite positive he will brook no opposition."

Miles almost breathed a sigh of relief, but he wasn't out of the woods yet. There was going to be hell to pay when Blythe—and Varya—discovered what he had just done. Regardless, it was for Blythe's own good. She couldn't stay hidden in the country for the rest of her life just because one man had disappointed her. She deserved better.

And "better" was Devlin Ryland.

* * *

"You are buying Rosewood?" Blythe tried to keep her horror hidden as she stared at Devlin. "Lord Dartmouth said yes?"

Apparently she did a good job of hiding her reaction because Devlin smiled as though he hadn't just dashed all her hopes and dreams. "Not yet, but Mr. Adams is certain he will."

They were in the middle of dessert alfresco, all of Miles's guests gathered around almost a dozen canopied tables in the courtyard as the sun began its leisurely descent into the western sky. Were it not for those many, many guests Blythe very well might have screamed.

But she wasn't the kind of woman who screamed, so she kept her tone as even as possible as she pushed a grape onto her fork with her knife. "I am surprised there were not other offers. It is a very pretty property."

"There was another offer," he surprised her by replying. "But Mr. Adams said the person could not afford to buy right now."

Was it her imagination, or had Miles just winced? She cast a sharp glance at her brother. Did he know? Had Mr. Adams told him? Two things were for certain: If Mr. Adams had told Miles, he hadn't told Devlin. And if Miles knew, then it was he who had talked the solicitor into backing his friend rather than his sister.

Bastard.

"When will you know for certain?" Oh, she sounded calm and completely disinterested, but inside she seethed and shook. Was Miles capable of such meanness? Would he be so deliberately cruel and callous?

Yes, he would. Especially if he had some twisted notion that he was acting in her best interest.

But now wasn't the time to ask. She would corner him later. For now, she had to put on a pleasant face and pretend to be happy for Devlin, but later she would write a letter to Mr. Adams demanding to know why he was so ready to sell to someone else the house he had, for all intent and purposes, promised to her.

"I hope to hear in a few days," he replied.

One thing was for sure, Devlin didn't know he had yanked Rosewood out of her hands. She didn't know him that well, but she had an idea of what kind of man he was, and he was not the kind who would revel in destroying someone else's happiness.

Blythe shoved another forkful of fruit into her mouth and considered reaching for a pastry or six. Her house might very well be lost to her if she couldn't think of a plan quickly. And the man who had ruined her hopes was the same man who had unknowingly ruined her hopes two years ago. Had fate purposely put Devlin Ryland on this earth to foil her at every turn?

And if so, why did he have to be so dangerously attractive? Why did the setting sun have to turn his skin a delicious rosy gold? Why were his eyes so very dark and attentive? If he was her nemesis, why did his smile make her heart jump as it did? And why couldn't she stop remembering the feel of his hands on her leg—and stop imagining those long, supple fingers elsewhere on her body?

"How is your leg today, Lady Blythe?" he asked softly once the attention and conversation of the tables had turned elsewhere.

Blythe almost choked. Had he read her mind?

She managed a smile as a blush crept up her cheeks. A gentleman would have used "limb" or perhaps the more suitably ambiguous "injury" rather than being so scandalous as to call a leg a leg. But Devlin wasn't like most gentlemen, a trait Blythe liked better and better as she came to know him.

"It is still sore, Mr. Ryland, but well on the mend thanks to your doctoring."

They were, of course, seated at the same table, side by side, nothing between them but a few dishes and a bright white tablecloth. It seemed that Miles or Varya put them together whenever they could. Their efforts at matchmaking did not escape Blythe's notice. She hoped they escaped Devlin's.

Oh Lord, had Miles helped him buy Rosewood thinking it would make him more attractive to her? No. Even Miles wouldn't be that controlling. Or stupid. Would he?

He would. But it was difficult to be angry at him when Devlin's leg brushed her uninjured one beneath the table. Would anyone notice if she dropped her hand to his thigh? Would it be as hard and unyielding as his shoulder had been the night they'd danced? Or would the muscle give ever so slightly beneath her fingers? And what would his reaction be to her brazen touch?

Oh dear. Swallowing hard, she shoved such thoughts aside and turned her mind back to the topic of their previous conversation—Rosewood. She was just going to be honest with him. Surely they could come to some sort of agreement.

Such as that he would agree not to buy the house so she could have it.

"Mr. Ryland, I—"

"Will you be looking for a wife now that you have found a home, Mr. Ryland?" It was Lady Chillinghearst, a commanding viscountess with three daughters of marrying age.

"I hadn't given it much thought," Devlin replied, slicing into the pear on his plate with slow, deliberate strokes. "Perhaps."

Perhaps? *Perhaps*? What did that mean? Either he was going to look for a wife or he wasn't. There was no perhaps about it. Was there?

Unless he already had someone in mind but wasn't certain if the lady returned his feelings. What woman wouldn't? Honestly. He might not be classically handsome, nor was he fabulously wealthy, but he was an attractive man with an ample fortune. And he was good. Blythe didn't pretend to know many things for certain, but one thing she knew without a doubt was that there were very few men in the world as decent, giving, and good as Devlin Ryland.

A woman could do far worse. She glanced at Carny. He was watching her. Plastering a false smile on her face, Blythe waved.

"Do you still love him?" whispered a voice beside her ear, so low, so soft that at first she thought she'd imagined it—until she felt a warm brush of breath against her neck.

Heartbeat accelerating, Blythe slowly turned to her right. A faint scratch of stubble stopped her from going any further. She should turn back around and ignore it. It was the height of impropriety for him to be this close. Why, she could smell him, feel the warm spiciness of his skin near hers.

She liked it.

This would be one aspect of marriage she would find appealing. Intimacy, sexual or not, was something lacking in her life. And while she might not want a man telling her what to do, she would be lying if she didn't admit to having an abundance of curiosity about the pleasure a man and woman could share. But was it enough to risk her freedom? Was it enough to take that gamble on ending up happy like either Miles and Varya or Carny and Teresa?

He drew back so that they were eye to eye, but there was still way too little distance between them. His gaze was dark, framed by those insanely lush lashes. He searched her face, then her eyes for an answer to his question. Try as she might, she couldn't look away. He held her captive just as surely as if his hands had seized her.

"I beg your pardon?" Her voice was hoarse.

His gaze never wavered. Had he no concept of impertinence? "Do you still love him?"

"Who?"

"Carny."

"That is none of your business."

His lips curved in a half smile. "That's not a yes or no."

It was as good as he was going to get right now! Why should he care how she felt about Carny? Unless . . . unless she wasn't alone in this strange pull she felt toward him. She had felt a strong sense of possessiveness when Lady Chillinghearst asked about his marriage plans. Did he feel the same when Carny looked at her?

"Do you have a fiancée waiting for you at home?"

Both of his brows lifted. "No. No, I do not."

"Someone hoping to be your fiancée, perhaps?" She'd be lying if she didn't confess to at least part of her wanting him to say yes so she could set aside this dangerous infatuation.

Now he frowned. "No one hoping or willing to be my anything anywhere that I know of."

So then he couldn't tell that she wanted to touch his cheek where the high ridge of bone stood out in sharp relief beneath his skin. He didn't know that she was tempted to lean ever so much closer so that the smell of him could invade her senses, and press her lips to his. Her gaze dropped to his mouth. Yes, she wanted to kiss him, taste him, press her body full against his and marvel in the length of his limbs, to know what it was like to be engulfed by a man.

At the moment, it made marriage seem almost appealing, but her happiness did not hang on her body's urges. She'd work around the demands of her body—or she'd ignore them. One thing was for certain, she wasn't going to marry just because a man made her itch in places she alone couldn't scratch.

Not that Devlin Ryland had asked to marry her. For all she knew, the thought hadn't even crossed his mind.

Her gaze came back up to his. His eyes had darkened and yet somehow seemed brighter, as though lit by an inner flame.

He knew. Somehow he had sensed the direction of her thoughts. And now his thoughts were in the same place.

What did he want to do to her? She shivered just thinking of the possibilities.

"No," she whispered, unable to tear her gaze away from his. "I do not love him anymore."

His mouth opened—

"Are you joining us in the drawing room, Blythe?" It was Varya. Dear, sweet, savior Varya.

God only knew what he might have said if not for this timely interruption. God only knew what Blythe might have agreed to in return. It was becoming more and more difficult to think straight when she was around Devlin. Already she felt as though she had known him a lifetime. Somehow she knew—or thought she knew—that he would never hurt her. But she had thought that about Carny as well. Would Devlin prove true, or would her poor judgment steer her wrong yet again?

"Yes," she replied, pushing back her chair. "I am coming."

Devlin handed her the cane she'd been using as she stood. Their gazes locked for a second of eternity as she took it from his hand.

"Thank you, Mr. Ryland." For those short minutes he had given her the knowledge of what it was like to be a woman desired by a man. It shook her right down to her toes.

He smiled, his eyes still dark with emotions better left unexplored. "My pleasure."

And Blythe knew that he was very much aware of what she was thanking him for. She also knew that he wasn't done with her yet.

Much later that evening, when the entire house was quiet and most of the guests asleep, Blythe lay awake in her bed, staring at the ceiling, murky blue in the bright darkness. Thoughts of Devlin and Rosewood kept sleep firmly at bay.

She had to tell him about her own feelings for Rosewood. Had to tell him how much the house meant to her, what it meant for her independence and her future. Surely once he knew that he would decide against buying it for himself. Surely she hadn't misread him that much.

She had to talk to him when there was no one else around to hear. She couldn't risk Miles finding out and trying to thwart her again—if he had truly done so to begin with. She would have to do it soon, not just because the clock was ticking on her, but because it was driving her mad.

She could go now. It was so late no one would see her, and if someone did, chances were he was doing something he wouldn't want anyone else to know about either. It would be dreadfully scandalous if she were caught, but she could always lie and say she heard a strange noise and wanted to make certain everything was all right. Once she had wished for someone to come along to make her want to behave in a scandalous manner. She would have to be more careful with her wishes in the future.

If she went to him now, when he was sure to be sleeping, perhaps she could talk him into letting her have Rosewood. She'd seen Varya use the same ploy on Miles from time to time when her brother was being particularly hard-headed about something. Dull-witted with sleep, Miles readily gave in to his wife's wishes. He hadn't seemed to mind the deception once he awoke either. Surely if it worked on one man, it could work on another?

With a sigh, she threw back the blankets and swung herself into a sitting position on the edge of the bed. Going to his room was the only thing that would give her any peace this night.

Maybe once she had seen to Devlin, she would finally be able to sleep.

* * *

Devlin jerked awake with a strangled cry.

Heart thumping wildly against his ribs, he sat in a puddle of moonlight, the sheets tangled around his legs and hips. Perspiration covered his body with cool stickiness.

Slowly, he raised his shaking hands to the light. They were eerily blue—not red—in the silver beams. Not a trace of blood to be seen.

It was all a dream.

This time.

He lay back against the mattress, grimacing at the dampness beneath him. As usual the dream had him sweating like a block of ice in the desert.

It had been different this time. This time it had been his own face staring back at him. He realized it as he drove the knife home, when the pain and realization of death dawned in the eyes of the man before him. He'd watched in horror as his own mouth dropped open, his own eyes widened. He'd let go of the knife then, staggering backward in horror at what he had done. Then he'd just stood there, unable to move, unable to speak. He couldn't help himself, and he couldn't run for help. He stood, rooted to the ground by some invisible force, and watched himself crumple to the ground, blood leaking from his gut around the bone handle of the blade.

He hadn't been able to look away either. Just as he hadn't been able to look away that day. And just as on that day he could feel the blood soaking through his shirt, mixing with his own from the wound in his side, could feel it drying on his hands as it cooled. It had been so warm, almost silky as it ran out of the other soldier. Then it became sticky and nearly impossible to wipe off.

Some of it had come off on Carny as Devlin carried him to the surgeon—Wellington's own, of course. Nothing but the best for a peer of the realm. By time Devlin placed Carny on the cot, he no longer knew what blood was his, he was covered in so much of it. He stopped long enough to allow the surgeon to clean and stitch his own wound and then went back out to continue fighting.

He didn't remember much about the rest of the day, only that his gun shoulder ached at the end of it and that England had won. Looking out over that field and seeing the sea of bodies lying there, he hadn't felt it was much of a victory.

Flinging back the covers, Devlin threw his legs over the side of the bed and stood. Nude, he crossed the carpet to the washstand and lifted the pitcher to his mouth. The water wasn't cold, wasn't even cool, but it was wet and that was all that mattered. A part of him longed for something stronger, something that would give him sleep without dreams, but he refused to give in to it. He did not want to end up like his father and Brahm, spending most of his days in a stupor, losing what was left of his dignity.

He didn't crawl back into bed. There would be no more sleep for him until the sun rose. Daylight always chased the night demons away. Until then he would read or clean the Baker.

He chose the Baker. Sometimes just sitting with it in his hands, polishing the butt, made things seem clearer. He wasn't certain what kind of person that made him. He wasn't certain he wanted to know.

After pulling on a pair of trousers, he took the rifle from its case and sat down with it near the window. As he polished the gleaming wood and metal he turned his thoughts to the one person who seemed to occupy them lately—Blythe.

She hadn't seemed very pleased that he would soon become a neighbor. Or rather, she hadn't seemed as pleased as he would have liked. Of course it would be unseemly of her to express such feelings in front of all the other guests, but she had never struck him as a stickler for propriety before.

Perhaps this attraction he felt between them was strictly one-sided. Perhaps that look she gave him as he bared her leg hadn't been one of curious desire. Perhaps he had frightened her with his crude handling of her. Perhaps his hands on her flesh hadn't sent the same lightning bolt of awareness through her that it had through him. Perhaps she wasn't the woman who was going to teach him what it was to love and be loved.

And yet . . . he wanted her to be.

He wanted *her,* every delicious, long, round inch of her.

But what about the desire he had seen in her expression earlier that evening during dessert? Surely he hadn't imagined that? The widening of her clear eyes, the soft parting of her full lips. That she hadn't much experience with men was evident in the hesitancy of her movements, the innocent way she unknowingly set him aflame by staring at his mouth, the direction of her thoughts acutely obvious. He wanted to be the man who gave her her first taste of pleasure. He wanted to be the *only* man to know what it was like to feel those long, strong legs wrapped around him. He wanted her strength and her innocence. Wanted to bury himself inside her and let her fill him with her light.

He had stitched a hundred men back together. He had tried to keep the blood in their bodies with his bare hands. He had even delivered babies when there was no one to attend the camp women, but his power to heal was nothing like the way Blythe made him feel. She made him want to be whole again. When he was with her there seemed to be some shred of promise in his life.

They had known each other but a few days, and it was getting to the point that he didn't care that she was Miles's sister, a lady, while he was a mere mister.

He thought about the farmer who had smiled at her that day they toured the park. The young, muscular man who had eyed Devlin like competition. He might feel threatened if Blythe had given him any reason to feel that way, but she hadn't.

That farmer was nothing to her, he had seen it in her eyes.

A knock on his door brought his brows together. It was after three in the morning. Who could be knocking at this hour? If it was Lady Ashby again, he was going to have to get a little more persuasive with her. Women who went from man to man were usually looking for something no one could give them but ended up with plenty of other things, such as the French pox, for their trouble. *Not* an arousing thought.

He opened the door, prepared to deliver a convincing refusal. His eyes widened.

There was a God. And He was good.

Standing in the doorway, like an angel or a gift from heaven, was Blythe. She wore a plain, ivory satin wrapper, and from what little he could see of it, a matching nightgown beneath. But this was hardly a planned seduction—her hair was mussed from bed and the wrapper was wrinkled, as though she had pulled it from beneath a bunch of pillows or perhaps other clothes.

Still, it had been a long time—if ever—since he had seen a woman as seductive as Blythe.

"May I come in?" she asked softly.

He didn't have to think of an answer; he simply stood back and allowed her entrance. Even if he had been capable of speech, he didn't think his mind would have been able to think of the words to say. What else could he say but "please"?

She strode purposefully into the room and turned to face him. "Shut the door."

He did, never taking his eyes off her lest she disappear when he wasn't looking.

She didn't face him. "I realize this is very improper of me to come here, to your room at such an hour, but I simply *had* to speak to you."

She did?

She began pacing, her gaze darting about the room as she moved. "Earlier this evening, during dessert, I discovered something that concerns you. I thought I could wait to discuss it with you, but it would not leave me alone. I had to see you."

He stared at her, his mouth so dry it seemed glued shut.

She looked at him, her eyes widening. It was then that he remembered he was naked from the waist up.

"Why . . . are you holding a rifle?"

Devlin's gaze shifted to the Baker in his right hand and then back to her. "Sometimes cleaning it helps me sleep."

"You could not sleep either?"

He said nothing, but shook his head as he leaned the rifle against the wall.

She came toward him. "Devlin, did you hear what I said? I said I had to see you. There is something we need to discuss."

Yes, yes, he had heard her, but talking wasn't what was on his mind right now. He didn't care what she wanted to discuss, whether it was the weather or her feelings for him didn't matter. All that mattered was right now and the chance of a lifetime being offered to him.

Reaching out, he trailed the tip of a trembling finger down the high curve of her cheekbone, to the hollow beneath and finally to the strong jaw below. Her skin was so soft, so delicate and smooth. Never in his life had he felt anything as fragile and perfect.

His hand slid around her neck. The downy hair at her nape brushed his fingers as heavier, tangled silk caressed his knuckles. In this light her hair was like the richest mahogany, almost black in the dark until the icy moonlight illuminated the red.

She offered no resistance as he pulled her closer. Only the widening of her eyes signaled that she felt any alarm at all.

"I'm going to kiss you," he murmured, his gaze boring into hers. He could feel her shiver in response.

Her hands came up between them, but they didn't push as

he expected. Instead, her cool fingers splayed across his chest, finding two of the many scars that served as constant reminders of the war. One she found high on his left shoulder was from a Frenchman's shot. The other just above the waist of his trousers was from the blade of a woman who hadn't wanted his assistance.

"They hurt you." Her voice was little more than a hoarse whisper.

He wrapped his hand around the one on his chest. "They shot me and they cut me, but it is nothing compared to the way I ache whenever you're near."

Blythe's lips parted, and he acted. He didn't want to talk about his scars or the war. He didn't want to hear her say how sorry she was or ask how he got them. He simply wanted to taste her, to show her just how much of an effect she had on him. Surely a kiss would appease the craving inside.

Pulling her flush against him, he claimed her mouth with his. Soft and supple, her lips accepted his invasion. Her free hand slid around to his back, her fingers whisper-soft against his skin.

Her teeth were slick against his tongue, opening to allow him access to the deeper recesses of her mouth. Tentative and unskilled, her tongue moved against his, and Devlin groaned despite himself, tightening his fingers on the back of her neck.

Her breasts pressed full and heavy against his chest. Her pelvis cushioned his upper thighs. She was so tall, so perfectly matched to him. He'd hardened to full arousal almost instantly the moment she first touched him, and now the ache in his loins was taut and insistent.

It had been forever since he had wanted a woman this badly—so badly that he didn't care if clothing was removed or if she was ready for him. He wanted Blythe so desperately he trembled with it. Could she feel it, the shivering beneath his skin? The quivering of muscle beneath her hands?

He wanted her to quiver too. He wanted to make her knees weak, wanted to make her blood so hot her entire body flushed.

He released her fingers against his chest. His heart hammered against her palm. Did it inflame her to know what she did to him? Did that salty-sweet furrow between her legs moisten with the knowledge? She owned him at this moment. If she ordered him down on his knees to worship before her, he would fall willingly and offer his amazon deity every praise his body could give.

Right after he took her to heaven with his tongue.

Devlin slid his hand under the neckline of her wrapper, inside her nightgown. Blythe made no effort to stop him as his fingers claimed her breast. Warm and firm against his palm, she pressed against him, her nipple hard and pebbled. His thumb and forefinger closed around it, pinching.

She gasped against his mouth, her hands grasping at his flesh as her hips moved against his. Her thighs parted beneath the slippery satin, taking his leg between her own. She pressed against him, her heat searing his skin as she set a slow, hesitant rhythm. He could only imagine the ache inside her, the insistent tightening of that sweet spot that held the key to her pleasure. His fingers pinched again as he imagined releasing the tension in that hardened nub. She moaned again. This time it sounded more like a whimper.

His thoughts were becoming more and more base. Need unfurled within him, driving his feral nature—his baser instinct—closer and closer to the surface. He didn't want to make love, he wanted to fuck—hard and fast and with no other emotion than pure aggression—and Blythe deserved better than an animal.

Somehow he managed to find the strength to remove his hand from her breast and drag his mouth away from hers. As her eyes opened, heavy-lidded with passion and wonder, he released his hold on the back of her neck.

"You have to go," he murmured, inching his leg from between hers. His body cried out at the loss of hers. "Or you will not leave this room a virgin."

She opened her mouth to speak, but he silenced her with the touch of a finger against her lips. She was going to tell him she didn't care, he could see it in the brightness of her eyes. But he would care when his selfishness made her first lovemaking less pleasureful than it should be.

"Please," he continued when she didn't move. "Go."

Something in his voice must have gotten through to her because she backed away from him then. Slowly, she edged toward the door, her gaze never wavering from his. She didn't speak, nor did he. He simply watched as she opened the door and retreated out into the dark corridor. The door followed after her, inch by inch obscuring her face from view until it clicked closed.

Shaking and still painfully hard, Devlin collapsed onto his back on the bed and waited for the wanting to go away.

He waited for a very long time.

Chapter 6

Blythe climbed out of bed two mornings later having lain awake all night, still unable to get the memory of Devlin and his kiss—his touch—out of her head. She had managed to avoid him for two days out of embarrassment, but she couldn't do it any longer—not if she wanted to take advantage of any chance of talking him out of Rosewood.

It wasn't the fact that he had kissed her that bothered her, nor did she find it overly troublesome that she hadn't been able to talk to him about Rosewood. No, what bothered her was that she would have let him make love to her if he had wanted. *He* had been the one to put a stop to things before they went too far. It should have been she.

His restraint—and his gallant assumption that she was indeed a virgin—made him very much the sort of man she believed him to be, which meant that while her behavior might be called into question, her judgment could not. Devlin Ryland was as much a decent man as she was a virginal miss, and until the other night no man had ever touched her breast. Who would have thought that such a simple thing as a touch could feel so sublime?

No man's touch—no man's kiss—had ever affected her as Devlin's had. No man had ever made her want to toss all her propriety and caution to the wind. Not even Carny. And she had thought that Carny's betrayal had cured her of her impulsiveness when it came to the male sex. She had thought Carny had destroyed her inclination toward romantic thoughts and hopes of being swept away by an all-consuming passion.

He had. He had destroyed it. And nothing would make her believe such foolishness again. Nothing. *No one.*

His kiss and his touches aside, Blythe still had to talk to Devlin about Rosewood. How she was going to face him this morning she had no idea, but if she didn't want to wave good-bye to all her plans for the future, it had to be done.

She washed and rang for Suki. She would be so glad when these guests were gone so she could go back to not being concerned with her hair and jewelry and gowns. It was so much easier to toss on a pair of trousers and not worry about them for the rest of the day. How many times would she have to change today? At least three or four, perhaps more depending on the entertainment planned. It was so very bothersome.

Bothersome because there was a part of her that liked it. There was a part of her that liked being feminine and fretful about her appearance. She didn't have to be brilliant to figure out why.

Because Devlin Ryland seemed to appreciate her efforts to look pretty.

As she waited for her maid she thought of the scars she had touched on Devlin's chest and stomach. There were more of them, of that she was certain. Thankfully the light had been too dim for her to see them. She didn't want to know how close he had come to dying or how many times it had happened.

He said the wounds he had suffered were nothing compared to the ache he felt for her. Dear heaven. Was it true? Did she really want to know? Men would say anything to get what they wanted—Varya had once told her that. Perhaps he had simply wanted to soften her up, make the temptation of surrender all that more eminent.

No, if that had been his intention, she didn't want to know. Despite her caution where her heart was concerned, she didn't want to believe Devlin capable of such deceit. Not him.

But she did want to know why he didn't boast about his war "trophies" as other men would have. He was a national hero and yet he never talked about the war unless asked. And that day while he was shooting, he looked so shaken, so scared.

Something had happened to him over there. And if Miles was right, it had happened at Waterloo.

Miles. *Ugh*. She didn't want to think of her brother right now. She was still raw from thinking he had plotted against her. His constant conviction that he knew what was best for her was not only one of the reasons she was so often angry with him, it was also one of the reasons she loved him as she did.

After dressing in a simple morning gown of apricot muslin, and having Suki twist her hair into a tightly braided knot, Blythe straightened her spine and went downstairs to the dining room. It was empty. Breakfast was outside this morning, a footman informed her.

Varya and Teresa were the only ones in the courtyard when Blythe entered. Blythe was relieved to see the pair of them. Her sister-in-law was her dearest friend, and Teresa, despite her unfortunate choice of husband, had already worked her way into Blythe's good graces. She liked the little tiny woman, liked her inner strength and her kind nature. Teresa was just a good person and Blythe couldn't fault her for it. Nor could she fault Carny for wanting to have her in his life.

Both women smiled brightly when they saw her, and Varya poured her a hot, strong cup of tea.

"Where is everyone this morning?" she inquired, seating herself at the table with them. "Umm. This tea is heavenly."

"Carny is out with some of the other gentlemen touring along the cliffs," Teresa informed her with a roll of her dark eyes. "You would think these men have never seen the sea before."

Varya cut into her poached egg. "The ladies are still abed and your brother is with his son. It seems Edward now has his own pony."

Despite her soreness where Miles was concerned, Blythe couldn't help but chuckle. "I'm surprised Miles waited this long."

"And the wonderful Devlin has taken a ride over to his new home," Teresa supplied, stirring more sugar into her tea. Her accent made his name sound like "Dev-lahn."

Did he already think of Rosewood as home? Blythe raised a brow. "Wonderful?" Extraordinary, perhaps. Wonderful didn't seem appropriate.

The Spanish woman nodded. "*Si*. He saved my Carny's life so I call him wonderful." She smiled. "You agree, no?"

"Oh, she agrees," Varya replied, flashing Blythe a knowing look. "She just will not admit it."

Blythe flushed under the weight of their stares. They laughed at her blush, and even though she told them they were foolish, she couldn't help the suspicion that they knew exactly where she was going not twenty minutes later when she decided to go for a ride.

And what of it if they did know? she thought as she limped toward the stables, her leg more stiff than sore. There was nothing wrong with their suspecting that she was attracted to Devlin Ryland. She *was* attracted to him. And they had no idea what had happened between them the other night. So far as Varya and Teresa were concerned, she was infatuated with England's giant war hero. She certainly wasn't alone there.

But she'd wager none of those other women had ever been held in his arms while he trembled and tried to control his desire. Even she couldn't dismiss his reaction to her. No matter how long it had been since he'd been with a woman, *she* had made Devlin Ryland tremble just as surely as he had done the same to her. She'd felt the rampant beating of his heart beneath her hand. He had wanted her and not just as a man taking what was offered, but as a man who knew what was being offered to him.

She would have given him her virtue without a blink. Perhaps that was why he stopped. He hadn't wanted the responsibility of being her first lover.

And perhaps he had second thoughts about ruining a good friend's sister. Not that she would mind being ruined. Miles might then leave her alone about getting married.

Or try to make her marry Devlin.

Halfway to the stables, Blythe froze in mid-limp. Marry Devlin. They'd no doubt make a very good match, but she was hardly in love with him—she hadn't known him long enough, nor he her. On the other hand, they liked each other well enough to stick their tongues in each other's mouths. Well enough that they would have shared their bodies. Surely that counted for *something*.

Whatever it was, it was more than she ever got from Carny, and he had actually *wanted* to marry her at one time.

But enough bashing Carny. She started walking again. She wouldn't have been happy married to him nor he to her, not once the polish wore off. He would have wanted her to be a lady all the time. He didn't like her wearing men's clothing any more than Miles did. In fact, the only man who seemed to like it was Devlin. Carny wouldn't want her shoeing horses or helping the tenant farmers. Given the way Devlin had looked at John Dobson, he probably wouldn't like that much either, but at least he seemed to like her just as she was.

"You're perfect just as you are," he had said to her. Wouldn't it be amazing if he actually meant it?

No, no, no. She would not think it. He was a man. She was a woman. They liked each other, were attracted to each other, but that was not love. And a man would have to prove his love to her several times over before she allowed herself to trust its validity. She had been stupid in the past, she would not be again.

Just for a second it occurred to her that her determination and stubbornness might be construed as stupidity by someone who believed in grabbing life by the tail and running with it. Life was too short to always worry about making mistakes.

Of course, marriage to the wrong man would be a *huge* mistake. Not like wearing puce when one looked better in russet.

A groom saddled Marigold for her immediately but Blythe refused when he offered her a lift up. Her injured leg was still a little sore, and lifting herself into the saddle hurt, but she was fairly certain that she would hurt the groom if he tried to lift her. She'd be surprised if he weighed as much as she did.

And she wanted Devlin to be the only man who assisted her. If she let others do it, it might become a habit, and the last thing she wanted to become was a useless female.

The ride to Rosewood was a reasonably quick one. She let Marigold run for most of it. Devlin had assured her that he and the grooms would make certain Mari was used to her new shoe by the time she was able to ride again. They had done a good job. The mare was anxious to run.

Devlin was standing in the drive when she came galloping up it. Flynn stood not far away, his reins wrapped around an obliging tree branch.

Devlin smiled when he saw her. Not one of those little lop-sided smiles, but a full grin. Long dimples appeared in his lean cheeks. He looked so young when he smiled.

He came right up to Marigold's side, holding his hands up to help her from the saddle. If it weren't for the fact that she already knew he could support her weight, Blythe never would have entertained the thought of sliding into his arms as she did.

He caught her around the waist, lowering her to the ground as though she weighed no more than a child. Her heart swelled foolishly as her hands slid down his shoulders. He was so very strong.

When he didn't release her immediately, she raised her gaze to his. "Hello."

He didn't reply, but Blythe knew exactly what he was thinking by the light in his eyes. She closed her eyes and lifted her chin, meeting the kiss halfway, even though every instinct screamed for her to break away.

His lips were soft and smooth yet firm. This kiss was far different from the one they'd shared in his room the other night. This time his mouth moved languidly over hers. His tongue teased and tantalized, slowly dancing with her own. He tasted of coffee and cream. She had never liked the taste of coffee before, but now she thought perhaps she could learn to like it, especially if Devlin was attached to it.

His long hands splayed across her back, pulling her flush against him. How incredible it was to know that the entire length of her could cover him and there would still be more of him left. The size of him was overwhelming, exhilarating, and a little frightening all at the same time.

How long they kissed Blythe had no idea. It seemed to last forever, yet ended far too soon.

He pulled back but didn't release her. "I've been wanting to do that ever since you left my room the other night, but you've been hiding from me."

Hiding. Yes—from what had happened in his room. She had gone there for a reason; the same reason she was here this morning—Rosewood.

She stepped back. "Devlin, about that night . . ."

He let her go, some of the pleasure leeching from his expression. "It was all a mistake and shouldn't have happened?"

"No," she replied, her voice shaky. This was ridiculous. When had she become such a ninny? "That was not what I was going to say."

He looked relieved, but still uncertain. "Good. Then whatever it was can wait. Come inside and see my house."

The bottom fell out of her stomach. "The sale has been finalized?" Aside from a slight husky edge, her voice sounded perfectly normal. Amazing.

Taking her by the hand—yet again something no other man had ever done—Devlin fished a key out of his waistcoat pocket as they walked up the steps.

"No, but Mr. Adams gave me a key so that I might have a look around and assess how many repairs are needed. The house has been empty for some time."

Blythe stood behind him as he unlocked the front door. "Any word from Lord Dartmouth?"

"Not yet. Ah, here we go."

As the heavy oak door swung open Blythe had a sudden and vivid vision of Devlin sweeping her up into his arms as he had that day in the stables and carrying her over the threshold like a bride.

His bride.

But he didn't sweep her up into his arms, he simply stood aside and waited for her to enter ahead of him as any gentleman would.

He picked the damnedest times to be like other gentlemen.

Truthfully the vision scared her. As she stepped inside the cool, slightly musty interior of Rosewood, she realized that for the first time since Carny she had imagined herself married to a specific person.

A man who had to kiss her senseless before he could even say hello, even though he knew that kiss might prove unwelcome. And she had let him because she wanted him to kiss her, even though she knew she shouldn't. A man who seemed destined to dash her hopes.

A Palladian glass dome made Rosewood's great hall bright and inviting despite the lack of direct sunlight. Huge alabaster columns, veined with a golden brown, lined both sides of the hall and flanked the doors at either end. Grecian statuary stood with dusty dignity among arches carved into the cream-colored walls. The ceiling was high, intricate plasterwork curving and winding its way to the dome, which looked far more fragile and delicate than it actually was.

Blythe's half boots clicked softly on the pale rose stone floor. The stone was smooth and unpolished, and the high luster of the marble made its circular patterns stand out all the more. Even though she had stood in this hall many times, it never ceased to take her breath away.

She snuck a glance at Devlin. Part of her wanted him to share her love for the house, while another part wanted him to hate it so that it might still be hers.

He gazed around the hall in unconcealed wonder. "It is amazing."

Blythe smiled at his awe. "Yes. It is. Come. Let us look around."

She should be trying to talk him out of buying the house rather than asking him to tour its rooms and share his plans for them, but she loved Rosewood. Even if it was against her best interest, she wanted Devlin to see its beauty as well. Of course there were things that needed to be repaired—the staircase banister, for example, and some plasterwork in one of the drawing rooms—but nothing serious.

First they walked through the curved corridor with its collection of Dartmouth ancestor portraits.

"I hope Dartmouth plans on taking these with him," Devlin remarked, staring at one particularly sour-looking woman.

Blythe couldn't help but smile. "I imagine he will."

They then moved through the large, welcoming library, several small parlors and drawing rooms, a gentleman's study, dining room, games room, music room and then up the stairs to the family rooms. Devlin looked at each room and their covered furniture with obvious pleasure, but it wasn't until they reached the master suite that Blythe knew she was in trouble.

He entered first, stripping the holland covers as he went. Blythe was right behind him, coming around on his left so she might see the expression on his face when he saw the room in all its splendor. His face lit up like a child's at Christmas.

Mahogany furniture complemented a blue, gold, and wine Axminster carpet with a simple diamond and fleur-de-lis pattern. Deep blue velvet curtains draped the floor-to-ceiling windows. The walls were a soft beige with no other accent except a few paintings, each of which was crafted with bold strokes in deep jewel tones that matched the carpet. The ceiling was pale cream with delicate yet simple plasterwork, but it was the bed that was the true focal point.

The frame and posters were made of solid, beautifully carved mahogany. The mattress was almost three full feet off the ground, with polished steps at the bottom for those who needed assistance climbing up. The bed itself was also long enough and wide enough for two large adults to lie down and not touch unless they wanted to. There were no hangings to take away from the beauty of the wood, only a dark blue velvet bedspread that matched the drapes and several gold and wine cushions to add more color.

Devlin immediately went to the bed. "*This* I'm keeping."

Blythe didn't tell him that Lord Dartmouth intended to include the bed, as well as most of the furniture in the house, with the sale. She wanted to tell him, wanted to be the one to give him the happiness such knowledge would bring, but she couldn't bring herself to say the words.

She watched, a large lump in her throat as he tossed himself onto the bed. He lay there, across the width of the mattress, his boots hanging over the side.

"You have to come try this," he enthused.

"I cannot lie down with you," she admonished, even though she wanted to. "It wouldn't be proper."

No, it would be downright *dangerous*.

Smiling, he left the bed and came toward her. His smile was entirely too cocky and mischievous for Blythe's liking.

"What are you doing?" she demanded, backing away from him as a mouse might from a cat.

He moved quickly—so fast she couldn't even defend herself. He grabbed her around the waist and half twirled, half carried her protesting to the bed. Instead of tossing her as she suspected he would, he lowered her to the counterpane gently, almost reverently. He followed her down, settling his weight on top of her, pressing her into the mattress.

So this was how it felt to have a man lie on top of her. It felt good—naughty and right at the same time. He wasn't as heavy as she would have thought, even though the full length of him was upon her. He held her hands above her head, pinned her skirts with his legs. She couldn't escape even if she wanted to.

His gaze was dark and bright and he stared at her as though he had never seen a woman before.

"You're beautiful," he told her, his voice rough.

Blythe opened her mouth to automatically disagree, but he cut off her protest with a kiss—a slow, deep, aching kiss.

"I'll think of this," he murmured when he eventually lifted his head. "Each night when I climb into this bed, I'll think of this moment when you were on it with me."

The lump in Blythe's throat turned into a mountain. Tears burned the back of her eyes as she gazed up at him and his wonderful, sadly beautiful face.

That moment she decided not to tell him about her own claim on the house. She could tell he had fallen in love with it, and she would rather have him crawling into this bed and thinking of her than crawl into it herself, alone, and think of him.

* * *

Devlin was quite busy for the next week. The deal for Rosewood went through without a hitch, and he divided his days between Brixleigh and his new home. When he was at Rosewood, he spent the hours preparing to take over the household, making note of repairs and purchases. The repairs needed weren't major, but several were quite extensive and would take some time. More time for him to spend at Brixleigh, he supposed. When he was at Brixleigh, he spent most of his time sleeping, eating, and stalking Blythe.

It was difficult to find her alone. Sometimes when he was at Rosewood, she would come and join him. He allowed her to pick out all the new carpets, draperies, and other furnishings. It made perfect sense to him, seeing as how he was entertaining the notion of making her mistress of it all.

When the thought had first occurred to him, he couldn't quite say. Perhaps it was that day a week ago when he'd kissed her on the bed, or perhaps it had happened sometime after that. Perhaps the day when he secretly bought her a new pair of trousers because her old ones were almost worn through in the knees. The kiss she had given him as thanks kept him in a state of semi-arousal for much longer than a man his age should have to suffer through.

Or perhaps it was the day he saw her running around the lawns at Brixleigh with the estate dogs playfully nipping at her heels. Some hair had slipped from the knot on the back of her head, and her cheeks were flushed with exercise.

Then again, perhaps it had happened the day she had looked at him as though she thought he could do anything. He had run out into the tide after two local boys and their boat had been carried out farther than they intended. It was hardly an act of bravery. He was one of the only men there who could actually swim. He just did what had to be done, but when he brought the boys to shore, Blythe had gazed at him with such open appreciation in her green eyes that Devlin had almost grabbed her and kissed her right then and there. The only thing that stopped him was the boys' thankful mother throwing her arms around him in a very tearful and exuberant hug.

Yes, that was more than likely the day he decided that he wanted to possess Blythe Christian. He wanted her to love him, if such a thing were possible. He wanted to be worthy of such devotion, even though he knew it was impossible.

If only he could decipher her feelings on the subject. He knew she liked him—that was obvious enough—and he knew without a doubt that she wanted him physically just as much as he wanted her. Some of those days at Rosewood it had been a chore for both of them just to keep their hands off each other.

And it didn't look like he was going to get her alone tonight either. He was dying to kiss her, but he couldn't just jump up and do that in the middle of Varya's performance even if it would be vastly more entertaining.

It wasn't that he didn't enjoy the music; he did. Varya's playing of the pianoforte was incredibly accomplished, but unless she broke into a round of bawdy ballads or old folk songs, it wasn't likely that he'd recognize any of it. It was another reminder that for a son of a viscount, he was shockingly lacking in culture.

However, he wasn't lacking in taste, a point that was proven by his acute attraction to Blythe, who sat very near the front in an evening gown of sapphire silk. He stared at her openly, not caring who saw the depth of his regard. He didn't believe in the social rule of hiding one's feelings as his parents had.

But he did believe in hiding one's past—something he was going to have to do if he was going to win Blythe. He didn't want to lie to her, but he wasn't prepared to admit to being a murderer, not when it would mean seeing disgust in her eyes.

"This is rich," purred a voice to his right. "The lion has fallen for the lamb."

Devlin didn't even spare Lady Ashby a glance as she slid into the empty chair beside his. Lion? Lamb? He certainly didn't see himself as much of a lion, and Blythe was far from being a lamb.

"She will never have you," the blond woman whispered. "You know that, do you not? You are a little too rough. A little too *much* for such a naive innocent."

Still Devlin did not look at her. He focused solely on Blythe and tried to keep the muscle in his jaw from tensing.

"You have competition," Lady Ashby went on, her breath hot against his ear. "See how a certain *ram* looks at her?"

If he gave her a good shove, would she go away? Even as he thought it, he found himself listening to her babble. His gaze drifted across the crowded music room, lighting from head to head until he found the one she meant.

Carny. Obviously he found Blythe more interesting than the music, or even his own wife. And while Devlin wouldn't call the expression on the fairer man's face lovelorn, it was definitely—*something*.

"She will never take you over him, even if he is married. I think you know that as well."

No, he didn't know that. Blythe had told him she didn't love Carny anymore and he believed her. She might still harbor some feelings for him—bitterness for one—but nothing he was worried about. Or rather, nothing he had been worried about until Joyce the Jackal sat her scheming arse down beside him. Carny's feelings really didn't matter. He was already married.

"If you marry her, how long do you think it will be before she runs off to have an affair with one of her own kind? How long before the novelty of your rough, quiet nature wears off and bores her to tears?"

The muscle in his jaw was twitching now. Damn it, he shouldn't let her see that she was getting to him. He knew better than to allow a tactician like Lady Ashby to get the upper hand over him. If this were a battlefield he'd simply put a ball between her eyes.

Christ, did he actually think that? Yes, he had, and he felt no remorse for it either.

"You need someone who knows how to stroke your fur."

Oh good Lord. Did the woman always talk such foolishness?

"What I need, Lady Ashby, is something you are incapable of giving." He turned to look her straight in the eye. "Loyalty."

He thought Lady Ashby might have actually hissed at him before getting up and swishing away, but he couldn't be certain. He was just glad she was gone. That woman made him feel dirty in a way no one else had ever managed—not even himself.

He sat for another few minutes, his arms folded across his chest, legs crossed at the ankles, and watched Blythe—and Carny—some more.

He was jealous. Jealous because she had once loved Carny. Jealous because Carny had known her longer. It didn't matter that he probably knew her *better* than Carny did. It wasn't the same thing.

Thank God Carny hadn't been awake to see him kill the soldier, or he would be able to tell Blythe all about it. He didn't want to think Carny capable of such betrayal, but when a woman was concerned, friendship often suffered.

The tune Varya was playing tinkled to an end. Devlin joined the applause, his gaze still focused on Blythe. He lost her for a moment as guests stood and the talking started.

Rising to his feet, he quickly caught sight of his quarry again. Being tall had its advantages on occasion.

Blythe was among a small group of women drifting toward the music room door. No doubt they were on their way to the ladies' retiring room. He almost turned away, but then

Blythe's gaze met his, and he knew in an instant that she wanted him to follow.

He did. When the ladies turned right in the corridor, Blythe turned left and headed for the French doors that led out into the courtyard and garden.

He caught up with her near the maze. "In here," she whispered, taking him by the hand and leading him through the dark twists and turns with the smooth skill of someone who knew the path like the back of her hand.

In the center of the maze was a fountain surrounded by benches and illuminated with softly flickering torches. A mermaid arched up among stone waves in the center of the fountain, water raining from her hands and tail. It was lovely. And Devlin couldn't have cared less about it.

As soon as they reached the fountain, Blythe turned to face him. Neither of them spoke. They wrapped their arms around each other as their lips met in a fierce, breathless kiss.

An eternity seemed to pass before they broke apart, each of them breathing a little more shallowly.

Blythe spoke first, leading him to one of the benches where they could sit. He enjoyed this part of being alone with her almost as much as the kisses. They could talk about anything. He never felt boring or silly around her. They had similar interests, and even when they didn't, Blythe was always interested in hearing what he had to say and would then share her own opinion.

"We cannot keep doing this. We are going to be caught."

He brushed the velvet lobe of her ear with his finger. She shivered. "So?"

"I do not want people to talk about us like we did something wrong."

He could remind her that sneaking away like this was wrong as far as society was concerned, but he didn't. What they did was none of society's business.

"All right," he agreed. "We will be more careful."

He could be so agreeable because the house party would end soon, and then he would take possession of Rosewood. Once all the guests had returned to town, Devlin would set about courting Blythe properly. Miles wouldn't object, not after all the not-so-subtle matchmaking he and Varya had attempted over the last week.

"I saw Lady Ashby talking to you. What did she want?"

Devlin smiled. "Jealous?"

Blythe arched a brow. "Of her? Hardly." She paused. "What did she want?"

His smile twisted wryly. "I think she wanted to be my lioness."

"She likened you to a lion?" If her expression wasn't dubious enough, her tone was.

He nodded. "She did. What are you doing?"

She scratched behind his ear with a smirk. "Seeing if I can make you purr."

Laughing, he wrapped his arms around her waist and hauled her up into his lap. "Try it now."

She kissed him instead, locking her arms around his neck and pressing her soft lips to his. A jolt of sheer sensual pleasure washed over him as she explored his mouth with her tongue. Over the past few days she had become more and more aggressive with him, initiating or taking control of much of their intimate contact. Devlin liked it. It aroused him to know that she wanted him as much as he wanted her.

It was time to take things further. He'd been waiting for this moment ever since their first kiss. Since then he'd not dared go any further than touching her breasts, even though he ached to feel the rest of her. Now it was time. This would be the beginning of her seduction into becoming his wife.

Returning her kiss with equal ardor, Devlin kept one hand around Blythe's waist as the other one crept beneath her skirts. She jumped as his fingers skimmed the silky length of her stocking-clad calf, but made no move to stop him.

Her calves were long and muscular, firm beneath his palm. He explored further, sliding his hand past the garters above her knees. Delicate embroidery rubbed against his fingertips.

Her round thighs were warm—and closed—to his touch. Undaunted, Devlin eased his hand up further as his tongue slid against hers. Tenderly, he twined his fingers through the soft curls at the apex of her legs, tickling the sensitive flesh there and slowly, ever so slowly, easing his hand closer and closer to the desired spot.

Her thighs relaxed under his gentle coaxing and parted as he pressed the pads of his fingers high against the warm cleft.

"Open for me," he whispered against the hot sweetness of her mouth.

Her eyes opened, heavy-lidded and bright. Her gaze locked with his, and he saw the desire and uncertainty there.

"Let me touch you." Another stroke. "Please."

Whether it was the pleasure or the "please" that convinced her he didn't know and didn't care. Her buttocks pressing down on the aching length of his erection, Blythe parted her legs as far as her narrow skirts would allow. It was enough.

Devlin's hand stroked downward, easing his middle finger between the swollen lips of her sex. Hot, wet flesh met his questing touch and he groaned against her mouth.

Deeper his finger slid, the muscles of her slick passage clutching it tightly. There was no barrier against his intrusion— Blythe's active lifestyle had no doubt long ago ridded her of the thin membrane that often made a woman's first sexual experience a painful rather than pleasureful experience. He could enter her easily, without worrying about hurting her. Good.

When his finger was as deep within her as it could go, he began moving it: slowly, in and out, in and out. Blythe squirmed in his lap, pushing against his hand, dampening his palm with her juices.

He added another finger, plunging them inside her as

though it was actually his cock thrusting there. She clung to his shoulders and whimpered at his sensual assault.

But he wasn't done with her yet. As she soaked and gripped his fingers, he slid his thumb up her slick furrow to the small nubbin of erect flesh that he knew ached for his attention. He touched it reverently with the tip of his thumb.

Her hips arched as she gasped into his mouth. He could feel her body tensing as she pushed against his hand, writhing on his lap until her skirts rode high on her thighs and Devlin thought he was going to go mad with desire. He throbbed beneath her, and every time she moved it made him want her more. If this continued he was going to come without her even touching him.

As though she read his mind, Blythe lifted herself off his lap and onto the bench, her knees straddling one of his. Breaking their kiss, she gazed down at him—the most beautiful, sensuous creature he had ever seen.

"I want to touch you," she rasped, her thighs spreading of their own volition as his fingers continued to play her. Her hands went to the falls of his trousers. "Let me give you what you are giving me."

He should refuse. Not doing so could be dangerous, especially if they got any more carried away than they already were, but her fingers felt so good as they freed him from the confines of his trousers. He wanted her to touch him.

"Will you teach me?" she inquired with sexual innocence, her fingers skimming the throbbing length of his cock.

"Like this." His free hand wrapped around hers, showing her how to pump him with just the right amount of pressure. "Ahh, sweet Jesus, Blythe, that feels good." So good he almost forgot that he was supposed to be pleasuring her as well.

He released her hand and gripped the edge of the bench with all his strength. He had to regain some control or he was going to come too soon. It had been too long since anyone had made him feel this way.

In fact, no one had ever made him feel this way before. Never had he risked discovery by having a sexual encounter out of doors, not even in the army when the times he'd found a woman had been few and far between.

Her lips claimed his again as she rode his hand. Her fingers dug into his scalp as her mouth bruised his. The faster she undulated her hips, the faster she pumped him. The pressure in his loins increased. He wasn't going to last long. Not at all.

Increasing the tempo of his thumb on her sweet spot, he crooked his fingers inside her, until he felt the tiny ridges of flesh on the front wall of her vagina. As he stroked them, Blythe made a low keening sound against his mouth, her fingers tightening around him, stroking harder and faster as her thighs tensed around his forearm.

They exploded together. Devlin just managed to pull his handkerchief from his pocket and cover himself with it as his climax hit. He caught his seed in the soft linen as Blythe fell against him, shivering with spent pleasure. Only their breathing was audible in the quiet darkness.

"My God," she said sometime later as he righted first his trousers and then her skirts. "I never knew it could be like that."

"It can be better." He thought of how it was going to be when he was finally able to spend himself inside her. "Someday I'll show you."

She smiled shyly as he kissed her. Tenderness engulfed him as their lips clung together. She was his.

"What the hell is going on here?"

Chapter 7

*S*hite.

Slowly, Devlin rose to his feet and turned to face the wrath of his future brother-in-law. Blythe stood as well, but he shielded her as much as he could with his body. Her hair was mussed, her gown was wrinkled, and the lower half of her face was red with whisker burn. One look at her and Miles would call him out.

But that aside, he didn't want to subject her to any more embarrassment than necessary, especially since Miles had people with him. And not just any people, but Varya, Carny, and Teresa. At least they could be counted on to keep their mouths shut. Blythe's reputation would remain intact.

Still, it was an unpleasant situation to be caught in.

"Miles," Blythe began. "It is not what you think . . ."

Devlin didn't even look at her. He kept his gaze fastened on her brother, who already knew the truth of the situation.

"It is *exactly* what you think," he admitted, watching his friend's green eyes narrow.

"Devlin!" Blythe's outburst proved her shock. Her use of his Christian name also proved him right.

Teresa and Varya were silent, their expressions serene and supportive. It wasn't them Devlin was concerned with. Miles and Carny looked positively murderous. Correction, Carny looked murderous. Miles's countenance had a bit too much smugness in it to be completely dangerous. Still, Devlin didn't doubt for a minute that if the heavier man suspected his sister's virtue had been breached, Devlin would be in danger of serious bodily injury.

"We will discuss this someplace less open," Miles announced, his voice tight. "Ryland, I'll see you in my study. Blythe, you go to your room."

"No," came the unwavering reply from over Devlin's shoulder.

Her brother's jaw tightened in the torchlight. "You will do as I say."

Blythe stepped out from behind the protection of Devlin's body, a stiff-shouldered amazon ready to do battle. She was an amazing woman. He'd seen men back down from Miles's anger, but she was his sister, and she did not fear him.

"You cannot order me about like a child, Miles. If you want to discuss this, then you will discuss it with me."

"I intend to." Miles's gaze flickered to Devlin. "But first I will discuss it with Ryland."

Blythe stepped forward. His beautiful amazon warrior. "If you hurt him—"

Devlin silenced her with his hand on her shoulder. When was the last time anyone had stepped forward to defend him? "He will not hurt me, Blythe," he said softly.

She turned to face him, fear and anxiety blazing in her eyes. "How do you know?"

He smiled. "Because he can't." He meant no disrespect toward Miles. It was simply the truth. Miles couldn't hurt him. In a fight they would be well matched, and even if Miles beat him to a bloody pulp, it wouldn't change a single thing.

Other than his brothers, the only person alive in the world

with the power to hurt him was Blythe, and she had no idea.

"Dearest, why do you not come inside with Teresa and me?" Varya suggested, stepping forward with an offered hand. "We will have some tea, and the gentlemen can join us when they are finished talking."

Blythe slid a hesitant glance in his direction. God love her, she didn't want to leave him alone and unprotected. He nodded for her to go. Once he explained that he would happily make Blythe his wife, everything would be all right. Miles simply wanted to ensure that his sister wasn't being trifled with. Truly, Devlin couldn't blame him.

"Fine. I will go drink tea." Blythe pointed a warning finger at her brother. "But do not think for a minute that you are in a position to decide my life for me, Miles."

"I am your guardian," came the haughty reply. "Those decisions are mine to make."

His sister scowled. "Even you are not so daft as to believe that." With that parting sally, she lifted her skirts above the grass and strode toward the maze exit, Varya and Teresa scurrying behind in an effort to keep up.

Devlin gestured for Miles to follow. "After you. I am afraid I do not know my way out."

"You got in here, did you not?" Carny asked.

Devlin studied the fair man as he came up beside him. Carny's tone had been sharp, sharper than a man who had broken Blythe's heart had a right to sound.

"I had help," was his quiet reply. Let Carny chew on that for a while. Devlin wasn't completely certain, but his friend's surly attitude seemed an awful lot like jealousy. Perhaps it was a protective instinct given that he had known Blythe so long, but it seemed more than that—

He walked between Miles and Carny, like a prisoner, as they exited the maze. In silence they made the torch-lit trek back to the house, entering through one of the many sets of French doors off the courtyard. From there it was a short walk down the softly lit corridor to Miles's study. They saw only two other guests on the walk, and despite the tension between them, managed to put on a good enough show so as not to arouse suspicions.

The wall lamps were already lit, illuminating the room in a golden glow. Miles offered Devlin a seat, which he took, and a drink, which he didn't. The other two men remained standing in a subtle attempt to intimidate. It was all very civilized.

Until Miles spoke.

"Damn it, Dev! Give me one good reason why I should not beat you senseless!" His eyes blazed with repressed anger.

Both of Devlin's brows rose. "Because I've done nothing you haven't encouraged?"

Carny snorted. Both Miles and Devlin shot him a silencing glance.

"Is my sister still a virgin?"

"That's none of your business," Devlin responded softly. He nodded in Carny's direction. "Nor is it his."

Carny looked very much as if he wanted to reply to that, and Devlin was most interested in hearing it. There was nothing Carny could say regarding Blythe's virginity that wouldn't tempt Devlin to knock his teeth out.

Miles ran a hand through his hair. "Let me rephrase. Is there any chance of my becoming an uncle in the near future?"

Telling Miles that was none of his business either might be pushing his luck too far, so Devlin opted for the truth. "No."

The big man's shoulders visibly sagged in relief. "Thank you."

"Why are you thanking him?" Carny demanded. "You and I both know that doesn't mean he did not take advantage of her! Just that he was smart about it."

"Smart about it," Devlin echoed coolly. He made it sound so emotionless, so cold. "Doesn't that mean screwing someone else while Blythe believes I'm thinking of her?"

Carny's expression was part amazement, part fury. "I beg your pardon?"

The left side of Devlin's mouth lifted as he leaned back in his chair. "You heard me. What's crawled up your arse anyway, Carny? This doesn't concern you."

Now the blond man looked affronted. "I have known Blythe for years. I care very much about her well-being."

"How much?"

He obviously didn't know how to answer, and Devlin's smile thinned. "Maybe you should figure that out."

"This is not about Carny," Miles barked. "It is about your actions toward my sister."

Reluctantly, Devlin dragged his attention from Carny and transferred it to Miles. "I haven't done anything you haven't pushed me toward since my arrival."

Miles's cheeks flushed. "I wanted you to court her, not seduce her!"

"Who says I seduced her?"

"You must have done something," Miles insisted. "She never would have gone into that maze with you if you had not. She is not that kind of woman."

It wasn't Devlin's nature to kiss and tell, so he wasn't about to tell Miles the maze had been Blythe's idea.

At his silence Miles's expression became even darker. "Have you asked her to marry you?"

"Not yet, no." There had been no opportunity, and at the time, he hadn't really thought of it. He planned to do that once he was more certain of her feelings—and his own.

"You must have made her a promise of some kind," Carny snapped. "You must have at least hinted at marriage or an engagement. Blythe would never act that way without some kind of provocation."

Devlin was one of those men whose temper was slow to ignite, but when it did it had a very short fuse. He scowled at Carny. "Why? Because she didn't act 'that way' with you?"

There it was. A guilty flush crept up Carny's cheeks as he averted his gaze. He *was* jealous. The son of a bitch. He had no right.

For the first time since the two of them met, Devlin was angry at Carny. Not just for thinking so little of him, but for thinking Blythe such a twit that she couldn't think for herself. And for his arrogance. Did he fancy himself such a fantastic lover that if a woman didn't fall into bed with him she wouldn't fall for anyone?

And, he had to admit, he was angry because now he knew that Carny had *tried* to get Blythe to act "that way" before going off and marrying someone else. If he had succeeded, would he still have cast Blythe aside after using her in such a manner?

To think that he believed he knew this man, that he had saved his life. He had taken the life of someone else in the process, bloodied his hands and damned his soul so that Rowan Carmichael, Earl Carnover, could come home and break Blythe's heart and then have the balls to try to pass off his jealousy as "caring" for her.

At that moment he didn't think very much of Carny. Not very much at all, and he didn't like it.

He liked Carny's possessiveness toward Blythe even less. The man was married. He had no business sticking his face into Devlin and Blythe's relationship. No business being jealous. Teresa deserved better. She deserved a man who respected his marriage vows, just as Devlin's mother had deserved such a man.

And Blythe deserved more than being dallied with.

"You intend to marry her, I hope?" There was no "hope" about it. Miles expected it; it was in his voice.

Careful to keep his expression bland, he glanced toward his future brother-in-law. "If she'll have me."

"Have you!" the red-haired man bellowed. "She will have no choice!"

Carny nodded in agreement, even though he looked as though he had swallowed something bitter.

Devlin couldn't help but chuckle. "The two of you really know nothing about her, you know that? You can't *make* Blythe do anything."

"Hmpf." Miles looked decidedly smug. "I managed to put an end to her plans to buy her own estate the day I convinced Adams to sell Rosewood to you."

Devlin froze. He couldn't have heard him right. "Blythe wanted Rosewood?"

Miles nodded, some of his smugness fading.

How could Devlin not have seen it? All Blythe's ideas for improving the house, the color swatches, the easy way she helped him pick furniture and staff. She had already planned it out for the day she owned it. Yet she didn't tell him. He wouldn't have bought it if he had known she wanted it, and yet she never tried to stop him from making it his own.

For a split second, he entertained the idea that the reason for Blythe's attentions was her desire for Rosewood. Did she want the house badly enough to take the man as well? No, that wasn't right. She liked him. She respected him and wanted him. He knew these things to be true. Perhaps she even loved him, but that was something he rarely let himself think about. Blythe's love was something he aspired to, something he longed for like some men longed for fame or money. He wanted for nothing in this world, not even a clear conscience, like he wanted Blythe.

He also knew that if he did win her love, it would be under false pretenses, because she didn't know the real him. Didn't know the horror he was capable of, or the darkness in his soul. She thought he was a good man. If only that were true.

He stood up, glaring at Miles. "You used me to disappoint your own sister?"

Miles's eyes widened. "Of course not. I wouldn't have even found out about it had it not been for your own interest in the place."

Well, that was small comfort, knowing that hadn't been Miles's reason for showing him the place to begin with.

"What's to stop her from finding another house?"

Miles's smug expression returned. "I have since changed the details of her inheritance. If she does not marry she gets the money in installments rather than one lump sum."

And Devlin had thought he knew this man! How could he do something so underhanded, so deliberately controlling? His disgust and horror must have shown because Miles added, "Do not look at me like that, Dev. You do not understand."

He watched the shorter man carefully. "You are right. I don't."

Miles's expression changed to that of a man at the end of his rope. "For years my sister has hidden away here at Brixleigh. She rarely socializes and she never comes to town anymore."

So far Devlin didn't see anything wrong with Blythe's choices. He planned to do the same. Miles must have seen that in his expression, because he went on.

"She used to like parties and balls. At one time she was just as at home in a pretty gown as in those awful trousers she prefers now. We used to talk, we used to laugh." His expression hardened. "And I will not allow her to hide in the country until she dies an old maid just because of—"

"Of me," Carny finished softly. "Because of me."

Miles looked at him. There was no blame, only regret in his features. "Yes."

It was then that everything became crystal-clear to Devlin. He wasn't the villain after all. Miles blamed himself because Carny was his friend, and Carny blamed himself because he hadn't loved Blythe the way he thought he should have. And maybe he didn't want anyone else to love her either. Maybe knowing that he was the reason she left society gave him power on some deep, selfish level.

Neither Miles nor Carny was a villain, not really. Each did what he believed was right and suffered the consequences for it later, if there were any to suffer. Carny had to follow his heart, and in return broke a heart that obviously had meant a lot to him, even if it wasn't enough. And Miles loved Blythe so much that he was willing to risk her hatred to protect her from herself.

And then there was Devlin himself. He hadn't seen anything wrong with his and Blythe's secret meetings, their stolen kisses and clandestine embraces. Now he saw them as Carny and Miles did. He thought of how he would react if it was his sister. Many people would see him as the worst kind of rake for taking such liberties with a lady without the benefit of marriage. An engaged couple *might* be excused, but he hadn't even asked Blythe to marry him yet.

No, he hadn't handled this situation very well either. He had no one to blame for his current condition but himself. He didn't have to follow her into that maze, but he had because he wanted to be with her. He wanted to touch her as he had and have her touch him in return.

"We're a fine lot," he said finally, breaking the silence in the room.

Both Miles and Carny chuckled tightly. There was still a lot of tension among the three of them, but nothing that wouldn't eventually go away. They were friends, after all.

Carny offered him his hand. Devlin took it. "My apologies, Dev. I should have known better than to think the worst of you."

Miles stepped up as well. "As should I, but she is my sister after all."

Devlin smiled. "And my future bride."

Miles's gaze was piercing. "You genuinely want to marry her?"

"I do."

Clapping him on the back, Miles chuckled. "Then I wish you luck, my friend."

"He is going to need it," Carny quipped, but there was something in the smaller man's eyes that continued to make Devlin uneasy. He couldn't help the suspicion that Carny was still jealous.

Despite Carny's marriage and despite Blythe's insistence that she no longer had feelings for Carny, Devlin couldn't help but wonder which one of them she would choose if given the choice.

"I sincerely hope neither of you intends to give me a lecture." Blythe flopped onto a pale blue silk-brocade chaise and stared at her companions with a countenance of extreme boredom. It was the only way she could get past the complete and utter humiliation she felt at having been caught with Devlin at such an intimate time.

Thank God they hadn't been found a few minutes earlier. Now *that* would have been terrible!

Varya and Teresa exchanged glances.

"I do not think either of us is prepared to lecture anyone on proper behavior, dearest." Varya seated herself in a dainty tapestry chair.

Teresa followed suit, taking the identical chair next to Varya's. "Now, if you wanted to know how to act *improperly* . . ." The two women laughed.

Blythe's gaze went from one to the other. When had they become such good friends? It used to be that she was Varya's only real friend. Of course it used to be that she despised Teresa without even knowing her. The two of them had become friends as well. In fact, other than Varya, Teresa was the only friend Blythe had.

Varya's expression sobered. "No lectures, but I would like to know what you intend to do now that you have been caught."

Ahh, she'd wondered when they'd get around to putting her on the spot. Picking at the fringe on a cream silk cushion, Blythe shrugged. "I do not see that *I* have to do anything."

Varya and Teresa exchanged another glance. This time, it was a tad more worried than before. So much for giving her pointers on improper behavior. The two of them had become paragons of propriety since marrying.

"But Blythe," Varya began, "you were caught with Mr. Devlin in a very . . . suggestive manner. Surely you know how that could damage your reputation."

Another shrug. "What care I for reputation?" But she did care, blast it all. She cared more than she wanted to. "Besides, 'twas only the four of you who stumbled upon us. No one else needs to know."

A glimmer of concern shone in Varya's dark blue eyes. "Yes, but what if it happens again and someone else sees you?"

"First of all," Blythe defended, holding up a hand, "there was nothing to see. Devlin and I were not doing anything but sitting together with his arm about my shoulders. There was nothing improper about that. Secondly, we will just have to ensure that such a situation does not happen again." Meaning they would have to be more careful. She'd just had a taste of the pleasure a man and woman could share, and she wasn't ready to give it up just yet, no matter how dangerous it might prove to her heart.

Teresa laughed at that. "Oh my dear friend, we all say that and then it happens again!"

Varya nodded sagely. "That is true. Dearest, you must consider that if you are caught with Mr. Devlin again your reputation will be ruined, and if you do not marry him, no one else will want you."

Blythe arched a brow. "I cannot believe the woman who

once warned me of the evils of marriage is now an advocate for the state. I have no more hope or intention of marrying than you once did, Varya."

That was true. At one time Varya swore marriage was the worst thing a woman could do. Back then Blythe hadn't believed her, but that was before she'd learned a few valuable life lessons courtesy of the Earl of Carnover. The first lesson was that women hang too much on the hope of getting married. The second was that a woman could be far more independent without a man telling her what to do. Blythe simply could not imagine putting her life, her habits, and her pursuits into the power of a man who might very well decide he didn't want his wife running about in trousers.

Her sister-in-law appeared unperturbed. "I know very well what I used to think of marriage, thank you, and I was wrong. Marriage to the right man can be quite wonderful."

If you love him and he loves you. Blythe didn't bother to speak the words out loud.

Varya obviously decided to get right to the point. "Has Mr. Ryland proposed?"

Good thing they had decided against having tea or it would have been Blythe's turn to choke on it.

"No!" How she felt about that was too confusing to bother trying to decipher.

That apparently wasn't the answer Varya had been hoping for. Her smooth pale brow furrowed. "Has he made you any promises, expressed any hopes for the future?"

Blythe shook her head. *Only to think of me whenever he crawls into his bed.* Devlin didn't have to make her any promises. She wasn't looking for any.

Although marriage to Devlin wasn't a wholly abhorrent thought, even if he hadn't declared his feelings to her. Making love with him whenever she wanted would probably be very pleasant, and he liked her just as she was, or so he claimed. And it would get her Rosewood. Funny how that was on the bottom of her list of reasons to marry Devlin. At one time it would have been on top.

"No, and I have not asked for any."

Now Varya looked completely and utterly perturbed. "Whyever not? You like him, do you not?"

Wasn't that fairly obvious? "Yes, I do. Very much." Very much indeed. How much, she had no way of saying, for these feelings were very new to her. Never before had she felt so comfortable yet discomposed with a man. Never had she felt both calm and anxious at the same time. It was as though they had known each other forever even though they'd just met. Each new discovery was a surprise and yet expected.

It was as though heaven had sent her the perfect man for her, yet she was terrified to believe it lest it prove untrue.

Lest *he* prove untrue.

"But I do not know if I love him," she added. "Nor do I know how he feels about me."

Poor Varya was good and truly flustered. "You do not know if you love him? Blythe, ladies do not engage in *intimate activities* with men they do not love!"

Blythe laughed; she couldn't help it. "Oh, Varya! I think we both know that is not true at all!" Why, she could name several women who were staying under that very roof who were engaging in such activities with men they didn't love.

Her sister-in-law flushed a dull red. "Regardless, it should be true for *you*. At one time it was. What changed you, dearest?"

Did she really have to ask, in front of his wife? Carny had changed her. Carny had opened her eyes to a world outside her romantic notions of how things should and shouldn't happen. A nice little slap in the face that taught her that not everything worked out how one wanted it to.

She glanced at Teresa. It had also taught her that sometimes the person you thought was right for you was really right for someone else.

"I grew up," she finally replied. "You were not in love with Miles when the two of you first became intimate, were you?"

If anything, Varya's flush darkened. "No. I was not aware of the depth of my feelings when I married him either, but we were lucky to find such love together."

"That is what I want," Blythe informed her, "but I am practical enough to realize that not everyone is lucky enough to find such love in their life, and I will be damned if I will spend my whole life waiting for something that might never come. I will take whatever happiness comes my way now."

It sounded crude and harsh and cold, but she didn't know how to explain it any better.

She rose to her feet. "The fact remains that I refuse to marry for anything but the deepest love, and a few minutes' folly in a garden is not something I am prepared to decide the rest of my life on!"

Her head starting to ache and her nerves frayed, Blythe turned to make her exit, only to find the door blocked by Miles, Carny, and Devlin.

Her silly heart leaped at the sight of Devlin. How much had he heard? Judging from the rueful expression on his face, he'd heard enough to know that she didn't want to marry him. That she didn't love him.

Damnation.

He turned his back on her and walked away without a word. No one else watched him go but her. Everyone else was watching her, studying her reaction. Did she look as bloody stupid as she felt? She had to go after him, but first she had to get past the sentries at the door.

At least Miles had lost some of his ferocity. There was no disappointment on his face, no damnation, just concern and

so much love that Blythe's throat tightened at it. She might
have preferred his anger to this softness—it would be easier
to walk away from.

But it was Carny who made it easier for her to leave. His
blue eyes were dark with displeasure, his mouth thin with it.
It was all directed at her—not Devlin. Just her.

How dare he look at her that way!

"Don't you dare judge me." Her voice was low—lower
than it had ever been in her life, and colder than a Scottish
winter. "You do not have the right, no right at all."

"You judged me," he replied softly. He didn't have to say
when.

Her fists clenched tightly at her side, Blythe stepped up to
him. Eye to eye she faced him. Were she a man she would
plant him a facer so hard he'd feel it well into the next week.

"You hurt me. Tell me, Carny, did I do something tonight
to hurt you?"

What could he possibly say to that? Either she had or she
hadn't. If she had, he would have an awful lot of explaining to
do to Teresa. If she hadn't, he was going to have to back down.

"No," was his tight reply.

Without another word, Blythe turned away. She left the
room without a backward glance. Miles didn't say a word.
That should have been her first clue that her life had been ir-
revocably changed by the evening's events.

She didn't have to go far to find Devlin. He was in her
brother's study—Miles's private sanctuary—standing with
his back to the door, staring out one of the many long windows at the darkness beyond.

"Can I talk to you?" she asked, her voice weaker than she
wanted.

He glanced over his shoulder, a sad version of his normal
smile twisting his lips. "I don't know. Can you?"

His glibness was as amusing as it was irritating. Now was
not the time for a grammar lesson.

"I am sorry you had to hear that," she said, closing the door. "I was angry and tired of having my life decided for me. Of course I do not think of what happened between us tonight as little more than a folly." Lord, all she had to do was think about it and she wanted to do it again! Perhaps that was the folly of it right there.

He turned from the window, his hands clasped behind his back. His expression was carefully blank, no hint of emotion anywhere. A soldier's face.

"Folly," he repeated. "Perhaps it was, but I don't regret it."

An invisible band tightened around Blythe's throat. "Nor do I." They were in agreement, so why did it feel as though she had hurt him somehow?

"Are you all right?" he asked. "No one said anything to hurt you, did they?"

She shook her head. "No. Varya and Teresa are merely concerned for my reputation. You?"

He smiled. "It was tense for a while. What concerns does Varya have for your reputation? No one else saw us, did they?"

This distance between them was more than physical. He stood just a few feet away, and yet it might have well been a mile. "Not that I know of. They played the 'what if' game with me. What if someone else had found us. What if we are caught again."

Finally, his eyes sparked with interest. "What if we were?"

His question startled her. "Don't you start too!" *Oh damn, damn, damn!* Could she possibly shove her foot any further into her mouth?

Closing the distance between them—the physical distance—Devlin took one of her hands in his, and placed the other against the small of her back. He applied the slightest pressure, and she began to move where he led as he danced her around the room in a slow, sensuous waltz that would certainly scandalize every society matron in London.

"Seriously," he prodded. "What if someone else caught us together. What would you do?"

She shrugged. "Accept the consequences, I suppose."

He guided her around a chair. "And what might those be?"

She thought for a moment. "Social ostracization. Nothing I would not welcome anyway." Once a woman was ruined, that was it. Nothing else she did could ruin her any further, not really. Miles and her mother would hate it, but she would truly be free.

"You could avoid being ostracized."

"How?" she asked with a smile. "Bribe our discoverers to keep them silent? Stomp on them?"

He chuckled as he guided her in a gentle swirl. "Miles expects us to marry."

Blythe stopped dancing. She shook her head. "I beg your pardon?"

He gazed at her, his eyes filled with a softness and a determination she had never seen before. "He wants us to marry."

Pulling out of his arms, she tried to stifle nervous laughter. "Did he threaten you?"

He shook his head, but he made no move to come after her as she backed away. "No, but he made his wishes clear."

She put a large leather chair between them. "He's pressuring you then. He's trying to force us." She really shouldn't be surprised. What surprised her was that Devlin wasn't angrier about it.

Devlin was offended. He didn't bother trying to hide it. "No one forces me to do anything. I make my own decisions."

And was he going to decide to propose to her? To spend the rest of his life with her after such a brief acquaintance?

It struck her then that while they seemed to know so much about each other instinctively, there was very little she knew about him in actuality. She didn't even know the names of all his brothers, or whether his parents had been happy together.

He slipped between the chair and a table beside it to stand next to her, so close that she could count the whiskers starting to come through on his jaw. He lifted a hand to her cheek. He was so gentle for a man so big.

"I would never try to force you to do anything," he whispered. "You know that."

Yes, she did. She wanted to share his bed, wanted to be a part of his life, but was it enough? Was this love? It felt nothing like what she had felt for Carny, yet he seemed to run deeper into her bones than Carny ever did. Devlin made her feel whole and complete, and yet she knew that she could live without him. She didn't have those feelings that she would simply die without him. Wasn't that what love was supposed to be?

"Do you love me?" she asked.

He seemed surprised by her question, and he thought about it a lot longer than she thought he should have.

"I don't know what love is."

Now *that* was something totally unexpected. "What do you mean you don't know what love is?"

He ran a hand over his face. "How could I know? My parents didn't even like each other. To be honest, I don't think they cared much for me either."

"That's ridiculous!" How could a mother not love her child?

There was a starkness in his eyes, a pallor to his cheeks that Blythe didn't like.

"I'm the result of my father forcing himself upon my mother, Blythe. How could either of them love the reminder of that?"

She stared at him in horror. Not because of what his father did to his mother but because he blamed himself for it— and for whatever hell they put each other through because of it. No child—no man—deserved such a thing.

"I don't think love really exists," he admitted. "If it does, I've yet to see it last."

There it was. The best man she had ever found, the most incredible person to ever enter her life, and he didn't believe in love—the one thing that could induce her to marry. The one thing she wanted.

She raised her gaze to his. "I cannot imagine marrying someone who does not believe in me." Oh, it hurt to say it, but his words, his confession about his parents and his own lack of belief in love scared her more than anything ever had before. How could a person not believe in love? How empty did he have to be? Yet her heart knew Devlin wasn't empty at all. In fact, he was a man bursting at the seams with so much to give.

An odd brightness lit his eyes. "I have not asked you to."

Oh, that was a low and sharp blow! Cold heat flooded Blythe's cheeks and limbs. He hadn't asked because he already knew the answer. He had heard her declaration in the drawing room, and he had been hurt by it. Hurt badly enough that he needed to hurt her too, just a little.

She could forgive him for it. She had wanted to hurt him a little just now as well.

He placed both hands on her shoulders. "But what if I did ask? What would you say?"

He knew the answer, she could see it in his eyes.

Say you love me. She'd say yes if he said he loved her, even though she wasn't certain of her own feelings. She was such a hypocrite, demanding love from him yet not knowing if she'd ever return it.

Tears filled her eyes. "My answer," she whispered hoarsely, "would be no."

Chapter 8

It was a good thing he hadn't asked then.

Devlin had expected her answer, of course. After her outburst in the drawing room he could have no doubt; still, he had hoped . . . Well, it didn't matter what he had hoped or expected.

Her refusal was real, as real as the tears spilling down her cheeks. His amazing Blythe was weeping. What was he supposed to do now?

He put his arms around her. She resisted, but he was bigger and stronger. Poor thing; she was too done in even to fight him. Or perhaps she didn't want to fight him. Perhaps she wanted him to hold her, because he couldn't help but feel that her refusal was his fault—that he had done something wrong.

He rested his cheek against the top of her head as his governess used to do when he was a child and had hurt himself. It had been so long since he cried. He didn't think he was capable of it anymore.

"Shh." He rubbed her back. "Princess, don't cry. Everything will be all right."

She shoved free of his embrace. "No it won't! You asked me to marry you and I cannot!"

No, he hadn't asked her, but now wasn't the time to remind her of that.

Blythe swiped at her eyes with the backs of her hands. "You do not love me."

"I will learn to love you." It wouldn't be a hard lesson if he was capable of the emotion. If he wasn't . . .

Didn't she deserve someone who could love her?

Obviously she hadn't forgotten his earlier doubt. Her eyes widened, her tears gone. "You do not even know what love is! You admitted so yourself."

"You could teach me." He was grasping at straws now.

Blythe stomped her foot, her fists clenched. "That is not what I want!"

"What do you want?" His was the quiet, pathetic tone of a man who would do almost anything, agree to almost anything to get what he wanted, even though he had already been told he couldn't have it.

Crossing her arms, she made it impossible for him to come any closer. "I said yes before to a man who did not love me. The result was heartache and humiliation. I won't allow that to happen again."

Ahh, it came back to Carny once again. What a surprise.

"It won't." He would make sure of it, damn it.

"How do you know?"

Yes, how did he? He had already said he didn't think he loved her—that he didn't even know what love was. Why couldn't he have just lied? He felt more for her than he had ever felt for anyone before in his life. Did she not understand that?

"I would never do anything to intentionally hurt you." It was the one truth he could give her.

The pain in her wide green eyes cut him to the very quick. "You do not love me. That is hurt enough."

Until now this conversation had been terribly one-sided. It all seemed to revolve around how *he* felt, *his* shortcomings. He wasn't the one who had announced in front of witnesses that no "folly" would induce him to marry.

His lips formed the question he could scarcely bear to ask. He had never asked it of anyone else, not even his parents. Especially not his parents. "Do you love me?"

She looked away. "I do not know."

Now he understood that rawness in her gaze, the whiteness of her features. This wasn't just about him, it was her own indecision that scared her—possibly even more than his own.

But still it hurt. It wasn't quite rejection, but it felt like it. He wanted her to say yes, even though he was uncertain of the strength of such a volatile emotion. Any love he had seen had been fleeting and painful. It rarely lasted—truly happy couples were those who had a good solid friendship as well as a healthy attraction for one another. He thought he and Blythe had been well on their way to building such a foundation.

He didn't want her to see his pain. "We understand each other, we feel the same way. So what if it's not love? What we have is better."

Christ, was that pity he saw in her gaze? She looked truly sorry for him. He didn't want her goddamn pity. "Did your parents honestly not love each other?"

"Yes." They hadn't even liked each other very much. Tolerate—that's what they had done with each other.

"Mine did." It was as though she was pleading with him to understand, but he truly didn't know what it was she was trying to say. "I want what they had. If you do not love me, I do not want to marry you, and if I do not love you, you shouldn't want to marry me."

He took a step toward her. He never said any of this made sense. "I have yet to say whether or not I want to." And he wouldn't either; why admit that he wanted to marry her when she so obviously didn't want to marry him? Still, he couldn't seem to help himself. "Would it be that bad?"

She pulled out of reach, backing up enough to put several feet of space between them. Her frustration was almost palatable. "What could possibly make it good? Because I am big enough? Because you desire me? Because you like me? It is not enough, Devlin."

What could possibly make it *good*? It sounded good to him. What did she want? Flowers? Poetry? He could try, but he wasn't good at that sort of thing.

"I can give you trust. I can give you respect. You already know I can give you pleasure." His own frustration drove him to thrust one hand toward her in supplication. "Christ, I can give you Rosewood. I know you want it."

"I will not have you thinking I married you for a house." Wonderful, now she was indignant. Would someone please just tell him what it was he was supposed to do so he could do it?

"I wouldn't mind." So why did it feel so wrong?

"You should." She sighed and suddenly she looked very tired. "And eventually you might."

Devlin moved toward her again. All this space between them made him anxious. "Blythe, you can't just walk away from what we have."

This time she didn't move, but there was an emotional wall so thick around her he couldn't get close even if he touched her. "I'm not, but neither am I going to marry you."

She wasn't going to leave him but she didn't want to marry him either? That didn't leave much. He clung to the remnants of his pride. "I haven't asked you to."

Her smile was patently sympathetic. She saw through that thin defense.

Another tactic was in order, even though he hated treating this discussion like a battle. It shouldn't be that way. She was not an enemy to be conquered, yet he was treating her as such. "We cannot go on as we have been."

"Why not? No one of consequence saw us tonight."

Now she was the one who didn't seem to understand. He hoped he would have better luck explaining to her than she had to him. "Because I don't want you to be my mistress."

"Your mistress, your wife. Without love there is no difference."

He scowled at her vapid tone. What did she mean there was no difference? She wasn't a simpleton, she'd been out in society. Lord, after a decade in the army *he* still knew the difference. "You do not have to be a wife to be loved. My father loved his mistress more than he ever loved my mother."

"Then he should have married his mistress."

For the second time that evening, Devlin's temper threatened to snap. "Damn it, Blythe!" His voice cracked. "If we're caught again you will be ruined."

Now she was back to pitying him. Why could she not take pity on him then and just agree to be his? "I would rather live by my own rules than society's, Devlin. As long as I am happy I do not care what anyone else thinks. Ruination is preferable to an unhappy marriage."

"I do not believe that." He shook his head, a dubious smirk tilting his mouth. "You care too much what society thinks. That's why you've been hiding here in Devonshire these past two years."

Her shoulders straightened defensively. She could stand as tall as she wanted—she wouldn't intimidate him even if she stood on a frigging chair. "Believe what you will. I will not marry you because society says I should."

"And I refuse to play hard and fast with your reputation just because you refuse to be rational!"

She looked as though he had slapped her. Wonderful. Just frigging wonderful.

"Rational or not, it is how it has to be."

Maybe this wasn't about just them. Maybe there was someone else figuring into this skirmish. Maybe she didn't love him because there was someone else in the way. "Do you still have feelings for Carny?"

"I told you I did not." He wanted to believe her, but he didn't know what to believe anymore. He thought she wanted him as much as he wanted her. He had been wrong about that. What else had he been wrong about? "Do you think I would kiss you and touch you if I loved another man?"

He sucked his cheeks against his teeth. His hold on his temper was slipping. He didn't want to fight with her, not like this. "You've said yourself that you do not love me. Yet I've had my fingers inside you."

She flushed a dark red as he held up the hand that just a short while ago had coaxed cries of pleasure from her throat. "You do a pretty good job yourself, but then men seem to have no trouble making love to women they do not truly love."

"I have found the same in many women." Why did it hurt so much to hear her words and reply in kind? They'd already established they weren't in love, so why did it feel like a knife in the gut every time either of them spoke of it?

Obviously it hurt her too. "I cannot speak of this anymore. We are going to end up saying things we both will regret, if we have not already. I am going to bed."

"Who are you going to think about?" Why couldn't he just leave that wound alone?

She shook her head sadly, that damn pitying expression back in her eyes. If he never saw it again it would be too soon. "I am going to think of you, Devlin. The same as I have done every night since we first met. But I will not marry a man who cannot love me as I deserve. And I will not marry a man who deserves the same just because I cannot stop thinking of him."

The first time he'd been shot hadn't hurt as much as those softly spoken words. Not even his parents' rejection had cut him as deeply as she had.

"Go then." He almost choked on the words, the lump in his throat was so hard.

She did, and he watched her go with a strange burning behind his eyes.

But he didn't—wouldn't—cry.

"You said no?"

Blythe looked up at the thunderous and incredulous expression on her brother's face with unconcealed weariness. How could one say no when she technically hadn't been asked a question? As Devlin pointed out, he hadn't officially proposed.

"Yes."

"Why in the hell did you do that?"

They were in her room, so at least there was little chance of any of the guests hearing his yelling—not that she cared if they did. She didn't seem to have the energy to care about anything this morning, which was why she was still in her nightgown, sitting on her bed at eleven o'clock.

She managed to push herself to her feet. "Because I have taken complete loss of my senses." At least that was how it felt. She knew she had done the right thing by refusing to marry Devlin, but a part of her—all right, her heart—felt that it was all wrong.

But what did her heart know? It had been wrong in the past when it came to men and their feelings.

"Well," Miles huffed, "at least we are in agreement there."

Blythe shuffled to the washbasin and splashed cool water on her face. It helped a bit, but it took far more effort than it should have to walk from there to her dressing table, where she plunked herself down and started unbraiding her hair.

"Just what the devil is wrong with you anyway?" her brother demanded as he yanked a silver-backed brush from her hand. "You are going to end up with a head full of tangles if you brush before all the braid is out."

How he knew that, Blythe didn't want to know. She just sat there, like a lazy cat on a hot day, wanting nothing more than to go back to sleep, and let him unwind the rest of her braid.

She didn't even let her shock show when he started brushing her hair in long, gentle strokes. Miles hadn't brushed her hair since they were children, and even then he used to hit her with the brush more than anything else.

"You are not going to strike me with that, I hope." It took all her strength to inject humor in her tone.

He scowled into the mirror at her. Goodness, but he looked like their father. "No—not that you do not deserve it. Perhaps it might knock a little sense into you."

"Doubtful." Her smile was rueful. "But perhaps you could cosh me hard enough to make me sleep for the next month."

Miles paused in his brushing long enough to meet her gaze in the mirror. "What happened, sweet? I was under the impression that you liked Devlin."

The softening of his tone brought a tremor to her chin. She would not cry. Not now. "I do, but I do not know if I love him, and he is quite certain he does not love me."

Her brother nodded as though he understood, even though Blythe was positive there was no way he could.

"Ah yes, love. The emotion women claim to be such experts on but know so little about."

Now it was Blythe's turn to scowl at his reflection. "We know considerably more than a 'little'!" And women ultimately knew more about it than men, but she wasn't about to remind him of that when he had a weapon in his hand.

"You *think* you know more than you really do." He held up a hunk of hair in his big hand and ran the brush through the ends. "But in actuality, all you know is how you think love should be, not how it really is."

How unimpressive his philosophy was. Another treatise

on how men were superior in every manner over women. If he went into a tirade about how gothic novels were to blame, Blythe would hit him with the hand mirror.

"Oh really? Then tell me, oh wise one, how is it really? Ow!"

Miles smirked in the mirror. "Tangle. Sorry."

Tangle, her foot! He'd done that on purpose, and perhaps she'd deserved it. He was trying to give her advice after all—and he wasn't yelling, which was a lovely boon.

"Love isn't something you can dissect or dictate, brat. It is unexpected, quiet, and will sometimes wait till the last possible moment to let you know it has arrived. Today you do not think you love him. Tomorrow you might wonder how you ever lived without him, and he you."

Blythe sincerely doubted that, but she would give Miles the benefit of the doubt. He was much older than she, and had been wildly in love with Varya for three years now. Surely he knew something on the topic.

"And if tomorrow comes and I still do not know whether I love him?"

His smile was kind. "Then it might happen the next day."

She raised both brows. "I could go on like that for a long time."

Miles nodded. "Yes and it could still happen two months from now. Let me ask you something, when Devlin proposed to you, what was your first reaction?"

He hadn't proposed. *Sigh.* It's not like it really mattered now. How could she admit this, even to Miles? It was like admitting to a weakness or deformity.

"*If* he had actually asked"—she had to cling to it, it was the only thing saving her pride—"I suppose my first thought would have been to say yes."

His eyes lit up. "Then I say you already have your answer."

Her tone was dry. "If I had my answer, I wouldn't have announced in front of him that I have no intention of marrying over a mistake."

A mistake. No, what had happened in the maze had been a lot of things—rapturous, for one—but not a mistake.

Miles brushed her hair back from her face, gently tugging at her scalp. Were it not for the agitation brought on by their conversation, he could easily put her to sleep. "You think he does not love you."

"He told me he does not love me!"

That made him frown. "He actually told you that?"

"Oh yes!" She laughed bitterly as she stood and walked away, leaving him standing there with the brush in his hand. "He said he did not know if he loved me."

Her brother's sigh of relief was as loud as a winter wind. "That is not the same thing at all, as you well know. That is what every frightened man says when he is backed into a corner. We are like rats, you see; all we can think of is escape."

Blythe turned her head, staring at him in disbelief over her shoulder. "Rats? You liken your own sex to rats?"

He nodded agreeably. "Varya thought it a very appropriate analogy. Devlin does not know his feelings any better than you do, but unlike you, who initially wanted to say yes, his first thought was not to do anything that might trap him in a bad situation."

She turned to face him, fists on her hips. "How might marrying me be a bad situation?"

"My darling baby sister." Miles tossed the brush on her dressing table. It clattered against her cosmetic jars. "There is not an unmarried man alive who truly believes marriage to be a good situation."

He was mad. "That is ridiculous!" But didn't she feel the same way on some level? She had felt backed into a corner by the overwhelming conclusion that she and Devlin would have to marry, and so she had done everything she could to fight her way out—including hurting Devlin's feelings.

He shrugged. "Women are taught from the cradle that marriage is something to be aspired to as soon as possible. Men are taught that marriage robs them of all freedom."

"At least you have freedom. Women do not have any!"

The smile that curved his lips was condescending at best. "I think you have enjoyed plenty of freedom in your life."

Perhaps he had a point, but that didn't make any of this easier.

"He said he didn't believe in love."

Miles didn't seem surprised by that either. "I do not doubt that he believes that now, but if he truly did not believe in love, he would not have spent his entire life trying to earn it."

"Earn it?" What did Miles know that she didn't? Probably a lot. He had known Devlin for several years.

Her brother ran a hand through his thick russet hair. "Did Devlin happen to tell you anything about his parents?"

Blythe nodded. "A little." It wasn't her place to share the details.

"He never spoke much about it, but it did not take a genius to figure out that he was out to prove himself to them. He became the perfect soldier. It did not matter what the mission was. Devlin would volunteer for it and he would do it, and afterward you would find him sitting off alone somewhere, cleaning his rifle. Nothing he did ever seemed to please him, as though he was holding himself up against an invisible standard."

Blythe saw where he was going with this. "You think it was his parents' approval?"

Miles shrugged. "I think so, but his mother died while he was away and his father died not too long ago."

He hadn't mentioned that. When her father died Blythe had gone into full mourning for a year. Devlin came to a house party.

"Do you remember Viscount Creed at all?"

Blythe's eyes widened. "The drunkard?" Hadn't there been some scandal attached to the oldest son—the heir? Something about him doing something very rude at a party—something that included a punch bowl.

He nodded. "That was Devlin's father. His mother was of course Lady Creed, who became known as one of the coldest, unhappiest women in England. The only love in Dev's life came from his brothers and what he saw of his father with his mistress—an often volatile relationship."

No wonder Devlin had such a horrible notion of love and marriage. He'd grown up in a house where two people who should adore each other couldn't stand each other.

"Oh Miles." She sighed. "I do not know what to do." Did she go to Devlin and tell him she'd changed her mind about marriage—when she really didn't know if she had or not—and hope he'd actually ask her to become his wife? Or did she wait? And if she waited, did she run the risk of losing him in the process?

He laid a warm hand on her shoulder. "I will make it easy for you. You either marry Devlin or you come to London."

She raised her gaze to his with a smile. "And if I refuse to do either?"

"You do not have a choice."

He wasn't joking. "Miles—"

"I mean it, Blythe." His tone brooked no refusal, and she knew better than to try. "For two years I have watched you hide away here in the country, and I will not stand for it any longer. You will either marry Devlin or you will come to London when Varya and I return. It is your choice, but those are your only choices."

What was worse—marriage to a man who might never love her or returning to London long enough to figure out what she wanted?

Marriage, definitely. She would rather lose Devlin forever than enter into a loveless union.

She believed that. Truly. She just had to keep reminding herself of it. She had almost married a man who didn't love her once, and he made a fool of her. It would not happen again. She had too much pride to let it happen again.

"I need to think about it." She covered the hand on her shoulder with her own. "Would you mind if I let you know later?"

He smiled sympathetically. "Of course not." He kissed her forehead. "I love you, brat. I am sorry if it does not always seem that way."

Blythe's eyes stung with tears. She was turning into a watering pot. "I know."

Miles left the bedroom just as Blythe's maid entered.

"Good morning, Suki. Oh, you brought tea, bless you."

"Some of Lord Wynter's guests are leaving today, I see," the young maid remarked later as she separated Blythe's hair into thick sections to be twisted and pinned.

Blythe took a sip of tea. "Yes, thank God. It will be nice to have a little peace and quiet again."

Suki twisted a thick chunk of hair. "I daresay you are right, my lady. I hope you do not mind me speaking so freely, but things will be a lot more comfortable belowstairs without us having Lady Ashby to deal with."

Chuckling, Blythe set her cup and saucer on the vanity. "She has left, has she?"

"Oh yes." Suki wound Blythe's hair into a smooth coil. "She and Lord Ashby departed this morning shortly after Mr. Ryland."

Blythe froze. Devlin was gone? "Where did Mr. Ryland go, Suki?"

The maid seemed surprised by her question. "Did you not hear, my lady? He's gone to stay at his own estate. At Rosewood. He said he could oversee the repairs from there."

A cold chill settled over Blythe's heart. Devlin was gone.

She felt his absence as surely as she would feel the loss of a limb. He had left her.

Perhaps the thought of staying under the same roof as the woman who refused to marry him was more than he could bear. Or perhaps he didn't care for her as much as he claimed. No, she didn't want to think that.

It really didn't matter one way or another. Devlin's leaving didn't change things. He still didn't love her and she didn't know how she felt about him. Right now she was a little miffed that he had left without so much as a farewell.

However, knowing that he was gone made her decision that much easier. In fact, she decided right then and there what she was going to do. She wasn't going to chase after him to Rosewood. He knew where she was if he decided he loved her. In the meantime, she would do something about her future. Miles was right. It was time to stop hiding.

"You will need to start packing for us, Suki," she said as the last pin was slid into her hair. "Make sure you take enough to do us both for quite some time. We're going to London."

The day Blythe was to leave for London, Devlin rose earlier than normal. Hell, who was he trying to fool? You couldn't rise when you hadn't slept.

Miles had sent him a note the day before, detailing the particulars of their departure. No doubt the marquess hoped Devlin might still talk his younger sister into being his bride.

If only he could, but he knew that nothing he could say could change Blythe's mind. Unless he lied.

They would be leaving at ten o'clock. They would wait until five minutes past ten if Devlin wanted to say good-bye—or anything else of importance. If not, they hoped to see him in town at a later date.

Him, in London? It was laughable. He hated London—not so much the city but the society. People treated him like a trained parrot, only interested in his war activities, never in him. Well, he knew how to fix that, didn't he? He could tell them he was a killer.

He wasn't going to think of that now. He had more important things to tend to.

A leisurely soak in the bathtub, followed by a close shave and a strong cup of coffee, got him feeling some semblance of normalcy. The war and the dreams that followed once he returned home from Waterloo had made him used to getting very little sleep at night, but he didn't want to look like shite when Blythe saw him.

He dressed in soft buckskins and a dark green jacket. His cravat was tied in a simple knot because he didn't know any other styles, and his boots were polished to the highest shine old leather could achieve.

"I still look like a frigging farmer," he muttered at the reflection in the mirror.

After breakfast and another cup of coffee, he went out to the stables to talk to the groom and ready Flynn. He wasted as much time as he could before anxiety finally drove him onto the massive horse's back and on the road to Brixleigh.

He hadn't seen her for days, not since the night she'd made her opinions of love and marriage clear. It had been hell to stay away; even more hellish was the waiting—and hoping—that she would come to him.

But he had kept his promise. Every night as he climbed into that huge mahogany bed in his chamber, he thought of her and that day he had held her and kissed her on the counterpane. Each night the scene had grown and changed in his mind, until finally it wasn't just a kiss they shared. He removed her clothes, she removed his, and then he made love to her until they were too exhausted to move.

No wonder he was having trouble sleeping. All he could think about were those full, wide lips; strong, slender hands; and long, firm legs—and everything else, of course, even her narrow, bony feet.

He missed her. Missed her more than he had missed England or his family when he first went to the Peninsula. In fact, he'd come to realize that Blythe was a lot of "more thans" for him.

Missing a person eventually went away, did it not? Back then he had gotten used to his new surroundings and made friends to replace his brothers. Some of those friends had died, and few filled the void Brahm, Wynthrope, and North had left, but they had made being away from home easier. Someday he might find someone to fill the void Blythe left behind as well.

The very idea of never holding her again, never touching her again, made his chest ache, but it wasn't unbearable. Shouldn't it be unbearable if he loved her? Perhaps if he didn't know he would be seeing her in a little while it would be harder to accept. Perhaps love didn't hurt as much as the poets claimed.

Or perhaps he was no closer to believing in the elusive emotion, or trusting in it than he had been before coming to Devonshire. Perhaps the only thing that had changed was that since meeting Blythe, since becoming obsessed with Blythe, he hadn't dreamed about the war as much as he used to. Now he dreamed about her, which was almost as tormenting.

He'd be a good husband to her. He wouldn't stray—not ever. He would be loyal until the day he died. He would never get drunk and say horrible things. He wouldn't be cold and unforgiving. And if they had children, he would make sure they all knew that he loved them. He would spend time with them and let them know that they could always come to him, always trust in him.

Odd, how he believed so deeply in the love of family, but not in the love between man and woman. He loved his brothers and knew they loved him. Of all the things he had doubted in his life, his brothers had never been among them, even when it looked as though Brahm was headed down the same dark road as their father. He had kept his faith.

It was that same faith that had him in the saddle, bound for Brixleigh. He might not be smart enough to understand them, he might wonder at the depth and meaning of them, but he had faith in his feelings for Blythe. And he had faith in her feelings for him, despite the little voice in the back of his head that insisted of *course* she would never marry a man like him, not when she deserved so much better.

The carriage was sitting in the drive when he rode up to the front of Brixleigh Park. Footmen loaded luggage on top of it and into a second cart already piled high with boxes and trunks, no doubt more than half of which belonged to Blythe and Varya.

The front door opened as he slid off Flynn's back to the gravel. Miles and Varya came out first, followed by a towering vision in dark forest green. Devlin had to smile when he saw the bonnet in her hand. He knew full well it would never make it onto her head. She would carry it all the way to London if she had to, but she would never wear it.

He watched them as they approached the carriage. Miles saw him first, then Varya. They exchanged pleased glances before smiling at him. Miles knew enough not to approach. He simply helped his wife into the carriage and followed her in, leaving Blythe alone outside.

She looked up just as she reached the open carriage door. For a second Devlin thought he would have to call out for her attention. She stared at him, seemingly uncertain if he was real or not.

Then she came toward him, her steps quickening the closer she came, until finally she broke into a run. She stopped not even a foot from him, her gaze as questioning as he knew his own must be.

As had become habit with them, they didn't even speak. He took her face in his hands and she clutched at his forearms, the unwanted bonnet bumping against his hand in the breeze.

It's going to rain, he thought absently as his lips touched hers, and then he thought of nothing but Blythe and how damn good it felt to kiss her again. She tasted like tea and cinnamon, two things he'd never really liked until meeting her.

She kissed him like a thirsty man drank water—as though it was the last time she would ever kiss him. It scared him.

Their lips broke apart, but he didn't release her. His forehead rested against hers, his hands still holding the sides of her face. She kept her gloves wrapped around his wrists.

"Don't go." His voice was little more than a hoarse whisper.

She sniffed, and he knew she was crying. "I have to."

"No, you don't."

She pulled free of his hold, her eyes red and her chin quivering. "Yes. I do. It is time for me to stop hiding."

It wasn't said maliciously, but it stung all the same. How could he have accused her of hiding from life? Even if it was true, who was he to criticize her? He'd spent enough time hiding from the truth about himself.

He offered her his handkerchief and she took it, pressing it to her eyes and nose.

"I'm going to want that back," he informed her, surprised at how strong his voice sounded, especially since his chest and throat were so tight.

She nodded, not even acknowledging his reference to how he had returned her handkerchief. "I shall send it to you." Her gaze locked with his. "Good-bye, Devlin."

She spun on her heel and dashed away before he could say anything in reply. That was all right. He hadn't planned on saying good-bye.

He didn't wait for the carriage to leave before spurring Flynn into motion. He had things to do that morning and no time to waste in doing them.

He was going back to Rosewood and then he was going to pack because he was going to London. And once in London he was going to visit his brother Wynthrope's tailor and get some new clothes made, because every soldier needed a good uniform when going into battle, and that's what this was—battle. Blythe had started it when she refused to marry for less than love, and he was determined to finish it.

If there was one thing Devlin Ryland knew how to do, it was win a war.

Chapter 9

L ondon was better than Blythe remembered.

For one thing, the season was over, so there wasn't the endless stream of balls and parties to attend. There were a few, of course; there always were. No matter the time of year, one could always find good *ton* in London, though perhaps not in great abundance. Blythe attended what events she wanted and passed on the rest.

The people seemed friendlier as well. Matrons who once seemed intimidating and ladies whose friendship she once questioned seemed genuinely happy to see her. After two years of near solitude in Devonshire, it was a bit overwhelming to suddenly be in such demand.

Still, that restless feeling that had started at Brixleigh continued at Wynter Lane. Despite her busy schedule, the company, the shopping, the entertainment, she was undeniably lonely. Surrounded by people, many of whom she enjoyed being with, she longed for something—someone—different.

Pleasure came in quiet teas with friends, both new and old, in dinners where the conversation touched on more than just the latest gossip, and in soirees where the card play was low, the music soft, and the topics ran to important current events, such as what to do with all the poor soldiers who had returned from the Peninsula unable to find work and were now reduced to begging and worse to feed themselves and their families. In the last two years the situation had gotten worse, not better.

Of course, as was bound to happen, the topic of soldiers eventually led to the one man Blythe was trying not to think about. This happened at a soiree held by the Countess Wickford at her London town house one Thursday evening.

They were in the drawing room—a serenely peaceful room of cream, rose, and taupe, filled with sturdy yet feminine furniture. Every chair and sofa was filled with a female body, enjoying cake, biscuits, little sandwiches, tea, and sherry. Some of the women hardly spoke at all, some only when spoken to, and then there were those who never seemed to stop.

Lady Letitia Rexley lowered her plate of thickly frosted cake, chewed thoughtfully, and swallowed. Letitia was a few years younger than Blythe, shorter and more slender, with brown eyes and a wide mouth. Her hair was a similar shade to Blythe's, but that was the end of any resemblance. Still, Blythe liked her. Letitia liked to talk—a lot.

"I hear Devlin Ryland hired quite a few former soldiers to work on his new estate in Devonshire," Letitia remarked innocently after washing down her cake with a sip of tea.

Blythe's heart broke into a gallop at the sound of his name. She had to grip the smooth arm of her chair to keep her fingers from trembling. Soldiers working at Rosewood? Why had he not mentioned it to her? She remembered him saying he wanted to hire some men from London, but it hadn't occurred to her that they might have been men he fought beside.

"That does not surprise me." Lady Wickford, a frigate of a woman despite her short stature, took a sip of sherry. "He talked his brothers into doing the same."

Lady Jersey nodded her dark head. "I hear no one else would work for the oldest Ryland. Horrible man."

Horrible? Viscount Creed? Scandalous maybe, but horrible? The few times Devlin talked of his family, he had nothing but good things to say about his oldest brother Brahm. Brother or not, Blythe couldn't believe he would be so generous if the viscount were unworthy.

"I hear Lord Creed is quite reformed," Lady Letitia informed them. "He has turned over a new leaf since assuming the title."

"As well he should," Lady Jersey retorted with an indignant sniff. "He showed every sign of following in his father's footsteps, and the other boys are *such* gentlemen, especially Wynthrope."

"Even Northam?" Lady Pennington joined the conversation with such a deceptively innocent tone that Blythe almost scowled at the snooty matron. Early in Miles and Varya's relationship, Lady Pennington had made her true nature known, and despite the fact that she tried to make herself agreeable to the Christian family, Blythe couldn't stand her.

Lady Jersey affected a very feminine shrug. "The poor boy cannot help what he is. At least Creed acknowledged him and raised him with the others."

"Of course he did!" Lady Pennington took over again. "He was the old lord's favorite."

Blythe was confused. Again she had no idea what they were talking about. Devlin had never mentioned his father having a favorite—at least not that she could remember. Nor had he given her any reason to suspect the old viscount held any of his sons above the other—he seemed to ignore them all. "What is wrong with Northam?"

"Nothing is *wrong* with him," Lady Wickford replied, slanting an annoyed glance at ladies Pennington and Jersey. "The boy was the product of Creed's long-standing affair with an actress named Nell Sheffield. Creed never tried to conceal his birth and often took Northam into his own house."

"Much to the displeasure of the viscountess," Lady Pennington added.

Lady Wickford shot her another dark look as she lowered her cup to her saucer. "When she was there long enough to be displeasured. Those Ryland boys were raised by a succession of nannies and governesses. Lord and Lady Creed were too busy with their private pursuits to bother much with their children."

From the sound of it, Lady Wickford didn't think much of either the viscount or his viscountess. Blythe would love to know more—she hadn't even known that North was illegitimate! But asking now would just invite gossip. Lady Wickford might be discreet, but Lady Pennington wasn't, and Lady Jersey hadn't earned the tongue-in-cheek nickname of "Silence" for knowing when to keep her mouth shut.

Trust the two of them to turn what was supposed to be a discussion of the plight of poor, unemployed soldiers into foolish gossip. If it hadn't been about Devlin's family, Blythe wouldn't have listened to a word.

Lady Letitia obviously thought it was time to turn the direction of the conversation. "I wonder if Mr. Ryland will continue his advocacy for the soldiers now that he is back in town."

This time Blythe's heart actually stopped. She almost dropped her cup. Suddenly tea wasn't enough. She wanted something stronger. Devlin was in town? No, he couldn't be. She'd been there for over a week and hadn't heard a word from or about him.

Lady Jersey raised her glass to her lips. "I would imagine so. He had a *private* dinner with Wellington the other night, you know."

A private dinner with Wellington! Devlin truly was in town! Why hadn't he come to see her? Did he not want to see her? Perhaps he had discovered the answer to whether he loved her, and the answer was no.

Oh dear. She was going to be ill.

"I hear he plans to attend Lady Homewood's ball tomorrow night."

"Oh good! He will add some enjoyment to an otherwise drab affair."

Blythe didn't even look up as Lady Jersey and Lady Pennington spoke. She couldn't even tell who had said what. Devlin was going to be at the same ball as she tomorrow evening. She would see him again. She would have to ensure that he saw her as well—not that a six-foot-tall woman was easy to miss. If he had decided he didn't love her, she would have to look good enough to make him regret that decision.

Because even though she had yet to make up her own mind, she wasn't prepared to let him go so easily, even though she had willingly walked away from him.

And didn't she kick herself for it at least once a day? Coming to London had been the right decision—the only way to find the strength she needed to make order of her life. Being in town had taught her an important lesson already—there were gentlemen who found her appealing. She could no longer blame her infatuation with Devlin on the fact that he paid attention to her. Many men had begun paying attention to her lately, and not one of them compared to her sweet, gentle giant.

"—Lady Blythe?"

Her head jerked up. "Hmm? Oh, I beg your pardon, Lady Jersey. What was that you asked?"

Sally Jersey raised a disapproving brow. "I asked whether Mr. Ryland was invited to your birthday celebration."

Her birthday. It was just a little over a week away. She would be five and twenty and come into her inheritance. It didn't matter that Miles had decided that her money should come to her as a monthly allowance while she remained unmarried. It was still enough for her to lease a nice little town house, should she decide to stay in London. She could still be independent.

"Yes, I imagine he will be on the guest list." He certainly would be! And perhaps the rest of his brothers as well. Now that she had heard more about them, she was exceedingly interested in meeting the rest of the Ryland family.

"Excellent," Lady Jersey enthused. "As if your return to society was not enough reason to come out, an appearance by Mr. Ryland will certainly add to the evening's pleasure."

She made it sound as though Blythe and Devlin would be on display, like exotic animals in a menagerie.

Well, Blythe would have to make certain she looked the part. Why settle for just Devlin's attention when she could attract the notice of all the *ton*? Perhaps then Devlin would realize that she was more than a woman tall enough to dance with. That she was a woman worthy of loving.

She wanted him to love her. The realization came as no real surprise. Of course she wanted his love—everyone wanted love. Why his meant so much to her, she could only attribute to the fact that she cared very deeply about him. She had missed him terribly since leaving Brixleigh. She missed the sound of his voice, the earnestness of his gaze. She missed the loose-limbed way he walked and the way he treated Flynn more like a friend than a horse.

She wanted him to love her because no man had ever loved her before—other than Miles and their father—and she wanted to know what it was like to be an object of such affection. Perhaps if he loved her it would be easier to decipher her own feelings for him, although she was beginning to suspect they ran deeper than she'd first thought. She was waiting for what Miles told her was going to happen, for the realization to suddenly strike her. It hadn't yet. The fact that she wanted it to was more than telling.

But her feelings didn't matter at the moment. Right now

she had more important things to worry about than how deep her feelings for Devlin ran.

She had to figure out what she was going to wear tomorrow night.

The twenty-plus hours until the Homewood ball dragged by like a boat adrift on a sea of cold molasses. It wasn't until Blythe started to fuss with her appearance and worry whether she had chosen the right dress that the time seemed to pass with any speed at all.

She left with Miles and Varya at a fashionable hour, dressed in a low-cut gown of bronze silk and matching gloves and slippers. Her hair was styled in the Greek fashion—with the sides and some of the back pinned up on her crown and the rest trailing down her back in thick spiral curls that had taken Suki hours to accomplish. For jewelry, she wore her grandmother's four-tier pearl choker and matching drop earrings.

Miles's eyes had widened when she came downstairs. For that matter, so had Varya's. They stood on the chessboard marble floor, both in their evening finery.

"You look beautiful!" her sister-in-law gushed. "I have never seen you so fashionable."

Miles frowned. "You are showing too much bosom."

His wife swatted him on the arm with her fan. "She is not!" Clad in a gown of rich green satin, Varya was showing just as much if not more skin than Blythe was.

"Shall we go?" Blythe suggested as Forsythe, the butler, brought her shawl. She had put too much energy into getting dressed to have Miles order her to change now.

Grudgingly, Miles agreed, shrugging into the greatcoat and top hat Forsythe offered him.

Outside Blythe didn't even stop long enough to appreciate the August night, but bolted into the shiny burgundy lacquered carriage as if her very life depended on it. Varya and

Miles followed, seating themselves on the opposite side of the carriage from her.

It was a beautiful night, warm enough for light wraps but cool enough that the dancers at the ball wouldn't become overheated. The scent of rain and damp flowers hung in the evening air, along with the ever-present smells of London—some more pleasant than others.

As usual, the streets were alive with activity. The sound of turning wheels and clopping hooves echoed off the cobblestones, voices occasionally rising over the chaotic rhythm with incoherent verbosity. Acutely aware of the pounding of her heart and the dampness of her palms, Blythe tried to fix her attention on these sounds, or on Miles and Varya—anything but where she was going and who she was going to see once she got there.

Devlin. She was going to see him again. It seemed forever since they'd last met.

They arrived at Lord and Lady Homewood's Berkeley Square home along with a small group of other guests. They greeted family acquaintances and good friends as they filed up the stone steps to the door.

Inside the blue and white marble hall, chattering guests milled about the thick Grecian columns. There were several maids and footmen to take their outerwear, followed by another servant to direct them toward the receiving line. Lord and Lady Homewood and their son and two daughters shook hands, bussed cheeks, and greeted everyone in the same jovial manner. Lady Jersey might find them dull, but Blythe thought they were just very nice people who had the good sense to throw a party when the lack of society in town made an outing all the more appreciated.

The wide double doors between several other rooms had been opened up to accommodate all the guests, with the gallery serving as ballroom and a drawing room as a supper room. The butler announced everyone who entered the long, spacious area decorated with dozens upon dozens of white and yellow flowers and yards of white and butter yellow fabric, glowing warm and inviting beneath the chandeliers. The carpets had been rolled up and stored elsewhere, leaving the gleaming polished floor open for dancing. It was the perfect look for a late summer ball and brightened what had been a cool and rainy day.

As soon as she entered the ballroom and her name was announced, Blythe was aware of the stares. Some of them were appreciative, others were not. But there were more smiling faces than frowning ones, and more than one person was heard to remark favorably on her appearance.

There was no sign of Devlin. A man his size couldn't possibly hide at such a gathering, no matter how he tried. He wouldn't try, however. He would be where everyone could see him and be damned if they didn't like the view. It was she who was accomplished at hiding, even in a room full of people.

Not tonight, however. Tonight she was going to stand with her shoulders back and her head high. She was going to dance with every man who asked, no matter how short or tall. She was going to make an effort to talk to other ladies her age, and especially to those who were younger and more shy. Tonight she was going to show everyone that she knew how to be a lady, and show Devlin Ryland that she wasn't at home crying over him.

She'd cried before she came.

She danced the allemande with Letitia Rexley's brother Julian, Lord Wolfram. He was a nice gentleman, a little taller than herself, but far too pretty for Blythe's liking. That was all right; she didn't think she suited his preferences either.

As Lord Wolfram escorted her back to Varya and Miles, a ripple of excitement ran through the crowd. Blythe didn't have to hear the whispers to know what had everyone so agitated. Devlin Ryland had arrived. She knew it as surely as she knew how to breathe.

Like everyone else she turned her attention toward the door, watching as a path cleared through the little crowd. People stepped back to let him through.

He came into view seconds later, a lean giant with shining sable hair. He'd had it cut recently, she noted. It was a little shorter than she remembered, and neater.

Unlike the other gentlemen present, most of whom wore the standard black evening dress, Devlin wore the "rifle green" jacket of the Ninety-fifth Rifle Corps. The dark jackets were made to fit snugly, and only a lean man with a broad chest and shoulders could carry it off successfully. Devlin was such a man. The horizontal black braid accentuated the width of his chest just as the accompanying red sash showcased the leanness of his waist. Silver buttons lined both sides of the braiding, glinting like newly minted coins under the chandeliers.

His cravat, stock, and gloves were black, as were his trousers. New and crisp, they hugged his long legs without being the vulgarly tight style many gentlemen preferred. Even his shoes were polished to a high gloss.

He must have shaved just before leaving because only the faintest shadow showed along his jaw. Good Lord, he cleaned up well. Never at Brixleigh had he succeeded in looking as sharp and handsome as he did now.

Even though she liked it, Blythe's chest pinched at his appearance. Where was her Devlin? The scruffy, slouching giant who didn't give a fig about his appearance?

Perhaps he would wonder the same about her. Had he taken these extra pains for the same reason? Had he sought to impress her?

He'd certainly succeeded.

He was headed straight toward them. His path never faltered even as he slowed to respond to the greetings called out to him or shake hands with someone who stopped him with a hand on his arm.

He was probably coming to say hello to Miles. Everyone knew they were friends. Carny and Teresa were present as well. Perhaps he wanted to inquire after them. It had to be something other than her, because Blythe would not—even if he was dressed to impress—allow herself to believe that Devlin's sole purpose in coming there that night was to see her. Not when he'd been in town for a week and not come to call.

He smiled at ladies Jersey and Pennington—not his real smile, but that patently fake one that curved his mouth on both sides—before stopping in front of Miles. Was she disappointed or relieved that he hadn't come straight to her?

Activity started back up again, even though much attention remained fixed on Devlin. Being out of society so long, Blythe had no idea that his effect on the general populace was so strong. If the usually fickle *ton* held him up so high, what did his fellow soldiers feel for him?

"Good evening, Lady Blythe." He bowed.

Heart hammering, she raised her gaze to his. Lord, he was so tall! And his eyes—they seemed to see deep within her. They shone as though they knew all her secrets and darkened as though he wanted to tell her all of his.

She wanted to know them, the topmost on her list being how a man so adored could think he had never known love. The second was whether he still wanted to marry her, because seeing him right now, looking at her the way he was, she'd be very tempted to toss her principles to the wind and say yes.

If he ever asked, that was, she thought with an inward smile.

Somehow she remembered to curtsy. "Good evening, Mr. Ryland."

His lips curved—into a real smile this time. How she loved that little lopsided smile. "I wonder if anyone has claimed you for the first waltz of the evening."

Claimed her. Not the dance, but her. A shiver thrilled

through her. She didn't have to consult her dance card to answer. "No, that dance is open."

Just for a second his gaze dipped to her cleavage, and a warm rush of blood flooded Blythe's cheeks as his gaze once more met hers. "Then I ask that you save it for me."

From the pounding of her heart someone might think he'd asked for her soul rather than just a dance.

"It would be my pleasure, sir."

His smile grew, causing the same warmth that was in her cheeks to blossom elsewhere in her body.

"I assure you, Lady Blythe, the pleasure is all mine."

Something in his tone of voice, the possessive way he looked at her, made warning bells go off in her head. Blythe didn't know what he had in mind, but she did know one thing for certain.

She was in trouble.

Was the orchestra ever going to play a damn waltz?

Devlin watched moodily as Blythe danced with yet another gentleman. It was an entirely proper dance, of course, but that didn't matter. Another man was touching his woman. As archaic a notion as it was, he wanted nothing more than to walk out onto the dance floor, swing her over his shoulder, and carry her off to his lair—or rather Brahm's house, where he was living during his stay in London.

Apart from that, it was good to see her again—too good. The sight of her in that shimmering dress, her breasts high and bountiful, was enough to make suffering an evening in an itchy cravat and a tight jacket worthwhile.

She was beautiful, his amazon queen. Others saw it as well. He could tell by the way they looked at her, the things they said whenever she walked past. They noticed a change in her, the way she carried herself, the grace and ease with which she conducted every movement.

It was because of him—he knew it even if no one else did.

Whether Blythe's confidence was a result of his attention or in spite of it, he wasn't certain, but he knew that he was responsible for this change everyone spoke of. Good. If it made people see just how truly amazing she was, then he was proud of whatever involvement he had in it.

He wasn't afraid of someone else seeing her true worth and pursuing her. They would pursue the lady they saw here tonight. They would try to win her with flowers and poetry—all the things she distrusted. They would compliment her looks and figure—things that meant very little to her. None of them would have the insight to know that she would rather talk of horses than gossip, or that the way to her heart was to treat her as a woman, not as a proper lady.

His Blythe was a mixture of sweet fragility and overwhelming strength, and the secret to winning her was to acknowledge that fragility while respecting the strength. So if she wanted to cry, he would let her cry, and if she wanted to arm wrestle, he'd accept her challenge and he would be serious about trying to defeat her, just as she would with him.

But right now he'd settle for a waltz.

The current dance ended and Devlin threaded his way through the crowd toward where Blythe and her partner were standing, chatting to Miles and Varya. Miles noticed his approach first and flashed him a grin so big Devlin almost laughed at it. His friend should have known that he wouldn't give up on Blythe so easily.

He had left her moments after securing the first waltz. He hadn't wanted to seem too eager for her company, and he had wanted her to see that he was considered something of a "good catch" by many of the mamas present. Perhaps she'd even be a little jealous when she saw him dance with other women.

If she was jealous, he didn't know. She'd been too busy dancing with other men and making *him* jealous for him to notice.

She didn't really *like* some of these fops, did she? Good

Lord, the one she'd just finished dancing with had diamond shoe buckles! What kind of man wore diamonds on his shoes? He was wearing heels as well. With them he was just barely the same height as she was. No, she couldn't be interested in him at all.

Nor would she be interested in that last one—the one with lace on his cuffs. It was all Devlin could do not to grimace as he remembered it.

She looked up as he drew nearer, as though she sensed his approach. Her feline eyes brightened at the sight of him, warming his heart in a way he never thought possible. She couldn't completely hide her feelings for him any more than he could hide his for her. His fingertips tingled at the thought of touching her, and his heart tripped heavily against his ribs.

She was his, even if she wouldn't admit it. And soon, he would have her as his wife. Strong and stubborn Blythe might be, but he was stronger and even more stubborn. He hadn't survived more than a decade in King George's army just by being a good shot. He wanted her, in every way a man could have a woman, and he wanted to give himself to her. No matter that he wasn't worthy of her love—he'd deal with that later. Love, if it existed, was secondary to having her in his life.

As luck would have it, the opening strains of a waltz began the moment he reached her. He nodded politely to her former partner, who still hadn't left her side, and offered Blythe his arm.

"I believe this is my dance, Lady Blythe."

"So it is, Mr. Ryland," she replied, laying her hand on his sleeve. "Excuse me, Lord Mackleford."

Heads turned as they approached the dance floor. What a picture they must make, he the tallest man in the room and she the tallest woman. Would the gossips consider them a good match? Or would they wonder why she would waste her time with a battered old soldier who had neither looks nor title to recommend him?

She pushed against his shoulder. "You are holding me closer than is proper."

He held tight to her hand and waist, refusing to allow her any more room. "I know."

"People will talk."

He shrugged. "Let them."

She relaxed some in his arms, as he steered her into the first turn. "It feels good to hold you again."

Her lashes fluttered. How odd it was to see her so coy and flustered. "It feels good to be held."

His heart thrilled at the words. Was it folly to feel this way? Did it make her as happy to say it as it did for him to hear it?

"How are you enjoying London?" He guided her closer to him as he asked the question. She didn't seem to notice.

Blythe's generous lips curved into an ironic smile. "It is not as I remembered."

"Is that good or bad?" Bad would be good.

Her smile never faltered. "It is good, I think."

Good meant that he would have to spend more time in London if he was going to court her. He hated London. The only thing that made all the stares and adulation bearable was knowing she was there as well. Going back to Rosewood without her, however, was not an option.

"How are you finding your time in the city?" Her tone was noticeably hesitant, as though she was afraid to hear his answer.

"Tolerable."

She seemed genuinely bewildered. "Then why are you here?"

He gazed into the clear, unclouded depths of her eyes and allowed himself a smile. Did she truly not know? Or did she simply want to hear him say it? "You know why."

Her lips parted in an inaudible gasp of surprise, perhaps at his bluntness or perhaps because she didn't think he would answer honestly.

"I'm not leaving without you," he continued. What had he to lose by being completely upfront about his intentions?

Some of the color left her face, then rushed back twofold. "Devlin, I thought we already discussed this."

"We did, but I have always been more a man of action than a man of words." How cocky that sounded! But it was true. He had always believed that what a man did meant far more than what he said.

The set of her jaw told him more than any words could have. She was not going to make it easy for him. "I cannot enter into a marriage without love."

He opened his mouth to reply, and she cut him off, "I know, I know. You have not asked me to marry you."

He smiled at her sweetly caustic tone and rolling eyes.

"But if you *did*, I cannot marry without love."

He guided her through another twirl. "Then I shall just have to make you love me."

Her steps faltered. Only his arm about her kept her from stumbling. She gazed up at him with frustration in her eyes and tension in her jaw. "That is a cruel jest."

Poor amazon. She didn't understand at all, did she? She had no idea how she affected him.

"I'm serious," he replied, turning her yet again.

She stared at him, disbelief bright in her wide eyes. "What about you? Am I to attempt to make a man who does not know the emotion love me in return?"

He smiled. "That's up to you, isn't it?"

"And if it does not work?" Her eyes blazed with emotion—defiance, anger . . . hope.

"I would be more than happy to oblige you, my lady amazon, if only you would endeavor to try."

She didn't seem to know how to respond to that, and perhaps it was just as well. The music came to an end, and their time together was over. He released her.

"Are you available for the next waltz, Lady Blythe?"

Mutely, she nodded, her eyes still wide from his challenge. He had shocked her. Truly, he had shocked himself. He still wasn't certain he believed in love, and even less certain that he deserved it, but by God, if it was that important to her, he was willing to give it a shot. He would do anything to call her his own. Surely she could see that now.

Devlin offered her his arm and escorted her back to Miles and Varya, both of whom smiled at him encouragingly. It was an action that did not go unnoticed by interested spectators. People liked to watch him, and he had called a lot of attention to himself by dancing with Lady Blythe, who had also garnered public interest with her sudden return to society. Tongues would start wagging when he collected Blythe for a second waltz—especially since he had no intention of dancing with anyone else for the rest of the evening.

Let the gossips talk. He would walk down Bond Street in nothing but his unmentionables and a ladies' corset if it would help persuade Blythe to be his.

He would do anything to have her—even if it meant eternity in hell for lying to her about his past. He would hide it forever if it meant having her love him. Even having her eventually discover the truth would be worth knowing just a day of being loved.

She was his. She would always be his. He just had to convince her of that.

He was just about to leave Blythe with her family when a very drunk young man swaggered up to him with two friends in tow. He saw this sort of thing so often, it didn't surprise him anymore. Why did young men come to such parties if all they wanted to do was drink? They should be at a club instead.

The young man jabbed a finger into Devlin's shoulder. "So you're the big war hero, what?"

Oh Christ. Not this again. It wasn't the first time a little man had tried using him to make himself look bigger. Heads were beginning to turn. "Let me guess—I don't look that big to you?" The young man didn't stand much higher than Devlin's shoulder.

Red-rimmed blue eyes tried to focus on his face. "Thas right."

Devlin sighed. What made some men act this way when they were in their cups? Brahm had never gone looking for fights. Of course, Brahm never had to; they usually found him of their own accord. Pissing in a punch bowl was good for that.

"You are foxed." Nothing like stating the obvious, but perhaps the young man didn't realize just how impaired his judgment was. "You should go home."

Obviously the young man didn't like being told what to do if the loose-muscled sneer contorting his face was any indication.

"I think I sh'd put you in your pl-place." The youngster belched, sending a whiff of noxious fumes in Devlin's direction. "You're just a youn'r son. I'm going to be an earl som'-day."

A younger son he might be, but Devlin didn't bother to remind the boy that he was also almost a foot taller, two to three stone heavier, and almost ten years older. The boy had something to prove to himself; he could understand that. He just didn't want to be part of it.

He had met many men like this one—young and old—who felt small within their own lives, either physically or emotionally. They all had one thing in common—they wanted to prove their virility, their power, by taking down the big fellow. For some reason, Devlin was often that fellow. It was odd, because he had spent much of his own life trying to prove himself as well.

The young man turned to grin at his equally foxed friends before addressing Devlin again. "I'm going to hit you so hard y'ull wish you were back fighting Boney."

Devlin allowed himself a smile. "Little man, *nothing* could make me wish for that."

In hindsight, it hadn't been the best thing to say to diffuse the situation. The future earl drew back his fist and let it fly in a wide, drunken arc.

Devlin caught it with his left—his weaker hand. He closed his fingers over the young man's knuckles, the muscles in his arm barely straining under the pressure. The poor boy really was drunk.

He was aware of the stares leveled upon him. Someone in the crowd shouted, "Let the pup have it, Ryland!" But the only gaze he was concerned with was Blythe's. She certainly wouldn't be impressed by his beating a drunk boy, and even if she would be, he wouldn't do it. There was no honor in defeating something smaller and less powerful than yourself. The boy knew that.

What the boy also needed to learn was to pick his battles a bit more wisely.

"There," he said softly as the young man stared at him in open distress. "You did it. You took a swing at me. Now be proud of that and go home." He relaxed his fingers, releasing the fist in his.

The young man staggered backward, staring at his hand as though he didn't recognize it. As his friends—who had obviously decided against any more attempts at violence—dragged him from the ballroom, he kept his gaze fastened on Devlin until the doors closed behind him.

The conversation and music started up again. A few gentlemen slapped Devlin on the shoulder and complimented him on his "gentlemanly" behavior. Others told him he should have taught the boy a lesson.

"I think I did," he replied with a patient smile. These people fancied themselves so wise to the ways of the world, so knowledgeable of how things should be, so why did he, an uneducated soldier, sometimes feel as though he knew so much more than they did?

A gentle pressure on his arm had him turning his head to his left—to Blythe.

Her eyes shone with something that looked very much like pride. "That was a good thing you did."

He shrugged. What was he supposed to do, agree? Disagree? He wasn't certain how to do either without looking like an idiot.

Their gazes locked. He gave her a glimpse inside. Did she see the darkness in his soul? Did she know how much light she'd brought into his life? Before he met her he hadn't dared dream that life would ever be better for him, that he would ever find a reason to dream or hope. Before her he had no goals except to find a place of his own. Now he knew that what he really wanted was to find where he belonged, and where he belonged was with her.

"I want you," he told her in a tone too soft for anyone else to hear.

Her eyes widened as a soft blush bloomed in her cheeks. "You should not say such things in public."

"Then let's go somewhere private."

The blush deepened, but he could see a spark of desire in her eyes. She wanted to go with him. Her heart might not know what it wanted, but her body did. "You know we cannot take such a risk again."

"I want you," he repeated. "Not just in my bed but in my life and in my future. I will do whatever it takes to get and keep you in all three."

She arched a brow, but he could see her trembling. "Even fall in love?"

He smiled. He had nothing to lose by risking everything; eventually she would learn that. There was nothing in his life that wasn't worth losing except for her. "If that is what it takes."

"It is." The bravado in her voice was touching. The sheer

tone of it was enough to tell him that she was very much in danger of falling in love with him.

"Then I am prepared to risk it."

Her jaw dropped.

He couldn't help touching her. It was the briefest contact, simply running the tip of his finger along the back of her hand, but it was enough to make her shiver and to send a jolt of awareness shooting through every nerve and fiber of his being.

"What about you, my fierce amazon?"

She seemed genuinely confused. "What about me?"

"Are you prepared to risk falling in love with me? Because I will not settle for anything less."

She swallowed, and he knew she was afraid of risking her heart again. Damn Carny, he hadn't deserved her love in the first place.

"I am prepared," she whispered.

Devlin smiled again. "Good. Regardless of the outcome," he murmured, leaning close to her ear. The scent of cinnamon and sandalwood filled his senses. "We both win."

He left her then with a stiff bow and a smile that was cockier than he felt. He wanted Blythe to love him, and dear God, if he was capable of it, he wanted to love her. There was only one question niggling at his conscience.

Could Blythe bring herself to love a murderer? And if she did, would she continue to love him even after learning the truth?

Chapter 10

The morning after the ball, Blythe sat at the small, round breakfast table chewing thoughtfully on a piece of toast with jam and sipping a cup of strong, hot tea. What had she been thinking when she accepted that absurd challenge of Devlin's? Make him fall in love with her indeed! As if she could.

He proclaimed it a winning situation for both of them, but what if one fell in love and the other didn't? How could that be a victory? It would be hollow at best, and potentially painful for the besotted party—which she greatly feared would be she.

She couldn't go through loving and not having that love returned. Not again. At least if they were lovers and he lost interest, he could walk away from her. Marriage would bind them forever.

"These just came for you," Varya announced, as she swept into the room in a morning gown of garnet muslin. She carried a Wedgwood vase filled with lilies.

"Oh, how pretty." She preferred roses. "Who are they from?"

Varya set the vase on a table next to the morning's other offerings. Oddly enough, she was suddenly quite popular among London bachelors, or so it seemed. "These are from Montrose."

"Ahh, the young viscount. Good height. Too skinny, though." Blythe sipped her tea.

Her sister-in-law regarded her with her hands on her full hips. Her pregnancy was becoming increasingly more noticeable. It wouldn't be long before she would be forced to give up appearing in public. "You have found fault with every man who has sent you flowers this morning."

Blythe shrugged. "I cannot help it." Was it her fault that these men were flawed in some major way? Certainly if she noticed, then their flaws had to be large indeed.

Varya looked dubious. "Well, if you bother to start a list of their virtues, please add the fact that they were considerate enough to send flowers. The size of a man's waist is nothing compared to the size of his heart."

She was right, of course, and Blythe was duly chastised. "I am certain they are all the best of men."

"Oh, I wouldn't go that far." Varya seated herself at the table and poured a cup of tea from the silver pot. "Although I am certain they are each fine in their own way. I think in your estimation there is only one man who deserves to be called 'the best.'"

An uncomfortable heat seeped into Blythe's cheeks. "Is it that obvious?"

Varya dropped two lumps of sugar in her cup. "Dearest, it was that obvious the night we found you in the maze. You are not the type of woman to be easily swept off your feet."

"No," she replied with a bitter chuckle. "I am too large for that."

The other woman pinned her with a penetrating gaze. "I meant too sensible, but do not let me stop you from belittling yourself. It is such an *attractive* trait, after all."

What else was there for Blythe to do but laugh? She picked at her toast. "Do you ever get tired of being right all the time?"

Varya waved a dismissive hand but her blue eyes twinkled with laughter. "Your brother makes it positively exhausting."

"I have no idea what you are talking about," Miles announced as he entered the room, "but I am going to assume it has to do with my overwhelming virility."

Both his sister and his wife rolled their eyes. "Think that if it makes you happy, my love," Varya replied with a warm smile.

Blythe watched the two of them with unquenchable envy. They gazed at each other with a mixture of love, lust, and friendship that she desperately wanted for herself. She wanted someone to look at her the way Miles looked at Varya.

She thought of the way Devlin had looked at her last night when he told her he wanted her, not just in his bed but in his heart. It wasn't the same look, but it was close. Could she make it closer? Could she make him look at her the way she wanted him to look?

"Congratulations, brat." Blythe jumped as Miles tossed the morning paper in front of her, the corner narrowly missed the thick layer of jam on her toast. "You made the scandal sheets *again.*"

He made it sound as though it was a regular occurrence. If it were the season, the gossips wouldn't pay any attention to her at all, but since it wasn't the season and *on dits* were in short supply, her return to society was being treated like news.

She picked up the paper, careful not to get ink on her fingers, or jam on her brother's paper. "What are they discussing this time, my glorious hair, my poignant lips?" Two days ago someone had rhapsodized about her "Junoesque" figure and "jade-like" eyes.

"No," Miles replied with a smirk as he seated himself beside his wife. "This morning's topic is how attractive you and Devlin Ryland look together."

"Oh." Was it possible for one's heart and stomach to trade places?

Tightening her grip to keep the paper from shaking, Blythe scanned the page for her name. Miles had kindly left the paper open to the society pages. Hmpf, as if kindness had anything to do with it. He was on Devlin's side.

"Although the decorations were sublime, no one gave them much notice once war hero and favorite of Wellington, Mr. Devlin Ryland, entered Lady Homewood's ball looking splendid in his Rifle Corps uniform."

Blythe snorted. He wasn't wearing the whole uniform. Did this writer not know anything? If he'd been in uniform he would have been wearing a sword and different trousers. At least then she could have fooled herself into thinking it was the hilt of that sword brushing her hip when they'd danced and not something else.

"Mr. Ryland's arrival caused more than one female heart to flutter in anticipation, but it was all for naught, for once the daring gentleman shared the waltz with Lady Blythe Christian, he refused to stand up with anyone else! Who can blame him? Lady Blythe not only looked remarkable in shimmering bronze silk, but she has the height and grace to display today's fashions to the peak of elegance."

"Elegant." Blythe didn't even bother to lower the paper. "Two years ago my height was pitiable, now it's enviable."

"Society is fickle," Varya remarked, followed by the gentle clink of a cup meeting its saucer.

"One has to wonder, dear reader, if there will soon be an announcement from Wynter Lane of what could be-

come the social event of the year. A mere glance is all
that it takes to ascertain the rightness of the match,
for where else would such tall, graceful personages
find a better mate? After watching them last night,
this author can only surmise that some people are indeed made for each other. A celebrated hero and a
lovely heiress—oh my dears, my heart is positively
aflutter!"

"This person is an idiot." Blythe tossed the paper onto the
table and wiped her fingers on her napkin.

Varya grabbed the paper. "What did she write?"

Blythe focused on her toast. If she looked at Miles he would
see the anxiety and joy in her eyes, and she didn't want that.
She knew better than to believe the writer actually thought her
lovely, but the fact that she suspected a match between herself
and Devlin, well . . . that was something else entirely!

He was a hero. He was popular and liked. Despite the fact
that he was the youngest son of a viscount, his family con-
nections were reasonably good and his fortune impressive.
He could probably have his choice of bride.

Obviously one person thought that choice was she. If society were a bit thicker, if the women at these parties weren't
either dowagers or young debs practicing for the next season,
Blythe wouldn't even be considered for the short list of Devlin's prospective wife. It was only because she was the oldest, the tallest, the . . . whatever she was, that the gossips
were making such a fuss over it. They had to fuss over something, after all.

But Devlin claimed *she* was his choice as well. Wasn't
that worth the risk? Carny might have made her more cynical and jaded, but she was still a hopeful romantic underneath it all.

"Oh." Varya grinned as she looked up from the paper.
"This is good!"

Miles, who had since seated himself at the head of the table, sliced an apple with a silver-handled knife. "It certainly sounds as though you have impressed someone, brat. How, I have no idea."

Blythe shot him a narrow glance despite the humor in his tone. Miles just couldn't be happy unless he made fun of her at least once a day.

"This should ensure that your birthday party will be a huge crush," Varya gushed, buttering a slice of toast. "Lady Pennington will be so jealous!"

The rivalry between Lady Pennington and Varya went back to before she and Miles were married. Blythe didn't know all the particulars, but she was in perfect agreement that Lady Pennington deserved whatever misery she got.

Blythe grinned at her sister-in-law's enthusiasm. "I hope they all bring gifts."

It was at that precise moment that Forsythe entered the room carrying yet another bouquet of flowers. This time they were roses—at least two dozen long-stemmed blossoms, their petals a delicate russet color.

"These just arrived for you, Lady Blythe." He offered her the note.

"They are so beautiful!" Varya enthused. "Quick, who are they from?"

Blythe instinctively knew the sender before she even opened the note. Who else would know her well enough to guess her favorite flower and to pick such an unusual color? The spidery handwriting inside only confirmed her suspicion, especially as it was addressed to "My Amazon Princess."

"They are from Devlin," she replied before reading the rest of the note.

"I would like to see these against your skin, Dev."

Heat flowed throughout her body, sending a shiver down her spine. Thank God neither Miles nor Varya had opened the note first! His words were positively scandalous. She tingled in the most embarrassing places, and yet she wanted him to see them against her skin as well! Her skin and nothing else; she wasn't so innocent that she'd believe otherwise.

It was then that Miles reminded Varya that they had to take little Edward to the park. Blythe didn't often want to kiss her brother, but she did just then. He knew Varya would want to see the note, and he knew Blythe well enough to know she would want to keep it private.

Once they were gone, Blythe left the table and crossed to where the tea-colored roses sat in a simple alabaster vase. Gingerly touching a petal with the tip of her finger, she inhaled the velvety fragrance. She loved them.

They did not belong in the breakfast room where she would see them but once a day—where other people would see them as well. She wanted them where she could enjoy them whenever she wanted, and where they would be hers and hers alone.

Cradling the vase against the front of her cream-colored morning gown, she took it and the note upstairs to her room and placed them both on the small stand beside her bed. Now she would have a reason to think of Devlin every night as she went to bed, and every morning when she awoke.

Other than the fact that she missed him.

"Will your lady friend like it?"

Devlin smiled—as much at the hopeful note in the jeweler's voice as in his own pleasure at the finished product.

Would Blythe like it?

"I'm certain she will," he told the older man, even though he wasn't totally confident. Who really knew what women liked and what they didn't? The most minute, obscure details often made a huge difference between acceptance and pleasure where females were concerned.

"I shall get a box for it. Would you like it wrapped?"

"Yes please." Devlin handed the delicate horseshoe-shaped pendant across the gleaming counter, the chain tangling around his fingers. It was an expensive gift for a birthday present, especially when the woman concerned wasn't his wife or even his betrothed. He had to have it specially made as the jeweler had nothing like it in stock, and of course plain gold wouldn't do. He had to have diamonds set along the shoe—eight of them, one for every nail.

Would she appreciate the meaning behind the gift? That it not only symbolized the day he taught her to shoe Marigold, but that it was to serve as a talisman against ill fortune and further injury?

Of course she would appreciate the sentiment. Blythe wasn't stupid by any stretch. Eventually she would learn the truth about him—she would see the blackness in his soul—but he'd already decided to make the most of the time he had with her. If she married him she would never be able to walk away from him. He would never lose her, not completely.

He refused to think that marriage might make her as miserable as it had his mother. He would treat her well, no matter what she thought of him.

The clerk returned with the pendant boxed and wrapped in pretty blue paper with a pale blue ribbon. Devlin thanked him and left the shop with the gift in his coat pocket.

His brother Wynthrope was waiting for him outside in the damp, gray afternoon, smoking a slender cigar and smirking in his usual manner. Wyn came across as cool and aloof, but Devlin remembered the little boy who used to drive himself to tears trying to be what he thought their father wanted him to be. He never said anything, but Devlin knew that was part of Wyn's resentment toward Brahm—he was the second son and always felt second best against his older brother.

"You should never buy a woman anything she can sell later, little brother."

Devlin looked down at him. He didn't have to look far, but it still gave him pleasure to know he was bigger than the brother who used to get him into so much trouble.

"What would you have bought? Cheese?"

Wyn's usually hard blue eyes lit with laughter. So many people thought him void of emotion. Only his brothers knew the truth, that Wyn felt too much so he protected himself by building a wall.

He flicked his cigar butt into the street. "Perhaps flowers, or a fine wine, but not cheese. No."

"Flowers die and wine gets drunk," Devlin lamented, as they began to walk, weaving in and out among other shoppers, "and then she's nothing to remember you by."

Wyn's expression was that of the typical arrogant dandy, and his tone twice as jaded. "If she does not remember you by your skills in the bedroom, then you might as well give up."

Trust Wyn to have such an answer. Never mind kindness or wit or strength. Prowess was a man's most valued skill. Domination, power, superiority, those were the things a man measured himself with in Wynthrope Ryland's world. Poor Wyn.

"The woman in question is a lady. My 'skills,' as you call them, have not yet been put to use." Not completely, anyway. That night in the maze he'd made her shudder with spent passion, but then she had reduced him to a trembling mass as well.

Wyn made a scoffing noise. "Call her a lady if you will, brother, but they are all the same in the dark. Touch her the right way, find out what makes her scream, and she will be yours for as long as you want her."

This conversation was quickly slipping into the vulgar. Devlin didn't like this bitter side of his brother. "Ah, so women are just like men then?"

Laughing, Wyn elbowed him in the arm. "Precisely!"

Devlin grinned. He much preferred his brother when he

was laughing and jovial. His mean side was better avoided. Wynthrope was the type of man whom others wanted as a friend, but was better avoided as an enemy.

"Here is a twosome I wouldn't want to go up against."

Devlin smiled at Carny as he approached. All the bad feelings churned up by his "indiscretion" with Blythe had passed, and things were easy between them once more. Devlin knew his friend's feelings for Blythe were nothing more than brotherly. It was only his own insecurity that tried to make them something more.

Or so he hoped.

"You wouldn't stand a chance with one of us, let alone attempt both," Devlin replied, shaking the smaller man's hand.

Today Carny was dressed in the height of fashion, as usual. Wyn could give him a run for his money as far as appearance went, but Devlin felt positively lowbrow next to the two of them. His polished boots were scuffed by comparison, his jacket less perfect, his trousers less snug, his cravat more simplistic. He was comfortable, though, and he doubted either of the other men could claim the same.

"You will attend the ball at Wynter Lane this evening, I assume?" the blond man asked, nudging Devlin in the leg with the side of his walking stick.

Devlin nodded. "I was just picking up my gift for the guest of honor."

Carny's smile seemed a little forced, but his gaze met Devlin's easily. "That is precisely what I am about this afternoon. I bought her a pair of emerald ear bobs. Thought the stones would match her eyes."

Match her eyes? Blythe's eyes were no more emerald than Devlin's were! They were more like jade, but even that was muddy by comparison. Had Carny never looked at them?

"That is a lovely gift," Wyn remarked smoothly. "Are you close to the young lady?"

Carny might have missed the edge in the older Ryland

brother's voice, but Devlin didn't. He shot Wyn a warning glance.

Carny merely smiled—a little sheepishly, Devlin noted. "She is as dear to me as my own sister would be, but I did something that wounded her grievously some time ago and hope the emeralds will help ease my way back into her good graces."

Well, that made perfect sense. It was quite nice, actually—in a "buying someone's affection" kind of way.

"I'm sure they will do just that," Devlin assured him. Why burst his bubble by informing him that Blythe was hardly the type of woman whose good opinion could be bought? It was as pointless as informing Carny that emeralds would not match her eyes, not unless they were paler than any such stones he had ever seen.

"Well, I shall see you tonight then." Carny smiled. "Will you be in attendance as well, Ryland?"

Wyn shook his head, his expression that of a man who had seen more of the world than he wanted and found it amusingly disappointing. "I have an appointment with an opera dancer that will not wait. Have a piece of cake for me, will you, old man?"

Carny chuckled. "Better ask that of Dev here. He always could hold much more eatables than I."

They took their leave of Carny after a few more minutes' banter and continued down Ludgate to Fleet Street, where they ambled toward a coffee house.

"You are oddly quiet," Devlin remarked as they stepped inside. "What are you thinking?"

Wyn pulled a chair out from a table. "I am thinking that you should be wary of your friend."

Devlin frowned as he sat. "You mean Carny?"

Wyn smoothed a hand over his neat black hair and seated himself. "The same." He set his hat on the table's polished surface.

Devlin gestured to a waiter for two coffees before turning his attention back to his brother. "Why do you say that?"

Wyn looked at him as though he was a simpleton. "You are taken with this young woman whose party you are attending tonight?"

Devlin nodded. "Lady Blythe Christian."

Wyn gave a dismissive wave. "It makes no matter who she is; the point is, Carnover has an interest in her as well."

"You're wrong." It came out more fiercely than he intended. He continued in a more casual tone, "Carny could have had her years ago. He didn't want her."

Wyn smirked. "There is nothing quite so tasty as a bone another dog wants."

Scowling, Devlin shook his head. "That's stupid. Carny loves his wife."

Something very much like wonder lit the depths of Wyn's eyes. "Even after all the horror you've seen, you still want to believe the best of everyone, don't you?"

"It was the only thing that kept me from putting the Baker to my head," Devlin replied softly. He met his brother's gaze evenly. "What I want to know is what you've seen to make you always think the worst."

Two hot cups of coffee appeared on the table before them, along with sugar and a tiny pitcher of cream.

Wyn tossed two lumps of sugar into his cup and stirred with a shiny silver spoon. "You have seen the evil man is capable of, little brother. I have seen the deceit. You go ahead and believe there's good if it makes it easier for you. I believe my way is safer."

Devlin lifted the creamer and shook his head. What had happened to his brother? "Safer perhaps, but does it make you happy?"

For one split second there was nothing but bleakness in Wyn's countenance. "Nothing makes me happy." Then it was gone, replaced by the cool façade once more. "Just do me one favor, Dev."

Devlin licked his spoon before laying it on his saucer. "What's that?"

"Do not turn your back on Carnover. It wouldn't surprise me if he tried to put a knife in it."

His brother's words still rang in his ears when Devlin arrived at Wynter Lane that evening. Wyn was wrong about Carny. He had to be. It was foolishness to think otherwise.

Still, the seed of doubt had been planted. Wyn was good at that.

"Stop thinking about it," Brahm whispered as they stood behind other resplendent guests waiting to enter the noisy ballroom. "Wynthrope just wants to make everyone else as bitter and distrustful as he is."

Devlin couldn't imagine Wyn intentionally doing anything to upset him—he would to Brahm, but not to him. Brahm was right about one thing, however. Thinking about it didn't make it truth. And Wyn *was* distrustful of almost everyone. Devlin didn't know if his brother even trusted him completely. The only person Wyn would ever put that much faith in was their other brother North. The two of them had a special relationship.

"How do you feel?" Devlin asked as they stepped up to be announced. "Is your leg all right?"

"It's fine," Brahm replied through a forced smile. "Although it may not get me very far if the vultures decide to attack."

This was Brahm's first social outing since the accident that killed their father. Even more importantly, perhaps, it was his first outing since giving up drink. He had no idea how the society he had often humiliated himself in front of would accept him.

Devlin smiled. "Do not worry. I'll protect you."

Brahm thumped his cane on the marble floor. "I am the Viscount Creed. I can protect myself."

Devlin nodded. "That was very good. Very haughty and masterful."

The older Ryland brother chuckled. "Shut up."

Happy to have made his brother smile, Devlin faced the room as their names were called. He couldn't help but notice the gasps at Brahm's name, nor could he miss the scandalized glances that were directed at them.

"They hate me," Brahm muttered, his smile still frozen on his face. He leaned heavily on his cane as they entered the ballroom.

"You don't have to stay if you don't want to."

His brother shot him a look of mock horror. "And have put on my best clothes for nothing? No thank you. I will remain until I'm certain my welcome has been overstayed and then I will go home."

"Just stay away from the punch."

The tip of Brahm's cane came down hard on his foot. "Beg pardon." His expression was all innocence, but there was a gleam of laughter in his eyes.

Devlin led him toward the highly piled gift table where Brahm deposited his gift—a book on horses that he had chosen at Devlin's suggestion. Devlin kept the necklace he had bought in his pocket. He would save it to give to Blythe later.

"Do you need me to stay with you?" he asked his brother.

Brahm made a face, his russet eyes hardening with determination. "I most certainly do not. I would rather chew off my own arm then give this lot the satisfaction of seeing me falter. I shall remain sober and strong on my own, thank you."

It did Devlin's heart good to hear his brother speak in such a manner. For years he had watched Brahm follow in their father's footsteps, and even while he was away in the Peninsula, letters from North kept him informed of the oldest Ryland's descent into drunken debauchery. He wasn't surprised that some of tonight's guests had looked on Brahm with disdain. Given what Devlin had heard of his brother's escapades, it was a wonder that Miles hadn't appeared and asked him to leave.

"Devlin!"

He turned. Speak of the devil. Miles and Varya were coming toward them. It had been Varya who called out his name.

"Damn," Brahm whispered. "Do you suppose I'm to be tossed out before I even make it to the lemonade?"

He might sound glib, but Devlin knew his brother was incredibly anxious about the next few minutes. How Miles and Varya—a marquess and his princess wife—treated him could set a standard for the rest of the *ton*.

"Good evening, Miles, Varya," he greeted as they approached. "May I introduce you to my brother, the Viscount Creed?"

Miles, bless him, was exceedingly polite, even though he had to know all about Brahm's legendary reputation. Varya, on the other hand, went above and beyond Devlin's hopes.

"Lord Creed!" she exclaimed happily. "I have been exceedingly anxious to meet you."

Brahm's surprise was evident. "You have, Your Highness?"

"Do not call me that," she replied with a tiny frown. "It sounds so stuffy. Call me Varya." She took his arm and continued in a conspiratorial whisper, "I heard what you did in Lady Pennington's punch bowl. I must have all the particulars."

Devlin almost choked on his own breath, the urge to laugh came upon him so strong. Trust Varya to be the one person who wanted to acknowledge Brahm's scandalous past—and ask for details.

Brahm cast a bemused glance over his shoulder as Varya led him away. Devlin turned to Miles.

"Where is your sister?"

Miles smiled. "Always to the point. I like that about you, Dev. I really do. My sister is chatting with Carny and Teresa. I am sure she will be pleased to see you."

Devlin was loath to approach Blythe with Carny present, but perhaps it would be easier to lure her away with Teresa there as well. He excused himself from Miles and crossed the Italian marble to where she stood, magnificent in a gown of shimmering emerald silk, with delicate chains of gold woven through her upswept hair. Her eyes and skin glowed like warmed alabaster beneath the chandeliers' sparkling light.

Miles was right. She did look pleased to see him. Her breath caught in her throat—he could tell from the way her breasts lifted against the low neckline of her gown and stayed there. She stood wary and still—like a lamb looking at a wolf.

As he hoped, Carny and Teresa left them alone. It was Teresa's idea. She slanted him a sly smile as she led her—reluctant—husband away. He had to stop this. There was nothing suspect about Carny's actions. Nothing at all.

"Happy birthday."

Blythe smiled, the wariness leaving her eyes as genuine pleasure took over. "Thank you." She gestured to her ears. "Carny and Teresa insisted that I wear their gift."

The emerald ear bobs dangled from her earlobes with glittering brilliance. These were no little "forgive me" ear bobs. These were "you're incredible, I must have you" ear bobs. If it weren't for the fact that they were supposedly from Teresa as well, Devlin would be very tempted to break Carny's neck.

Suddenly his little diamond pendant didn't seem so special.

"They're beautiful," he remarked, his throat dry.

Silence settled between them. It had never felt this uncomfortable before. What the hell was wrong with him? He was thinking the worst of his friend, actually entertaining Wynthrope's cynical and distrusting comments. There was no need. Carny had known Blythe for a long time. He had said himself that she was like a sister to him. Of course he was concerned about her—and Devlin's intentions. It made perfect sense.

"Do you have a partner for the first dance?" he asked.

She nodded. "Miles. It is something of a tradition with us."

"Ah. What about the second?"

Her gaze fell away, and he knew without her answering who had already spoken for the second dance. Carny.

Brotherly concern—that's all it was.

Brotherly, his arse.

He swallowed. "I suppose your dance card is fairly full."

"Fairly, yes." She looked up. "But not completely."

Was that hope in her eyes or pity? He couldn't tell. And he had bought a new suit just for this night, damn it all. He'd even had Brahm help with his cravat—it was tight and stiff with starch, and it was difficult to move his head. Now he was going to spend most of the night standing against the wall watching other men dance with the woman he wanted.

Well, shite.

He nodded. "Perhaps you might save one for me later in the evening then?"

She smiled—in relief, it seemed. "I have the quadrille open."

He hated that one. He didn't know the steps well at all. "Wonderful."

Silence followed. He counted to six before she spoke. "Thank you for the flowers. They were beautiful."

"You're welcome." He'd sent her three batches of roses over the past few days.

More silence. This was ridiculous. Simply stupid. Why were they acting this way? Why was it so awkward? It struck him then that even if he danced with her later, this was probably the only time alone he'd have with her.

"Here," he said, taking the small wrapped box from his pocket. "I wanted to give you this personally."

Her eyes were wide as she accepted the gift. "Oh. Thank you."

The anticipation in her face was almost enough to make up for everything else. Almost. But his little offering couldn't compare to Carny's, and he didn't want to see her disappointment.

His fingers clenched into tight fists at his sides. "Do me a favor. Don't open it now. Open it later—when I'm not around."

She frowned, her confusion evident as she raised her gaze to his. "Why?"

"Just promise me you won't open it in front of me." Lord, she probably thought it was a severed finger or something.

She nodded, albeit hesitantly. "All right."

"Thank you. I shall leave you to your festivities then."

Her face fell even more. "Of course."

Instead of leaving immediately as he planned, he reached down and gave her hand a quick squeeze. "Happy birthday, princess."

Then, without waiting for her response, he released her hand and walked away. He had to find Brahm. Brahm was the only person who could keep him from giving in to what he truly wanted—

Have a drink and forget all about Blythe Christian. At least for tonight.

Tired from dancing and pleasantly full from supper, Blythe wearily closed her bedroom door behind her. The last of the guests had finally left and now she could wrestle out of her gown, pull these blasted pins from her hair, and blessedly go to bed.

Her room was dark save for one candle on the bedstand. The dim light was a welcome respite after the brightness of the chandeliers and outdoor lanterns that had lit the evening's festivities. She didn't bother to light a lamp or any more candles; she knew this room like the back of her hand.

Stifling a yawn, she removed the pins and fragile gold chains from her hair and let the mass tumble down her back. Her scalp ached from the elaborate hairstyle Suki had designed, and she massaged it gently before lifting her brush to the heavy waves. After ensuring there were no tangles, she worked her hair into a loose braid and secured the end with a bit of ribbon.

Then she crossed the soft carpet to the wardrobe. Leaning on the open door for support, she removed her slippers and tossed them inside. Ahh, it felt good to have them off. She wriggled her stocking-clad toes as she shut the door.

Her hands then went to work on the hooks on the back of her gown. She loosened them enough to shrug the bodice down around her waist and then unfastened the rest. The silk fell to the floor with a faint whisper of protest. She picked it up and draped it over the trunk at the foot of her bed for Suki to take to the laundry in the morning.

Lifting a foot to the trunk, she raised the hem of her shift to untie the garter just above her right knee. As the silk stocking rolled down her calf, her thoughts turned to Devlin. Where had he gone when he left earlier? Why hadn't he said good-bye?

Shaking out the stocking, Blythe dropped it on top of her gown and bent to remove the garter from her left leg. Had she said something to offend him? Had someone else done something to anger him? It wasn't like him to leave without speaking to her. It hurt—more than she wanted to admit.

Perhaps he was losing interest in her. Perhaps that was why he'd never come back to collect his dance, why he had seemingly disappeared.

Her fingers went to the pendant around her neck after she added the second stocking to the pile. That couldn't be. If he was truly losing interest in her, would he have given her such a personal gift? He must have had it made especially for her—she couldn't imagine diamond horseshoe pendants being heavily in demand in London.

It was the perfect gift, touching her heart with its simplicity and thoughtfulness. He instinctively knew how to please her. He knew the very soul of her, faults and all, and didn't find her lacking. He was the only person to ever think that, and just now she realized what a rarity it was to find a person who liked you flaws and all. It was a precious gift to have such a person come into one's life.

Please God, don't let her have done something to lose him. Panic swarmed the edges of her mind. She didn't want to lose him. She couldn't lose him.

Why? The question echoed through her head like a shout across a mountain valley.

Trembling fingers fumbled with the hooks on the font of her demi-corset. They wouldn't budge. She sucked in a deep breath. Her fingers wouldn't work properly.

Why did it mean so much to her to have a man who didn't know if he loved her in her life?

Because . . . because she . . .

"Oh, damn these hooks!"

"Allow me," came a low, velvety-rough voice.

Blythe's head snapped up as her heart jerked against her ribs. The pounding filled her ears, thrummed through her blood, and trembled her legs with the sheer force of it. Out of the darkest corner of her room—where a comfortable chair sat before the fireplace—came Devlin. He had removed his coat and his cravat, revealing the golden expanse of his neck and upper chest.

How long he'd been there, she had no idea, but he had been there since before she walked in—long enough to watch her undress. Long enough to intrude upon her privacy. If she hadn't cursed her corset, would he have sat silent still? Would he have waited until she was entirely naked to announce himself? The idea both angered and aroused her.

In the flickering candlelight, his hair was black as pitch, his eyes almost as dark, save for the warm reflection of flame within their depths. His features were sharper, rougher, and somehow he seemed taller, wider.

For the first time since meeting him, Blythe realized that Devlin Ryland was a dangerous man. He was flesh and blood, heat and strength, and some part of her responded to that—it trembled and thrilled to it.

"How dare you invade my privacy like this," she whispered, her voice pathetically hoarse. "You should not be here."

He nodded, his lips curving into a mockery of his normal smile. "I know that. I shouldn't have done a lot of things in respect to you." He stepped closer. He was right in front of her now, so close she could smell the warm spicy scent of cologne and flesh.

"If we are caught I will be ruined," she reminded him—feebly.

He was so close she could feel the heat of him through the thin lawn of her shift. "I thought that didn't matter to you."

"I lied." No she hadn't, but he had her emotions so raw right now, she didn't know what she wanted.

He ran his fingers through the heaviness of her hair with surprising gentleness for a man so large. "You're lying now. Do I frighten you?"

"No," she whispered. He didn't frighten her. Her reaction to him did.

"I should never have kissed you that first time." He touched her cheek with the back of his hand, and she shivered. "Because all I've been able to think of since then is kissing you again. That's why I'm here."

She gazed at him, swallowing against the lump of fear—no, anticipation—in her throat. "Because you shouldn't be?"

He chuckled and dropped his hand. "No, because I want to kiss you. I want to do more than kiss you." His gaze flickered to her chest.

Blythe's nipples tightened in response. How could he do that? Make her want him without even touching her.

What could she say? If she told him she didn't want him to kiss her, it would be a lie. "Devlin—"

"But first . . ." He cut her off, his hands sliding around her ribs, his thumbs resting just below her breasts.

"Let's get you out of this."

Chapter 11

The second his hands touched her, Blythe knew she wasn't going to stop him. Was this not what they had been working toward with all their secret embraces and clandestine meetings?

Still, she hadn't been quite prepared for the effect his touch would have on her. No man had ever seen her in her underclothes before, and here she was standing before a man who was also in a state of undress, in nothing but her shift and corset.

He had watched her remove the rest.

That was why he hadn't danced with her, why he had disappeared earlier in the evening. He'd snuck up here to wait for her, easing his obvious jealousy with thoughts of what would happen when she joined him. What he'd been jealous of didn't matter.

He hadn't lost interest in her.

"Take a deep breath," he commanded.

She did, her hands going to the hooks on the front of her corset. As he squeezed against the boning, she popped the hooks one by one, until finally the offending garment fell to the floor, leaving nothing but a thin layer of lawn between his hands and her body.

She shivered, her nipples tensing in response. His hands slid up her ribs, across the tips of her breasts, to the ribbon at the neckline of her shift. He wound one delicate length of satin around his finger and tugged. The knot let go, and the flimsy fabric it had held together gently gaped.

"Wait."

His hands stilled, just seconds away from loosening the ties even further. His gaze was dark and sweet as it met hers. "Second thoughts?"

She knew without a doubt that if she told him to stop, he would, but that wasn't what she wanted to tell him.

"It isn't fair that I'm standing here in next to nothing while you still have so many clothes on." It didn't occur to her to put a stop to this madness. She didn't want to stop it. She wanted him to show her how it felt to be a woman.

A woman loved by a man.

He smiled, that slow little smile that she'd come to adore. "What would you like me to remove?"

"Your shirt," she replied without hesitation. It was less intimidating than his trousers, but would still give her ample opportunity to touch him. "Take it off."

He did as she bade, first removing his ivory-colored waistcoat and tossing it on the floor by her corset before grasping the fine linen in both hands and pulling it over his head.

With his arms up, his stomach was concave beneath the arch of his ribs. A fine dusting of silky hair trailed into the waistband of his trousers from the thicker crop on his chest. His golden skin was smooth and would have been completely unmarred, were it not for the awful scars that claimed it.

His shirt joined the rest of their clothing. Arms lowered, he stood before her, gold and dusky in the flickering candle-light. He must have noticed her stare because he reached down and took one of her hands in his and lifted it to the twin patches of white, puckered flesh high on his chest and left shoulder.

He placed her fingertips to the scars—they were smooth and satiny to the touch. "French musket fire, one at Talavera, the other almost exactly three years later at Salamanca."

Blythe swallowed. Two shots, so close together in target, but so far apart in time. She couldn't imagine what it was like to be shot once, let alone twice.

Devlin guided her hand down further, to his right side, along the bumpy ridge of his ribs. A long, thin scar slanted across there. "Knife wound, from a woman I thought I was saving from a fate worse than death. She hadn't wanted to be saved."

"Oh," was all she could think of to say.

Over to the left side now, high on the side of his ribs just underneath his arm. "Bayonet. San Sebastian." He dropped his hand.

"What about this?" Her fingers dipped to his left hip, where a rough, jagged scar disappeared beneath his trousers.

He stilled. "Waterloo."

She knew from the tone of his voice not to ask any more questions about it. Instead, she placed both hands flat against his stomach and slid them upward, feeling the heat of his skin and the delicious tickle of his chest hair against her palms. She went up to his shoulders and then down his arms, feeling the solid, ropy strength of muscle beneath flesh.

She should stop. She should tell him to go while there was still time for them to turn back, but she could not. She was going to see this as far as it would go because she wanted him. Because when she'd opened the pendant earlier that evening she had realized that he knew her better than some people who had known her for her entire life. Maybe he didn't know her favorite color or her favorite food, but he knew her in her soul, or as her grandmother used to say, "right down to the bones."

He was the man for her. He was her match, her mate. She knew it in her heart. The future didn't matter—not at this moment.

"Kiss me," she whispered.

She didn't need to ask twice.

His lips came down on hers with a gentleness that surprised her. Beneath her hands his muscles trembled with restraint. He didn't want to be gentle, but he would be because he knew she had never done this before, and he didn't want to frighten her. It was the way a man treated a delicate woman. Not just that, it was the way a man treated a woman he cared about the first time he made love to her.

Blythe clung to his shoulders as he tilted her head back further. His fingers cupped her jaw and slid around her head into her hair, holding her still as though he was afraid she might try to run.

She had been kissed before in her life. Over the course of her acquaintance with Devlin she had become quite familiar with the feel of his mouth on hers, his taste, the texture of his tongue. What was so amazing was that it was different every time he kissed her. Her heart sped up and her blood warmed, of course, that was nothing new, but every time he kissed her it felt like the first time. There was a spark, a jolt, a feeling that nothing like his kiss had ever happened to her before, even though it had.

Pressing herself against his beautiful, scarred chest, she opened her mouth to the warm intrusion of his tongue. Slowly, he drank of her and she of him. This was what a kiss should be.

He picked her up—not just off her feet, but swept her up into his arms like a knight with his lady fair. How light he made her feel. She was in awe of his strength. She was used to being able to do a man's work, hold her own with any man, but Devlin was stronger than she was. He could protect her if the need ever arose. She hoped it never did, but she liked knowing she had someone to run to, someone to hide behind and tell her everything would be all right—that *he* would look after her and that he meant it.

A few steps and then he was lowering her onto the bed— her bed, and yet she'd never noticed before just how wonderfully firm it was, or how soft the coverlet was against her skin. Even the pillows seemed plumper.

In the dim, wavering candlelight, she watched as he stood beside the bed, her battered warrior. He kicked off his shoes, his fingers going to the fastenings on the front of his trousers. Was it just she or had the temperature suddenly gone up? She was so warm, her mouth so very dry. She licked her lips.

Devlin kept his gaze locked on hers as he opened his trousers and slid them down the long length of his legs. She told herself not to look when he straightened, but how could she not when he had bared himself to her like a humble offering?

His legs were strong and hairy, just as she expected. His hips were narrow, the golden flesh taut across jutting pelvic bones. The scar on his left hip ended near the top of his thigh. It had been a nasty wound.

And then there was nowhere else to look but at the one place she'd tried to avoid. Her gaze moved toward the center of his hips, to the thick springy hair that surrounded his penis— cockstand, some of the tenant men liked to call it, rod, or John Thomas. Those seemed silly names now that she was confronted with the actual organ.

It was fairly long, not that she would know short if she saw it, and thicker than she'd imagined. It grew under the weight of her stare, stiffening and rising, the sheath around it pulling back to reveal the blunt, round head. Awed, she sat up on the bed and reached for it.

"Jesus!" Devlin hissed as her fingers closed around him.

Blythe would have let go but he grabbed her hand when she loosened her grip and held it around the warm, hard length of him, moving it up and down. "Touch me," he murmured.

She did. Her fingers stroked the satiny shaft, marveling in its smoothness and the veins that ridged it.

"What do you call it?" she asked, raising her curious gaze to his.

His eyes were heavy-lidded and she knew it was because of her touch, but he smiled all the same. "You mean me personally?"

She nodded.

"Usually I refer to it as my prick."

"Prick." The word felt odd on her tongue. *Pah-rick.* "I don't like that. It sounds painful."

His smile faded. "I would never hurt you."

Blythe's heart seized. "I know."

Devlin shoved his hips against her hand. "Name the damn thing whatever you want, just don't let go of it."

Thrilling at the power she had over him with just a touch, Blythe leaned closer to his groin and studied the shaft of flesh in her hand. Slowly, she pumped the foreskin. A drop of clear fluid beaded on the tip. She touched it with her finger. He groaned in response. Ahh, this was the sensitive spot, just as when he touched her so intimately.

"Enough," he said, pulling himself free of her inquisitive fingers. "You can play with it all you want to later. Right now I want to see you."

Blythe raised a coy brow. "All of me?"

"Fuck, yes."

She should be offended by his vulgar language, but she wasn't. The harshness of it reminded her of what he was—a man, a soldier. It also told her just how utterly desperate he was to have her. What woman could possibly object to that?

Brazenly, she shrugged the straps of her shift off her shoulders, loosening the ties at the neck even more as she did so. It took only a few tugs to send the lawn pooling around her waist.

She lay back on the bed revealing her exposed flesh to his gaze, offering herself up for his approval and his will.

"My God," he rasped, crawling onto the bed with her. He knelt over her, his dark gaze leaving a trail of blazing heat along her sensitive flesh. Her breasts tightened under his scrutiny, her nipples puckering into hard, aching peaks.

Those black eyes met hers. The need on his face was so stark, so incredibly humbling. He looked on her as though she was the most amazing thing he'd ever seen, as though his very existence depended on having her and the pleasure her body offered.

"You're beautiful."

Even though he made her want to believe it with the sincerity of his gaze, Blythe said the first thing that came to mind—the thing that always came to mind. "No, I'm not."

"Yes, you are. You are light and peace. There's nothing more beautiful—and unobtainable—to a man like me."

How was she supposed to respond to that? How could anyone even begin to think of a worthy response?

"Make love to me," she whispered, her throat clenching with emotion. "Don't tell me how you feel, show me."

His fingers, reverent and warm, slid down her stomach to the shift twisted around her hips. "We could stay like this for a hundred years and I would never find the right words to tell you."

Whatever Blythe might have thought of in reply was nullified as he grabbed her shift and pulled. She arched her hips to accommodate him, feeling the soft fabric brush against her legs as he pulled it free.

She was naked. Naked and vulnerable before a man whose opinion of her mattered above all others. Her breasts were large as were her hips, and her belly was far from flat. Her arms and legs were stronger than a woman's should be and had the musculature to prove it. It was far from what society would call the "ideal form." Would he find her lacking? Or would he find her perfect in all her imperfection just as she found his scarred chest?

His attention slipped to the vase on the nightstand. Was this the third or fourth bouquet he'd sent? She couldn't remember, but every one since the first had come without a note. They hadn't needed one. She knew who they were from—and what he wanted to do with them.

He plucked a rose from the arrangement, its stem dripping tepid water on the bed and Blythe's chest. She gasped as it hit her heated flesh.

"I knew as soon as I saw these roses that they would look magnificent next to your skin." Inching closer, he straddled her legs. The hair on his legs tickled hers; the head of his sex brushed the curls at the juncture of her thighs, sending a flood of warmth swirling through her lower abdomen and loins.

The petals of the rose touched her cheek first, velvety soft, whisper light. She breathed the heady fragrance as it trailed along her jaw to her neck, down her chest to circle one breast.

Bracing himself on the other hand, Devlin leaned down, brushing his lips along the same path the flower had taken. His beard scratched the skin of her throat and shoulder as he drifted downward.

The rose tickled her left nipple. She gasped. Devlin's tongue flicked the puckered flesh. She groaned. The hot wetness of his mouth engulfed her breast, sucking and laving until the throbbing between her legs grew to a fevered rhythm. Then he took the rose to her other breast, and his mouth repeated the exquisite torture on that side.

Blythe arched under his ministrations. She wanted to part her legs, to press her pelvis against something hard until she achieved the release she sought, but Devlin held her prisoner between his own thighs, making it impossible for her to arch against the sweet weight pressing against her dampening curls.

This was how she knew it would be with him. This insistent ache, the driving need to have his body inside hers was so incredibly overpowering that it robbed her of all propriety and reason. She didn't care what he did to her, she just wanted him to do it and do it now.

The rose slid down her stomach, circling her navel before dipping lower still. Devlin shifted his weight; he straddled only one of her legs now, down by the knee, and the rose drifted between the spread of her thighs, teasing the inflamed cove there.

Now she could lift her hips and she did, but the pressure wasn't enough, not nearly enough.

"I want to go slowly," he whispered, tossing the rose aside and slipping his hand between her legs instead. His fingers parted her flesh, rubbing the slickness there, spreading it further and further along the cleft. "But I'm too impatient to have you."

Impatient? If this was impatient, she'd go insane with lust when he decided to take his time! She spread her legs even further, inviting him to slide his fingers deep within her as he had that night in the garden maze.

"If this were my tongue," he murmured, the velvet roughness of his voice raising gooseflesh on her skin as his finger slid closer to the center of her ache, "I would lick you until you ground yourself against my mouth, begging for release."

The throbbing between Blythe's legs intensified. She was considering begging now!

Then Devlin's finger touched that hardened spot high up within the hidden recesses of her body, and a cry of delight escaped her lips.

"I would lick you here." His breath was hot against her mouth as his finger worked its magic. "I would rub that sweet spot with my tongue and suck it until you came."

Oh Lord, the things he said! They shouldn't inflame her the way they did, but oh! She wanted it. Wanted him.

As if reading her thoughts, he moved his leg, positioning himself between her splayed thighs. He knelt there, at the opening of her body, the thumb of one hand stroking her "sweet spot" while the other guided himself inside her.

For a second she tensed as his flesh parted hers, but the pressure of his thumb and the incoherent whispers of encouragement coming from his lips made it impossible for her to do anything but relax. As she did, she could feel her interior muscles softening against his intrusion, and her back curved in a supple arch as she opened herself up to the full length of him.

He stretched her, filled her, and it wasn't enough. She wanted friction, wanted the push and pull of his body thrusting into hers. Her hips began to move.

Moaning, Devlin stretched himself over her, pressing his pelvis fully against hers. He was as deep within her as he could possibly be. He was part of her, and she never wanted to let him go. He braced his forearms on either side of her head as she wrapped her legs around his hips, holding him tightly to her.

Slowly, he moved. She could feel his arms quivering with the tension of every controlled thrust. Her hands pressed on his lower back, urging him on, but he just continued his lazy stroking until she thought she might scream. The ache within her was excruciating. Tighter and tighter it wound, sweeter and sweeter the pressure. It was like melting a piece of chocolate in your mouth even though you really wanted to bite and chew it.

"Devlin, please," she pleaded. She wanted him to give her what only he could. Not even on those dark nights when she gave in to temptation and pleasured herself had it felt this good, this right. If this was a sin, then she was ready to spend eternity swimming in hellfire just as long as she had Devlin and his magnificent body with her.

He stilled. She opened her eyes to gaze up at him. His face was mere inches above her own, so close that she could feel his breath and see that his eyes were not really black, but a deep, rich brown.

He withdrew from between her thighs, only to plunge back in again, thrusting his hips hard against hers, increasing the delicious friction between their bodies. It grew and it grew until finally it exploded in an eruption of sensation unlike anything Blythe had ever experienced before. It tore through her entire body, radiating from that part of her that held them together. Pulse after pulse shook her until she muffled her cries of release with his mouth.

Above her, Devlin stiffened, quickening his thrusts until his own stifled moan joined hers and he was still, his body slumping onto hers. She cradled his weight with her arms and legs, reluctant to let him go, even as he rolled to the side.

He slid from between her legs, leaving a warm wetness behind. Blythe wasn't worried about the possibility of pregnancy. She might have been inexperienced, but even she knew there was little chance of her becoming with child at this stage in her monthly cycle, and to be honest, even if there was a chance, right now she didn't care.

It was odd, but after all the little things Devlin had done to make her feel delicate and feminine, *this* was what made her feel like a woman. His woman.

His face was almost completely hidden in the shadows, far from the glow of the candle, but she didn't have to see him to know that he was gazing on her with the same wonder with which she gazed on him.

His hand came up to cup her cheek. "Marry me."

Blythe's throat tightened as she wrapped her fingers around his. She couldn't. Could she? Making love to Devlin had changed everything and yet it changed nothing. She wanted love. She wanted to be sure.

The light in his eyes dimmed, as though he sensed her uncertainty. "I will not continue to play with your reputation. You say you don't care what the *ton* thinks of you, but I do. I either wed you or I stay the hell away. You decide."

Oh, how could he be so unfair? Bound to him forever or not at all. She should have known he wouldn't settle for anything in between. It was all or nothing with Devlin. She was the one who wanted the best of both worlds. Perhaps she was the one who was being unfair—or at least unrealistic.

He cared what people thought of her. He cared—period.

Was it enough? Could it keep them going forever? It was then that an epiphany struck. There were no guarantees in life, just chances taken or ignored.

Which would she rather risk—a few months or a few years of something special, or a lifetime of nothing at all?

Tears filled her eyes—tears of relief, of happiness, and something she couldn't quite put her finger on. "Yes," she murmured. "I will marry you."

"How long are you going to make me wait?"

Blythe stretched in his arms, pushing the soft curves of her long, supple body against his. "It will take three weeks to have the banns read."

"Frig the banns. I'll get a special license."

Instead of admonishing him for his vulgar language, she laughed—a low, throaty sound of delight. "I want a proper wedding. It will take me at least three weeks to arrange everything."

It was dark, their candle having sputtered away to nothing sometime during their second session of lovemaking, but even in the watery moonlight, Devlin could see the set line of her jaw. She was determined.

"Fine." He sounded sullen, even to his own ears.

Her fingers brushed his face. "Why are you in such a hurry to marry me?"

"I don't want to give you a chance to change your mind," he replied honestly.

Her tone was soft. "I'm not going to change my mind."

"You might." *You would if you knew the truth. If you knew what I am.*

Her hand came down to his hip, just above that damn scar, the one the Frenchman's blade had made as he fought for his life. He wanted to move her hand, but she might become suspicious if he did. She already knew he didn't want to talk about that one.

"Tell me the real reason you want to marry me, Devlin."

"Why did you agree to marry me?"

"I asked you first." He could hear the smile in her voice.

He shifted beside her. "You'll think it's foolish."

"I will not."

Sighing, he wrapped his arm around her, slipping his thigh between hers as he caressed her lush hip. "When I'm with you I feel alive." There, he'd said it. It hadn't been all that difficult. The world hadn't ended.

She slid her leg further over his. "Did you feel dead before?" It was said lightly, like a bit of a joke.

"Yes."

"Oh." It was a choked sound, and Devlin instantly regretted his candor. He brought his hand to her cheek and felt the tiny drop of wetness there.

"Are you crying?" As if he even needed to ask.

"Yes."

"What for?"

"For you."

She hadn't cried for her lost virginity, hadn't wept in his arms for her innocence, but she wept for his. Good God, could she break his heart any more easily? When was the last time anyone had wept for him? *For him?*

Love me, he wanted to beg, but his mouth wouldn't form the words. It was probably just as well because she had already given him so much—it would be wrong of him to demand more when he didn't know if he could return it.

He kissed her instead, rolling her onto her back as he did so. He was rock hard and desperate for her, and all because of two little words: *"For you."*

Blythe's thighs fell apart easily. She arched her hips toward him, wanting him inside her just as he wanted to be there. She was ready too, slick with their previous lovemaking and her own need. Sweet Jesus, he hadn't made love three times in one night since his youth.

He plunged into her, heedless of how sensitive he knew she must be, but if he caused her any discomfort at all, he couldn't tell. Her long, strong legs gripped his flanks, urging him to thrust and thrust again.

A tingling that started at the base of his spine shuddered through Devlin's entire body. It felt so good to be inside her, so right. He was home, where he belonged.

Hooking his arms under her knees, he pushed her legs upward so that his stomach pressed against the backs of her thighs. She took him deeper into her body, her internal muscles flexing sweetly, gripping his cock in the most exquisite of embraces.

Love me.

He arched his back, thrusting inside her with every ounce of strength in his possession. The bed actually moved with it. Blythe cried out with it, digging her heels into his back and her nails into his shoulders.

"Oh God, Devlin," she panted. *"Oh yes!"*

She wasn't ready to come yet, but she was getting there. So was he. There was no finesse to this coupling, no sweetness or tenderness. This was pure need, pure instinct. He couldn't tell her how her words or tears had affected him, but he could show her the ferocity of his passion, that she was so deep inside him that no matter how much his body pounded hers, he could never hope to plunge to the same depth in her.

He was giving her everything he had, all his strength, all his darkness, all his anger and despair and restlessness, and she took it, arching herself upward, begging for more.

She engulfed him, beckoned him deeper with the promise of light and peace. He didn't care who heard them, didn't care if they were caught. He should, if not for his own sake then for hers, but he couldn't bring himself to think of what they were doing as wrong, not when it was so damn right.

He released his hold on her legs, holding them in position with his chest instead. Her knees hooked over his shoulders, pressing him down. His hands seized hers, holding them out to the sides in a gesture of complete supplication. His full weight was upon her, centered on the spot where their bodies were joined. This was as deep, as connected as they could possibly be, and still it wasn't good enough. He thrust harder. The bed protested. Blythe whispered words of encouragement, urging him onward.

"That's it," she whispered. "Faster. *Yes.*"

His back was beginning to cramp. Sweat beaded his brow and yet he plunged forward. The desperation that drove him was spiraling downward, focusing itself into a smaller and smaller space as sensation flooded his veins. He shoved once . . . twice . . . thrice . . .

He exploded. A torrent of pleasure seized him, robbing him of speech, thought, and breath. Like a giant fist it shook him, stiffening his body and arching his back as Blythe cried out wordlessly beneath him, as though the vortex whirling between them had sucked the sound from her throat.

Her muscles pulsed around him, wringing the tension from him, taking everything that poured out of him into the absolving vessel of her body. Her legs lowered, little shivers jerking her body against his. Every clench of her sent him gasping for breath. He was spent, completely drained.

He was completely and utterly at peace. Still, he managed

to find the strength to withdraw from her enveloping warmth. Shaking legs carried him to the washbasin whose outline he could vaguely make out across the room. Wetting a cloth, he came back to the bed and gently washed between her thighs.

"You do not have to do that," she murmured.

"Yes I do." How could he explain to her that it was more than removing what he had put there? It was a kind of worship, cleaning that part of her that had taken so much from him and given so much back. How could he explain that this night with her had made him feel as though a thousand sins had been lifted from his soul?

All sins but one.

After he washed her, he took the cloth back to the basin, rinsed it, and washed himself. Then he returned to the bed, crawling under the covers and pulling her against him even though he should be dressing. He needed to sneak out before the servants awoke. Didn't he?

But he didn't budge. Instead, he made her slide over to where he had lain so she didn't have to sleep where the sheets were damp and placed a kiss to her forehead. She was already drifting off to sleep. He'd stay with her a little while and then he'd go.

As his eyelids closed, as he drifted into what would prove to be a deep and dreamless sleep, one thought echoed in the peaceful cavern of Devlin's mind. It was like a voice whispering in his ear.

Love me.

Dear God, was it possible that she could?

Miles stumbled downstairs at his usual time, despite having been up late with Blythe's birthday celebration. The sun was still low in the sky, much like the state of the lids over his eyes. Why couldn't he be more like Varya, who seemed to sleep as long as she needed and woke almost every morning at a different time, refreshed and sometimes more than a little cranky? She was still slumbering peacefully, snoring softly even though she claimed she never snored at all.

There would be no one else up and about but the servants. He would sit at the breakfast table, sipping his coffee alone until Blythe joined him an hour or so later. It would be nice to have some time alone with her. He wanted to know if she'd enjoyed her party. And he wanted to know if anything had transpired between her and Devlin. Lord, by the time the two of them got around to marrying each other he'd be an old man.

Rubbing one eye with the heel of his hand, he entered the breakfast room on a yawn, only to find someone already sitting at the oak table, a pot of hot, fragrant coffee before him.

"Ryland. Lord, man, but you're up demmed early." Many years in the army would do that to a man, he supposed, but did he have to sit at the table looking no different than he did any other day, save for a growth of beard far too long for London standards? Really, the man didn't look tired at all. In fact, he looked as energetic and invigorated as a newborn colt, despite the seriousness of his expression.

"Sit down, Miles," Devlin said, pushing the chair across from him from the table with his foot. "We need to talk."

He hated those four words. When Blythe said them, it usually meant she had done something stupid. When Varya said them, it usually meant he had. But when a man like Devlin Ryland said them, the whole country could be going to hell in a handbasket.

Miles did as he was bid, accepting the cup of coffee his friend poured for him without question. He felt better with the first gulp—even if it did burn his tongue.

"I'll get right to the point. Your sister has accepted my offer of marriage, and we would like to set the date at three weeks hence."

That woke him up. His tongue forgotten, he straightened in his chair. "Three weeks!"

Was that enough time to plan a wedding? How long had it taken to plan his to Varya? Surely it must have been longer than that? Even if it hadn't been, his baby sister deserved better than a rushed affair. She deserved St. George's and all the trappings.

Devlin smiled. "Your sister demands that the banns be read and I reluctantly agreed. The date is set. I know Blythe is of age, but I should like to know we have your permission and blessing."

Miles nodded. So many questions buzzed through his brain, but he couldn't seem to decide which to ask first. Perhaps now wasn't the best time to discuss particulars. All that mattered was that Ryland and Blythe had finally made up their minds. He couldn't think of anyone who was better suited to his handful of a sister. Ryland was more than a match for her physically and while he would treat her like a queen and indulge her eccentricities, Ryland wouldn't allow her to manipulate or control him either.

"Of course you have my permission—and my blessing. This is exactly what I've hoped for since the two of you first met."

Devlin's smile grew. "I know. If you will excuse me, I will leave you to your breakfast. I've much to do today."

"You're welcome to stay," Miles told him, gesturing at the otherwise empty table. "The company would be nice."

But Devlin was already on his feet. "I'd take you up on that if my morning weren't now so busy. I will see you later though, at dinner. Blythe thought you and Varya might want to celebrate."

Miles chuckled. "Indeed." He offered the taller man his hand. "Welcome to the family, Ryland."

It wasn't until Devlin had left that Miles realized what it was that had seemed so strange about the other man's appearance. It wasn't just the growth of beard . . . *Son of a bitch.*

Ryland was still wearing the evening attire he had worn the night before.

Chapter 12

Word of their betrothal spread throughout the *ton* like tea through a lace tablecloth. It started the day after Miles discovered Devlin at the breakfast table. The marquess had made the decision that the sooner these two were married the better, seeing as how they could not seem to avoid inviting scandal. Some expressed surprise, others expressed boredom at what *they* had already suspected. And some, like Lady Ashby, were bitterly cruel and catty with their remarks.

"Is it not wonderful for Lady Blythe that she has *finally* found someone who will have her?" Lady Ashby was overheard asking someone at the theater that evening.

Blythe would be the first to agree that it was wonderful indeed. Devlin, on the other hand, would be sorely tempted to remind Lady Ashby that he certainly hadn't wanted *her.*

And of course, Blythe had many callers during those three weeks as the banns were read in church every Sunday. Old friends and acquaintances came with genuine wishes of happiness, gossips came to ferret out if perhaps there was a *reason* for the speedy engagement, and others came simply because it was bound to be the wedding of the year and they wanted to guarantee their place at it.

Teresa called often. Sometimes Carny accompanied her and sometimes he did not. He always went in search of Miles, and the two of them engaged in their own conversations while the women busied themselves with preparations and excited chatter. It seemed like things were better between Carny and his wife, and Blythe for one was glad.

"Lingerie," Teresa announced one morning over tea. "A woman must have lingerie."

"I already have nightgowns," Blythe replied.

Varya and Teresa shared a secretive chuckle and immediately put aside all other projects to go shopping. By the time they were done, Blythe had ordered much more than nightgowns—including a few items that were so shocking, she just knew Devlin was going to love them.

Devlin. She saw him every day, and yet it felt as though she rarely saw him at all. They were rarely alone—no doubt that was Miles's doing—and when they were they were almost always in a public place, such as Hyde Park or a social engagement.

Every time they were together, every time she thought of him, memories of their lovemaking inevitably surfaced. How could she forget his gentleness during the first time? His adoration during the second, and his passion during the third? He was a man of startling emotion, running so much deeper than she had originally suspected. He spoke of her innocence, her light, as though she was something he didn't quite deserve.

How could he possibly think that? He was the best of men, at least in her estimation. A man worth his salt, as it were. Was it the war he spoke of, and the horrors he had seen? Or was it something else? Something that made him hold himself at a distance at times, as though he was scared she'd see it if he got too close.

She'd discover what it was eventually. She hoped he

would be the one to tell her. Someday he would trust her with all his secrets. He would love her enough to tell her. He would have to. She wasn't about to settle for anything less. Their marriage would be built on a foundation of respect, trust, and love, just as her parents' had been—just as his parents' should have been.

The more she discovered about the late Lord and Lady Creed, the less she liked either of them, especially the viscount. Devlin had told her how his father forced himself on his mother, resulting in Devlin's conception. How could they ever have let him know this? Even if they had been unaware of him listening, it wasn't something that should have been discussed so openly. And how could they allow a little boy to blame himself for such violence? How could they allow him to feel unwanted and less loved than his brothers? They should have been horsewhipped, the pair of them.

She would do her best to make up for all those years of loss. He would never feel unwanted or unloved again. She told him that during one of the few times they were allowed any privacy in the days leading up to the wedding.

He looked at her with the strangest expression, as though he wasn't certain it was really she and not an illusion.

"You cannot promise me those things, Blythe."

"Yes I can."

"Perhaps you shouldn't."

When she demanded to know what he meant by that, he changed the subject, but Blythe didn't forget it. It wasn't just his parents' love Devlin felt unworthy of, it was love in general. He would not make it easy to give love to him. He would have to learn how to give love in return, although Blythe suspected he did that instinctively already. He just didn't realize it. What he thought of as loyalty—like naming his horse after a dead friend—was actually an expression of love. She just had to make him realize it. And make him realize, she would. The consequences of failure were too potentially painful.

But perhaps the strangest visit leading up to the wedding came from Carny. He appeared by himself the morning before the wedding was to take place. And this time, Miles wasn't the Christian he came to see.

Blythe was in the parlor with Varya, discussing details of the wedding.

"But dearest, you cannot have only *one* kind of flower in your bouquet!"

Blythe smiled. "I can and I will. I want roses. Tea-colored roses." She wasn't about to tell Varya why these flowers were suddenly so very special to her, or why the very thought of them sent heat rushing to her cheeks. They just simply had to be the ones she carried on her wedding day, and she would save at least one from the bouquet for the wedding night.

"Lord Carnover is here to see you, Lady Blythe," Forsythe announced from the doorway.

Blythe and Varya exchanged startled glances.

"By all means," Blythe said, "show him in, Forsythe."

When the butler left the room, Varya turned to her sister-in-law. "Do you want me to stay with you?"

Smiling, Blythe patted the other woman's hand. "Of course not. I am fully capable of facing Carny on my own." In fact, she almost looked forward to the meeting, as she had a long time ago, long before her feelings for Carny became more than friendship. Perhaps it would be possible for them to have a friendship once more. Just dispelling the tension between them would be a big help. After all, Carny was one of Devlin's closest friends. She would hate to be the reason for any discord between them.

Varya left the parlor just as Carny entered. He looked splendid in wheat-colored breeches and dark blue coat. Odd how at one time Blythe would have sighed over his impeccable appearance. Now she thought he looked stuffy. He said hello and kissed Varya's cheek, making the proper small talk before allowing her to be on her way. Then he turned his attention to the woman standing beside the sofa, and his easy expression turned somewhat anxious.

Blythe made the first move. "Carny." She went to him, taking both of his hands in greeting. "It is good to see you."

He looked at her as though she had bitten him, he was so surprised. "Blythe. It is good to see you as well."

"Come, sit down. May I offer you tea? Or would you prefer something stronger?"

He crossed the carpet to a small chair, flipping out the tails of his coat as he sat. "I am fine, thank you."

Blythe sat as well. "What brings you here alone this morning? Teresa is not ill, I hope?" She hated to think her friend might not be able to attend her wedding.

"No, she is well." Carny's brow puckered. "Or at least as well as she has been of late."

Averting her gaze, Blythe pretended not to hear the softly spoken remark. She knew very well that Carny and Teresa had been having some difficulties in their marriage, but things seemed to have gotten better. She strongly suspected the trouble had something to do with Teresa's obsession with having a child. Teresa talked of it often when it was just the two of them. She so desperately wanted to have one and thought Carny alarmingly uncaring on the subject. Blythe didn't know what to tell her friend except to be patient. She didn't bother to add that when little Edward was born, Carny had been right there demanding to hold the infant and expressing a desire for a son of his own. It would only upset Teresa more.

"Have you come hoping to see Devlin? He will be joining us for luncheon." And he would be taking her for a ride in the park if he knew what was good for him. It had been too long since they last had any time alone—not that Hyde Park at five would offer any privacy whatsoever, but at least they'd be together.

Carny shook his head. "No. I came to see you."

She stared at him expectantly. He was silent. "About?"

A pained expression crossed his handsome features. "Blythe, you know Devlin is one of my oldest friends. I would not be alive if not for him."

"You would not have Teresa either," she reminded him when it became clear he wasn't going to mention it himself.

Judging from his countenance, he wasn't sure if that was something to be entirely thankful for. Good Lord, had things deteriorated to that point? Poor Teresa, she so obviously still loved him.

What was it about this man that inspired such devotion in women? Whatever it was, she was glad it no longer affected her.

"I am not so certain my wife would thank him for that right now," he surprised her by saying. "In fact, I think she'd rather have attended some other soldier in that hospital, but that is beside the point. I am not here to discuss my marriage."

Well, that was good. "What are you here to discuss?"

He took a deep breath. "Yours."

Now *that* was surprising! "Mine?"

He nodded, sliding forward in his chair until he was perched on the edge. "Blythe, we used to be good friends, did we not?"

"The best," she replied honestly, despite her growing wariness.

"Then tell me, as a former and hopefully future friend, are you marrying Devlin to spite me?"

Blythe's jaw dropped. "I beg your pardon?"

If he realized just how preposterous his question was, he didn't show it. "You didn't agree to marry him because of what happened between us, did you?"

"Of course not!" She could hit him for even suggesting it. "Lord Carnover, your arrogance is astounding."

He actually smiled at that, the blighter. "You only call me 'lord' when you are angry with me."

"You had better believe I'm angry with you!" She was practically shaking with it. "How dare you imply that you have any involvement at all in my decision to marry! You may take credit for my spending the last two years intent on *not* marrying if you need credit at all!"

He laughed. He actually laughed! Good Lord, it had been forever since he'd laughed at anything she said. This was not a good time to start again.

"Oh thank God," he murmured when his laughter ebbed.

Blythe sat board-stiff on the sofa, glaring at him. "I think you had better explain yourself, Carnover. *Now.*"

His smiled faded as he faced her, but merriment continued to light the bright blue of his eyes. "I was worried that your engagement to Devlin was some kind of retaliation against me—not that you would deliberately use him," he was quick to add, "but that you might have said yes to show me that you could land a husband."

Her anger slowly—very slowly—ebbing, Blythe raised a brow. "Carny, I wouldn't have wanted to show you that I could land a fish let alone a husband."

"I know that." The gleam in his eyes dulled. "Despite what you may have thought of me these last couple of years, I never stopped caring about you, Blythe. I care about both you and Devlin. I only want to see you happy."

She wasn't about to let him off that easily. "And you think I am determined to make him miserable, is that it?"

"No. I do not think you would consciously make anyone miserable."

Ahh, touché. A subtle yet effective reminder that she would have made *him* miserable, and that he would have returned the favor.

"Neither of us is going to make the other miserable," she informed him. "I am marrying Devlin because I want to marry him. You may console yourself with that, if you wish."

Carny smiled, his eyes warm again as they gazed at her.

"Then I believe the two of you will be as happy as you deserve."

She didn't understand him at all, and while it was petty of her, she couldn't help but respond with "I expect we shall be. Devlin Ryland is truly the best man I have ever known."

"Thank you," came a seductively familiar voice from the doorway.

Blythe's heart jumped in joy. Leaping from her chair, she ran to him, arms outstretched as though it had been four and twenty weeks since she'd last seen him rather than that many hours. "Devlin!"

He caught her in his powerful arms, lifting her off her feet as he planted a quick, hard kiss on her lips, heedless of their audience.

"Carny came to wish us happy," she told him when he set her down, her head spinning from his kiss.

Her fiancé smiled, but the same surprise Blythe had felt lit his eyes. He turned his attention to his old friend. "Thank you, Carny."

The blond earl was on his feet, a slight flush high in his cheeks. Obviously, he was embarrassed by Devlin's sincerity. "You deserve it. Now, I will leave the two of you alone. I doubt you've had much time to yourselves recently."

Devlin protested. "Stay for a bit, at least until Miles returns."

Carny shook his head. "No, thank you. I promised Teresa I'd be home in time for luncheon. I will see you tomorrow at the ceremony. Good day."

With that he departed, leaving Blythe and Devlin staring after him, their arms wound around each other's backs.

"That was the oddest visit I've ever had," she confided. "He wanted to make certain I wasn't marrying you as some kind of revenge against him."

Devlin's lips curved. "He has that little faith in my charm, eh?"

"Or mine." Her tone was dry. "It was odd. I've spent so long being angry with him, and now . . ."

Turning, Devlin slid both arms around her, pulling her close against his chest. "Now what?"

She shrugged, laying her head against his shoulder. She could hear the faint, reassuring pounding of his heart through his clothes. "Now I feel almost sorry for him. Is that silly, do you think?"

He squeezed her. "No. I don't think it's silly at all."

She glanced up. All she could see was his ear. "Did you see how he looked at us as he was leaving? It was almost as though he was . . ." She couldn't bring herself to finish.

Apparently, Devlin could. "Envious."

Yes, envious.

"Who do you suppose he's envious of?" Devlin asked, glancing down at her with a slight smile. "Both of us, or just me?"

She kissed his chin. His stubble was rough against her lips. "Both of us, of course."

"Of course," but he didn't sound convinced. Not at all.

It was his wedding day.

"There," Wyn announced, giving Devlin's cravat a final adjustment. "Now you look fit to be seen in public."

They were in Devlin's bedroom at Creed House, the four of them. Wynthrope agreed to put aside the tension between himself and Brahm for his youngest brother. Brahm tried to make the best of it, and Devlin loved them both for trying. North sat on a trunk at the foot of the bed, legs splayed wide, watching the goings-on with an expression of amused boredom. He would no doubt rather be chasing criminals around the city than sitting around waiting to sit around and wait some more.

"I can't breathe," Devlin gasped as his brother tightened the starched linen around his throat. "Loosen it."

Rolling his eyes, Wynthrope did as he was commanded. An arbiter of fashion, Wyn had never understood why his youngest brother couldn't bother to learn more than one way to tie his cravat. "Better?"

Devlin nodded. "Much."

He was dressed in buff trousers, gold embroidered waistcoat, and dark blue jacket. Wyn had tried to convince him to wear breeches, but Devlin refused. He felt silly dressed up like some dandified nob. He wasn't Beau Brummell by any stretch.

"I have something for you," Brahm spoke when Wynthrope was done fussing. Leaning on his cane, he came forward with slow, uneven steps. His leg was healing, but not fast enough for Devlin's liking.

Like the other brothers, Brahm was dressed in his finest daywear, but he wore trousers to hide his lame leg. In his free hand he carried a small black box, which he held out for Devlin to take.

"I know you bought Blythe a betrothal ring rather than give her one of Mama's, but I thought you might want to give her this one. It was Grandmother's."

Their grandmother Ryland had been a favorite of all the boys. She adored them all equally. She was long gone now, and her loss was a hollowness in his chest. She would have liked Blythe.

Devlin took the box. It was so small, so dainty in his hand, but inside was a large, square-cut topaz on a slender gold band.

"I thought it would suit Blythe," Brahm said, a hopeful note in his voice.

"It will." Both bold and delicate, simple yet elegant, the ring would be perfect for Blythe's hand. Trust Brahm to understand that on such short acquaintance.

"Nice touch, Brahm," North said from his perch on the chest. His pale blue eyes sparkled at his eldest brother. "Well done."

Even Wynthrope, who would rather cut out his own tongue than utter a kind word to Brahm, nodded in agreement. A look passed between first and second born. Devlin couldn't quite decipher it, but it appeared as though a truce had been reached—for his wedding day at least.

Brahm pulled his watch from his pocket and flipped it open. "We should be going."

The wedding was to be held at St. George's—at Miles's insistence—with a breakfast to follow at Wynter Lane. Varya had offered them her town house for the wedding night and the remainder of their time in London, and they had readily accepted. Time alone was what they wanted most. Once preparations and renovations at Rosewood were complete, they would return to Devonshire for their honeymoon. Blythe had refused the offer of a trip abroad. She wanted to be at Rosewood, *their* home. Traveling could wait. Devlin didn't mind; as long as he never had to step foot in Spain or Portugal again, they could go wherever Blythe wanted. They would be in London for perhaps another month, but no longer.

Truth be told, Devlin couldn't wait to return to the country. London's bustle and harried atmosphere were beginning to fray his nerves. The city was so loud, voices and sounds and smells all pushing in on one another. It was like cannon fire, complete with smoke.

And perhaps at Rosewood, where things were quiet and secure, Devlin might take Brahm's advice and finally confide to Blythe the truth about Waterloo. It was a terrifying prospect, revealing himself as a murderer, but Brahm was right—it was the only way they could truly have a future together. A braver man would tell her before the wedding, but Devlin never laid any claim to bravery. The chance of losing her was not something he was prepared to risk. Even if she turned away from him, she would still be his wife, and there would still be a chance he could win her back.

Slipping the ring into his jacket pocket, Devlin pushed

thoughts of what the future might hold from his mind. Today was his wedding day. Soon Blythe would be his. He wasn't going to spend the day worrying about what might ruin it.

"Let's go."

As far as ceremonies went, it was quick, simple, and relatively painless. The breakfast was longer, definitely more ornate and incredibly filling. But it was the time alone with Blythe that came later that Devlin would remember with the most fondness.

They left Wynter Lane late in the afternoon, with plenty of hours to go before they had to return for the "small gathering" Varya was throwing in their honor. Small by Russian standards, perhaps. The guest list had at least two hundred people on it. People had actually traveled up from various parts of the country to attend the wedding and the following festivities.

Devlin carried his bride over the threshold of their borrowed town house, and when she suggested he put her down, he simply laughed, kicked the door shut with his foot, and carried her up the stairs—two at a time.

The master bedroom was filled with vases of roses of all different kinds and colors. The covers were turned down, and a bottle of champagne sat chilling near the bed. Varya had thought of everything.

"Shouldn't we wait until tonight?" Blythe asked, laughing as his big fingers struggled with the tiny buttons on the back of her pale blue gown.

"No." Damn buttons.

"But I have lingerie!"

Lingerie? Devlin paused. Seeing Blythe in some lacy confection was definitely tempting, but seeing her naked was even more so.

"You can wear it later. I want you now. Frigging buttons!"

He offered to slice the gown off her with a knife, but she adamantly—laughingly—refused. In the end, she managed to undo enough of the buttons so that he could remove the gown over her head.

Stripped down to the skin, they fell onto the bed together, the afternoon sun warming their bodies as it slanted through the windows. Their coupling was quick and needy, driven by the twenty-plus days they'd waited for this moment. They made love a second time before sharing a bath and a luncheon of cold meats, bread, and cheese. The bath took longer than the luncheon and lovemaking combined as they leisurely explored each other's bodies without the haze of passion taking over. They talked and they laughed, and Devlin was sorry when the water turned cold.

The luncheon they ate on the rug by the hearth. They ate with their hands, feeding each other with their fingers, and acting like children.

Devlin couldn't remember the last time he'd acted like a child—not even when he was one. Blythe made his heart feel light and free. He wasn't going to think about the darkness in it, not now when there seemed to be so much promise in his life. He wanted to enjoy it while it lasted.

When it finally came time for the evening, Devlin was loath to leave their private sanctuary, but he wouldn't put it past Varya to personally come and collect them, so he donned his evening attire, allowing his wife—his *wife!*—to tie his cravat.

"Wynthrope did a better job," he teased with a grin.

Fastening the horseshoe pendant around her neck, Blythe stuck her tongue out at him. "Too bad you hadn't the forethought to marry him then."

It was then that he remembered the ring. "I have something for you. Brahm gave it to me."

Her eyebrows arched upward. "That was nice."

So was the look of surprise on her face when she opened the box. "Devlin, it's beautiful!" Taking it from the velvet, she slipped it onto her finger.

"It was my grandmother's," he explained with a smile.

"She was a statuesque woman too. Very tall and very bold. Brahm thought it would suit you."

"Remind me to give Brahm a kiss when we see him tonight."

Such a public display would go a long way in easing his scandalous brother back into society.

He hauled her close. "What do I get?"

Her clear eyes lit with sensual mischievousness. "I'll give you that later."

"In lingerie?" Lord, he was growing hard already!

Soft hips pressed against his. "If you are good."

Smiling, he released her. She was an amazing woman, his amazon princess.

I love you. The words came unbidden, almost blurting themselves into the air between them.

Devlin swallowed, taking the words deep inside him, back where they belonged. It was a reflex, the urge to say them. Hadn't he said them before, to a woman whose face he couldn't remember? A woman who had offered him comfort and solace after Waterloo—a woman who had washed the blood from him, stitched his wounds, and allowed him to use her body for a night of forgetting? He had told her he loved her and in a way perhaps he had, but not the way he was supposed to. Not in the way he should love Blythe.

He supposed this meant that he believed in love after all. Or maybe he just wanted to believe. Right now he wasn't sure there was a difference, but he knew better than to go making such a vow when he wasn't certain of it—and when he wasn't certain it would be returned.

They made the journey to Wynter Lane in the carriage Miles had loaned them. Devlin had wanted to hire his own, but his brother-in-law insisted. He said it would make him feel better knowing they would be driven by someone he trusted.

They were among the last to arrive, entering the ballroom to a roar of applause. Holding Blythe's hand, Devlin glanced at her, wanting to see her reaction to all this sudden adoration.

She was like a rose blossoming under the attention. How could she have ever felt like a wallflower? Everyone he met seemed to adore her, as was evident by their happiness for her.

Clad in a gown of shimmering copper silk, her hair swept high on top of her head, her cheeks blooming with delight, Blythe was easily the most beautiful woman there. How could she not know it? He knew it—like a sharp blade in the heart he was so acutely aware of her beauty.

A crowd soon gathered around them, many of them guests wanting to extend their felicitations and well wishes. Devlin smiled and nodded politely, saying the appropriate words whenever he was spoken to, all the while waiting for the crowd to disperse. There was nothing more suffocating than the feel of too many bodies pressing around one's own.

Finally the music started and the crowd around them thinned, everyone drawing back to watch them make their way to the dance floor for the first set of the evening. Thankfully, it was something simple so Devlin didn't have to worry about flubbing the steps with so many eyes watching.

They were joined in the set by Carny and Teresa, who then accompanied them off the floor when the dance ended. Devlin and Carny were then charged with the responsibility of fetching refreshments for their wives—not that Devlin minded.

"Blythe is in good looks tonight," Carny commented as Devlin poured a ladle of punch into a glass for him.

Devlin nodded with a smile. "She always is."

Carny grinned as well. "Spoken like a besotted husband."

Devlin couldn't quite put his finger on it, but something about Carny's attitude toward Blythe bothered him. It was strangely proprietary, but not exactly threatening. It made him uneasy but not quite jealous. He wasn't certain whether it was he Carny envied or his situation. One didn't have to be a genius to notice that things were not as they should be with Carny and Teresa. But why was that? And was it their trouble that seemed to make Carny gravitate toward Blythe, or was it Carny's attention toward Blythe that was the cause of their trouble?

And how had he gotten to the point where he would trust a man with his life but not with his wife?

"Would you mind if an old friend stole her for a dance?" Carny asked—innocently as far as Devlin could tell—as they walked back to the women.

"You will have to ask her yourself," Devlin replied easily. "It is not my decision to make."

Carny chuckled again. "Oh yes, you have learned quickly how to be a proper husband!"

Devlin only smiled, uncertain if he had been complimented or not.

Blythe seemingly had no opposition to the dance. "Do you mind?" she asked him.

Devlin shook his head. "Of course not." Really, he didn't. Regardless of Carny's motives, he was certain of hers. Blythe had no interest in Carny other than possibly being friends again. He knew this because his wife was not very good at hiding her emotions. If she was nervous about dancing with Carny, it would be obvious in the way she held herself. If she still had feelings for him, Devlin would know just by the way she gazed at Carny, but there was nothing in her gaze to cause alarm. No, it was only Carny he couldn't quite read.

Teresa excused herself to go talk to a friend as Blythe and Carny walked out onto the floor, leaving Devlin alone to watch his wife dance with another man. If Teresa had stayed he might have danced with her, but apparently she hadn't thought of that. Or maybe she had and didn't want to risk having his huge feet tread on her much smaller ones.

He wasn't alone for long, however. Wynthrope soon joined him.

"I told you to keep an eye on that one," he remarked, lifting a glass of champagne to his lips. "He's not to be trusted."

Devlin opened his mouth to reply, but another voice beat him to it. "Don't tell him that!"

Brahm.

Wynthrope shot a sharp glance at their oldest brother. "You lost the right to tell me what to do years ago, Brahm."

Wonderful. The two of them were going to use him as an excuse to fight—not that they hadn't done so before. Any excuse to exchange heated insults seemed to suit his eldest brothers.

Brahm's gaze was just as cool as Wyn's. "No one could ever tell you anything. Perhaps if you pulled your head out of your ass and stopped blaming everyone else for your life you wouldn't judge people so harshly."

Wyn drained his glass. "I do not blame 'everyone' for my life. I blame you."

The oldest Ryland stiffened, and Devlin held up a hand to both of them. "Not here. If the two of you ruin this party with a fight I swear I'll personally pound you both into the ground." He might very well be the youngest, but he was the biggest, and they both knew he'd do it.

"Sorry," Brahm mumbled.

"Beg pardon," Wyn added, likewise. But neither looked at the other.

Devlin shook his head. "You should be apologizing to each other, not to me."

Silence as the two stared in opposite directions.

"Oh for Christ's sake!" Looking from one to the other, Devlin couldn't decide which backside to kick first. Why were they like this with each other? Ever since they were children it seemed they had been at each other's throat.

"I will decide who I can and cannot trust," he told Wynthrope.

"I do not need you to defend me," he said to Brahm. "The only person I am concerned with is my wife and I trust her completely. Carny is not my concern."

Wyn shrugged. "Suit yourself, but I still wouldn't turn

my back on him if I were you." With that parting remark, he turned his own back on his brothers and strode away, depositing his empty glass on a footman's tray as he passed.

"I hate to say it," Brahm said softly, "but I agree with him. You are right to trust Blythe, but there is history between the two of them, and there is nothing more appealing to some men than the woman they can no longer have."

Devlin raised a brow. Hadn't Wyn said something similar not long ago? He refused to be baited. He already doubted Carny enough. "Speaking from experience?"

Brahm smiled ruefully and nodded across the room. "Remember her?"

Devlin followed his gaze to an elegant blond woman. He didn't remember her name, but he recognized the face. "Didn't her father and ours try to arrange a marriage between the two of you?"

Brahm nodded. "Lady Eleanor refused to marry the drunkard son of an even worse drunkard."

It was said in such a rueful tone that Devlin frowned. "But you didn't want her anyway. You said she was colorless and cold."

Brahm's whiskey eyes were bright with irony. "That's right. And ever since she refused me I find colorless and cold becoming more and more my taste."

Devlin stared at his brother. It had been years since she had refused Brahm, and *now* his brother decided she was attractive? Because she was out of his reach?

"That is precisely what I mean." Brahm tapped his cane on the floor and took his gaze off the graceful blond. "You do not have to distrust your friend, Dev. Just be careful you do not give him more trust than he deserves."

And then Brahm left him as well, so that Devlin was once again alone, watching his wife dance with another man.

A man he had killed for, and now one he did not know if he could trust.

Chapter 13

"**D**o you trust Carny?"

It wasn't exactly the kind of conversation Blythe would have planned for her wedding night, but since it was her husband asking, she decided the question deserved an answer.

"I would certainly trust him to tell me whether a gown became me or not, but I suspect that's not what you are asking."

They were in the master suite—the one they planned to share while at Varya's town house. Blythe sat at the vanity in her nightgown while Devlin, clad in shirt-sleeves and trousers, stood behind her, brushing her hair with an ivory-handled brush. He seemed to have a fascination with her hair—not that she minded, of course.

His high, ebony brows knitted. "My brother thinks I shouldn't trust Carny with you."

Blythe was tempted to ask which brother, but a little voice in her head told her it was Wynthrope, the cool one who seemed to find the whole world one big cynical joke.

"I have a feeling your brother does not trust anyone but himself."

He ran the brush through her hair, following it with his fingers. It felt nice. "He trusts me. And North."

"Not Brahm?"

Another stroke. "Not that he would ever admit."

Her gaze met his in the mirror. "Whatever happened between the two of them?"

Devlin shrugged. "If I had to blame it on one thing, I'd say my father."

Blythe stared at him. What kind of life had these boys had? "I am afraid that right now I am very glad that your father is dead."

He stopped brushing, his gaze falling to the top of her head. She could see his solemn expression in the mirror. "Don't be happy that he's dead. Be happy that he's not in our lives."

What was the difference? Before she could ask, he spoke again, "You never answered my question. Do you trust Carny?"

"With me?" That was what he was asking, was it not? At his nod, she thought about it. "I have no reason not to. What do you think?"

Another gentle pull of the brush. "I think I would prefer to give him the benefit of the doubt."

She smiled at his reflection. "You do not want to think ill of him, do you?"

He set the brush down. "I know he's not perfect, but he is my friend."

Rising, Blythe turned to face him, her arms twining around his neck. "He is my friend as well, and I do not believe he would do anything to injure either of us."

Devlin smiled. "Good."

She realized that was what he had wanted—to hear her absolve Carny so he wouldn't have to wonder anymore.

"Now no more talk of Carny," she murmured, pressing herself against him. The thin silk gown she wore shifted coolly against her skin. "It is our wedding night. Remember?"

Devlin's arms closed around her, his fingers sliding down to cup her buttocks. "How could I forget?"

His lips came down on hers and Blythe shivered, as much from the cool night breeze drifting from the open window as from his touch.

"Are you cold?" his asked against her lips, his right hand sliding up to capture her breast. His thumb rubbed the tightening peak, drawing a gasp of pleasure from her lips.

"No," she answered, leaning into his touch. "I think it is about to get very warm in here."

He toyed with her breast some more, pinching the nipple and lowering his head so that his mouth closed around it. He suckled through the silk until her knees were weak with desire and her body throbbed with need.

His hands slid up her legs, taking the gown with them, until she could feel the night air swirl around her thighs and higher. Then he lifted her, setting her on the vanity.

The flimsy nightgown was rucked high above her hips, baring her from the waist down. Her legs were golden in the warm candlelight, the hair at the juncture of her thighs far too visible. Flushing with embarrassment, Blythe pressed her knees together. She could smell herself, smell her desire for him.

Devlin stood before her. He pulled his shirt over his head and faced her, clad in nothing but his trousers, the front bulging with his arousal. His fingers wrapped around her knees, his thumbs pressing between.

"Spread your legs for me." The sensuous timbre of his command turned the muscles of her thighs to jelly. She couldn't—wouldn't—resist as his hands slid her legs apart, the backs of them pulling on the vanity's polished surface.

He stepped between her splayed knees, hooking his hands beneath them. He lifted, pulling her hips closer to the edge. Blythe reached behind for balance, shifting her weight so she wouldn't fall off onto the carpet.

"What are you doing?" she demanded, her voice shaking.

He dropped to the floor, kneeling between her anxious thighs. There was no doubt in her mind that he could smell her now as well. But he didn't seem the least bit repulsed by her body's reaction to him. In fact, he seemed only further inflamed by it.

"Your skin is the color of cream," he murmured, sliding a finger down the quivering expanse of her belly. "And this"—his fingers delved into the damp curls at the base of her abdomen—"this is exactly the same color as cinnamon. I want to taste."

Taste? He had mentioned putting his mouth there before, and she'd tingled at the thought. What would it feel like to have his tongue torment her as his fingers had?

As though answering her unspoken question, Devlin parted the slick folds of her sex with his thumbs. Sitting as she was, Blythe caught a glimpse of glistening pink flesh as he moved purposefully toward it. She watched as his tongue slid from between his lips—

"Oh!" Her hips jerked, her muscles tightened. He had licked her—right in her most sensitive spot. And she liked it!

Breathless, she sat, muscles straining, unable to tear her gaze away as he flicked his tongue against her yet again, sending a shudder of pure sexual delight coursing through her. Wantonly, she spread her legs wider, angling her hips upward to give him better access to the private recesses of her body—recesses that were swollen with heat and need.

His tongue entered her, hot, firm, and insistent. Moaning, she writhed against it, digging her heel into the vanity chair to the right of her for purchase. Softer and smaller than his erection, his tongue was ten times as insistent and infinitely more agile, stroking her with a velvety texture that had her entire body quivering.

Then he withdrew from inside her, leaving her breathless and wanting for more. His tongue slid upward, until the tip once again toyed with that aching crest he called her "sweet spot." It felt sweet indeed, but it was because of his exquisite mouth, not because of her!

Gently he licked, rubbing her with the slick roughness of his tongue, stroking her until she was almost mad with desire. It coiled deep within her, tight and insistent, desperate to release its tempest throughout her. She wanted that storm as well. Wanted it so badly that she lost all concept of proper behavior. All that existed was Devlin and the pleasure he gave her. Blythe gripped his head with one hand, her fingers pulling at his hair as she held him between her legs. She lifted herself with the heel on the chair and the arm still on the vanity. Her hips moved with his stroking, her need driving her rhythm until even the vanity itself swayed with her motions.

Brushes tumbled to the floor. Bottles rattled against one another, all punctuated by Blythe's moans of sensual delight. "*Ohh* . . . I'm . . . oh, Devlin!" The tempest whipped through her, barraging every nerve and fiber with a torrent of pleasure that had her crying out in wordless wonder, her body arching like a fork of lightning in the summer sky.

She slumped on the vanity, numb and boneless in the calm following the storm. But Devlin wasn't done with her yet. She should have known there would be more.

He lifted her off the vanity, turning her so that her back was to him. God, he didn't expect her to stand, did he? Her legs couldn't support her weight.

He pushed against her shoulders, easing her torso over the vanity so that she rested on her wide-spread forearms. He nudged her thighs apart with his own legs, the blunt head of his sex pressing against her swollen, sensitive flesh.

Surely he didn't mean to take her like this, did he? Was it even possible?

Looking up, Blythe caught their reflection in the vanity mirror. The height of the vanity was such that she was bent at an angle that put her hips level with his groin. Once again she was unable to look away. The expression on his face held her captive. His fingers closed over her hip as he stroked himself. At first she thought he meant to find his own pleasure that way, but then he moved and she felt him nudge the opening of her body with the hard length of him.

Slowly, he slid inside, parting her tender flesh with gentle insistence. She shuddered, sparks of intense sensation flooding her groin. She was still feeling the effects of her climax. Deeper and deeper he forged, until his pelvic bones pressed against her buttocks and her breasts flattened against the vanity top.

Their gazes met in the mirror and the familiar tightening started anew in the core of Blythe's being. Every languid thrust, every heavy-lidded look sent it spiraling lower and lower.

"You're mine," he told her, his voice husky and strained, his body deep within hers. "Mine alone."

She didn't respond. She only closed her eyes in pleasure as his hips ground against her buttocks. She was his. She would always be his.

And he was hers.

He withdrew only to thrust again. Her body was so tight around his she could feel the head of his organ stretching her, filling her. It was almost too much to bear and yet she would rather die than have him withdraw.

Fingers drifted across the front of her thigh, to the spot where his mouth had been not long before. The sensitivity had ebbed somewhat and he easily stroked her into preparation for another star-seeing release.

Blythe spread her feet, angling her hips upward to better receive him. Devlin bent over her, one hand gripping her hip, the other rubbing her ruthlessly. Her neck bowed. Her breath came in short, harsh gasps, fanning against the vanity's polished surface. She was up on her toes as he shoved himself within her, so insistent that sometimes her feet left the carpet altogether. In and out, oh and God.

And then she came again, with no warning, only the on-slaught of mind-numbing pleasure that had her gripping the vanity with all her strength and stars dancing before her tightly squeezed eyes.

Devlin quickened his thrusts. The only thing that saved her from being slammed against the vanity mirror was his hold on her. Holding her by both hips now, he plunged in and out of her without mercy as her flesh became increasingly sensi-tive, until she felt him stiffen, heard him groan something that sounded very much like an obscenity. Then he slumped against her, and somehow she managed to keep from falling to the floor.

A few moments later, as their breathing began to return to normal, he withdrew from her, taking her arm to help her stand upright again.

They cleaned up at the basin before snuffing the candles and crawling into bed. Blythe snuggled contentedly against him, sated in both body and spirit.

"Did you like that?" Devlin asked as she rested her head on his shoulder.

She slid her arm across his chest. "You have to ask? I thought it was fairly obvious."

"I just want to know that I please you."

It was such a simple admission, certainly nothing like pledging undying love, but it hit Blythe square in the chest all the same. "Of course you please me." Then a shard of panic struck. "Do I not please you?"

Devlin chuckled, squeezing her with the arm around her shoulders. "If you please me any more you're going to kill me."

A smug smile curved her lips in the darkness. "So you won't be looking to take a mistress anytime soon?"

It was meant as a joke, but she realized how poor a one it was when he stiffened beside her. "I will never take a mis-tress."

Blast, she forgot all about his father's infidelity to his mother. It was something Devlin obviously felt very strongly about, having discussed it in the past. Even though it didn't sound as if his mother made it easy for the late viscount to be faithful to her, she could understand why Devlin wouldn't want to repeat history in his own marriage—which suited Blythe just fine. The idea of his bedding another woman filled her with an inexplicable rage. He was hers, and no other woman would ever find joy in his arms again—not while she lived.

"I am sorry." She rubbed his chest. "I forgot."

"I know." She couldn't see his face, but she could tell by his voice that he was himself again.

A comfortable silence stretched between them.

"Devlin, do you trust me?" she asked when the question refused to stop swirling about her mind.

"With my life," came the sleepy response.

"Good." Smiling, she snuggled against him again.

He didn't ask her if she trusted him. No doubt he took for granted that she did, given his thoughts on infidelity. Oddly enough, she did trust him. With Carny she had always been waiting for him to find someone he liked better than her. It hurt like hell when he did, but it hadn't surprised her—not really. But with Devlin she didn't have that feeling. It wasn't that she thought no other woman would want him; she knew for a fact that others did—Lady Ashby, for instance. And it wasn't that she had come to think of herself as such a prime catch either.

No, it was something she couldn't explain. She couldn't quite put her finger on how it had happened, or when, but she knew deep down inside that he would never stray—not just because he said he wouldn't, but because she didn't believe he would ever want to. She was the only woman for him, and if that wasn't love, it was something very close to it.

She couldn't deny that she very desperately wanted to hear

him say the words despite not knowing what her own reply
might be. Oh, she had an idea of what she would say, but she
didn't want to think about it too much just in case the idea
took hold in her mind and blossomed out of control. She
didn't want to fall in love with him before he fell in love with
her. She didn't want to be the one to give her heart without
knowing if there was one waiting for her in return—not
again.

And so she wouldn't reflect too heavily on her feelings.
She would simply feel and give him a chance to understand
his own feelings, give him a chance to fall in love with her. If
it was the last thing she did she would win his poor battered
heart. It was too tempting a prize for her not to want it. What
woman wouldn't want to be the one to teach this seasoned
warrior, a man who had seen and suffered so much, to feel
the joy of love? To have Devlin's love would be to have a
fierce and unswerving loyalty that nothing could ever de-
stroy. He was so solemn, so quietly passionate that it was
easy to dismiss him as reserved or even shy. Perhaps his
emotions were slow to stir, but make no mistake, once they
were roused, they ran deeper than the average man's.

She wanted to be the one to stir them.

Feeling the even rise and fall of the chest beneath her
hand, Blythe smiled. He was asleep, and in a few hours they
both would awake to their first full day as husband and wife.

It was the perfect time to start making him fall in love.

The dream returned two days after the wedding, just when
Devlin was foolishly allowing himself to believe that maybe
it was gone for good. He should have known better.

This time the dream was different. Instead of seeing the
soldier's face, he saw Blythe's. It scared him so badly he
lurched upright in their bed as he cried out her name.

He sat there, moonlight icy bright in his eyes as he gasped
for breath. His skin was slick with sweat, the sheets beneath

him damp. He shoved at the blankets, desperate to cool himself, and swung his legs over the side of the mattress.

A soft, dry hand touched the small of his back. "Devlin?"

"It's all right," he assured her over his shoulder, his gaze unseeing. He couldn't look at her. Not now. "Go back to sleep."

He should have known she wouldn't.

Out of the corner of his eye, he watched as she sat up, holding the sheet against her breasts in an innocent display of modesty. She had no problem baring herself in front of him during their lovemaking, but turned the demure miss at any other time. Usually he found it cute, but tonight he thought maybe it was smart of her to try to use whatever defenses she had against him.

"Did you have a nightmare?" she asked.

His heart lurched, even though it was a legitimate question. What else was she to think when he bolted up in bed screaming in the middle of the night? It didn't mean she knew his secret. Didn't mean anything.

"Yes," he replied honestly, surprising himself.

"Do you want to tell me about it?"

No. "I hurt you." Christ, why not just tell her the whole sordid tale then?

Her arm crossed his chest, the flat of her palm pressing against his breast, urging him back down onto the bed. He grimaced at the clammy sheets. Then she tugged on his arm. He rolled toward her, out of the dampness and into the warm haven of her arms.

He let her hold him, cradling him as a mother might a child. It felt good to be held this way. It felt safe.

"Everything is all right now," she assured him, stroking his back. "You have not hurt me."

Not yet. But he would if he told her the truth. He didn't think he could hide it from her for the rest of their lives. What hope did he have of winning her trust when he didn't trust her feelings for him? Yet had he any more hope of winning her if he told her the truth? What if it ruined any chance of her ever loving him? What if it drove her away? He couldn't lose her—not when he had just claimed her.

Every decision he'd ever made in his life—even the decision to kill that soldier—had been made quickly, without hesitation. His reflexes had been all that kept him alive on more than one occasion, but now, when it really mattered, he didn't know what to do. Didn't know what path to take.

Blythe fell back into slumber long before he even gave thought to it. There would be no more rest for him tonight, not when images of the sins of war flooded his mind, reminding him of the countless lives he'd taken.

He climbed out of bed, careful not to disturb his sleeping wife. Dressing quietly, as only a man once used to a life of stealth could, he crept from the room and down the stairs like a thief.

It was a nice night, cool for September but not so chilly that a man missed his gloves. He walked with his jacket open, letting the gentle breeze strip away the last vestiges of the dream that clung to him.

Varya's house, while in a good West End neighborhood, was still a fair distance from the pomp and circumstance of Mayfair. The streetlights were few and the surroundings became less and less inviting the farther he walked. That was good; it was what he wanted. He needed to go where the edges were less smooth, the people less polished. He needed to be someplace where who he was didn't matter.

He walked for another twenty minutes before he found it.

A small building, not fancy but not run-down either. Simple and sturdy, it was the only building with any lights burning within, aside from the local tavern. Perhaps he would find honest guidance here.

Other than his wedding, it had been a long time since Devlin had entered a church seeking solace. When he first joined

the army he had gone into every church he could find, praying for strength, for answers. It hadn't happened overnight,
but eventually he had stopped asking. On the day when his
friend Flynn had been killed, Devlin had given up church altogether. What was the sense in praying when no one was listening?

He'd seen a lot of things that made him wonder just what
God was thinking up there on His ivory throne. Maybe there
was a grand plan, or perhaps it was all a game. Whatever it
was, someone kept changing the rules.

But now the church and what little it offered was his last
resort. It was either here or the tavern, and he hadn't fallen
that low yet. He hoped to God he wouldn't. He hoped this
time, God was listening.

The door was unlocked. It creaked as he pushed it open.
The inside of the church was small and cozy, warmly lit by
several candles at the altar.

That he could see, there was no one else inside but him.

Slowly, he walked toward the front of the church, to the
first pew on the right. The floorboards groaned softly beneath
his weight, his boot heels falling with heavy thuds. The floor
dipped in places, worn by countless numbers of feet, but they
were highly polished, as were the pews, and the air was
sweet with lemon and beeswax. This little church was neither large nor grand, but it was loved and well looked after.
Odd how people often took better care of a building than of
themselves.

"Good evening, sir."

Were he the type to frighten easily, Devlin would have
jumped clear out of his skin at the soft greeting, but years of
living with every nerve on edge, his awareness heightened,
had taught him to remain perfectly still even if his heart was
in his throat.

He angled himself toward the voice. Out of the murky
shadows came an aged man, with a kind round face and a

thick head of snowy white hair. Folding his hands in front of his robes, he paused near the altar and favored Devlin with a smile.

"May I help you?"

He felt like a child caught snooping where he oughtn't. "I was walking. The door was unlocked."

The old priest continued to smile. "The house of God should not bar His children entrance."

"And so you get stuck playing butler all night?" One would think a priest of his age would have a nicer, more pleasant occupation.

The old man seemingly took no offense at his tasteless remark. "We usually have someone here at night in case a soul such as yourself wanders in, and to dissuade the vandals."

"If there are vandals, shouldn't you lock the door?" God might want His house open to His children, but what if those children pilfered the place?

Still the old priest smiled serenely. "What hindrance is a lock if someone wants in bad enough?"

It made a strange sort of sense, but it still seemed pretty stupid to Devlin. "But you could be hurt or killed."

The bushy white head shook slowly. "I am not afraid of pain or death."

Spoken like the truly naive. Devlin had fought with many boys who had such faith. It tended to disappear when one was slowly dying of a gut wound. Where had their God been then, when they begged and wept for the peace of death and it took so long to come?

He turned away from the priest's kind gaze. "You haven't seen enough of it."

"But you have. Far more than you should." The priest moved back into his line of vision and gestured to the front pew. "Come, sit. May I offer you a cup of tea?"

Devlin shook his head as he moved to sit. "No, thank you."

"Something stronger?"

Yes, that was what he really wanted. He sat down. "Tea is fine. Thank you."

The priest poured him a cup of tea from a service on a small table near the altar. Did he do this every night? Make tea and offer it to any lost soul who crossed the threshold?

A china cup appeared before him. It was white with yellow roses. There was a small crack running through one of the flowers.

"Tell me, what brings you here tonight? Most of the people I see are either unfortunates or drunkards. You are obviously neither."

No, he certainly wasn't a whore. Neither was he drunk, but he'd trade his soul for a little peace. What did that make him?

"I'm looking for forgiveness," he responded, taking the cup the priest offered. The tea was hot, and even though he didn't care much for the beverage, he drank it.

"Are you?" The priest sat down beside him. "You do not have the look of a man seeking absolution."

"Don't I?" What did he look like then?

The priest folded his arms across his chest. "You look like a man seeking damnation."

Devlin didn't respond immediately. The church was perfectly still, save for the sound of their breathing. The candles at the altar flickered and jumped. It was like this sometimes at night in the Peninsula—quiet darkness that made it all too easy to forget there was a war raging around you.

Or inside you, as the case might be.

"Perhaps I am," he answered finally, resting his forearms on his thighs, the cup small and fragile in his hands.

"If you want someone to punish you, then you have come to the wrong place. We do not do that here."

"What about Him?" Devlin spared the briefest of glances for the darkened church ceiling. "Doesn't He punish those who have sinned? Doesn't He send them to hell?"

The priest shook his head, that patient smile still curving

his lips. "Hell and punishment are the domain of Lucifer, my boy. God deals only in heaven and forgiveness."

That wasn't what he'd heard. "How do you know if He'll forgive you?"

Spreading his arms, the priest held his hands palms up in a gesture of supplication. "You only have to ask and it will be done."

"Just like that?" When had he become so cynical? He'd read the Bible as a child, he'd gone to church, he'd believed. When had he lost his faith?

Once again the old man folded his hands in the lap of his robe. "Just like that."

Devlin sipped his tea, staring straight ahead at the low oak wall that separated the pews from the front of the church. "What if you don't deserve to be forgiven?"

"Everyone deserves forgiveness."

It was all he could do not to snort. "Even someone who has taken life?"

The priest nodded. "Even him."

If it was truly that easy, Devlin would have earned his absolution long ago. How many times had he begged for God to forgive him? How many times had that forgiveness been denied? He still felt the same, still felt the weight pulling at his soul.

"How long were you a soldier, my boy?"

Was it that obvious? "More than ten years, sir." Closer to twelve.

"Ten years." The priest shook his head again. "You must have been a child."

Devlin shrugged. "I was old enough."

A smile colored the kind tone. "You must have seen some horrible things."

Oh he was so tired of people saying that! As though all the things he'd seen and survived somehow made up for everything else. They didn't. They were just a convenient excuse for those who couldn't face their past.

"I've done some horrible things."

"For your king and country." More kindness, the benefit of the doubt from a man who didn't know him from Adam.

"For my life." He turned his head to regard the priest. "You would be surprised at what a man will do to stay alive, Father."

"You think me a naive old fool," the priest admonished with that damn serene smile. "You think I spend all my time shut up in this old church untouched by the real world."

"I didn't say that." No, but he had thought it. He drained his cup.

"Young man, I have seen things that have broken my heart, curdled my blood, and made me question my faith on more than one occasion. But He always forgives me and He always restores my hope. All I have to do is look for it."

Devlin's defenses immediately went up. "I did ask. I did look. It never came."

"Oh, it came." The priest patted his shoulder. "You just did not notice."

Devlin scowled. "How could I have not noticed? I don't *feel* forgiven."

"That is because it is not His forgiveness you seek."

He was coming to despise that all-knowing, kindly mocking voice. "Whose then? Yours? King George's? Tell me who and I'll damn well seek it."

The old man seemed not even to notice his blasphemy. "Getting God's forgiveness is easy. It is forgiving yourself that is the true challenge."

"Myself?"

The priest stood, plucking Devlin's empty cup from his hands as he did so. "Your own forgiveness is all you wait upon. How much longer will you make yourself suffer before you grant it?"

Devlin only stared at the old man as he set the cup next to

the pot. He hadn't forgiven himself; the priest was right. He didn't know if it was possible for him to do so now.

"You had better get yourself home, my boy," the priest said as Devlin rose. "Your wife will be missing you."

Devlin froze. "How did you know I have a wife?"

Again the priest smiled. "The other ones usually end up at the tavern rather than here. Go home, son. Forgive yourself. Be happy. Sleep."

Not daring to take his gaze off the spooky old man, for fear he might prove to be an apparition or a dream of some kind, Devlin backed into the aisle.

"Thank you for the tea."

The priest nodded. "Thank you for the company."

Devlin put a few more pews between them before finally turning his back. When he stepped out into the night it seemed oddly cold, as though the temperature had dropped drastically since he'd stepped inside. It seemed darker as well, even though he knew dawn could be only a few hours off.

He walked quickly, hailing a hack as soon as he stumbled upon one. He was in a hurry to get home and didn't relish making the walk back, not when he had wandered so far.

Blythe was still sleeping when he entered their room. She rolled onto her back, a soft snore escaping her lips as his boots fell to the floor with a thump that made him wince. Still, she did not wake.

He sat down in the chair by the window and took the Baker from its case. He was just about to start cleaning it when his wife spoke.

"Are you all right?"

Was he? "I'm fine. Go back to sleep."

"Only if you come back to bed too."

He glanced down at the rifle in his hands. It had been there so often for him in the past, it didn't feel right to walk away from it now, but there was a real person waiting to give him comfort, a woman who had already changed his life in a thousand immeasurable ways.

The decision was surprisingly easy to make. He put the Baker away and stood. Quickly, he stripped down to the skin and slipped into bed beside Blythe's warmth. At least the sheets didn't feel damp anymore.

Blythe shifted toward him, rolling onto her side and curving against him. "You are cold," she mumbled, draping her arm over him regardless.

"Sorry," he whispered.

He allowed her to snuggle against him, all heat and soft skin. The feel of her in his arms and the sound of her even breathing gently lulled him into slumber. His last thought before drifting off to sleep was to ask whether he could forgive himself for his sins. The answer was simple.

Not if those sins cost him Blythe, he couldn't. He'd never forgive himself for that.

Chapter 14

Blythe didn't know if the dream Devlin had the night before was to blame or if something else had happened. All she knew was that the next morning, her husband was even quieter than usual. He seemed to have withdrawn further into himself, as though trying to work through some great internal struggle. A struggle that she was not privy to, even though she was his wife.

At least he kissed her before leaving the house after breakfast. He said he had to go see Brahm and she didn't ask why, even though she wanted to. He would tell her when he was ready. She had to trust in that.

Where had he gone last night? What had happened to him while he was out? Was this secret outing the reason for the change in his behavior? He hadn't told her where he'd gone, and when she asked he'd been deliberately vague. She trusted him. She thought he trusted her as well, so why keep his whereabouts the night before hidden?

Perhaps it was too early to expect him to divulge his secrets. Did she not have things she kept from him? No, not really. She wasn't exactly a secretive kind of person. She had a tendency to let everything out rather than hold it inside for too long.

Which was why she was very frightened of this growing intimacy with Devlin. Soon she was going to blurt out her feelings, and then she would have to wait in horrible silence for his reply. She could only hope that when the time came he would return her sentiments. Having her heart rejected by another man would be just too awful, especially now that she was beginning to discover what love really was.

So she would keep those feelings to herself and wait until she had a better understanding of Devlin's emotions before blurting them out. She could not bear having her love tossed back in her face again. It would be even more painful and humiliating than when Carny rejected her.

It seemed the height of irony when at that moment, the housekeeper announced that the man responsible for her caution had come to call.

Blythe found him in the drawing room, looking entirely too comfortable on one of Varya's plushly padded sofas. He was the picture of perfect gentlemanly elegance—smoothly shaven, impeccably dressed, his hair immaculately groomed. At one time she would have sighed in rapture at the sight of him; now she simply smiled. The smile wasn't for his benefit either; it was because of the realization that she actually liked her men—her *man*—a lot less polished.

"It is a little early for you, is it not?" she inquired with a smile as she entered the room.

Carny stood, his gray coat and buff pantaloons a perfect complement to the pale blue and cream decor. He belonged in such a setting, with the delicate French furniture, gilt picture frames, and elaborate Axminster carpet.

"I confess I dragged myself from slumber this morning with the express purpose of calling on you."

Now that she drew closer, she could see the lines of fatigue on his face, but they were from more than simply rising early. Carny looked tired and weary—bone weary.

"A compliment indeed," she replied easily, knowing how he liked his sleep. "Please sit. I shall ring for tea. You look as though you could use a cup." Not the most polite of greetings, she knew, but if she couldn't be so blunt with Carny she might as well not speak at all.

He reclaimed his seat on the sofa. He was so sure of himself. Her Devlin always seemed afraid of breaking such spindly furniture.

Her Devlin.

Seating herself on a cream brocade chair on the opposite side of the low tea table, Blythe made small talk until their refreshment arrived. Once the door had shut behind the maid she poured them each a cup of tea and fixed her companion with a direct gaze.

"Why are you here so early, Carny?" She kept her tone soft, not bothering to mask her concern. He might have broken her heart once, but even that couldn't change the fact that beneath it all, Blythe still cared about him as one friend cares for another.

He looked mildly affronted. "There is no law against paying a friend a morning call, is there?"

"In the entirety of our acquaintance, I've scarcely seen you twice before ten in the morning. What is it?"

He stared at her strangely, a kind of wonder in his expression that both pleased and alarmed her. "Marriage agrees with you, Blythe. You've the look of a happy woman."

A well-pleasured one, he meant. Blythe fought a blush. "I am happy. Devlin is everything I have ever wanted."

Carny's smile was rueful. "Certainly much better than what you could have ended up with."

"Perhaps," she replied, gracing him with a similar smile. "Carny, we have been through a rough two years, but I would like to think we can put that behind us and be the friends we once were."

He nodded. "I would like that."

Setting her cup and saucer on the table, Blythe leaned forward, her hands folded on her knees. "Then tell me what it is that is distressing you. You have not been yourself of late."

"It—" He stopped and took a large swallow from his cup. His countenance was that of a scared man. "It is my marriage."

"Your marriage?" Blythe knew from Teresa that she and Carny were having some troubles, but she assumed they had worked themselves out. If Carny was prepared to discuss them, however, they were much, much more serious than Blythe had first believed, and obviously had not been solved.

He also set his cup on the table. He looked so tired, so old. "Teresa has been acting so strangely."

Did she leave bed in the middle of the night and come back cold and smelling of coal smoke and outdoors as Devlin had? Did she harbor more trust for a rifle than Carny? Blythe was willing to bet the answer was no.

"Strangely how?" She seemed well enough to Blythe, her unhappiness aside.

Carny sighed and ran a hand through his thick blond hair. "One minute she is happy, the next she is crying. She is always on the verge of the vexation."

Well, that didn't sound all that odd. Blythe spent several days out of each month feeling much the same herself.

"She has become obsessed with having a child," he continued, obvious worry in his eyes. "I try to tell her it will be all right, that it doesn't matter if we have to wait—it doesn't matter if it happens at all—but she gets so *upset*."

This wasn't something Blythe should be hearing. This was a personal matter between husband and wife, and yet she couldn't turn Carny away when he so obviously needed someone to listen.

"Perhaps she takes your words as disinterestedness," she suggested, knowing full well that was how Teresa took her husband's attitude. "Perhaps she needs to hear how you feel about having a child; perhaps she needs you to be upset as well."

He raised a brow. "I never thought of that."

"*Are* you upset as well?"

A dry chuckle escaped his lips. "Of course I am. What man does not wish for a son, a child of his own? I want a child very much, but I do not want Teresa to think I blame her."

It was Blythe's turn to arch a brow. "Do you?"

He glanced away. "I blame myself."

"Must either of you be to blame? Sometimes these things just happen." Vaguely, she wondered about Devlin and herself. Would they have children? The thought warmed her almost as much as it frightened her. That was why she had approached Varya for ways of preventing pregnancy. It wasn't that she didn't want children; she just wasn't ready yet. She wanted to give herself and Devlin time to get to know each other before they started a family.

"The problem must lie with one of us," Carny argued with a petulant tone. "One of us is defective."

Blythe refilled both their cups, shooting him a sharp glance as she did so. "No wonder Teresa is vexed! Defective, indeed. One is not defined by one's ability to produce offspring, Carny. If we were, three quarters of England would be a sorry lot."

He chuckled at that. "I knew coming to see you would make me feel better." He raised his cup. "You are delightfully blunt, my friend."

She stirred her tea. "Perhaps what you and Teresa need to do is just stop worrying about it so much. Think of other things. Take a trip abroad, do something you both will enjoy."

"Perhaps you are right. And what are you going to do?" He relaxed into the sofa, lazily crossing his leg. "Are you and Dev ever going to take a wedding trip?"

Blythe had forgotten how good Carny was at changing the subject when he wanted to be. "Perhaps someday. Once the renovations are finished we are going to return to Rosewood. That is more than enough for me. I do not care if we ever leave Devonshire."

Carny smiled warmly. "I can see Devlin wanting to put down some roots, and you—you have never once wanted to lift yours. The two of you will never come to town, will you?"

"Not if we do not have to, no."

He gestured at her with his cup. "I will expect weekly reports."

Blythe grinned. "Even if they are about nothing more interesting than the crops and the movement of the tides?"

"Even if."

"Then you shall have them." She took a drink. "And I will expect you and Teresa to keep me informed of all the good gossip."

They made small talk for the remainder of their visit until Carny announced that he had to be on his way.

"Thank you so much for listening, dear Blythe," he said as she walked him to the door. "I believe I shall take your advice and try to keep my wife's mind occupied with other matters."

"I wish you success."

He kissed her cheek before taking his hat and gloves from Piotr, Varya's manservant, and took his leave. Blythe watched him go with a light heart. It was nice to have Carny as her friend again. She had forgotten how much she missed him. And thank heaven he was more himself again. His own marital strife was undoubtedly the cause behind some of his strange behavior where she and Devlin were concerned. She hoped he and Teresa would work everything out between them.

Blythe wasn't back in the drawing room ten minutes before Piotr announced another caller. It was Teresa.

"You had better bring more tea please, Piotr," Blythe said

with a sigh as she sank down onto the sofa. "I have a feeling we're going to need it."

She also had a feeling that she was about to become better acquainted with the Carnover marriage than she wanted to be.

It was going to be a long morning.

"Someone needs to pound some sense into that head of yours."

Devlin started at his brother's exasperated tone. What the devil had gotten into Brahm?

"It is not like you to wallow in self-pity, Dev." Brahm thumped his cane on the carpet for emphasis. "That is my domain."

"I am *not* wallowing."

"Christ, you make *me* want to drink! You cannot possibly be so stupid that you do not realize what you are doing."

Devlin had no idea what he was doing, but he didn't want Brahm to know that. He also didn't like knowing he made his brother want to get foxed. He shrugged. There was nothing he could say that Brahm wouldn't find fault with.

"It was two years ago." Brahm rose to his feet, and for one fearful second, Devlin thought his brother was going to head for the liquor cabinet.

Brahm began pacing a small section of the drawing room carpet instead. His lame leg dragged slightly. "For years prior to that day you killed many men from a distance."

Devlin's stomach roiled. How thick was the blood on his hands? Too thick to be forgiven, unless the old priest was right. "Do not remind me."

His brother paused. "I do not have to remind you. You never let yourself forget. Yes, you killed men, other soldiers like yourself, who knew very well there was a chance they might die. If you had not killed them, they might very well have killed you."

"That might have been for the best."

Brahm's cane thwacked against his leg—hard. A jolt of pain ran all the way up to Devlin's hip. "Do not say such things! What would your wife say if she heard you speak such nonsense! Would you rather be dead than have her?"

No. He'd rather live with the guilt of all the blood he'd spilled than spend one day without Blythe's light shining upon him.

He rubbed his leg where his brother had hit it, but he wouldn't let Brahm know he was right. "What I did was wrong."

Brahm's scowl was unsympathetic. "You did what you have always done—what you had to do. Now I dearly wish you would stop whining about it! Everyone has done things they regret, little brother. It is part of living."

"That's easy for you to say. You've never killed anyone!"

Brahm fixed him with a dark and hard gaze. "You have no idea what I have done. You ran away for ten years, remember?"

Devlin's temper sparked, and he understood how Blythe must have felt when he accused her of hiding in the country. "I did not run away. I left a place where I was not wanted in the first place."

A scowl creased Brahm's brow. "Not wanted? You truly are an idiot if you believe that. Every day you were gone I feared the letter that would tell us of your death. Every night I prayed for you."

"Every night you weren't passed out drunk, you mean." Devlin hadn't meant to sound so bitter, but the words came out of their own accord. Hell, maybe he had run away.

Brahm did not recoil, even though he must have been stung. His rugged features were tight with emotion. "Do not think you were not wanted. You were wanted every damn day."

Devlin could ask if his parents wanted him, but that wasn't what he had come to discuss, and he didn't want this to grow into a fight between him and Brahm. He didn't like arguing with Brahm.

"Do you really think I pity myself?"

Brahm nodded. "I know self-pity when I see it. The priest was right. You need to forgive yourself. No one else can do it for you."

Had Brahm forgiven himself for the part he played in their father's death? Had he forgiven himself for all the offenses he'd committed while foxed that earned him the disdain of the *ton*?

"How do I do that?" He couldn't keep the desperation from his voice. "How do I make it all right?"

"It may never be all right," Brahm replied, sitting down again. "But you can learn to accept it. I think the first step would be telling Blythe."

Devlin shook his head. "I can't do that. Not yet."

"Then when?"

He stared hard at the toes of his scuffed Hessians. "I don't know."

"If you do not do it now, you never will. The longer you wait, the harder it will be to tell her the truth."

Devlin looked up, meeting his brother's calm gaze. "What if she leaves me?" There it was, the fear that gnawed at his insides. True, she would be bound to him forever by the marriage, but he could no longer fool himself into thinking that would be good enough. He did not want Blythe to be his wife in name only.

"If she leaves you then she's not the woman for you," Brahm replied softly. "Do you really think she would abandon you?"

After spending his entire life feeling as though he were alone in the world, Devlin was terrified of being left that way again, especially by Blythe. She brightened his life. She made him smile. Losing her would be worse than any torture he could ever endure. He would never forgive himself if he lost her, and if she left because of what he had done, then he would know he truly was the monster he feared he was.

Murderer. Killer. Never once when he'd pulled the trigger had he given thought to the man the shot tore through. Not until that fateful day, years after firing his first volley, had he realized just what it was he had become. He killed. It had become his job, his life. He was good at it.

Hell, a part of him had taken pride in it.

And he felt nothing when he did it, only the knowledge that he would kill again if he had to in order to save himself and Carny. He shouldn't have looked in the dying man's eyes. He shouldn't have watched the light fade.

But he had and he simply could not forget it.

"You have to face it, Dev. You know what you have to do. You have to tell her. It is the only way you can ever begin to forgive yourself. You do not believe what I tell you, so perhaps you will believe the woman you love."

"I don't love her."

Brahm laughed. It wasn't a cruel sound, but it cut all the same. "You truly are an idiot. If you did not love her, it would not matter what she thought of you."

Good Lord, was it true? Was love that simple? No. It couldn't be.

His fingers trembled as he ran them through his hair. He wouldn't think of love. "I don't understand how they can call me a hero, knowing that I've killed so many."

Brahm shook his head. "Because you were one of the many men who kept Bonaparte from taking over the world, and they are thankful for it."

Devlin had never thought of it like that before. When he had joined the army it had been with the foolishly naive notion that he was fighting for England, that he was protecting these emerald shores. But in truth he had run off hoping to earn the respect and love of his family—his parents. And both of them died without his ever hearing a word of praise. Perhaps if he had told his father what had happened at Waterloo, he might have said something that could relieve Devlin's guilt, but he hadn't told his father, because he'd been as afraid of his disapproval as he was of Blythe's.

"You must end this," Brahm said, stretching his lame leg out in front of him. "I cannot bear to hear it anymore, and you need to let go of it and get on with your life. It was two years ago, Devlin. *Two years.*"

A long time. Yet sometimes it was as clear as yesterday. What good did it possibly serve to keep thinking of it? He was sorry for it. If he could he would change it, but he couldn't. Surely that regret, the sorrow he would take to his grave, was enough penance?

But Brahm was right. The only way he could truly be certain that he deserved forgiveness was to tell Blythe. She was so good, so pure; if she forgave him then surely he could forgive himself.

And if she didn't . . .

Perhaps he would wait just a little while longer to tell her.

He met his brother's gaze. "Do I really make you want to drink?"

Brahm smiled faintly. "If the post is late I want to drink. Do not take it as a personal affront."

His humor did little to soothe Devlin's fears. "But you don't give in, do you?"

Brahm massaged his upper thigh, where the bone in his leg had been broken in the carriage accident that killed their father. "No. I want to, but I do not. If I have one I will not stop."

Drinking was a part of life for gentlemen of the upper ranks, and it was common for many said gentlemen to drink until they passed out. For Brahm, however, drinking was more a compulsion than a pasttime, and when he was deep in his cups, he became a different person. A person Devlin didn't like very much. That he had pissed in a punch bowl was a great joke among some members of the *ton,* even among their family, but it was just one of many incidents that had happened while Brahm was foxed that had led to his social ostracization.

"But I do not want to talk about me," Brahm said as he once again rose to his feet. "Walk in the garden with me and tell me all your plans for your new home. I am looking forward to visiting."

In the garden they talked some of family, of North and Wynthrope. They even talked a bit about their mother and father, and how difficult it was to believe the old man was really gone, especially when he had it written into his will that he did not want his sons walking about in black for a year in his memory. Without traditional mourning to continually remind them, it sometimes seemed as though he might stumble upon them at any moment.

They walked until the ache in Brahm's leg would allow him to walk no more and then Devlin took his leave. He sauntered out to the stables and hoisted himself up onto Flynn's back, setting off into the misty afternoon.

He hadn't gotten very far when a pretty little curricle pulled by matched blacks came up alongside him.

"Ryland, is that you?"

Turning his head at the familiar voice, Devlin was surprised to see that one of the curricle's occupants was James Bamber, a young man he had served with. He certainly had changed. The last time Devlin had seen Bamber he'd been dirty, thin, and covered in blood. Now he looked the part of a very respectable gentleman. He was obviously doing well for himself if the lovely blond sitting next to him was any indication.

"How are you, Bamber?"

"Better now that I've seen you!" the young man enthused as they pulled over to the edge of the street to let traffic pass them. "I wonder if I might introduce you to my betrothed, Miss Anna Watson."

Devlin tipped his hat to the dimpling young girl. "Miss Watson."

Bamber turned to his fiancée. "Ryland saved my life, dearest. If not for him I would have died a lonely death in Spain."

Miss Watson looked horrified. Devlin didn't blame her. "When did I save your life?"

Bamber turned to face him. "Do you not remember? We were sent into that old church to find a priest for Flynn, and a Frenchie tried to shoot me as we left. If you had not been so quick to fire first he would have killed me for certain."

Now Devlin did remember. It had been the day Flynn died. They had gone looking for a priest to give him the last rites he insisted on having. He hadn't shot the French soldier for Bamber, he had done it for Flynn, so they could get the priest back to him. Bamber didn't need to know that.

"How awful!" Miss Watson was a decidedly delicate shade of pale. Living with Blythe had spoiled him. He had forgotten just how fragile some females were. How did Bamber stand it? The girl looked as though she might faint at any moment.

Bamber took her gloved hand. "Forgive me, my dear. I did not mean to discomfit you with talk of violence."

"It is not the violence that disturbs me," Miss Watson replied, some color returning to her cheeks beneath the wide brim of her bonnet. "It is the idea that you almost died. What would I do without you?"

Such blatant sentimental talk normally would have made Devlin shift uncomfortably in the saddle, but it made him think of what Brahm had said about people thinking him a hero because he'd protected them and England, that some people were glad he had done all the things he did in the name of Wellington and King George. If he hadn't gone to war, Devlin himself never would have known men such as Patrick Flynn, and that had certainly been worth some of the bloodshed.

Perhaps when he started dwelling on all the awfulness

he'd seen he would be wise to remember the many good things he'd done as well. If not for him, Bamber would not have his Miss Watson. If not for him, Carny would never have found Teresa, and Blythe would still be mourning her lost love, thinking he had been the man for her. Devlin might never have met her, might never have won her.

"Thank you, Mr. Ryland."

Devlin's attention snapped back to young Miss Watson. She was staring at him as though he were larger than life—a hero—and for the first time, he didn't mind. He understood what his actions meant to this girl. If he met someone who had prevented Blythe from being killed, he would feel the same way, just as blessed and grateful.

He didn't know what to say when faced with such sentiment. Telling her she was welcome would seem trite.

"And God bless you," she added, reaching out to touch his arm.

It was then that Devlin realized God already had.

It was mid-afternoon before Devlin returned to the town house. Blythe was waiting for him in the parlor, a simple but ample luncheon prepared for them to share.

"How did you know I'd be hungry?" her husband demanded as he took her in a tight embrace.

"You are always hungry," she replied with a laugh, wrapping her arms around his neck. It no longer mattered that he had been away so long. All that mattered was that the burden he had carried with him that morning seemed to be gone. The dark weight in his eyes had lifted, leaving behind the intimate glow that made her feel so warm inside.

He nuzzled her neck, the sharp rasp of his stubble abrading her jaw. "Hungry for you."

Squealing, Blythe squirmed in his arms. Her neck was so ticklish, it was maddening to have him torment it so. Laughing, she tried to push him away, her shoulder squeezing up to her ear. Unfortunately, that only served to trap him even more tightly in the crook of her neck.

Finally, after sending what felt like a million shivers up and down her spine, he released her, shrugging out of his dark gray jacket as he walked toward the table she'd had prepared for them.

His jacket landed on a nearby chair in a crumpled heap. Blythe knew of several gentlemen—Carny was no doubt one of them—who would cringe at such a sight. But her unrefined husband wasn't finished. He rolled his shirt-sleeves up around his elbows, revealing strong, hairy forearms. She loved his arms—the tan of his skin, the soft black hair, even the knobby bone of his wrist that stuck out.

She was surprised he didn't strip off his cravat as well. He hated the feel of anything tight around his neck. Obviously he had tied his cravat loosely enough to suit him that morning. No wonder he didn't have a valet; he'd no doubt drive the man to distraction.

"How was Brahm?" she asked as he pulled out her chair for her. Unrefined he might be, but unmannerly he was not.

"Fine." He rounded the table to the other chair. "He sends his regards and wants us to come for dinner one night later in the week."

She offered him a platter of cold ham. "That would be lovely."

"How was your morning?" He speared a slab of meat with a fork and dropped it on his plate, going back for more. "Did you have any callers?"

"Actually, I did." She had no idea how he would react to Carny's visit, given his recent apprehension where his friend was concerned, but she wasn't about to start keeping secrets from him. "Carny came by."

Devlin barely glanced up from the bowl of boiled potatoes before offering it to her. "He did? Was he looking for me?"

It was an innocent enough question, but there was just the

slightest bit of an edge to it—an edge that tingled low in Blythe's spine, reminding her that while he was so sweet and gentle with her, her husband was a man who had kept himself alive by his sheer strength and determination. He was a fighter by nature.

That he would fight for her was a certainty—one that appealed to a decidedly feminine and primitive part of her nature.

"No. He . . . he was looking for me."

He nodded, seemingly nonchalant save for the ticking in his jaw. "What did he want?"

"Advice."

He moved on to the salads. Still he did not look at her. "On?"

Helping herself to the potatoes, Blythe sighed. "He and Teresa have been having some difficulties lately. He thought perhaps I might help him decipher what is bothering her."

Devlin finally glanced up, a frown drawing his brows together. "Why would he think you could help with that?"

Wasn't it obvious? "Because I am a woman."

Her husband snorted, mashing his potatoes violently with his fork. His mouth curved dubiously into what could only be described as a kind of sneer, although it didn't seem the least bit malicious. "You're a completely different sort of woman than Teresa."

That could be taken as either an insult or a compliment. Blythe decided on the latter. Knowing Devlin, that was how it was meant. "I am still a woman. We are very much alike under the skin."

He pinned her with his obsidian gaze. "I've never met a woman like you, below the skin or on it."

She froze with a bite of ham halfway to her mouth. It was impossible to eat with her ribs squeezing her stomach as they were. She lowered her fork. "How do you know just what to say to break my heart?"

He looked genuinely alarmed as he froze in the middle of buttering a slab of bread. "I'd never hurt you."

Her blood tingled warmly in her veins. "It is not a bad hurt."

Devlin smiled, and it was as though someone had lit a candle within the dark depths of his eyes. How she loved his eyes! So black she could get lost in them, and with lashes so thick any woman would envy them.

"What advice did you give your lovesick swain?" he asked, biting into his bread.

Blythe rolled her eyes and took a sip of her wine. "I told him to spend more time with Teresa and to talk of other things than having children."

"Ah." A wide grin split across Devlin's face as he cut a bite of ham and shoved it into his mouth. "Carny's pistol's not firing as it ought, eh?"

Heat rushed to Blythe's cheeks. It was one thing when Devlin talked in such a manner in their bedroom, and it was one thing when he did it in the middle of the day, but it was quite another when he did it in regard to Carny!

She took a bite of her own lunch, chewed and swallowed. "I do not want to think about Carny's 'pistol'!"

His grin faded a bit as he tore a chunk off his slice of bread, but his eyes still sparkled. "I don't want you thinking about it either. My trigger should be the only one that concerns you."

"If you ever want me to squeeze it again, you'll stop talking about it or anyone else's this instant!"

Some men would have been shocked, but Devlin only laughed. "If you weren't so far away I'd kiss that beautiful, vulgar mouth of yours."

Flushed, Blythe took another sip of wine. "I never used to be vulgar at all before I met you."

His gaze locked with hers over the table. He grinned. "You don't know what vulgar is."

She arched both brows. Now this was intriguing. Intriguing and decidedly dangerous for someone as ignorant as she. "No?"

"No." The light in his eyes brightened. "But if you're very good, after luncheon I'll show you."

That was all he had to do, simply make the suggestion of something carnal and she practically melted right into her chair. It was far from proper, but she refused to think that anything that felt so right could possibly be wrong.

She needed to change the subject before she cleared all the dishes off the table with one swipe and offered herself up as the main course.

"Anyway, Teresa came by after Carny left and I discussed things with her as well—I did not tell her about her husband's visit, though. However, I think if both of them take my advice, I do not expect to see either of them for some time."

Devlin chewed and swallowed. "Good. We're newly married, for God's sake. You have better things to do with your time than hold Carny's or Teresa's hand."

She knew it was asking for trouble but she couldn't help it. "Such as?"

His lips curved. "Such as taking care of me when I'm cocked and loaded."

A tremor shook her entire body. To blazes with luncheon. The parlor door was locked.

"Mr. Ryland, sir?" she said, rising from her chair, her plate of food forgotten.

He stood as well. "Yes, my lady?"

She grabbed him by the waistcoat. "I think you are due for a little target practice."

Chapter 15

Blythe had competition for her husband's devotion, someone else whom Devlin trusted with his innermost secrets. It wasn't her he turned to whenever he had something on his mind.

It was that blasted Baker rifle.

How much attention did a gun need? And why did he keep it around with him when the war had ended more than two years ago? It was almost as though it was his lucky charm, his talisman—his one link to a past he couldn't let go of. Every day he took the time to clean it, even though nothing had been done to dirty it in any way.

"It is enough to make a wife jealous," she informed him as he sat once again, pampering the gun as though it were an exquisite treasure. He stroked the barrel with hands that stroked her just as gently, touched the scarred wood as though every mark held a memory of its own.

"What is?" he asked, oh so innocently.

It was early morning. She was still abed while he sat by one of the windows, clad in nothing more than his trousers, the Baker in his hands and its oils and clothes within reach.

"The way you fuss over it, one would think it was a living being rather than a piece of wood and metal."

He frowned. "The Baker?"

Blythe pushed herself up on the pillows, tucking the blankets beneath her arms. "You spend more time with it than you do with me." She meant it to be teasing, but it came out a little more sharply than she intended.

His frown turned into a full-fledged scowl, but he didn't stop polishing. "Don't be ridiculous. It's a gun. You're my wife."

She'd seen rabid fox hunters pay less attention to their rifles. Some men paid less attention to their children, even their horses, than Devlin paid to the Baker. "It is not just a gun, it is your mistress."

He stared at her as though he thought her completely mad. "My mistress."

She hadn't even realized she resented the rifle so much until that moment. "Yes. Whenever there is something vexing you, you run straight to it when I wish you would confide in me."

His jaw slackened as his eyes widened. "That's not true."

"It is true!" She slapped her hand down on the bed beside her in frustration, her other hand catching the sheet as it threatened to slip below her breasts. "For the past few days you have practically doted on it! The only time you spend with me is at meals or in bed." Oh damn, she was going to cry. She hated crying. It was so missish.

But it was true. At least in Devon they had spent time riding or discussing Rosewood; now it seemed they hardly ever did that. Lord, she'd be happy if he took her to a party or to the theater, even to Tattersall's, but no.

Setting the rifle aside, Devlin stood, padding across the carpet toward her with his trousers riding low on his hips and his hair mussed. He was so rough-looking, so lanky and strong. Sometimes he seemed so old, not in body but in spirit.

He was only thirty years old, younger than Carny was when she first fell in love with him. Carny seemed like a boy next to Devlin, and yet there was a vulnerability to her husband that she had never seen in another living soul. He was wounded deep inside, and something wouldn't let it scar over.

And it was something that only he and the Baker knew the truth about. That's what bothered her the most.

Blythe withdrew as he sat beside her, but he caught her arm, preventing her from going very far.

"If you want my attention, all you have to do is ask," he informed her, his voice little more than a scratchy whisper.

His fingers had gun oil on them. She yanked at her arm, trying to free it. It was like touching her when he smelled of another woman's perfume, she reacted so strongly to it. He wouldn't let go.

"I should not have to ask." How whiny she sounded! If she were standing she would have surely stomped her foot.

He smiled patiently. "No, you shouldn't, but sometimes you'll have to. I cannot see inside your mind, no matter how much I might like to."

Her gaze snapped to his. "*My* mind? I am not the one who hides parts of myself, Devlin. I am not the one keeping secrets."

Tilting his head, his smile faded. "You think I'm keeping secrets from you?"

"I know you are."

She wanted him to argue, wanted him to prove to her that he wasn't keeping things from her, he just liked spending time alone, cleaning his gun. He didn't argue, though. He simply looked away.

"I thought you trusted me." Her voice trembled with the force of holding back her tears.

He rubbed his thumb along her upper arm. "I do."

She caught his hand. "Then tell me what it is that weighs upon you so."

"I can't."

Tears beaded on Blythe's lashes, threatening to spill onto her cheeks. "Why not?"

He looked up, his own eyes glistening. Her big, brave soldier was on the verge of tears. A drop of warm, salty wetness dropped onto her lips.

"I'm afraid," he whispered, squeezing her fingers.

"Afraid of what?"

"Of losing you."

It was as if two giant hands reached into her chest, seized her heart, and wrung it for all it was worth, so acute was the pain in her breast.

She touched his cheek, feeling the scratch of his beard beneath her fingertips. "You will never lose me."

"I might," he insisted, his stark gaze locked with hers, "if I tell you the truth."

"You might if you do not tell me the truth." It wasn't a threat, just a fact.

She could almost see him withdraw in defiance. Good Lord, what had happened to him?

"Devlin." She grasped his jaw in her hand, forcing him to look at her. "What is it?"

He was quiet. Too quiet. It was as though even his breathing had stilled. His eyes drifted closed, and for a moment—a stupid, irrational moment—it seemed as though he had simply up and died. It scared her to the point of trembling. Then she felt the barest brush of breath across the hand holding his face.

She released him, and after a few seconds, he finally spoke, "Have you ever done something that you wish you could go back in time and change?"

"No." At one time she would have said she regretted telling Carny she loved him, but now that didn't seem like such an awful regret. It was foolish and unfortunate, but she really hadn't suffered for it. Marrying him would have proven to be a much more serious mistake.

A bitter snort of laughter escaped him. "Of course you haven't. You wouldn't be my Blythe if you had."

She wasn't certain, but she was fairly convinced that was a compliment. He seemed to have this notion that she was innocent and full of light. She didn't feel it, but if he liked it, she wasn't going to argue with him.

"No matter what you have done, it will not change how I feel about you." Perhaps it was naive of her to cling to such a conviction, but she couldn't help it. She knew in her heart that he could never disappoint her unless she set standards for him that she had no business setting.

He stared at her, some of the color draining from his face. His expression was far from encouraging, but there was very little point in turning back when she had come this far. She hoped this wouldn't become her moment that she would go back in time to change.

"I love you, Devlin." What release to finally say the words! In her heart she knew she had been wanting to say them for a long time—longer than was possible. It was foolish, but looking back, it seemed as though she had fallen in love with him that first day in the stables, when he had stood with her as she patted Flynn. It hadn't taken long for her to fall, and she was tired of hiding it for fear of his reaction.

"Don't say that." He jerked to his feet. "Don't tell me that."

Blythe watched, wide-eyed, as he staggered toward the window. "Why not? It is true." Oh God, he didn't feel the same way about her. Was that why he didn't want to hear her declaration?

Bracing an arm against the window frame, he rested his head upon it. "Because you may very well want to take it back when you learn the truth, and I won't want to let you."

Despite his ominous tone, Blythe warmed at his words. He wanted her to love him, he had just said as much.

"I love you," she repeated.

There was real anger in his expression as his head whipped up. "Stop saying that."

"I will not." He was fierce and more than a little frightening when he was angry, but she refused to be scared of him. She had nothing to fear from him—not physically. And she would not fear him emotionally either. She couldn't, not if she ever wanted to win his love.

"I love you. Nothing you say can change that."

This time his laughter rang with defeat as he turned to face her. Despair, stark and unrestrained, harshened his features.

"No? I killed a man, Blythe. I murdered him. I stuck a knife in him and took his life even as he begged me not to. What do you say to that?"

That was it? That was his big secret? There was no other woman, no life-threatening illness? He had her imagining the worst, and *this* was what he finally revealed? He had taken a life. Hadn't he taken many during the war? She might not be the most intelligent of women, and perhaps she didn't know Devlin as well as she would like to, but she knew him well enough to be certain that if he had killed a man, there was a good reason for it.

She stared at him, uncertain whether to kiss him or kick him. "You were a soldier, Devlin. I imagine you killed more than one man." True, it wasn't a pleasant thought, but it wasn't new to her. Long ago she had accepted that her brother and her one-time fiancé had also taken lives for the glory of England; it wasn't that upsetting to her.

"Did you hear me?" He moved away from the window, coming toward her once again. "I said I killed a man."

She nodded. "You are going to have to tell me all the sordid details if you want me to damn you for it."

He pinched the bridge of his nose with his thumb and forefinger, squeezing his eyes shut as he did so. Then he sank into the chair he had occupied earlier. Blythe tried not to take it personally. Obviously he needed a little distance between them right now. At least he didn't pick up that blasted gun.

"It was at Waterloo," he said after a moment's silence.

Waterloo. Was he joking? How many men had died during that battle? For that matter, how many men had tried to kill Devlin that same day? That he lived to talk about it was a miracle in itself. Still, she was sensible enough to keep that thought to herself and simply allow him to tell his story.

"It was late in the battle. I had been among those hidden in the hills to pick off the French as they came into view earlier in the day, but by this time I was elsewhere on the field, doing my damnedest to stay alive."

She could have said how grateful she was for that, but he wouldn't hear her. He had the faraway look of a man reliving a painful memory.

"It's funny," he continued. "I can't remember the particulars. I don't know if I ever could. I remember turning around to see Carny on the ground. He'd been shot and a Frog with a knife was kneeling over him, ready to finish the job one of his fellows had started.

"I ran toward them. Why I ran, I don't know. I should have just loaded the Baker and shot the bastard, but I didn't. I dropped my rifle and grabbed the Frenchman with one hand, my own knife with the other. I hauled him to his feet. And when he turned around I stuck my blade in his gut. He looked so surprised."

Blythe's heart twisted as his voice cracked. She wanted to go to him, but she knew she couldn't. She had to let him finish this on his own.

Devlin blinked slowly, still in the past. "He begged me not to kill him. He even stuck me with his own knife trying to fend me off."

The scar on his hip that he didn't talk about. That was how he got it. Blythe winced. She could only imagine how much it had hurt.

"I killed him anyway. I held and gutted him like a fish. I remember the shock on his face and watching the life fade from his eyes. Sometimes, I can even remember how sticky his blood was."

Blythe covered her mouth in horror—not at what Devlin had done, but at the effect it had on him. No wonder he hated it when people brought up his saving Carny's life. He despised what he had been forced to do in the process. He hated himself for it, even though it meant keeping himself and Carny alive, even though it was an act of war.

He came back to the present then, his haunted eyes meeting hers. "I don't remember much after that, only taking Carny to the surgeon."

He made it sound so easy. He had run across a battlefield with Carny draped across his shoulders. And then he had gone back into the fray.

"You saved Carny's life," she reminded him.

"I killed a man in the process." His tone was frustrated, as though he couldn't understand why she didn't see it as he did.

"He wasn't the first man you killed. What makes him so different from all the others?"

He rubbed his eyes. "All the others. I think of them sometimes too, but they didn't beg me to spare them."

"Would you have listened if they had?"

"I don't know."

"Well, if you had, then you would be dead instead of them, so do not expect me to say you were wrong. I will not. I am glad you killed them, every one of them, because if you hadn't I might never have found you, and I refuse to let you have any regrets where we are concerned." No, she had no regrets, but she would do anything to take his guilt away, to relieve him of the awful responsibility the war with Napoleon had laid upon him.

He simply stared at her.

"Come here," she commanded, patting the expanse of bed at her side.

He hesitated for only a moment before standing and coming to her. He sat on the edge of the bed and faced her, his hands on his thighs. She reached out and took one of them in hers. His fingers were cold. He was never cold, except for that night he had left her in bed alone. He still hadn't told her where he'd gone. It didn't matter.

"You aren't disgusted by me?"

Her heart nearly broke at the pain in his tone. "I am sorry you had to do what you did, Devlin. I am sorry you had to experience all the awful things you did, and I am sorry you have carried this needless guilt around with you for the last two years, but I am not sorry you did whatever you had to do to stay alive. I could never be sorry for that."

"Then you forgive me?"

Her brow knit together. "You've done nothing I need to forgive you for."

He pursed his lips and squeezed his fingers around hers. "I need you to help me forgive myself. I don't know how."

Blythe drew him into her arms, not caring if the blankets fell or not. She cradled this great big man against her breast as though he were a child. She kissed his forehead and smoothed the hair back from his brow, all the while aching with the love she felt for him. She would give anything to take away his guilt and pain. She'd gladly take them upon herself if it meant setting him free, but that was impossible, and she had no idea how to help him.

"It is all right to regret it," she told him softly. "But you have to stop dwelling on it. You have to stop defining yourself with that one action. You are a good, brave man."

He lifted his gaze to hers; his eyes blazed with emotion. Before Blythe could react, he had her on her back on the bed, his mouth grinding against hers. Her body instantly reacted, some deeper part of her recognizing that this was how she could take the darkness away from him. She let him bruise her lips, returned his desperate caresses with sure and gentle ones of her own, and when he drove himself inside her, she wrapped her legs around his waist in a grip he would not be able to free himself from even if he wanted to.

She wrapped her arms around his neck, meeting every thrust of his hips with a lift of her own.

Moments later he stiffened above her as climax rocked them both. "Love me," he rasped against her ear. "Just love me."

She did love him. The question was, did he love her?

She didn't tell him she loved him again.

It was a trivial thing that he shouldn't even waste his time thinking about, but he couldn't seem to help it. It didn't matter that she had allowed him to make love to her or that she had held him for what seemed like hours afterward as he talked about the war; she hadn't repeated those three little words that she had given so freely before he confided his secret.

They'd been invited to dine at Wynter Lane that evening along with Carny and Teresa, and now the six of them were sitting in one of the drawing rooms chatting comfortably. Miles had brought up the first time he and Varya met—apparently she'd abducted him at gunpoint—and he and Blythe and Carny were having a chuckle at Varya's expense. She didn't seem to mind, however, as Miles told the tale in such a way that his wife looked very heroic and brave while he made himself look buffoonish.

No one seemed to notice that Devlin, slouched comfortably on one of the sofas, wasn't taking part in the conversation. Honestly, what could he possibly add to it? Teresa might be interested in knowing more, but he was happy with just the bare facts, although to be truthful, the idea of Varya pointing a pistol in Miles's face was amusing.

Carny made a remark and Blythe laughingly agreed with him, which led to her bringing up some other bit of shared history. Teresa didn't seem to mind not having been part of that past, and Devlin didn't either, not really. He couldn't shake this feeling of impending doom where Carny was concerned, and he didn't like it. Carny was his friend, a fellow soldier, and he had known him for years, and yet he just knew something bad was going to happen between them and that Blythe was going to be at the center of it.

Just as Devlin had never considered himself much of a hero, he had never thought of himself as a coward either, but he was when it came to Blythe. He was so afraid she would turn her back on him, afraid that he would lose her. He would do anything to be a hero in her eyes, to have her look at him as though he could do anything.

She wasn't even bothered by the fact that he had killed. She simply accepted it. Accepted him.

His life had been empty before her, and it would be emptier still if he lost her. He didn't feel as if he had to be anything but himself with her. She loved—or at least had loved—him for who he was, a love he'd been chasing most of his life.

He was terrified he was going to lose it—that he might have already lost it. Despite her assurances that what happened during the war didn't matter to her, there was still his conviction that for some reason he wasn't worthy of her affection. After all, he hadn't been worthy of his parents' affection. Blythe might very well feel differently about his actions once she had some time to think on them. She might decide that he wasn't what she wanted after all.

She had fallen out of love with Carny easily enough, and he hadn't deserved her either. It was unfair, but what did she know of love anyway? Her only experience with it had been Carny, and look how that had ended.

There was a knock on the drawing room door, and the governess entered with little Edward. He was a sturdy child with a thick head of unruly dark hair, touched with a hint of red, and wide blue eyes. A broad smile brightened his cherubic face when he saw there was company to fawn over him. He wasn't a shy child by any stretch of the imagination, and neither Varya nor Miles seemed to subscribe to the notion that children should be kept in the nursery at all times. They loved their son and enjoyed showing him off whenever the opportunity arose.

"Just set him down, Fanny," Miles instructed. "We'll ring when you can return for him."

"Yes, my lord." The young woman lowered the little boy to the carpet and smiled as he took off running as fast as his short legs would take him. She curtsied then and left the room.

Edward ran first to his mother for a kiss, and then before Varya could pick him up, ran off to his father for the same. When Miles tried to grab him, the little boy screamed with laugher and bolted once again.

Straight to Devlin.

Devlin stared at the robust, nightshirt-clad little man standing by his feet. Edward Christian, future Marquess of Wynter, stood just a little higher than his knee—fairly tall for his age, he supposed. He just stood there and regarded Devlin with round eyes sparkling with good-natured mischief.

"I am not going to kiss you," Devlin told him.

"Devlin!" Blythe exclaimed, her expression a mixture of amusement and censure.

Edward didn't seem to take offense, however, and since Blythe didn't sound *that* put out with him, Devlin didn't worry about it.

Giggling, the little boy held up his arms. "Up."

Up. As in, pick him up? He'd never held a child in his life. He looked to Miles for help, rescue, anything.

"Go ahead," was all his friend said, reclining leisurely in his chair. "He will not break, I assure you."

"Nor will he leave you alone until you do," Varya added with a smile.

Devlin's gaze went to his wife. She wasn't going to help him. She was gazing at him as though she thought this suitable retribution for his "no kissing" remark.

Sighing inwardly, Devlin reached down and slipped his hands around Edward's trunk and lifted. He was surprisingly light for such a stocky boy.

Instead of sitting, Edward stood on Devlin's thighs, his stockinged toes digging into the muscles—hard. Obviously feeling secure with someone holding him, Edward leaned forward and grabbed Devlin's nose.

"Nose," he said in a happy little voice. Then he squeezed. Devlin's eyebrows lifted. It didn't hurt, but it was a tad embarrassing. He knew very well his nose was long, but to have anyone, even a child, be able to actually grab it and pull . . .

With this fat little hand still wrapped around his nose and everyone around him laughing about it, Devlin took one hand from Edward's side and lifted it to gently squeeze the tiny button in the middle of the child's face. His hand was almost as big as the toddler's face. Edward laughed in delight and patted Devlin on the cheek, almost shoving all five fingers in his eye.

Then, releasing Devlin's nose, Edward spun on a surprisingly sharp heel and plopped himself down on Devlin's lap. Devlin winced. If he was still able to produce his own children after that it would be a miracle.

Edward glanced up at him, laughed, squirmed a bit, and then lay back against his chest and was still.

Devlin didn't even dare breathe for fear it would set the little monster squirming again. Then slowly he allowed himself a breath.

Edward took one of his hands and held it, his little hand grasping no more than one finger. Good Lord, that chubby hand was tiny compared to his own.

Well, this wasn't so bad. It was somewhat nice, actually. There was something oddly secure and comforting about this gentle weight against his chest, the soft, inquiring fingers that held his, occasionally stroking in an absent manner. Now as long as Edward didn't wet his nappie, everything would be fine.

Devlin looked up to find everyone else watching him.

"Someone likes his uncle Devlin," Miles remarked with a smile. He didn't seem the least bit bothered that his son had gone to someone else. Perhaps he was secure in the knowledge that he was Edward's favorite no matter who else might get a chance to hold him for a while.

Too bad Devlin couldn't bring himself to have that same kind of faith in his marriage.

There was no way in hell he was going to allow someone else to hold her. He'd kill whoever tried. That he meant it should bother him, but it didn't. *That* was what bothered him, that he could think about taking another life, even after all the guilt he suffered, and know that he could do it easily.

"I have been usurped," Carny remarked with mock wryness, but there was an element of seriousness to his expression. Clearly he was used to being the one Edward ran to. Did he think Devlin had usurped him when it came to Blythe as well?

"Would you like to take him?" Devlin asked.

Carny colored slightly. "No, no. He will scream the house down if anyone tries to take him from you. He is yours until he decides to move."

Which made the chances of being pissed on all the greater. Yet oddly enough, Devlin didn't mind that much. He'd had worse things on him than a toddler's wee.

"Have you much experience with children, Devlin?" Teresa inquired, her dark gaze bright with adoration as it fell on Edward.

She wanted her own child so badly, it was there for all to see in her eyes. Devlin couldn't help but feel for her.

"No," he replied. "This is the first time I've ever held one."

"Not the first time," Carny reminded him. "Did you not deliver a woman of her child once in the Peninsula?"

Three sets of female eyes pinned him to his chair, each one wide with wonder. If he admitted that yes, he had helped bring a child into the world, would they immediately start talking about it? It was a scary, messy business, and he had been terrified the entire time. It had been an incredible experience and he'd been filled with an incredible awe when he held the slippery little bundle in his hands, but that didn't mean he wanted to relive it any time soon, even in memory.

"Uh, yes. I did." When the women continued to look at him as though he truly was some kind of hero, he added, "I was the only one around to help her."

Still they stared at him.

"War makes it necessary for people to do things they wouldn't necessarily do," he explained. Such as killing, perhaps? "It doesn't make me special."

"I beg your pardon," Miles responded, "but I have been in the birthing room, and I find the fact that you did not pass out special indeed."

Varya chuckled, gazing at her husband lovingly. "Miles has no stomach for blood, I'm afraid."

Carny went white. "Blood? There's blood?"

Miles laughed. "That's enough talk of that. We do not want to scare Carny out of ever becoming a father."

Neither Teresa nor Carny responded, but their expressions said the same thing—*if* Carny ever became a father.

"Have you ever thought of becoming a physician, Devlin?"

It was Blythe who spoke. Startled, Devlin met her curious gaze. It was so soft, so warm, and so obviously affected by the sight of him with the child, that it was all he could do not to toss Edward at Carny and drag her home to bed.

"No. The thought never crossed my mind."

She seemed surprised by that. "But you would be so good at it, and you obviously have a lot of experience from your days as a soldier."

She spoke as though it was long over, but he still considered himself a soldier. Perhaps that was part of his problem; he spent too much time in the past and not enough thinking about the future.

"An excellent notion," Miles enthused. "I know for a fact that Brixleigh could use a new physician. All they have now is an apothecary and a midwife."

Two people more than qualified to do their jobs—certainly more qualified than Devlin was. Still, the idea of becoming a physician, of actually helping people, was starkly appealing after years of being paid to kill.

"I will think about it." It was the only answer he could give right now. Later, he would discuss it with Blythe, even though he could tell from her expression that she supported the idea wholeheartedly.

Varya brought up something that had happened at a party recently and changed the topic. Devlin listened with half an ear as the others talked. His attention drifted back to the little boy in his lap. Still wide awake, Edward had released his hand and watched the adults around him with unconcealed interest.

Devlin touched the tip of his index finger to the tiny curve of the child's ear. It was like the soft flesh of a peach, but warmer and more pliable. His cheek was downy, leading to a round jaw and a plump, warm neck.

Edward laughed, dropping his head to a shrugging shoulder and trapping Devlin's finger between the two. He was ticklish, just like his aunt Blythe.

Smiling, Devlin wiggled his finger, causing Edward to laugh even harder. Suddenly lifting his head, the child flipped his body over, and holding on to the lapels of Devlin's jacket, climbed to his feet, his toes digging into Devlin's thighs once more.

Edward launched himself forward, wrapping chubby arms around Devlin's jaw and pressing a big, wet openmouth kiss on his cheek. Devlin froze.

Good Lord, was that drool dribbling down his face?

Yes it was, he realized as Edward lifted his smiling face, his little cupid's bow lips and chin slick and bubbled with spittle. "Kiss!"

"Thank you." Devlin managed what he hoped was a sincere smile as he wiped his cheek with his hand.

Edward just stared at him expectantly.

"He wants you to kiss him back, Devlin."

Devlin caught his wife's laughing gaze over her nephew's head before dropping his attention back to the waiting child.

Kiss him back? He wasn't sure how he felt about that. Still, he was just a child, and children needed to know they were appreciated. This was the first time he'd truly met Edward, and the last thing he wanted was make the child afraid of him. He didn't want anyone in his new family to be afraid of him.

If he and Blythe ever had children—and the odds were in their favor—those babies would know they were loved and cherished. He would make sure of it. He had no doubt of his ability to love a child of his own.

Yes, he could give his heart to a child, someone who was the least likely to throw it back at him because he had yet to learn how to judge. And he could give it willingly to his family and friends, but giving it to his wife was the hardest thing he'd ever attempted, because if she rejected him, he'd be lost—forever bound to the dark with nothing more than a brief memory of his time in the light.

Gently, he pressed his lips to the little boy's forehead, his heart giving an unexpected jolt at the contact. He could smell the fresh scent of his hair, the soft soap cleanliness of his skin. There was none of this sour milk smell he'd heard people talk about, just warm, clean baby skin. God, it was beautiful.

This was true innocence, untouched and unsullied by the world. If Devlin could wish anything for Edward, it would be that he maintain his innocence for as long as he possibly could and not toss it away as he had. Then again, he didn't think he had ever been innocent himself.

Edward inched himself down again, his surprisingly sharp knees just missing Devlin's groin. He dropped himself on his belly on Devlin's chest. Devlin was slouched so that the child was able to lie against him without sliding further downward. Edward laid his cheek on Devlin's shoulder, his fingers curling around the ends of the cravat in front of him.

"Pretty," he said with a wide yawn.

Awkwardly, Devlin lifted his left hand to the boy's back and splayed his fingers there, feeling the gentle rise and fall of every breath. He rubbed softly.

Edward closed his eyes and was asleep within minutes. Ignoring those around him, Devlin contented himself with watching the child sleep. What peace this was, what trust.

Raising his head, he caught his wife's gaze. All the breath in his lungs stilled at the tenderness of her expression. She wanted this too; he could see it—and she wanted it with him.

Because she loved him. He couldn't say it in return. He could only hope she saw it in his eyes.

He dropped his gaze, not wanting anyone else to see his heart beating there. He looked at Carny and Teresa instead. Teresa's gaze lifted from the sleeping child on his chest to shine enviously at him.

Devlin moved his gaze to Carny. He wanted to give his friend a reassuring smile, let him know that he hoped their wish was granted soon.

But Carny wasn't looking at him. He was looking at Blythe, who was oblivious of the attention. Was that simply friendship on Carny's face, or something more? There was a certain wistfulness to it, as if looking at her was a reminder of something he couldn't have, as though there was something he wished he could change.

Devlin's smile faded. Whatever it was, he had a feeling Carny's wish was one wish that he would rather *not* see granted.

Chapter 16

It didn't make him special, he'd said.

Good Lord, the man had saved lives, lived through incredible odds and delivered babies. If that wasn't special, Blythe didn't know what was.

How could Devlin not realize just how astonishing he really was? He seemed to have no conceit at all, no vanity. One day Blythe came home from a bit of shopping to find Wellington and her husband laughing together in the drawing room! She had met the duke before, of course, but seeing him gaze at Devlin so fondly, so respectfully, made her see her husband in a whole new light.

He truly was a hero.

A hero who complained the duke had been excessively verbose that morning. Devlin maintained he was stiff from having sat for so long.

Blythe stripped off her gloves. Soon they would be back in Devonshire and she wouldn't have to worry about what she wore. "What did Wellington mean when he called you 'Sir Devlin'?"

A loud popping noise accompanied Devlin stretching his

neck to one side. "After the war he wanted to approach Prinny about having me knighted." He rolled his shoulders. "I refused, but he insists on calling me 'sir' anyway."

Blythe didn't hide her surprise. "You turned down an opportunity to be knighted? Why?"

He smiled. "I thought 'Sir Devlin' too foppish."

He was joking, of course. He had to be. Exasperation colored Blythe's sigh. "You turned it down because you did not believe you deserved it, did you not?"

Devlin's smile faded. "Perhaps."

"But you do deserve it. Do you not think it time to take him up on his offer to approach the regent?"

"Is it important to you?" He unfastened the frogs of her spencer. She turned so he could slide it from her shoulders.

"What is more important to me is that it seems so *unimportant* to you. A knighthood could open many doors."

"I'm not concerned with doors I can't open on my own."

She faced him. "You are the oddest man I have ever known." It was true. The things that drove and interested ordinary men seemed to have no effect on him. He had no ambition for riches or power or fame. He simply wanted to live a quiet life.

With her.

And yet he could not say he loved her, even though she was sure he did. Or rather, she *thought* he did, but then she had thought Carny loved her as well. Her declaration had obviously pleased him, if the way he'd made love to her was any indication, but he had yet to echo the words. Why?

Did he not love her? Was he afraid? If she had any courage at all she would simply ask. But then he would have to answer, and perhaps she was better off not knowing at this point. Perhaps she should just be happy that he was glad she loved him.

How could she possibly be happy when she felt so utterly vulnerable? She had offered him her heart, and like Carny, he had taken it without so much as a thank-you. The only difference was that if Devlin returned it, she could not run away and hide from him as she had from Carny.

She didn't want to run and hide. She wanted him to love her.

He was silent, regarding her thoughtfully with dark, bright eyes. "Odd, am I?"

She nodded, wishing she could disappear into the thick carpet beneath her feet. Why had she used that choice of words? She should have known they would wound his male pride.

"I cannot figure you out," she admitted. "I do not think I understand you at all."

His hand came up to touch her face. "You understand me—better than anyone else ever has."

Her heart thudded heavily at his words. It was obvious that he believed them, despite her own skepticism. "But I know so little about you. I've told you so much about my life."

Devlin was indignant. "I've told you about my past."

How to make him understand? "You have told me about a part of your past, about the war, and I understand how that shaped you, but you have seen my home and where I grew up. I know nothing about your childhood."

The light in his eyes snuffed out. "You know I was not close to my parents."

"Yes, but who were you close to?" It was true, she did not know who had raised him, whom to thank for his kindness or his honesty. He knew about her father, and of course had seen her with Miles. From what little she had seen of him with his brothers, he got along best with Brahm, but she hadn't spent much time with the eldest Ryland brother herself.

She knew he had joined the army to prove himself, but to whom? His parents? Himself?

"You really want to know?" he asked, raising a dubious brow.

She nodded, and the black arch dropped.

"Then come. If it is that important, I will show you."

"I will need to change first." Was it normal to be this anxious to learn about his life?

A shadow of his normal smile returned. "Of course you have to change. It is your one concession to being female. Since we've been in London I've not seen you wear the same gown twice."

She made a face. "That is not true."

"You cannot leave the house without changing your clothes."

Shrugging, Blythe led the way from the room. "It is expected—and is completely different from not wearing a gown more than once. I've worn several many times since coming to town." A member of the *haute ton* she might be, but frivolous she wasn't.

"Then you won't mind if I continue to wear the same clothes for the remainder of the day?"

Preceding him up the stairs, Blythe flashed him a seductive smile over her shoulder. "Provided you let me remove them tonight."

All it took was that tiny reminder of the intimacy they shared to darken his eyes. "I think that can be arranged."

As they entered their bedroom, Blythe realized immediately that something was different. Something was missing.

She looked around. All the green and gold furniture and draperies were accounted for. The bed was draped in the same fabric it always was, the carpet was clean and exactly as it had been earlier that day. Even Devlin's chair by the window remained untouched.

Her gaze snapped back to the chair and little table beside it. All of Devlin's "grooming" supplies for his rifle were gone.

The rifle itself was gone, its case no longer leaning against the back of the chair.

"Where is the Baker?" she asked. After having it always present, it was strange to find it gone.

Devlin stood near the vanity, where he had given her such pleasure on a night not long ago. He stroked the surface as though remembering the details as vividly as she. He did not look at her. "I put it away."

"Away?" There was no way to keep the alarm from her voice. That rifle had been with him for years. It would be no easier for him to put away than a limb. "Where is it?"

He glanced toward the trunk at the foot of the bed. "It is packed for our return to Brixleigh."

"But we do not return for another fortnight." Surely he could polish, buff, and dote on the rifle many times between now and then.

He shrugged the wide set of his shoulders. "I don't need it when I have you."

It might not be "I love you," but it was almost as good! A sharp tightness gripped Blythe's chest, squeezing until just to breathe was a struggle. It seemed a paltry thing, certainly something other women would scoff at, but she couldn't help but be humbled by the knowledge that *she* had replaced the Baker. He had put aside his most prized possession—his best friend, as it were—for her. How could she not be honored by that?

"You did not have to do that." The words almost caught on the lump in her throat.

He raised his gaze to hers, seemingly taken aback by her words. "I know I didn't *have* to. I wanted to."

"Why?" Why did she have to ask? Why couldn't she just be happy and leave it at that? Everything had to be questioned and dissected until any magic it possessed disappeared just because she found it so blasted hard to trust in anything that might mean she was cared for.

He closed the scant distance between them. Standing with

barely enough room for a whisper to pass between them, he cupped her face in his hands, holding her as though she were some delicate porcelain doll rather than a woman larger than most men.

"Because you are the most important thing in my life. Nothing, especially a gun, means as much to me as you."

Tears collected on Blythe's lashes. "You say the most incredible things."

His thumbs brushed her cheeks as his gaze bored into hers. "I've meant every one."

Of that she had no doubt. It was his honesty that wrenched at her heart, not the words themselves.

She would have told him she loved him again if he hadn't chosen that moment to kiss her. The second his lips touched hers, all capacity for thought disappeared. There was nothing in her mind but him. He filled her head, her senses, her very soul.

Tenderly, he held her, his incredibly strong hands cradling her face. Lips, soft and warm, moved against hers, claiming and surrendering in turn. She gripped his wrists, neither pulling him away nor tugging him closer, but simply ensuring for the thousandth time since he first kissed her that he was real and not some wonderful dream. He was strength and heart, and he was hers as surely as she was his. If he didn't love her yet it was closer than he'd ever come to love before, and knowing that she was the first woman to make him feel those fledgling emotions was the most powerful knowledge she'd ever been given.

"I need to change," she murmured against his lips as the kiss ended. She wasn't about to let him get out of showing her parts of his past.

"Allow me." He turned her around, his fingers going to the fastenings on her dress. Within minutes, it fell to the floor with a soft swish.

She should have known he wouldn't stop there. He didn't stop until he'd released her from her corset and shift as well. He left her stockings and shoes; he seemed to like making love to her with them on.

And make love to her was what he did. Even if he didn't realize it, she could feel it in his every touch, every brush of his lips against her flesh. He might not think he knew what love was, but in his heart he knew it as surely as he knew how to breathe. It was just a matter of time before he realized it. She simply had to wait.

She could only pray that he wouldn't keep her waiting too long.

The stables at Creed House had apartments for its head groom built above them. They were by no means elegant or fancy, but they were homey and comfortable. In fact, they sometimes felt more like home to Devlin than the house itself. He had spent much of his youth in this parlor, and after his return from the Peninsula, much of his time in London had been talked away within these walls. It seemed fitting, then, that he would bring Blythe there to meet the man who had so shaped his life.

What was she thinking as they climbed the rough-hewn stairs? Did she find such living arrangements disdainful? Somehow he couldn't imagine her being quite so delicate.

The wood creaked, giving ever so slightly beneath Devlin's boots as he climbed toward the simple door at the top. Sunlight poured in from a small window near the top of the landing, lighting what would have been an otherwise dark and narrow stairwell.

He knocked on the door, the latch rattling under the force of his knuckles. A dog barked from within, and he heard a woman's voice telling it to be quiet. Footsteps approached.

The woman who greeted them was tall and buxom, with

golden blond hair and pale blue eyes. Even clad in a gown of faded rose muslin and a stained apron, she was as pretty as any debutante.

"Devlin!" she cried, flinging her plump arms around his neck and squeezing for all she was worth. "How lovely to see you!"

He hugged her back. "Hello, Elsie. You're looking well."

As she released him, the voluptuous blond swatted him playfully on the arm and chuckled. "You'd say that even if I was covered in mud and drawing flies."

He grinned. "And I'd still mean it." Turning his attention to the woman standing in the door behind him, he held out his hand, bringing Blythe into the room. "I would like you to meet my wife. Blythe, this is Elsie. She used to trounce me silly when we were children."

Elsie smiled brightly, extending a pink, slightly chapped hand in Blythe's direction. "I couldn't trounce you now, it's for certain. It is a pleasure to meet you, my lady."

Blythe didn't have to do much to make him proud of her, but when she didn't even glance at Elsie's hand before stripping off her glove and taking it in her own, his estimation of her rose another notch. He hadn't thought it could rise any higher.

"Come in and sit down," Elsie commanded once pleasantries had been exchanged. "I'll fetch Papa and make tea."

"I know the way," Devlin reminded her when she started to escort them inside. "You go get your father. We'll wait in the parlor."

Elsie flashed him another grin before hurrying off to do as he bid. Holding Blythe's ungloved hand in his own, Devlin led her down the narrow corridor to the first room on the right, the Fieldings' "good" parlor.

"Pretty girl," Blythe remarked once Elsie was out of earshot.

Devlin nodded, his gaze taking in every detail of the small parlor. It was as unchanged as it had been during his last visit, and as untouched as it had been the twenty years before that. The furniture was of excellent quality but old, and all of it, right down to the peach and blue rug on the worn wood floor, had come from Devlin's mother. Devlin remembered helping Fielding carry some of it up the stairs the day the new furniture for the main house arrived. Both Fielding and his daughter thought they'd been given a treasure. Devlin's mother thought it garbage.

"The two of you seem rather close."

His thoughts still in the past, Devlin turned to face his wife's questioning gaze. "We were once."

"How close?" she asked, removing her hat as she stepped further into the parlor.

Devlin made for the sofa near the back of the room. It was the most comfortable seat for his frame. It never occurred to him to lie to Blythe—something Wynthrope would no doubt slap him in the head for were he present.

He sat down. "She was my first lover."

She had already suspected it, he could see it in her eyes, but she colored anyway. Her back stiff, she sank into the first chair she came to, her gaze carefully avoiding his.

"It was a long time ago," he heard himself continue, as if it made a difference. Blythe had to know it hadn't happened recently. "Before she was married."

Blythe merely nodded, setting her hat and gloves on the low table before her.

Should he be amused or worried by her uncharacteristic behavior? It was jealousy, even he could recognize that.

"You look as though you'd like to take her eyes out. She really is a nice girl."

She looked at him this time, her expression a mixture of sheepishness and unamusement. "How would you feel toward Carny if I had lain with him before I met you?"

Like I could take his eyes out. Point well taken.

"Does it bother you?" He already knew the answer—of

course it bothered her. That was obvious. His pride just wanted to hear her say it.

She shrugged. "It does make me a little uncomfortable, knowing she has known you in a way I never can. I have no such person to introduce you to."

And a damn good thing it was too. He didn't care how hypocritical it was of him, he'd be insane with jealousy if another man knew what Blythe felt like wrapped around him. And it wasn't just because he was possessive of her either; it was because he knew that she would never give herself to someone she didn't love, and the idea of her loving someone else as much as—or more than—she might love him was something he would not be able to accept.

"You could thank her," he suggested in a lame attempt to dispel her discomfort. "She taught me most of what I know."

Wrong thing to say. Two spots of dark crimson blossomed high on Blythe's cheeks. If the thought hadn't occurred to her earlier to compare herself to Elsie, it certainly would now.

How could she possibly think any woman—first lover or not—could compare to her?

"It was quick, messy, and not very memorable for her, I'm sure." Common sense told him it would be wise not to admit that their "lessons" had continued after that first time. The less he told her now, the better.

"What was it like for you?"

Of course she would have to ask that, and she would have to ask it here, when either Elsie or her father could walk in on them at any moment.

"Maybe we could talk about this later when we're alone?" he suggested.

Blythe nodded, her movements stilted. "All right." But it wasn't all right. That was obvious as well.

Sighing, he ran a hand over his face. "It was awkward and embarrassing and not something I'd ever care to repeat."

Her gaze was so hopeful he didn't know whether to laugh or sigh. "Really?"

He sighed. There was no way he could make her understand the mortification that followed coming before even getting one's cock wet. It was one of those amazing advantages that women held over men. "Really."

Thankfully, that seemed to appease her, and just in time as well, for not even two minutes later, Samuel Fielding practically skipped into the room with sparkling eyes, cheeks bright with color, and thick white hair that stood straight up on end. He looked like a gnome.

"Devlin, my boy!" he boomed in a voice bigger than he was. "Here ye are, here ye are!"

As was their custom, Devlin jumped to his feet and crossed the carpet to embrace the older man, and as usual, Samuel caught him in a grip that was surprisingly strong. He might be small, but he was wiry and younger than his white hair would have one believe. Devlin didn't know if he was even sixty yet.

"It's about time you brought your lovely wife to meet me," he chastised jovially as Devlin pulled away.

"You could have met her if you had come to the wedding," Devlin reminded him. "You were invited."

Samuel waved a dismissive hand as he pulled a face. "And wouldn't I have fit right in with all your fancy guests? No, it was better that I didn't go, but I appreciated the sentiment, m'boy, and the piece of cake you sent home with His Lordship."

Once Samuel stopped talking, Devlin introduced him to Blythe. As he'd hoped, the two of them took to each other immediately. He had no doubt that old Sam would adore her—the old groom was bound to like whomever Devlin married just because she was his wife, but he'd been a little fearful that Blythe might not appreciate this man he adored like a father.

God love her, she even went out of her way to be polite and friendly with Elsie, even though he knew it must be killing her to do so. When Blythe offered to pour the tea, essentially putting herself in the position of both lady and servant, Devlin knew she was trying to show him that she harbored no resentment toward Elsie, who was a dear friend and had never really been anything more, despite the physical turn their relationship had taken.

"So you have been with Devlin's family for many years, Mr. Fielding?" Blythe asked, after taking a sip of her tea.

"Call me Sam, my dear lady. Aye, I've been with the Rylands for as long as ever I can remember and my father before that. Why, I remember when this one here"—he gestured toward Devlin—"was born. His father brought him out to the stables that same day to meet us, despite the surgeon's orders. Biggest babe I'd ever seen."

Blythe chuckled at his humor. "I imagine he was."

Samuel nodded. "Lord Creed held him out to me and said, 'Look at this, Fielding, is he not a fine son?' I said, 'Aye, m'lord, but I cannot imagine him being anything but.' The next time he entered my stables, his father took him up on his first horse."

His wife seemed charmed by the old groom's reminiscences, but Devlin could only stare in stupefaction. His father had taken him out to the stables when he wasn't even a day old just to show him off? He'd called him "a fine son"?

"I remember the day when Devlin went off to war," Samuel went on, his face clouding with memory. "Oh, that was a dark day, my lady. Lady Creed kept to her rooms, weeping, and His Lordship looked as though the boy was already dead. He didn't like his boys being too far away from him, no sir."

His mother had cried? No, that had to be wrong. She'd been positively dry-eyed when Devlin left. Although she had been clutching a handkerchief in her hand as she waved good-bye . . .

"Every time His Lordship would get a letter from Devlin

he'd come up to visit and we'd have a drink while he read it aloud, and whenever they'd print something about him in the paper, it was the same thing. Lord Creed had to come boasting. He cut every mention out of the paper and tucked it aside in a little box. 'That's my boy, Fielding,' he'd say. 'That's my boy.' He was so proud of his son the hero." Samuel's gaze was full of emotion as it settled on Devlin. "We all were."

Devlin didn't utter a sound. It was as though the power of speech had been taken from him. He sat there, dumb and mostly mute for the remainder of the visit. Thankfully Blythe was comfortable enough to talk without him, and old Sam certainly had no trouble keeping conversation flowing. Devlin spoke when spoken to, and other than that, barely said a word.

He hugged both Elsie and Sam as they left, and mumbled a promise to return again soon. He thought he heard Blythe tell Elsie how happy she was to have met her, but he wasn't certain. She could have threatened to slit her throat for all his muddled brain knew.

His father had been proud. His mother had cried.

His silence continued as they drove home. Blythe didn't bother trying to get him to talk either. She seemed content to let him be silent until he decided otherwise. The quiet between them was far from uncomfortable. If anything, it seemed to bring them even closer together, because he knew she understood his silence. Normally someone knowing him so well would make him uneasy, but not so with Blythe. She might lament not knowing much about his past, but she knew him better than anyone, possibly even better than his brothers.

Once they were back at the town house, she led him upstairs to the privacy of their room, and with the door safely closed behind them, she turned to him and wrapped her arms around his waist.

"They loved you," she said softly. "Even you must accept that now."

She was right. Hugging her tight against him, Devlin pressed his cheek to her temple, trying to quell the storm of emotion raging within him. All these years he'd thought that they hadn't wanted him, that he hadn't mattered, and he had. He just couldn't see it, and his mother and father hadn't been very good at showing it, at least not to him. Then again, they hadn't been overly affectionate with any of their children, not really.

Christ, how could he have been so stupid? He'd gone off to fight in hopes of winning their love, love that was already his. What if he had died over there? He never would have known they cared.

All he had done, all he had seen and endured, had been for nothing. It had been an empty quest, a search for something he'd had all along. He could have avoided the whole war, could have eluded all the bloodshed.

He wouldn't have killed the Frenchman. He would never have killed at all.

"They loved you," she murmured once more, her hands stroking his back through his coat. "I love you."

A shudder wracked his body at her gently spoken words, and as the tears coursed down his cheeks, Devlin didn't know if they would ever stop.

"Where is Devlin?" Carny sat on the sofa, one leg crossed elegantly over the other.

"I sent him off to White's with Miles." Sent him off because she sensed he needed some time away after allowing her to witness the force of his emotion. Never had she seen a man weep as he had after their return from Samuel's. She had forgotten all about Elsie and her own jealousy and simply held him while he let it all out. He might have had other lovers, but Blythe was willing to bet he had never opened himself up to another woman as he'd opened himself to her.

"He is very fortunate to have such a considerate wife."

As she poured the tea, Blythe rolled her eyes at the blatant flattery in Carny's voice. "I have to disagree. I believe I am fortunate to have him."

He took the cup she offered. "Not many women would be so accepting of a man who has lived the life Devlin has."

Now she frowned. Lifting her cup to her lips, she met his gaze unflinchingly. "What do you mean?"

Carny, immaculate as always in a green coat and buckskin breeches, sipped his tea. "War changes a man, as you are well aware. Devlin has seen—and done—things that have a way of leaving a man scarred on the inside as well as out. It is not easy to love such a man. Nor is it easy for him to love in return."

He spoke as though he was such a man himself, and Blythe wanted to laugh. Carny was a good man, a brave man who never shrank from doing his duty, but he could never compare to her Devlin. He had entered the army as an officer and watched most of the action pass from the back of a horse. What did he know of the lower ranks? Truly, what did he know of Devlin or what he had seen? Her husband's biggest regret in life was having to kill a man in order to save Carny's life. The best Carny could do was regret jilting her, and that was only on days when his marriage wasn't quite what he thought it ought to be.

"Loving Devlin is one of the easiest things I have ever done."

Carny seemed as surprised at her words as she was. It was very bold of her to make such a declaration, but he had left her little choice.

He cleared his throat. "Then he is a lucky man indeed. I hope he appreciates it."

Blythe's smile was easy. Of that she had no doubt. "I am sure he does."

He studied her carefully, his azure gaze taking in every aspect of her countenance. She forced herself to sit still under his scrutiny.

"Marriage has changed you," he announced finally.

This should be interesting. She took another drink. Hot, sweet tea kept her from immediately asking, "Oh? In what respect?"

He watched as she lowered her cup to the saucer in her other hand. If he was looking for a tremor or some sign that he had discomposed her, he would be sadly out of luck.

"You seem more mature," he replied. "More content. Less rebellious."

Ahh, meaning that she was being nicer to him. Of course she was. It was easy to be nice to a person when his hold on you was gone. Carny was nothing more than an old family friend now. Despite his sometimes bizarre attitude where Devlin was concerned—he was often like an old stallion annoyed because the new male brought into the barn had the attention of all the mares—Blythe knew that Carny was her friend as well. He wanted only the best for her. And everything else aside, she knew he wanted only the best for Devlin as well.

"I suppose I am," she replied. "I feel more content than I have in years."

Carny nodded. He seemed genuinely happy for her, but there was an envy to his expression as well. Perhaps he did realize his hold over her was gone, after all. Perhaps that was part of his problem.

"Then I hope Ryland continues doing whatever he did to deserve you in the first place."

Sour grapes were not flattering on any man. Carny was not the exception.

"I will ask you to hope the same for me as well," she said good-naturedly. "I do not know what I would do without Devlin in my life."

Carny watched her carefully, as though he didn't quite believe her—or didn't want to believe her, the suspicious part of her thought.

"I am glad to see you finally happy, Blythe. I am sorry I wasn't the man to do it for you."

Blythe believed him. He truly was sorry. That he waited till now to let her know just how sorry he was wasn't what bothered her. It was the fact that he looked as though he'd take it all back if he could.

She couldn't shake the feeling that while he hadn't been the man to make her happy two years ago, he'd desperately like to be that man *now.*

Chapter 17

It was ridiculous.

Pretty soon she was going to have to place a sign in the window advertising advice for unhappy married people. Since when had she become an expert on marriage? She was still new to the institution herself. She had no idea how it was supposed to work.

One thing she did know was that as she sat there, listening to yet more oration on the trauma of a discordant union, Devlin was upstairs soaking in a hot bath, completely naked, and she wasn't there to enjoy the sight. Nor would she be able to join him in the tub, or coax him out of it, or let him show her all the amazing things he could do with his amazing hands, mouth, and body in a tub of soapy water.

They were newly married, for heaven's sake! Other people seemed to understand what that meant, but not so Lord and Lady Carnover. Carny had been by again the day before, and while Blythe had managed to tell herself that she'd been wrong in her misgivings about Carny's feelings toward her, that didn't mean she wanted to hear about his troubles every day.

"This has to stop."

Teresa blinked. "What does?"

Sitting in the drawing room, drinking her third cup of tea of the morning, Blythe tried to keep her tone kind and patient. "You know I adore you, but Carny is my friend as well, and the two of you really should be discussing your problems with each other, not with me."

Obviously her tone hadn't been as kind or as patient as she thought because Teresa promptly burst into tears.

"Oh blast." Rising from her chair, Blythe moved to the sofa where the other woman sat sobbing and awkwardly placed an arm about her slender shoulders. She wasn't good at this sort of thing. She wasn't good with women and their emotions in general.

Dealing with Devlin's tears the day before had come much more easily, although with a lot more pain on her part. It nearly killed her to see him suffer so, even if it had come with the happy realization that his parents had loved him after all.

She patted Teresa's shoulder, making shushing noises as she did so. "I am sorry, Teresa. I did not mean to upset you."

Pulling a handkerchief from her sleeve, Teresa shook her head before wiping at her eyes and nose. "I am not upset with you."

She wasn't? "Then why are you crying?"

The other woman's shoulders straightened as she visibly tried to put herself to rights. "I am with child."

"That is wonderful!" Carny must be ecstatic. So why did Teresa look so glum? Then somehow, Blythe understood—at least a little bit.

"You have not told Carny yet, have you?"

Teresa shook her head, a new batch of tears threatening. "I cannot bring myself to tell him."

"Whyever not?" Then a horrible thought occurred. "He is the father, is he not?"

That dried Teresa's tears quickly enough. "Of course he

is!" Her affronted expression spoke louder than her indignant tone.

Blythe was back to being confused again, and just a little exasperated that Teresa didn't come right out and confide in her.

"Teresa, I have no idea why this has you so upset when you have wanted it for so long."

"I am upset because my husband no longer seems to care!" She sniffed. "I do not think he loves me anymore."

Now that was just ridiculous. All Carny ever seemed to talk about was Teresa. Of course, he seemed to dwell mainly on the problems they were having . . .

"I am sure you are mistaken. Of course Carny loves you."

Teresa dabbed at the wetness in the corners of her dark eyes. It took a truly beautiful woman to retain her looks when trying not to cry. Blythe could hate her for that if she allowed herself. "I think he has fallen in love with another woman."

"Good Lord, what gives you such a foolish notion?" Fickle Carny might have been once, but he was not the type to deceive a woman in such a way. If he was in love with another woman, he would be honest about it.

"He hardly spends any time at home anymore, and when he does he seems distracted and preoccupied. And yesterday I overheard him talking to a friend about past regrets. I believe he regrets marrying me."

Or he regrets not marrying me. The thought raced through Blythe's mind before she could stop it. How could she even entertain such an awful, conceited notion? It wasn't true. It couldn't be true.

And yet, on some level, she knew it was. It wasn't because Carny realized he had feelings for her, it was because her marriage looked good and his seemed so bad. It was because she was what could have been, and in his head he made that something better than what he had.

Blasted idiot.

"Teresa," she said, taking her friend's hand. "Carny loves you, of that I have no doubt. If he seems distracted it is only because he believes you have fallen out of love with him." It was wrong of her to betray Carny's confidence, but she wasn't about to let him and Teresa ruin their marriage just because they were too foolish to talk about their problems.

Teresa raised her damp gaze to Blythe's. "Did he tell you that?"

Blythe nodded. "He did." She squeezed the smaller woman's dainty fingers. "Tell him about the child. Tell him you love him, and I promise everything will be fine."

The hopeful expression on Teresa's pretty face pinched Blythe's heart. The knowledge that she might somehow be involved in her friend's unhappiness, even by no fault of her own, laid a heavy guilt upon her shoulders. She didn't want the responsibility for their happiness. It was all she could do to pursue her own.

"You are right," Teresa agreed with a sniff. "I should tell him. Thank you, Blythe."

By the time Teresa finally left a little while later, Blythe felt as though she'd been wrung out and left to dry in a wrinkled heap. Lord, she'd be happy when she and Devlin could finally return to Rosewood. Why were renovations taking so long anyway? It wasn't as though *that* much work needed to be done.

Lifting her skirts, she climbed the stairs to the next floor, grateful to have just herself and Devlin—and the servants, of course—in the house. She wanted to talk to him more about what they had discovered yesterday. She needed to know that he believed it still, that it had made a difference.

She found him in their bedroom, fresh from the bath, naked from the waist up as he sorted through the wardrobe for a shirt. He'd gone over to Creed House to fence with Brahm earlier that morning, returning with his clothes drenched in sweat. Blythe only had to wrinkle her nose and he rang for hot water.

Closing the door behind her, she paused by the foot of the bed, leaning her temple against the poster as she curled one hand around the carved wood. Smiling, she admired the long, supple line of his spine, the dusky gold of his skin, even the dusting of freckles across the top of his shoulders. Dampness turned his hair to ebony silk, and the scent of cloves and sandalwood hung in the air between them. Every time she looked at him, she was struck by the sheer untamed beauty of him.

No, he wasn't beautiful in the classic sense. No sculptor would ever cast him in marble. His face would never grace a chapel ceiling, and it was just as well, for no one, not even Michelangelo himself, could capture the strength and grace that was Devlin.

He turned from the wardrobe, a questioning expression on his angular face. There were times when he seemed so weary and tired, so sad and alone, and then there were times like this—when the shadow of his past didn't darken his gaze, when the lines around his mouth were faint and his lips curved ever so gently upward. She didn't think it possible, but those were the moments when she loved him most, those moments when he wore his hope like armor.

"Like what you see?" he asked, turning to fully face her.

His hand rested high on the wardrobe door, the other on the jut of a narrow hip. His flesh pulled taut across his ribs, elongating the pale scar that arced into the crisp hair on his chest. He had to know that she loved to look at him, that she couldn't look without wanting to touch.

"I love it," she replied honestly. "I love you."

He looked as though she had punched him. Obviously he had yet to get used to hearing someone say those words. If it took the rest of her life, she was going to make sure he eventually believed he deserved to hear them.

Good God, if the man was any easier to love it would be

ridiculous. He'd snuck up on her and stolen her heart with that lopsided smile before she had a chance to defend herself. He had pursued her with reckless abandon after sharing just one late-night kiss—a kiss that had sealed their fate just as surely as that night she agreed to marry him.

"You do not know what to say when I tell you that, do you?"

He shrugged. "Usually I want to tell you not to."

Pushing away from the bed, she moved toward him. "We've had this discussion before. I thought we agreed there would be no more talk of it."

Chuckling self-consciously, he nodded. "I seem to remember being given that order."

Her arms went around his waist. "Then do you not think the time has come for you to start obeying it?"

"All right." His simple acquiescence warmed her, as did the smile curving his lips as he slipped his arms around her shoulders. "How was your visit with Teresa?"

Sighing, Blythe leaned her forehead against his shoulder. "I cannot decide whether it was good or not."

"Did you have a quarrel?" She could almost hear the frown in his voice.

"No." She lifted her head. "She is pregnant."

Devlin's brows rose. "Isn't that a good thing?"

"You would think so." Blythe shook her head. "She hasn't told Carny yet because she thinks he's having an affair."

She saw the frown this time. "With you?"

"No. Thank God she didn't make that assumption, but she did remark upon how much time he's spending away from the house lately. I find it somewhat discomfiting thinking he hasn't told her that he comes to visit me as often as he does."

"His silence does make his motives seem suspicious."

Blythe rolled her eyes. "You are determined to make a villain out of him, aren't you?"

"I am not."

She would have smiled at his indignation if she hadn't had

such thoughts about Carny herself. "I think I will tell Piotr to tell him I'm not at home the next time he comes to call. This needs to stop."

The humor left his eyes. "You do know why Carny's coming around, don't you?"

No, no. She didn't want to have these thoughts. She didn't want to think that Carny might have feelings for her—not because she wanted him to or because she doubted her own where he was concerned, but because she would have to kill him if he were truly that stupid. When she wanted him he hadn't wanted her, and if he wanted her now . . .

Well, she'd at least have to reap a considerable amount of hurt on him.

"He doesn't think Teresa loves him anymore." It was the only reason she was prepared to give.

"Of course she does."

He said it so easily, so determinedly, as though Carny should simply know it as truth. Was that how he thought Blythe should see it as well? Was she simply to assume that he loved her without ever hearing the words?

She couldn't do that.

"But that's not why Carny is coming to you."

She raised her gaze to his, unease tingling at the base of her spine. "Is it not?"

A cynical smile twisted his lips. "He wants you to know his marriage is in trouble. He's giving you a chance to come to him."

That was absurd! Her mouth opened to say so, but the words wouldn't come out. Good Lord, was it true?

"He wants to know if you still love him." He said the words matter-of-factly, but there was a glimmer of fear in his eyes—real fear. It wasn't that he distrusted her, that was without question, it was that he didn't trust his own ability to keep her affections.

Silly man.

Her arms tightened around his ribs. "There is room for only one man in my heart. You."

"Prove it."

Both of Blythe's brows climbed high on her forehead. Her eyes widened at his challenge. "I beg your pardon?"

"Prove it." He released her and took a step backward. "Show me you love me. Please."

It was the "please" that was her undoing. He needed a physical demonstration of her feelings. He needed it so badly, she could see the anxiety in his eyes. For some reason, it meant more to him than he could articulate to have her show him how much she loved him. It was almost as though he thought he didn't deserve it, or couldn't quite allow himself to believe that she loved him that much.

"All right," she murmured. "I will."

The moment Blythe said the words, something changed in her expression. There was a determination to her features that quickened Devlin's heart and sent a thrill of arousal spiraling down to his groin. She was going to show him, and it scared him a little.

She took him by the hand and led him to the bed, pushing him down onto the mattress. He stretched out on it, his arms at his sides as he watched her slip out of her blue morning gown. When she joined him on the bed she wore her corset and shift. He caught a glimpse of stocking and garter as she climbed up beside him.

She knelt by his legs, her hands sliding up his thighs to converge on his cock, already straining beneath the fabric of his trousers. Deftly, she undid the falls and tugged on the soft wool. He lifted his hips, allowing her to slide trousers and smallclothes down past his knees and over his feet. She tossed them to the floor—his stockings followed.

Completely naked, he lay still before her, scarcely daring to breathe. Her fingers started at his shins, dancing along his flesh until they once again stilled at his groin. She smiled as her hand closed around the aching, flushed length of him. She squeezed gently, firmly. Devlin groaned.

He watched as she pumped him, fluid beading on the blunt head. No other woman had ever touched him as though his pleasure was all that mattered. No other woman had aroused him as Blythe did, and when she lowered her head, wrapping her sweet, wide mouth around him, Devlin knew what it was to die. To be worshipped. To be loved.

Her tongue caressed him with long, wet, velvety strokes and swirls. Her mouth swept up and down the shaft—sweet suction on the sensitive tip, then sliding slowly down until he felt himself nudging the back of her throat. Muscles tensed with restraint, Devlin fought the urge to grab her by the head and thrust himself into that delicious mouth until he came with such force she wouldn't be able to swallow it all.

His fingers went to the back of her skull, but instead of pushing down, he plucked pins from her hair. He was far from gentle, yet she didn't stop what she was doing. She simply raised her own hands to the thick coil of hair and removed the pins herself. She allowed him to comb the silky mass with his fingers, spreading it around them, feeling it brush against his hips as it cascaded around them. He held it back with one hand so he could continue to watch her love him with her mouth.

"I'm going to come," he muttered hoarsely when the pressure grew to that familiar level. He wanted to give her plenty of warning.

She lifted her head; his cock quivered at the loss of the hot, wet suction of her mouth. He thought she was going to climb on top of him, take him between her legs, but she didn't. She merely smiled—a seductive, loving smile—and lowered her mouth to his trembling erection once more.

Oh God. She was going to finish him with her mouth. She wasn't going to take the pleasure he offered her, not right now. She was going to be selfless, thinking only of his gratification rather than her own. She was truly showing him that she loved him, by giving him something no other woman had ever given him—pleasure without the expectation of anything in return.

Her lips and tongue continued to stroke him, bringing him closer and closer to the edge until he cried out in release, waves of emotion washing over him.

It was, without a doubt, one of the most incredible sexual experiences he'd ever had. He lay there, unable to move as she came up to curl her body against his.

"Why?" he asked when he regained the ability to talk.

She didn't make him elaborate. "Because I wanted to."

Good enough.

"Has any other woman done that for you?"

Not for free, no. He almost smiled at the uncertainty in her voice. Sometimes it was easy to forget that she needed reassurance too. She seemed so strong at times, it was hard to remember that she was just as vulnerable inside as everyone else. "Only you."

There was pleasure in her expression. "Good."

"Thank you." Not for the climax, but for the unselfishness of the act.

Her eyes grew misty. She understood. There was a quiver to her chin as she spoke, "I love you."

Devlin nodded. "I know."

"Does it still frighten you?"

"The only thing that scares me is the thought of losing you."

"You never will," she promised, and he wanted to believe her, but he couldn't change completely all at once. He would simply be content to have her now and try not to think about the future.

He didn't want to think about the past either. So many things had changed since he first met Blythe. So many things he thought of as truth had been proven false, and lies believed too long were hard to forget. It had been hard to believe old Sam's casual remarks about his parents loving him, worrying about him, being proud of him, but earlier that morning Brahm had assured him it was all true.

His oldest brother had been astounded to learn that Devlin had felt unwanted. Perhaps the circumstances surrounding his conception had been unfortunate, but he had been as loved as any child of their parents' ever could be. Neither the viscount nor his viscountess was an affectionate person, enjoying parties and social engagements more than time with their sons, but they loved each of the boys in their own way.

Brahm had even shown him their father's box of newspaper clippings and other keepsakes, which included a miniature of North's mother as well as a curl from each of his sons' heads cut when they were but children. They'd spent an hour going through it before starting their fencing match.

It was impossible for Devlin to dissect how he felt having the truth put before him in such an undeniable fashion. Everything was happening so quickly—too quickly to think about. All he could do was sit back and let it happen.

There was one thing, however, that he couldn't allow to continue, and that was his distrust of Carny. This feeling of dread where his friend was concerned had to stop. It was getting to the point that every time Blythe told him she'd seen Carny, he waited for her to announce that Carny had made advances toward her. It was ridiculous and grounded in nothing more concrete than his own jealousy.

Except that now it seemed Teresa feared the worst as well. She believed Carny to be unfaithful. How long would it be before she suspected Blythe was the other woman? He didn't doubt Blythe's fidelity to him, not one bit. She loved him and she would never do anything intentionally to hurt him, but Carny had been her first love, and when held up against that, Devlin couldn't help but feel lacking. That cowardly part of him, that fearful part that he had been on such close terms with lately, didn't see how he could possibly compete.

He was going to have to speak to Carny; that was all there was to it. For God's sake, he'd held the man's life in his hands at one time; he should be able to speak to him about such a delicate manner. He didn't want Blythe to come between them—no more than she already had—but he'd be damned if he'd let Carny come between him and Blythe.

He'd kill again before he let that happen.

Blythe pulled a blanket over them, curling herself into his side as he wrapped an arm around her shoulders. The combination of the morning's exercise, the hot bath, and Blythe's lovemaking made his head heavy with pleasant fatigue, despite the direction his thoughts were taking.

"I could stay like this forever," she said sleepily.

Devlin yawned. "Mm hmm." He was already drifting off.

It shouldn't have been a surprise then, that the dream came once he'd drifted off into slumber, but the dream was always a shock when it came lately, because it seemed to change every time, and this time was no different.

This time when he killed the soldier there was no shock or horror at what he had done. This time there was a certain satisfaction to feeling the hot stickiness of blood flowing over his hand, especially as he yanked the blade upward. The knife digging at his own hip only spurred his blood lust onward. He was going to live. He was going to survive. He was going to *win*.

What was so shocking about this version of the dream was that he felt nothing for the man dying before him. There was no guilt, no remorse, only the slackening of muscle as the soldier's life slowly drained away.

What else was shocking was the fact that unlike every other time the dream came, Devlin did not awake with a start, or a cry of denial. His body didn't even give a jerk of awareness. He simply opened his eyes to find that afternoon had crept up on them and that his wife was still asleep in his arms.

But the most shocking realization was the identity of the

man in his dream. It hadn't been the French soldier he'd killed without feeling. It had been Carny.

And that realization didn't surprise him at all.

They took the carriage to Wynter Lane as it was raining and spent the drive laughing as Devlin entertained her with stories about himself and his brothers and the mischief they got into as children. It was amazing the change that had come over him recently. It would take a while before he came to terms with everything—a lifetime of negative thinking couldn't be dispelled in a few days—but she was confident that her husband would soon learn to accept the truth about himself and see things as those around him did.

He still refused to consider the knighthood, but admitted he was considering going into medicine as she had suggested. It would be something satisfying to keep him busy when they returned to Devon, and she knew he saw it as a way of atoning for all the violence he'd been a part of. If it made life easier for him to live, she supported it entirely.

They entered Varya's blue and white sitting room only to find her brother and sister-in-law weren't alone. They had Teresa with them. A very visibly distraught Teresa, who was sobbing in Varya's embrace on the sofa.

Blythe met Miles's worried stare with one of her own. "What has happened?"

"Carny did not return home last night," her brother answered, rising to his feet. "No one seems to know where he is. Has either of you seen him?"

Both Blythe and Devlin shook their heads, but while Devlin gravitated to Miles for more information, Blythe headed straight for her sister-in-law and friend.

She knelt by Teresa's feet, but the smaller woman was crying too hard to talk. "When was the last time she saw him?" she asked Varya.

"Yesterday morning."

Yesterday morning, but that was when Teresa came to visit Blythe. So then she hadn't been able to tell Carny how she felt, or about their child. And if Carny truly felt his marriage was over as he indicated to Blythe, he could have gone just about anywhere in the last twenty-four hours.

Varya's expression was plaintive as she laid a comforting hand on Teresa's shoulder. "He told her he had business to take care of, so she didn't think anything of his absence until late into the evening."

"Did he take any clothing with him?"

Teresa shook her head, obviously trying to regain control of herself. She pressed a crumpled handkerchief to her face. "Not that I know of, unless he came back for some while I was gone."

Blythe placed a hand on her friend's knee. "Teresa, did you notice anything out of the ordinary about the way Carny was acting? Did he do or say anything unusual?"

Another shake of her head, her ebony curls bouncing around her cheeks. "Nothing. Oh Blythe, I just know he is with another woman!" Her sobbing began anew.

Varya and Blythe exchanged troubled glances.

"He is not with another woman," Blythe insisted. Carny would never betray the woman he loved, but if he thought she didn't return that love, she believed him capable of great stupidity in the name of self-pity.

Standing, Blythe crossed the cream and robin's-egg blue carpet to where Devlin and Miles stood.

"We have to find him," she told them. "Teresa is convinced he's with a mistress."

Both men raised their brows in mirror expressions of astonishment.

"Did he take anything with him?" Devlin asked.

Blythe sighed. "No, but if he does indeed have a mistress he might already have belongings there."

Miles ran a hand through his russet hair, mussing it even

more. "I refuse to entertain such an outrageous notion. Carny would never take a bit of muslin."

"Regardless, he spent the night somewhere," Blythe reminded him. "I will stay here with Varya and Teresa for a bit longer, then I will return to the house and ask Piotr if Carny's been there."

Devlin nodded. "I'll go over to Carny's and see if he's returned home."

"I will come with you," Miles said in a tone that brooked no refusal. "I cannot stand to stay here and be useless another moment. If he hasn't been home we can check the clubs and his usual haunts."

Blythe could only imagine how helpless Miles felt. He despised being powerless and ignorant. If the apocalypse happened tomorrow, he would fight it just because he would have to try.

"We'll come for you when we are finished," Devlin told her. "If Carny hasn't turned up by then, the three of us will return here and decide what action to take."

She met his determined gaze with a loving one of her own. If anyone could find Carny it would be Devlin—especially with Miles's assistance. Neither of them would rest until their friend was found, and the fact that they included her in their plans made her realize just how much she was respected by both of them.

It also reinforced just how much she adored them both. She couldn't imagine either of them simply vanishing on her as Carny had on Teresa.

When Miles went to tell Varya their plans, Devlin wrapped his fingers around Blythe's upper arm, squeezing gently as he leaned down to kiss her cheek. "I'll be back as soon as possible."

She nodded. "I know. Just find him."

The look they exchanged was charged with a multitude of emotions, and Blythe felt as though she was sending him off to battle even though she knew the opposite to be true. It was the situation itself that made them all so grave. This just wasn't like Carny, and it was hard to keep one's mind from turning to the macabre for possible explanations.

After the men left, Blythe sat with Varya and Teresa. She poured Teresa a cup of hot sweet tea and forced her to drink it. Holding the cup gave her something to focus on other than her husband's disappearance and gave her a chance to catch her breath and dry her tears.

"Devlin and Miles will find him," she assured both women as she poured herself another cup. "They'll no doubt find him at a coffee house where he'll have spent the night talking politics with his cronies."

Varya's expression was dubious at best, but Teresa looked at her with such hope in her eyes that it very nearly broke Blythe's heart. Carny had better be lying somewhere bleeding because she was going to kill him for putting Teresa through this if he wasn't.

She sat with them for another half hour, until she was fairly certain Teresa wasn't going to burst into tears again anytime soon and that Varya would be able to handle it on her own even if she did. Then she set her cup and the saucer on the table and stood.

"I should get home in case Carny comes by the house."

At Teresa's startled glance she added, "He might think to come see Devlin." Teresa knew Carny had called before, and Blythe told her he had discussed their marriage, but it was obvious Teresa had been ignorant of just how often Carny came calling—and didn't know that it was Blythe he was truly coming to see.

"I will let you know immediately if he does. He may have stopped by already and be on his way home." It was unlikely, and she hated to give Teresa false hope, but she'd rather see her hopeful than weeping as though he were already dead.

Varya walked her to the door.

"Where do you think he is?" she asked as Blythe pulled on her gloves.

"I honestly have no idea, but if he's simply been off moping for the last twenty-four hours I will personally kick his posterior up between his shoulders."

Varya smiled slightly. "I believe you will have to get in line behind your brother for that."

Blythe's answering smile was grim. She gave her sister-in-law a brief hug. "Send word if he comes here."

She nodded. "I will. And dearest?"

Blythe stopped at the door and turned. "Yes?"

Varya's expression was of wry concern. "If you do find him first, try not to hurt him too badly."

She grinned at that—how could she not? "I will try."

Miles and Devlin had gone off in one of Miles's vehicles, leaving their borrowed carriage for Blythe to make her journey back to their borrowed house. Again she thought of how nice it would be once they were in Devon, in their own house, and not spending their time chasing after other women's husbands.

"You have company," Piotr informed her in his guttural accent as soon as she crossed the threshold. "Lord Carnover is in the sitting room."

Oh what relief! How glad she was that she hadn't given Piotr those instructions to turn Carny away if he came to call.

Now she could strangle the idiot for making them all worry about him!

Her stride full of purpose, her shoulders set with determination, Blythe made her way down the corridor to the sitting room. She opened the door expecting to find Carny waiting for her, all charm and sheepish smiles.

What she saw shocked her into stunned stillness in the doorframe.

Lolling like a rag doll on the chaise, a bottle of wine dangling from his pale fingers, was Carny, but it was a Carny Blythe had never seen before.

His normally perfectly groomed hair was a tangled mess, sticking out in all directions like the frayed edge of a hem. His eyes were so red she could see it from across the room, and heavy-lidded with drunkenness. A day's growth of stubble covered his cheeks and chin. He had lost his cravat, and his open shirt revealed a shocking amount of chest and throat for a gentleman of his station, and the rest of his clothing was dirty, as though he had fallen several times, or perhaps spent the night sleeping on a tavern floor.

If not for the smile he flashed when he finally saw her, Blythe wouldn't have believed this creature to be Carny at all.

"There you are," he slurred. He didn't attempt to stand. "I've been waiting."

"What's going on, Carny?" she demanded, finally crossing the threshold. She closed the door behind her, not wanting to give the servants fodder for gossip.

He heaved himself up into a sitting position, resting his forearms on his thighs, the bottle hanging between his knees. Perhaps he wasn't as foxed as she originally thought.

"Spent the entire night drinking," he replied. "Never did get drunk enough to forget."

"What did you want to forget?"

He sighed and took a deep swallow from the bottle. "That m'wife doesn't love me anymore."

"That's rubbish and you know it, although you have certainly put her through an ordeal with this latest stunt. She's terrified something awful has happened to you."

He laughed bitterly. "Perhaps it has."

She didn't even bother trying to decipher that cryptic remark. "I am going to send a note to Wynter Lane now so she will know you are alive and in one piece." She started for the small writing table on the closest wall. "By God, I hope you suffer for this. Do you know that Miles and Devlin are out searching for you?"

Now that she was certain Carny was unharmed, her anger came pouring forth like the cheap wine he was guzzling. To be so inconsiderate and put them all through such worry just because he was feeling sorry for himself was the height of selfishness. The worst part was that if only he had gone home yesterday, he would have discovered his foolish fears and insecurities were all for naught.

"They are? They are looking for me?" His bleary gaze followed her across the room.

"Of course they are," she replied, not bothering to look at him. "You frightened us all."

"Were you frightened?"

She shot him a sharp glare. "Of course I was."

The bounder seemed pleased by that. "And Teresa was frightened as well?"

"Teresa is more than frightened, you ass," she retorted, taking paper from the small drawer in the writing table. "She is hurt and confused and—" *pregnant*. "You'll be lucky if she forgives you for this."

Out of the corner of her eye she saw him rise to his feet. The paper forgotten, she turned to face him as he moved unsteadily toward her.

"Oh, Blythe." He sighed and tried to run his hand through the snarls in his hair. "I've made such a mess of things."

She wouldn't disagree with him there. "Yes, you have."

The bottle of wine hung precariously from his lax fingers as he came toward her on drunken limbs, and suddenly Blythe was nervous. She had never backed away from Carny in her life, but every instinct screamed at her to do so now. She did, but met unyielding hardness, and she knew she literally had her back to the wall.

"I should have done the right thing and married you," he

lamented, lifting the bottle to his lips for another drink. "You would not vex me as Teresa does."

Her hands slid clumsily over the table beside her, trying to find some kind of weapon just in case one became necessary. A weapon to use against Carny. Good Lord, it seemed impossible. "Only because you would not love me as you do her."

He nodded dumbly, too drunk to see the illogic of his statement. "But at least you loved me." His gaze met hers. "You would not be so fickle. You would love me still. I could make you."

Warning bells clanged in Blythe's head as she tried to inch away from the wall. He was almost upon her now. "But I don't love you Carny, not anymore. I love Devlin."

"But you did love me once. You could love me again. I'm so sorry, Blythe. I should have loved you. It would have been so much easier than loving Teresa."

"But you do love Teresa, Carny. *She* is the one you want." She tried to move past him, but he grabbed her by the arm with surprising strength for a man so deep in his cups. It was then that Blythe realized that while she might be big and strong for a woman, she still wasn't as strong as a man.

But that didn't mean she wouldn't try her damnedest to fight him if she had to.

He pushed her backward, throwing her hard against the wall, so hard that she couldn't stop the cry of pain that escaped her lips.

Carny seemed not to notice that he had hurt her, which didn't bode well for his awareness or his sense of reason.

She shoved at him, turning her face away from the liquor-sourness of his breath. It was no use; he was using his full weight to pin her against the wall. "Carny, you do not want to do this."

"But I do," he insisted. "I should have done it a long time

ago. He reached out and caught her jaw in his hand, forcibly turning her head so she had no choice but to look at him.

"I know you have wondered what it might have been like between us. Well, I've wondered too, and now I think it's time we both found out. Love me again, Blythe. Please."

He was the second man who'd demanded her love without offering it in return, but he didn't hurt her with his denial as Devlin did. He made her angry.

Before Blythe could reply, before she could insist that he leave her alone, or cry out for Piotr's assistance, Carny brought his mouth hard against hers. Even as she pushed against his shoulders, whimpering in protest, she couldn't push him away.

And she knew he wasn't going to stop at kissing.

Chapter 18

"Anything?"

Devlin shook his head as he climbed into the carriage. "No one's seen him." He had gone into a tavern that many former soldiers frequented on the off chance that Carny had gone there, but the search had proved fruitless, as had their visits to the clubs Carny belonged to.

"Damn." Miles slumped against the plush squabs. "What do we do now?"

Running his hands through his rain-soaked hair, Devlin sniffled. As if smelling like a wet sheep wasn't bad enough, he was going to catch a chill on top of it. "Return to Blythe and see if he's gone there." He didn't bother to voice his suspicion that Carny would eventually run to Blythe if he hadn't already.

But Miles wasn't a stupid man. "How long has he been visiting her?"

There was no use pretending ignorance, and he didn't want to lie to Miles. "Since shortly after the wedding."

"Christ." Miles rubbed a hand over his eyes. "And she's the woman he's been seeing—the one Teresa believes him to be having an affair with?"

Devlin nodded. "Blythe says they spend most of their time talking about his marriage to Teresa."

Miles shook his head in disbelief. "If you are having problems with your wife, you talk to *your wife,* not someone else's."

"Perhaps he simply wanted another female's perspective." Now he was defending Carny's actions even though they annoyed the hell out of him. Wonderful. It wasn't enough that he had saved the man's life, now he had to try saving the blighter's marriage as well.

Miles eyed him shrewdly. "You are a good man to say that."

A good man. No, he wasn't that at all, not really. People assumed that he was, but they'd change their tune if they were privy to the thoughts that drifted through the darkness that sometimes blanketed his mind.

"Look, we've both known Carny a long time," he began. "He's been acting strangely lately, but that doesn't mean we should believe the worst. You know how mad a woman can drive a man."

His friend appeared surprised. "My sister's driving you to distraction, is she? Well, good, she tortured me for a good many years. It is high time she vexed someone else for a change."

"Blythe could never vex me." Devlin squared his shoulders defensively.

His humor fading, Miles nodded. "I know. I never would have allowed you to marry her if I did not think you were her match."

It was on the tip of Devlin's tongue to inquire just how Miles would have *tried* to stop him from marrying Blythe once she said yes, but he didn't. Miles meant no offense; he was simply stating his regard for his sister.

Silence fell between them, marred only by the sound of the horses' hooves and the carriage wheels as they rolled over the cobblestones. The coach swayed and jostled gently, rain pitter-pattering on the roof. It was a comforting melody, despite the anxiety twisting in Devlin's chest. Was Carny all right? What if he did go to Blythe? Would she take him in?

"Are you jealous?"

A smirk curved his lips as he stared out the window. "Insanely," he replied, watching a young man with an umbrella run down the street. What was the point in denying his feelings any longer? No doubt Miles would know if he tried to lie.

"You shouldn't be. She never looked at him the way she looks at you."

An invisible hand wrapped around Devlin's throat, squeezing until it was a chore just to swallow.

"He was a youthful infatuation, nothing more. Why do you think I never sued him for breach of promise? If I thought he had truly hurt her, I would not have kept him as a friend."

Devlin turned from the window. "I've often wondered why you never beat the snot out of him."

Miles shrugged. "I wanted to, believe me, but it would not have done any good. It wouldn't have changed things. I had to forgive him just as Blythe has. She realizes what a poor match they would have been."

The carriage pulled up in front of Delvin's and Blythe's temporary home. He would be so glad when he could take her back to Devon and have her all to himself. No company for at least two months; he would make certain of it.

"I don't know about you," Miles said as they stepped out into the rain, "but I could do with a cup of cider."

Devlin flung open the door. "Something hot, definitely."

Piotr met them in the foyer. "Lord Carnover is here, Mr. Ryland. He is with Lady Blythe in the sitting room."

So Carny had come to Blythe after all. He should be pleased that his friend had been located, but he wasn't—not completely. The fact that Carny had come to Blythe was like a splinter festering deeper and deeper beneath his skin.

"Thank you, Piotr." He handed the burly Russian his coat and strode across the foyer in the direction of the sitting room, Miles hot on his heels. All thoughts of hot drinks and dry clothes were forgotten.

The door to the sitting room was closed but thankfully unlocked. If it had been bolted, Devlin would have kicked it into kindling.

Perhaps he should have kicked it in anyway. It might have been enough to scare Carny away from Blythe. It might have saved him.

Jesus Christ. It was more a prayer than a blasphemy. For a second, Devlin could only stand frozen in the doorway, watching as Carny, a wine bottle in one hand, tried to shove his other down Blythe's bodice. She struggled against him, God love her; she was trying to get away, but Carny was by far the stronger of the two, especially with obvious desperation on his side.

He was trying to force himself on Blythe. Just as Devlin's father had forced himself on his mother. In his estimation, it was the lowest thing a man could do.

"Devlin—" The cautionary voice came from behind him. It was Miles. Devlin didn't listen, he was already halfway across the room, and in the span of one unblinking second, he had slipped his left hand between Blythe and Carny, wrapping the fingers around the smaller man's throat.

He pulled. Hard.

Carny stumbled as he was yanked away from Blythe. Wine splashed over the both of them. "What's this?" he mumbled drunkenly. "Oh, Dev. It's you."

And that was it—no apology, no half-assed explanation. He didn't even try to explain himself.

Devlin snarled, the fingers around Carny's throat tightening.

Carny dug weakly at his fingers. "Can't . . . breathe."

"Devlin," Blythe's voice cut through the haze of rage. "Devlin, let him go."

He did what she told him. He let him go.

Then he slammed his fist into Carny's face with all his strength.

More wine sloshed out of the bottle as Carny reeled backward from the force of the blow. He went down hard on the carpet. The wine bottle smashed. Carny struck his head on the table beside where he'd had Blythe pressed against the wall and crumpled to the floor.

There was a few seconds of nothing—as though time had simply frozen, as the three of them who were still standing watched to see if Carny would open his eyes. He didn't.

Blythe gasped and rushed forward. It wasn't Devlin she rushed to. It was Carny.

"He was drunk," she said, shooting him an angry look. "He didn't know what he was doing."

Devlin stared at her. "He knew exactly what he was doing."

But she wasn't looking at him now; she and Miles were rolling Carny's limp form over onto his back. The neck of the wine bottle lay next to his lax fingers. The front of his brocade waistcoat was bright with crimson. Blood trickled from his nose. The hands that cradled his head—Blythe's tender hands—came away smeared and glistening with it.

What had he done? Good Lord, what had he done?

Devlin glanced down, a strange roaring in his ears. His own hands trembled; the right was already swelling a bit. Had he broken it when he hit Carny? He'd hit him pretty hard, hard enough that the skin over his knuckles had split and was bleeding.

Blood on his hands.

The front of him was spattered with deep red, several large splotches visible on the pale fabric and the white of his shirtsleeves. It was wine. Just wine. He kept telling himself that, but even though he knew it was true, his mind kept jumping back to another time when it hadn't been wine, when it had been something thicker, something warmer.

Blood on his clothes.

He had wanted to kill Carny, just as he had wanted to kill that French soldier, just as he had killed Carny in his dream. This wasn't a question of survival, it had been rage, pure and simple.

"His head is bleeding fairly badly," Miles said to Blythe. "Better send for a surgeon."

A surgeon. Not dead then. Hurt though. Badly hurt. His fault.

Blythe rose to her feet. She stopped to look at him as she moved toward the door. The expression on her face changed from grave concern to something deeper, something less calm.

"Devlin?"

He met her gaze, ready to face the damnation there, but there wasn't any. Her eyes were wide and fearful. Scared.

Of him?

Of course she was. She'd just witnessed him trying to murder someone, a man he used to call friend. A man whose life he had sacrificed another to save, and now would have snuffed out like a bug because he dared take liberties with her.

How could she look at him at all? He wasn't a man, he was a monster, a monster who didn't deserve her love, who had probably lost it anyway. He'd been kidding himself thinking he could ever be good enough for her, be what she deserved.

She deserved better.

She came closer. "Devlin?"

"I—" He jerked back as she tried to touch him. "No, blood!" No more blood on him, he couldn't stand any more. He was already drowning in it, couldn't she see that?

She froze, her eyes widening even more, until the iris sat surrounded by a wide border of startled white.

"I have to go," he heard himself say in a voice that sounded hollow and flat. "Have to . . . can't . . . I'm sorry."

Her voice rang out behind him as he bolted from the room,

but he didn't stop. He didn't dare stop. If he stopped, every-thing inside him was going to try to force its way out, and he didn't know if he could stop it. He wanted to cry, wanted to scream.

He wanted to haul Carny to his feet and pound on him some more.

He didn't bother with a coat. He ran out into the rain, the door hanging open behind him. He raced through the down-pour, his boots splashing through puddles, water seeping in through worn stitching. Water ran down his face, into his eyes, plastering his hair and clothes tight against his skin. He didn't care what happened to him. He just had to get as far away as possible from that house, from the blood.

From her.

"Blythe, are you listening to me?"

Dragging her attention away from the door through which her husband had just disappeared, Blythe turned to her brother. "Sorry, Miles. What did you say?"

He was crouched beside Carny's motionless body, his hand underneath his friend's head. "I said we will go after Devlin later. Get something to put under Carny's head to staunch the blood while I get him to the sofa."

Blythe glanced around for something to use. Her gaze fell upon the tea tray she'd rung for earlier. There were serviettes on it that should do the trick until the surgeon arrived.

Devlin momentarily forgotten as she leaped into action, Blythe snatched up the napkins and folded them into squares as Miles lifted Carny onto the sofa. She pressed one to the cut on Carny's head. It didn't look serious, but it was bleeding quite profusely. The other she used to wipe the blood away from his nose. It looked like the more serious injury of the two, as it was slightly off center and discolored.

"I'll take care of him," she told Miles. "Go have Piotr fetch a doctor."

As her brother left the sitting room, Blythe knelt on the carpet beside the sofa, holding the makeshift bandage to Carny's skull. He looked so peaceful, so familiar now that he was unconscious. Whatever had possessed him to act as he had?

"You are lucky Devlin did not kill you," she scolded, even though he couldn't hear. He was fortunate indeed. She had seen the look on her husband's face, seen the anger and betrayal in his eyes. It hadn't been directed at her, thank God. He didn't blame her for the incident, only Carny. It didn't seem possible their friendship could survive this.

Could her own relationship with Carny survive? Perhaps. Despite the violence with which he attacked her, despite his intentions, Blythe couldn't bring herself to hate him. It was the drink and his own desperation that made him act so. He never would have done it if he had been sober and thinking clearly, of that she was certain. Carny could never hurt her— not intentionally. He would have stopped. He wouldn't have defiled her. She was certain of it.

It didn't matter now. He hadn't hurt her, and she refused to think of what *might* have happened if Devlin and Miles hadn't arrived and Carny hadn't returned to his senses.

She'd been so angry at Carny when he released her that she could have punched him herself. And then Devlin had hit him, and the damage he'd done with just one blow was staggering. Even though part of her had thrilled at his primitive defense of her, she hadn't wanted him to hurt Carny further. That was why she had tried to defend Carny's actions by blaming the drink. Devlin hadn't believed it.

He'd looked so lost, so hurt when she went to Carny instead of him. But he wasn't the one in danger of leaving a horrible stain on Varya's carpet. And then when she had gone to him, he recoiled from her as though she were some kind of poisonous snake and ran from the room.

He'd run away from her, and she didn't know where he'd gone or when he'd be back, or if he would be. She couldn't even go after him because they had to deal with Carny.

"Idiot," she muttered at the unconscious form on the sofa. She pressed harder on his wound, hoping the pain might wake him up. It didn't.

How seriously injured was he? His breathing seemed normal, but she knew nothing of these kinds of wounds. Perhaps Carny wouldn't have passed out if he hadn't been so thoroughly foxed. Then again, he could be seriously hurt.

Dear Lord, Devlin would never forgive himself if he'd done irreparable damage to his friend, no matter what his initial reaction to the situation had been.

"Piotr's gone for a doctor," Miles announced as he reentered the room. "Has he woken up yet?"

Blythe was about to shake her head when a low moan escaped Carny's lips as if on cue. "I think he's about to."

Carny's fair lashes fluttered lazily, opening just enough for his bloodshot gaze to see the face in front of his.

"Blythe." His breath was so strong, Blythe felt lightheaded just breathing it. "What happened?"

She frowned. "Do you not remember?"

He shook his head. "I remember we were talking and then nothing."

"You fell," she lied.

"On my face? My nose feels strange."

She nodded. Later, when he was sober, she would tell him what he had tried to do. Just because she felt the slightest bit of sympathy for him didn't mean she was going to let him off with it. His actions had driven Devlin to lose control, possibly had harmed Blythe's marriage. There was no way she was going to let him forget that.

"Can I get you anything?" she asked, forcing a note of compassion into her voice.

"Teresa," he replied, a fresh trickle of blood dribbling from his nose. "I want Teresa."

Nodding, Blythe pressed the napkin to his nose again. "I'll send for her."

Carny patted her arm heavily, awkwardly. "Thank you." His eyes shut and he slept again.

"Go fetch Varya and Teresa," Blythe said to Miles.

He raised a brow. "Are you certain you want to be alone with him?"

Glancing at the unconscious man on the sofa, Blythe took the cloth away from his bloody nose. "He won't try anything again. Besides, he should have someone here who will actually feel sorry for him."

Miles's expression was somber. "Are you going to tell Teresa what happened?"

"God no. That's his decision, not mine. Hurry, my hand's starting to fall asleep beneath his head."

Turning to leave, Miles paused. "Blythe, you're not angry with Devlin, are you? He did what any other man would have done in the same situation."

A thin smile curved Blythe's lips. "No, I'm not angry."

He nodded. "Good. I think he's going to feel badly enough about this as it is."

Blythe didn't respond. There was no point; they both knew he spoke the truth. She could only hope that Devlin didn't emulate Carny and stay away rather than return home to talk to her. The damage a drunken, self-absorbed Devlin could wreak was far more frightening than Carny's kiss.

That thought alone was enough to make her want to leave Carny there by himself and run out looking for her husband. But she wouldn't know the first place to look. She could go to Fielding's or Brahm's, but that was it. Devlin wouldn't go to either place. He wouldn't want to talk about what happened as both men would try to force him to do. He would want to be alone to think about what he had done, to berate and punish himself for it.

No doubt he would convince himself that he wasn't good enough for her or was some kind of monster, knowing how his foolish brain worked. No doubt he would think losing her love suitable retribution.

And if he thought she didn't love him, he might not come back at all. It was silly, but unfortunately, it was probably very close to the conclusion he would draw.

How could a man who had faced death so many times be so frightened of his heart—of hers? Outside he might be hardened and scarred, but inside he had a wound that was raw and as unhealed as it had been when it first opened. It didn't matter that he knew the truth. It wasn't enough that he was forgiven for all his sins. He still found it hard to accept the fact that he was loved—first by his brothers and parents and now by her. Believing himself unlovable was easier than taking the risk of loving and being loved.

"He's a bigger idiot than you are," she growled at Carny's still form.

But he was the idiot she loved and she wasn't going to lose him—no matter how hard he might try to make her.

The room was starting to spin.

Sitting at a corner table in a dark, noisy tavern, Devlin stared at the bottle before him and wondered if maybe he shouldn't sit a little further away from the fire.

Wait. He was already sitting as far away from the hearth as he could get. Then why the hell was he so bloody warm? He wasn't wearing a coat and his clothes were still damp. When he'd first arrived at the tavern he hadn't thought he'd ever be warm again. Now it felt as though someone had dropped hot coals down his back.

If he'd been drinking he'd blame it on that, but the bottle

was just as untouched as it had been several hours ago when he'd ordered it. He had poured himself one drink, which he'd downed most of in one gulp. It had made his stomach roll violently in protest, and the rest remained untouched, but since he'd paid for the whole bottle, and probably because he looked half insane, the barkeep allowed him to stay.

Which was good because he didn't know where else he could go. Going back to Blythe was not an option.

He'd gone to the little church, but the priest wasn't the same one he had spoken to before so he'd left, hailing a hack to take him to the docks and this hopeless little tavern where light was as scarce as sobriety and cleanliness.

Nobody bothered him. It could be his size, it could be the state of his clothing, but more than likely it was because he already looked as though someone had tried to take him down and failed.

His right hand was swollen and discolored—or at least it looked it in the distant firelight. Dried blood crusted around his knuckles—whether it was his or Carny's he couldn't say. A little of both, perhaps.

Was Carny all right? As angry as he had been when he saw Carny kissing Blythe, he would never forgive himself for seriously hurting the drunken bastard. A broken nose was fine, and he was certain that he had achieved that, but he hoped nothing more.

Which of them was Blythe more worried about at the moment, him or Carny? He didn't even want to try to guess, nor did he have hopes in either direction. If she was worried about Carny, then he could feel sorry for himself over that, and if she was worried about him, he could torture himself even further for putting her through such worry. Whichever way he went he could heap himself in as much misery as he wanted. He was good at that.

"Seems we are related after all," came a voice from above him.

Devlin looked up. His older brother wavered before sliding into focus. "You doubted it?"

Brahm nodded at his glass as he slid across the bench opposite him. "What number is that?"

"It's my first."

"Bottle?"

"Drink."

His brother laughed happily. "Or perhaps we are not related at all."

Devlin smiled, knowing that Brahm easily could have finished six bottles in the same amount of time he'd been nursing one.

His brother had obviously come looking for him; it was the only thing that could draw him to a tavern now. Brahm was dressed in dark, simple clothing, hardly the kind of finery he usually chose. More important than his clothing, however, was the fact that Brahm was sober, Devlin would stake his life on it.

Just being that close to liquor must be difficult for him, yet he gave every indication of being completely unconcerned. That was why he was the viscount—he had control, unlike his stupid younger brother.

It was Brahm's supreme control that had led to his dance with the devil's drink in the first place. He drank to lose control, until finally drink controlled him. That same control was the one thing that kept him from giving in to temptation once more.

Devlin pushed the bottle and glass aside. Was it his imagination, or were his hands shaking?

"Are you certain you haven't had more to drink?" Brahm asked. "You do not look so well."

"I don't feel so well."

Like a nursemaid, Brahm leaned forward, stripping off his glove and placing his cool fingers against Devlin's forehead.

"You are feverish."

Devlin nodded. He wasn't surprised. "I've been out in the rain."

What did surprise him was the sharp cuff his brother gave him on the side of the head. Normally it would have merely stung, but this time it sent a large, throbbing ache all the way across his skull down into his neck.

He didn't ask what the slap was for. He supposed it was for any number of things, none of which he felt like discussing.

"You should be at home," Brahm berated. "Not in a place like this. You do not belong here."

"How would you know?"

"Because people like *me* belong here." Brahm shot him an exasperated glance. "You can't even finish one drink."

He didn't make it sound like an insult, but Devlin couldn't help but think his manhood had been deeply maligned.

Picking up his glass, he downed the rest of the whiskey in one swallow. It burned, hitting his stomach with a heat that made him shudder. Good Christ it was awful.

Brahm was unimpressed. "Now you are being an idiot— more so than usual, that is."

"I already know what I am," Devlin replied with a belch. He could still taste the whiskey. "I do not need you to tell me." He hadn't sunk that low yet that he wanted his brother to back up his own low opinion of himself.

"You really should stop this brooding self-punishment. It doesn't look good on you."

"I know." Devlin leaned back in his chair and regarded his brother thoughtfully with eyes that felt as though sand had been sprinkled into them. "I've always blamed myself, ever since I was a boy. Everything was my fault."

Brahm's expression was a careful mix of disinterest and brotherly concern. "Only because you made it so."

Devlin nodded. "I kept thinking that if I was better, stronger, braver, then everything would be all right and I wouldn't be to blame anymore, but it didn't work. I'm a coward."

"No one who fought with you could call you a coward, Dev."

Laughing bitterly, Devlin rubbed his burning eyes. "I'll tell you a secret. The only thing that kept me alive during that damn war was fear of death. I didn't want myself or any of my friends to die over there. Bravery had nothing to do with it."

Brahm shrugged. "What else is bravery but knowing what must be done and doing it?"

Devlin poured another drink of whiskey. "I don't look very brave right now, do I?"

His brother took the glass away from him before he could raise it, and for one split second, Devlin saw craving in his brother's eyes. As vile and awful as the whiskey was, Brahm wanted to taste it on his tongue, wanted it to burn his belly into sweet numbness.

Instead, the eldest Ryland brother set the glass as far away from both of them as he could.

"You look scared," Brahm told him. "It is all right to be scared, but you cannot avoid life forever. Eventually you have to face what you have done. Believe me, I know."

Devlin smiled understandingly at the rueful curve of his brother's lips. "How did you know where to find me anyway?"

Brahm toyed with the cork from the whiskey bottle, flipping it from one end to the other on the table's scarred surface. "When Blythe sent for me—"

"She sent for you?" Of course someone had to, otherwise Brahm wouldn't have known he was missing, but the fact that Blythe had been the one to ask for his help gave him an echo of hope.

"She is very worried. I should cuff you again for all you have put that poor woman through. First you leave her to deal with that idiot Carnover and then you stay away for hours. I thought you loved her."

"I do!"

"Then you should be with her. Christ, a man tried to force himself upon her earlier and you're off feeling sorry for yourself."

When he put it like that, Devlin thought he deserved another slap as well. He hadn't thought of himself as abandoning Blythe. He had thought only of the angry way she looked at him and knew he couldn't stand to be less of a man in her eyes.

He had proven himself less of a man by running away.

He met his brother's gaze across the table. "Take me home, Brahm."

His brother smiled. "With pleasure."

Devlin pushed back his chair and stood, only to have the world tilt unsteadily around him. Was he foxed? He couldn't be, not after one drink. Perhaps this fever had a deeper hold on him than he first suspected.

"Are you all right?" his brother asked. "You do not look well."

Raising a hand to his face, Devlin felt the dry heat of his skin. His head swam, and now that he was standing, the air seemed cooler, but it was a cool that went right to his bones.

"Get me home," he half pleaded, half ordered as he grabbed Brahm's arm.

Brahm put his arm around his back, taking the weight of both of them on his good leg and cane. "Lean on me, but for God's sake do not pass out. I won't be able to carry you."

Devlin only nodded, feeling his strength ebb with surprising swiftness. He never should have stood up. His vision blurred as they wove their way out of the tavern. The cool rain was sweet against his skin even as it made his bones all the colder. His teeth chattering, he stumbled into Brahm's carriage.

Someone tucked a blanket or something around him. It warmed him somewhat, but not enough.

This was a sweet way to be going home to his wife, he thought. And then he thought nothing as darkness swamped him.

Chapter 19

Blythe met them at the door when Brahm brought Devlin home. It had been hours since Miles and Varya accompanied Teresa home with a somewhat coherent Carny, and Blythe had spent the time waiting, alone, for Brahm to bring her news of her husband.

"Oh, thank God you found him!" She froze, staring at the dead weight forcing Brahm to lean heavily on his cane, his face white with the effort. "Is he drunk?"

"Fever," Brahm grunted, then audibly sighed in relief when she rushed to take Devlin's other arm, bearing half his weight across her shoulders.

"Can you help me get him upstairs, or should I call for Piotr?"

"I can do it." Her brother-in-law's tone was a little defensive as they practically dragged Devlin toward the stairs.

Blythe knew better than to argue. One thing she had learned about the Ryland brothers was that it took a blunt instrument to get an idea out of their heads once it took hold.

"Where did you find him?" she asked halfway up the staircase, her breathing becoming more labored under the strain of the climb.

"At a tavern." Brahm's breathing wasn't much better than her own. They really should save the conversation for when they got Devlin in bed.

"I thought you said he wasn't foxed!"

"He's not. When I found him he was still trying to get through his first drink." Blythe didn't miss the bitter irony in his voice.

They spent the rest of the climb in silence, both of them puffing from exertion by the time they dumped Devlin on the bed.

"Help me undress him."

Taking off his coat, Brahm tossed it and his cane onto the foot of the bed. "You might want to have a servant bring a compress and cold water up as well."

She unfastened the buttons of Devlin's waistcoat. "When we have him in bed I will."

Undressing Devlin when he was awake was an easy enough task, especially since he wanted out of his clothes as badly as she did, but when he was too weak to assist, it was an incredibly difficult job. He was six and a half feet tall, weighed over fourteen stone, with limbs so long she had to back up to pull the clothing off them.

"If I had known he was going to put me through this I would have cuffed him harder," Brahm muttered, hauling on one of his brother's stockings.

Blythe stared at him in shock. "You *hit* him?"

The viscount's expression was all innocence. "It was just a tap."

"What is it about your family that makes you brothers so inclined to hitting?" she demanded, relieving Devlin of his smallclothes. Her hand rested on his thigh. "It is like a compulsion. Hit first, think later."

Brahm graced her with a rakish grin as he collected his coat and cane.

Blythe divided her attention between her brother-in-law and her husband as she covered Devlin with blankets. "You are leaving?"

He shrugged into his coat. "I'm going home to change. I would like to return later if that is all right with you."

She nodded. "Come for dinner. Bring North and Wynthrope if you wish. I'm sure Devlin would appreciate having you near."

Brahm cast another glance at his brother. It was deeply affectionate, despite the mocking curve of his mouth. "He will sleep through our entire visit, but I would feel better being close by. Thank you."

It was then that Blythe realized just how much Devlin meant to his oldest brother. Perhaps the four of them weren't overly demonstrative in their affection, but there could be no denying the love between them, not when it drove Brahm to face his own demons in search of his brother.

"Thank you for finding him." Rounding the bed to where he stood at the foot, she kissed his slightly scratchy cheek.

He stiffened noticeably at the contact, his fingers going to the spot her lips had touched with a hesitancy that moved her. What a wounded lot these Rylands were if a mere kiss on the cheek could so discompose one of them.

"I just knew where to look for a self-pitying idiot," he replied, making light.

Blythe put on an expression of mock astonishment. "How ever would a Ryland know about such men?"

Brahm chuckled at that, his unease dissolving. "It is good to have you in the family, Blythe."

Warmed beyond measure at his words, Blythe said her good-byes, making him promise to return for dinner even if North and Wynthrope couldn't. She liked Brahm, and she wouldn't worry so much about Devlin if he was there with her.

As soon as Brahm left the room, vowing he could see himself out, she rang for a maid to bring cool water and compresses up to the room.

Devlin's flesh was hot and papery beneath her palm. A fever that came upon a person this suddenly was going to be difficult to tame, and would no doubt get worse before it got better.

Rolling up her sleeves, Blythe sat down on the side of the bed near Devlin's hip. Starting at his head, she soaked the compress in the basin, wrung it out, and began swabbing his skin with it. By the time she reached his waist, his forehead was dry again.

It was going to be a long night.

Time ceased to exist for Devlin as the fever took hold. In and out of consciousness he faded, uncertain how many minutes and hours had passed each time he slipped into dream-riddled blackness.

One time when he awoke he was hot, the next time he was cold. Then he was thirsty. No matter how he felt or how often he woke, Blythe was there beside him. She stayed by his side, wiping his hot flesh with cool cloths or covering him when he shook with chills. Even if he couldn't see her through the slits of his eyelids, he could smell her, the subtle spicy blend of her perfume, or he could feel her hands, so gentle and loving as they touched him.

She hadn't tossed him aside. She didn't despise him. She stayed by his side and nursed him. That was even more comforting than the blankets tucked under his chin.

Once he woke to find himself in almost total darkness, as silent as the tomb, and for a moment he feared that was exactly where he was. Then Blythe was beside him, candle in hand, and he winced at the light. He remembered asking her to move it from the bedside table last time he awoke because the light hurt his eyes. That was why the room had seemed so dark. And it was the fever that made him warm, not the flames of Hades.

He had done nothing to be damned for. His brain could finally accept that now. It seemed so simple to believe. Perhaps he hadn't always done the right thing, and Lord knew he had so many regrets, but God would never have given him Blythe if his soul was beyond saving. She was the one good, pure thing in his life and he was going to stop thinking he didn't deserve her—he *knew* he didn't deserve her—and start trying to be the man she did deserve. And that was a man who didn't run away, who accepted who and what he was, and who took responsibility for his actions.

He had been given a great gift, and he was going to hold on to it and treasure it. He was also going to give all his own love in return. It might not be as unsullied as Blythe's, but it was a rare and delicate thing, and it was all he had to give.

Her hand closed over his. "Devlin, are you all right? Did you have a nightmare?"

Yes, he had. He'd been living one entirely of his own making.

"I'm fine." He didn't sound fine. His voice was as rough and dry as sand in a boot.

"Drink some water." She pressed a cup to his lips as she lifted his head. The water was cold and sweet, and he wanted to drink it all in one greedy gulp, but she wouldn't let him. "Just sip it."

He did as she bid, taking one small sip after another until he felt the hand supporting his head start to quiver with exertion and his own neck began to feel the strain. Lord, his head hurt.

He raised his gaze to hers, despite the glare of the candle. The sharp glow surrounded her with a hazy halo, lighting on the red in her hair, making it look as though her whole head smoldered like embers of a fire.

She looked like an angel with her hair down and a prim nightgown buttoned up to her throat.

Her hand touched the one on his chest. Slowly, he opened his fingers and allowed her to wrap her own around them.

"I'm sorry," he said.

She smiled. "So am I." Her free hand smoothed the hair back from his brow. "You should go back to sleep. You need your rest."

His hand clutched at hers. "Don't leave me."

She squeezed his fingers. "I am not going anywhere. I will be here when you wake up."

Devlin held her hand to his chest, her words ringing in his ears. Despite the fever's hold, he managed to fall into a comfortable slumber.

A deep and dreamless sleep with his guardian angel watching over him.

The last person Blythe expected to have come to call was Carny.

It had been three days since that fateful afternoon. Devlin's fever had waned and eventually broke altogether the day before. Still, he had spent most of yesterday in bed and was there now, which was perhaps a good thing as far as their guest was concerned.

Carny looked very much like his normal self, save for the discoloration and swelling about his nose.

"It is broken," he said when he caught her staring.

Blythe nodded, hugging herself with her arms. "I wish I could say I'm sorry for that, but you did ask for it."

He rubbed the back of his neck as he seated himself on the drawing room sofa. She didn't want him in the sitting room—too many unpleasant memories that were still far too fresh.

"What exactly did I do? Teresa cannot tell me and I cannot remember."

She could lie. Seating herself in the chair farthest away from him, she folded her hands in her lap, her fingers twisting the delicate bottle green muslin. She'd never felt scared in Carny's presence before his drunken attack, and while she wasn't frightened of him at this moment, she wasn't easy with him either. She didn't know if she would be ever again.

"You kissed me and tried to force yourself upon me. Devlin walked in, and that's when he . . . hit you." Dropped him like a rag doll, more like. Never in her life had she seen an attack so quick and efficient in its brutality. It had scared her a little. It had also excited her. There was something about a powerful man, especially when one was the only woman in the world who knew just how vulnerable he was as well.

Carny looked horrified. His face was ghastly pale save for that awful bruise. "My God." He lifted a hand to his mouth as though he thought he might be ill. His gaze shot to hers. "Blythe, I do not know what to say. That I'm sorry seems so inadequate."

That he was sincere in his apology was obvious, and oddly enough, Blythe found it very easy to forgive him. Startlingly easy, given the fact that he had intended to molest her. Drunk or not, there was no excuse for that, yet she could almost understand the desperation that drove him to it.

"I accept your apology, Carny. Whether or not Devlin will is a completely different matter."

Carny's elegant fingers hovered just above his nose but did not touch. "Is he here?"

"He is upstairs in bed. He contracted a fever from being out in the rain that day. He is better now, but still a little weak."

If it was at all possible, Carny turned even paler. "He was out looking for me, was he not?"

Blythe nodded. "Yes." It wasn't a lie. Devlin had been out looking for him, but that wasn't what led to his fever. However, if Carny wanted to feel guilty about Devlin's illness, she wouldn't stop him.

"Do you think I might be able to go up and speak to him?"

Blythe didn't bother to conceal her surprise. Carny was many things, but obviously a coward wasn't one of them.

"Of course you may go up. Would you like me to announce you?"

"No." Carny shook his head. "I prefer to go alone."

Brave man indeed.

But rather than standing, he remained sitting, his gaze on the floor. He looked like a chastised child, so different than she was used to seeing him. Then again, she'd seen a totally different side of his personality a few days ago—a side she'd never known existed.

And to think she'd once wanted to spend the rest of her life with him. A man she didn't know even after all these years.

"Teresa is increasing. Did you know that?"

Blythe nodded, not sure how to respond to this change in subject. "I did. She told me the morning you left and did not return."

This news did not seem so shocking to him. "That was why she'd been acting so strangely—suspecting she might be, hoping she was." He looked up, his face ravaged by guilt. "She thought I had changed my mind about wanting a child."

Of course, none of this was new to her. She'd heard the whole sordid tale from both of them. "Had you?"

"Of course not! I wanted us to have a child so badly and when it didn't happen I thought—"

Blythe's hands stilled in her lap. "You thought what?"

His shoulders sagged. "That it was my fault. That there was something wrong with me."

Odd how that desolate confession tugged at Blythe's heart. Never in a thousand years would she have thought that Carny would lose that incredible confidence of his. Now she understood his odd behavior and why he had turned to her. Her worship of him had been such at one time that he had undoubtedly believed it could buoy him again. It hadn't occurred to him that her love for Devlin made it impossible to feel the same way about anyone else. Perhaps he hadn't given it any thought at all.

This generosity of feeling was odd—not unwelcome, just strange. He might have raped her, and yet she was less mad at him now than she had been when he jilted her two years ago.

"Now you know there is nothing wrong with either of you."

He nodded morosely. "Yes. And almost too late."

She didn't respond. If Teresa knew what he had tried to do to her, Blythe suspected it would be more than "almost." But Teresa would never hear the details from her, of that Blythe was certain.

"Oh Blythe." A long, gusty sigh escaped his lips. "I have made such a mess of things."

That was perhaps the biggest understatement she'd heard in a long time. "Yes you have. You are very fortunate to have been given the chance to make it all right again."

He ran his palms along the tops of his thighs. "Yes, I am—on all accounts." His meaning was clear. "Will you let me make it right?"

She smiled slightly. "I believe so."

"And Devlin?"

As much as she might like to assure Carny his friend would forgive him, it was something she couldn't give. No one could but Devlin himself. "You will have to ask him."

"Yes." This time he actually stood. "I will."

He crossed to the door, stopping and turning in the open doorway—she hadn't been able to close herself in with him a second time.

"I truly am sorry for any harm I may have caused you, Blythe. You are one of the people in my life whom I would never wish to hurt."

She nodded. "I know. Promise me it will never happen again?"

"I promise."

And unlike two years ago when he had made a similar vow, this time Blythe believed him.

* * *

"What the hell do you want?"

To his credit, Carny didn't even flinch at the rancor in Devlin's tone. Then again, how intimidating could he possibly be, propped up against a mound of fluffy white pillows, nothing covering his nakedness save for a few blankets?

The smaller man closed the door behind him. "I know you probably won't believe me and you certainly don't have to accept it, but I have come to apologize."

Devlin scowled. "Shouldn't you be apologizing to my wife?"

Carny folded his hands in front of him. "I already did."

Alone? Had Blythe been frightened to be in the same room with him? If he hadn't been stupid enough to get himself sick he could have been there with her, assuring her that she was safe. But he hadn't been, and one of the things he was learning from Blythe was that you couldn't change the past. You could only learn from it.

He pushed himself further upright. "And?"

"She accepted it."

Why didn't that surprise him? "She's much nicer than I am."

Carny actually smiled. "She does not hit as hard either."

Devlin's gaze fell on Carny's nose. Only now did he notice the swelling and bruising. There was a part of him that felt guilt at the sight. Another part felt a bizarre sense of pride and accomplishment. He had hurt him. Good. He deserved it for the hurt he'd almost done to Blythe. She'd tried to be his friend, trusted him, and he'd returned it by trying to violate her.

The memory of the scene was enough to fuel Devlin's anger. He didn't want to forgive the son of a bitch, not yet. "You tried to rape her."

Carny's smile faded at Devlin's harsh reminder. "I do not remember."

"I'm sorry to hear that." Perhaps he was being unduly cold, but he could not bring himself to feel sorry for Carny.

There was no excuse for what he tried to do to Blythe, but if she could forgive him, then he would try to as well.

As he folded his arms across his chest in a protective gesture, the effort to keep from becoming emotional showed clearly on Carny's face. "I care very much for Blythe. I would never want to hurt her."

"But you did. Maybe not physically, but you hurt her."

Carny nodded, his expression glum. "I know."

"I wanted to kill you that day," he admitted. "The only thing that kept you alive was her mercy."

Another nod.

"Never let it happen again."

"It won't." Carny laughed bitterly. "A hell of a thanks from a man whose life you saved, eh?"

Devlin shrugged. "It would be if you had thought of me while doing it, but I suspect that if you had thought of me, you might have thought better of touching Blythe."

Carny's fingers went to his nose. He smiled faintly. "Perhaps."

But there was no perhaps about it, Devlin knew that. If Carny had been capable of rational thought, he never would have acted as he did. He might have thought it—which was almost as disturbing—but he wouldn't have done it.

"I can forgive you because we've all done things we regret, but I'm not sure I can ever forget it."

Carny's expression tightened as he swallowed. Perhaps it was just as well that he didn't remember what he had done; he certainly seemed to be suffering enough without it. Still, Devlin would be lying if he didn't admit to wishing his friend's suffering was tenfold.

"I know I wouldn't forget it if the situation was reversed," he replied.

So there, they understood each other. Their gazes locked and held, and Devlin saw real remorse and regret in the other man's eyes.

"It's going to be a while before things are as they once were." Hell, things hadn't been the same between them since Waterloo. The difference was that now there would be tension not only between himself and Carny, but between Carny and Blythe. Miles and Varya would be a long time rallying around him again as well. This mistake was something Carny would have to live with for the rest of his life, just as Devlin had to live with his.

Perhaps it would become easier for Carny someday as it was becoming for him—but not too soon, he hoped.

"I understand."

Devlin allowed himself a small smile. It wasn't up to him to determine how long Carny suffered. "But I expect that whelp of yours to call me 'Uncle,' understand?"

Carny's face brightened. "Of course. I'll send him to you to learn how to shoot."

"You'll have to. He sure as hell won't learn from you."

It felt odd, joking with Carny when there was still resentment toward him in his heart, but it was what Blythe would want, and Devlin had a sneaky suspicion that forgiving himself his own sins would be much easier once he learned to forgive other people for theirs. No doubt Carny would continue to punish himself for his transgression long after everyone else had stopped.

"Have you seen Miles?" he asked, wondering if Blythe's brother had forgiven him as well.

"Yes. He was angry, but we managed to patch things up. Blythe is very fortunate to have the two of you looking out for her."

"I'm the lucky one to have her."

Carny regarded him closely. "You truly love her, don't you?"

Devlin did not respond, but apparently Carny took his silence as all the answer he needed.

"The two of you deserve one another. She should be loved by someone who means it."

His words struck hard in Devlin's chest. All this time wondering if he deserved Blythe, and he never once thought that maybe she deserved him as well. It hadn't occurred to him that he might have something to offer her, but he did. He was the man to love her as she deserved to be loved.

And that meant no more avoiding his feelings, no more hiding and running away whenever it seemed that things might become heated between them. Being married meant disagreeing sometimes, and occasionally driving each other to distraction.

He would rather have Blythe drive him anywhere she wanted than run there alone.

One thing was for certain, she'd run away from him if she could smell him right now.

"Do me a favor, Carnover," he said, tossing back the covers. "Make yourself useful and ring for a bath, will you?"

Smiling, Carny turned to do just that. Devlin threw his legs over the side of the bed and stood. Carny handed him his robe to save him having to get it himself. He wasn't as weak as he suspected. His legs hardly shook at all. Nothing a good, big meal couldn't fix.

Carny left when the bathwater arrived. The tension between them was definitely thinner than it had been when he arrived. Perhaps it was time for a fresh start. God knew they could both use one.

But first he needed to be clean.

Entering the dressing room just off the bedchamber, Devlin removed his robe and draped it over a chair. Then he lowered himself into the tub of steaming water, shivering and sighing as he did so. Lord, it felt good.

He soaked for a while, enjoying the soothing heat of the bath. Then, using both a cloth and a stiff brush with Blythe's sandalwood-scented soap, he scrubbed at his skin until it glowed pink. No part of him was ignored—not even his elbows or the skin between his toes. By the time he was done he felt like a new man.

Water ran down his body in rivulets as he stood, the evening air hitting his flesh with a slight chill. He toweled off briskly and slipped back into his robe, the soft velvet warming him. He padded back to the bedroom with every intention of dressing for dinner and joining Blythe in the dining room. Afterward, he'd apologize for being such an idiot, and maybe she'd allow him to make love to her. It felt like forever since he'd held her rather than just a few days.

There was a knock and the door opened. Speak of the angel.

She was already dressed for dinner—very well dressed in fact. She didn't normally get so fancy for their dinners alone, knowing that he preferred her comfortable over fashionable.

She looked surprised to see him. "You are up."

He smiled. Face to face with her he wasn't quite as confident as he had been a few moments ago. "I just had a bath. I thought I'd dress and join you for dinner." He spied the tray in her hands. "Or have you come to join me?"

Twin spots of color bloomed high on her cheeks. "Actually, I have been invited to Wynter Lane for dinner."

His heart deflated a little. "Oh." She was going out. Leaving him.

"I thought you would still be abed," she explained, turning even redder. "If you want to dress and come with me, I'm sure Miles and Varya won't mind. Or I can stay and we can dine together here if you want."

Devlin shook his head, taking the tray from her. He wanted to beg her not to go, certain that she would not return. He was such a coward. "I'm feeling somewhat tired. I'll have my dinner and take a nap. Wake me when you get home?"

She swallowed and nodded, her gaze locked with his. In her eyes he saw the same uncertainty he felt swimming in his chest. Good Lord, had he already lost her?

"I will not be away long," she promised, backing toward the door. Then, as though she had just thought of it, she came to him and kissed him swiftly on the lips. "Have a good night."

Devlin's heart went with her as she left. Taking the tray to the bed, he tried to read as he picked at a supper of cold meats, bread, and cheese. Then he put tray and book aside and waited.

Waited for Blythe to return—wondering if she would.

It was late when Blythe returned from Wynter Lane. She'd left as soon as she was able so she could keep her promise to Devlin.

She should have stayed home with him. She had wanted to, but then he told her to go and part of her was desperate to get out of the house, and another foolish part had thought maybe he didn't want her to stay with him, but that went away the minute she entered the carriage. Of course he wanted her around. He loved her.

It didn't matter now. She was home and they could finally talk. It felt as if he had been away for a week rather than sick just a few days. She wanted to know what he and Carny talked about, wanted to tell him how worried she'd been about him. Wanted to tell him she loved him and finally hear him say it in return, because that was really all that mattered.

He was asleep when she entered the bedroom. A candle, burned down to its stub, flickered on the bedside table; his supper tray and a book lay beside him. Quietly, she removed them both from the bed and went to the vanity to take down her hair. She didn't bother to ring for Suki.

Devlin didn't wake as she took the pins from her topknot and brushed her hair. He was the oddest sleeper of anyone she knew. There were some things he could sleep through as though he were dead, such as a ruckus outside or thunder, but if she dropped a pin, or stepped too hard, or if the door latch happened to click, he would instantly awake.

She undressed in silence, and for the first time since he'd

fallen ill, crawled into bed with him. The maids had made the bed up clean, she noticed as she slipped beneath the sheets. They must have done that while he took his bath.

The candle sputtered and spatted. She didn't bother to snuff it—it was almost to the end of its wick and would extinguish itself soon enough.

Snuggling her back to his front, Blythe closed her eyes and let the warmth of him seep through her thin nightgown into her flesh. How good it felt to be this close to him again. She had missed it so, and had slept poorly these last two nights because of it.

But sleep wasn't elusive tonight. Within minutes of the candle flickering its last, Blythe fell into a deep, peaceful slumber.

It was sometime later when she awoke, feeling as though something wasn't quite right. The murky hours before twilight were upon them, making it difficult, but not impossible to see.

Rolling her head to the side, she realized what it was that had woken her. Devlin lay beside her, his head propped in one hand, watching her. Only he knew how long he'd been doing so.

"You were supposed to wake me when you came home," he reminded her softly.

Blythe stifled a yawn. "You looked so peaceful I did not want to disturb you. You need your sleep."

"What I need is you."

Her whole body shivered at the words.

"Do you still love me?"

Smiling tenderly, she lifted a hand to his cheek. He'd shaved earlier, and his skin was satiny smooth. "Of course I do. How long do I have to keep telling you that before you believe it?"

"Forever."

"I had better get used to it then." It wouldn't take forever, she knew that. It might take a while, however, and she was more than prepared to accept that. It wasn't that he doubted her; he just wasn't used to having love offered to him. Eventually he would learn to trust it. She wouldn't give him any other choice.

Rolling toward him, she propped herself up on her elbow and placed her other palm against his chest, right above his heart, feeling its steady rhythm against her skin.

"Devlin, you know I never did anything to encourage Carny that day, do you not?"

He caught her hand in his own, holding it against the hairy warmth of his chest. "Yes." He hesitated a moment, as though wondering whether to tell her something. "When I saw him kissing you, I wanted to kill him."

"I wanted to kill him too," she replied lightly, but she knew what he meant. He had literally, truly, wanted to kill his friend for assaulting her. Did he expect her to damn or turn her back on him for such feelings? If the situation had been reversed, she would have wanted to kill whoever dared try to harm him.

His eyes were wide in the darkness. "Did I scare you?"

Was that what this was all about? That his violence might somehow have caused her to fear him?

"No, you did not frighten me. I could never be frightened of you, but you did scare me when you ran off like that."

"I thought I had disgusted you. You looked so angry."

Her fingers flexed beneath his, stroking the warm hairiness of his chest. "I was angry at Carny, not you. And even if I was angry with you, avoiding me is not going to make it disappear."

He nodded. "I know. No more running, I promise."

She believed him. Something had changed in him over the last few days. Slowly, he was beginning to realize he had nothing to fear by opening himself up to her, that she would accept him no matter what, just as he had accepted her.

"What did I do to deserve you?" she mused, stroking the warm curve of his muscled chest.

He stilled beneath her hand. "I often ask myself the same question."

Smiling coyly, Blythe inched closer, wedging her thigh between his. "If I tell you, will you tell me?"

She could feel his growing hardness against her hip as he returned her smile with a seductive one of his own. "All right."

"You were just you," she replied simply, almost echoing a sentiment he'd once told her. "That is all you did. That is all you will ever have to do. Now you tell me."

His smile faded as he stared into her eyes in the gray light. "You loved me. Even when I thought I made it impossible for you, you loved me anyway."

A hard lump in her throat, Blythe couldn't think of a suitable reply. Instead, she pressed herself against him, offering him her mouth.

Devlin took her kiss, covering her lips with his. Releasing her fingers, he touched her softly, first on the thigh, then up to her hip and around to her back, stroking her as though feeling her for the first time. Her own hand slid down his chest, past his ribs to the dip of his hips. There, her fingers found the ridge of scar tissue the Frenchman's blade had left. Gently, she stroked it, loving it with her touch.

Loving him.

Her hand stilled.

She pulled free of the kiss. "When were you planning to tell me?"

He tilted his head, his eyes bright behind the thick black fringe of lashes as he gazed at her. "Tell you what?"

"That you love me." Just saying it made her chest tighten in a most peculiar way. It was almost as though an invisible band was being wrapped around her.

Again he had that struck look. He just stared at her.

"You can say it," she assured him. "I want you to say it. I won't reject you, you know that."

He did know it; she could see it in his eyes. She could also see that old fear that he couldn't quite let go of.

"I already know it is true, Devlin. Even if you do not say it, I know it is true." Reaching up, she touched his cheek with her fingers. "But I would love to hear you tell me what I mean to you."

"Everything," he whispered hoarsely. "You are everything."

"Why am I everything?" It was like trying to coax a secret out of a child. In fact, that was exactly what it was—she was trying to get that child who thought himself unloved to make himself vulnerable again.

"Because—" He swallowed, his face ravaged in the dim light.

"Because I love you."

Blythe's heart swelled. Joy soared through her veins. He'd said it with words. He'd been saying it a hundred different ways since they met, but she'd never heard it until she realized that he touched her just as reverently as she touched him. He loved her. He always had.

As soon as the words left Devlin's mouth, the world shifted beneath him. He had said it, he'd actually said it. And he meant it. He knew it to be true as he had known nothing else in his life. He loved her. In a way, he believed that he had loved her since the first moment he laid eyes on her, or perhaps even long before that, when Miles and Carny used to tell him stories about her and he imagined her in his mind.

His hands went to the flimsy fabric of her nightgown, bunching it, hauling it upward until he could slide his palm along the silky softness of her hip and buttocks. Her hips arched against him, tempting him with the warm grotto between her thighs.

His cock hardened with the promise of sinking deep within her. He slid the nightgown up further, until she lifted herself off the bed and slipped the offending garment over her head. She tossed it to the floor.

She knelt beside him, every inch of her bare to him in the pearly predawn darkness. His fingers brushed over her shoulder, down her breast, thumbing the nipple into erectness. Then, down to her indent of her waist, the generous flare of her hips, and the subtle roundness of her belly. Finally, his fingers moved to the thatch of dark cinnamon between her legs.

Her knees parted, allowing him better access. She didn't try to cover herself, but simply locked her gaze with his as one questing finger parted the moist lips of her sex, sliding into her already slick, tight passage. He slid his finger in and out as his thumb toyed with the crest of her desire, stroking until she arched against his hand.

Then he withdrew his fingers and she lay down once more beside him. He rolled to face her. Cupping his hand around her thigh, he lifted her leg over his hip and then guided himself to the entrance of her body. Slowly, he slid the pulsating length of his hard, aching erection inside her, her muscles sweetly clutching.

He made love to her that way, face to face, with one hand pressed against her lower back, pushing her pelvis flush against his, stimulating the center of her pleasure with every roll and thrust of his hips.

"Love me," he whispered against her lips as the pressure mounted within himself.

"I do," she gasped, moving her hips against his. The tips of her breasts were hard as they brushed his chest. "I do love you, I do."

Those simple words were all it took to send him spiraling out of control. It had been too long since he'd felt her wrapped around him, and the excitement of this coupling was too much for him to bear for long.

"I love you," he groaned, thrusting hard as climax shook

him. Blythe's hips churned faster as well, meeting his frantic thrusting until she too cried out in release.

They lay in silence afterward, their bodies still entwined, impossible to tell where one began and the other ended.

Soon they would be returning to Rosewood, the house they both loved, where they would make their home—a place where they both belonged. Together. They would fill it with laughter and love and, someday, children. Lots of children, who would be certain of their parents' love from the day they were born.

"You own my heart," he murmured against her hair, a strange prickling sensation behind his eyes. "You claimed it the first day I saw you."

She squeezed her arm around his ribs, pressing her body even closer. "I think you have always owned mine, even before we met."

Her words wrapped tightly around his heart, squeezing until he could scarcely breathe, and yet it wasn't an unpleasant feeling at all. It was a good feeling—like being set free.

And as dawn broke over the horizon, spilling its bright glow into the room around them, Devlin Ryland found all the light, peace, and love his heart had ever wanted.

In the arms of his wife.